Trying Not to Drown

Cindy Horrell Ramsey

Published by Loggerhead Press
Oak Island, North Carolina

ISBN: 978-1-7360517-0-2

Other Books by Cindy Horrell Ramsey

Creative Non-Fiction

BOYS OF THE BATTLESHIP NORTH CAROLINA
ISBN-13: 978-0895873392

Adult Fiction

600 LETTERS HOME
ISBN-13: 978-0692639627

EDGE OF SANITY
ISBN-13: 978-1978406063

Middle Grade Fiction

MADDIE IN THE MIDDLE
ISBN-13: 978-1790431236

DEDICATION

This book is dedicated to all the heroes who come to the rescue of neighbors, friends, family, and even strangers during national disasters like hurricanes, floods, tornadoes, fires, and earthquakes. I am awed by you. It is also dedicated to the survivors who valiantly keep going – sometimes more than once in their lifetimes. May those who did not survive live on in cherished memories. My heartfelt prayer is that we as a nation and a world will realize the danger of global warming and all do our part to slow it down or stop it.

TABLE OF CONTENTS

ACKNOWLEDGMENTS

Many thanks to all the people who helped bring this story to life accurately. Loving gratitude to my sister Jean Walker who shared her emotional journey of living through losing her home to flooding twice—once with Hurricane Floyd, then again with Hurricane Florence. Her experience and insight were invaluable to this story. Beta reader extraordinaire Patsy Rivenbark is the absolute best at catching typos and things she thinks I meant to say. My cousin Robin Eldridge Roller offered her depths of knowledge on natural healing processes. Shawn Sanders is an expert on training horses, lending her expertise for my writing, then reading my work to make sure I got it right. Many thanks to Michael Sawyer for his timber expertise, Millard Murray for his contribution on why plants and trees bloom out of season after a serious storm, and my daughter-in-love, Sara Ramsey, for her knowledge of which men's cologne will linger longest. Mary Ames Booker and Kim Sincox helped me understand how to salvage documents, and Kim—an avid reader—also gave me encouragement and support by reading the full manuscript and offering her thoughts. Charlotte Baggett is my biggest fan, and I always love to hear her reactions to my writing—thank you my friend. Across the ocean in Hawaii, Ann Beach always provides excellent feedback and ideas on my books. Thanks to Mary Murray Croom for being a new beta reader for me—she also experienced the emotional upheavals caused by flooding as she helped her parents through the loss of their home more than once. Sherry Lyons and Carmen Williams served as proof readers of the first sample copies, and Carmen was a great sounding board for making the back copy better. Thank you! And many thanks to all of you who offered photo ideas or answered other questions. My failure to mention you by name does not diminish my gratitude. I hope everyone enjoys this story of survival and love.

Chapter 1

Saturday, September 8, 2018

The autumn atmosphere pulsed, and humidity thickened the air like an invisible blanket of fog. Seasoned Southerners understood. As Lucy dug her toes in the sand and closed the book in her lap, she looked down the beach in both directions. Not many people out today—probably all home getting ready. The breathtaking beauty of the beach belied what the forecast predicted. The waves rolled gently onto the sand, and the sky shone a clear Carolina blue.

She watched her boys building sand forts on the shore and playing in the small swells lapping at low tide. Benji was eight and Nathaniel ten. She gazed over at her thirteen-year-old daughter, Ella, stretched out on a blanket in the sand with her best friend, Amelia, and took a deep breath of soothing salt air.

Lucy placed her book in the pocket of her chair and called out, "Are you guys hungry?"

Even though the girls barely acknowledged the call, the boys scrambled toward her. She couldn't help but smile. She missed them like crazy since they started school a couple of weeks earlier.

With three active kids, a small farm, and an aging grandmother at home, Lucy had more work than she could complete—every single day—but never kept herself quite busy enough to prevent the memories from haunting her. And every single day, she wondered if she could have said something, done something, to prevent the tragedy that changed their future forever.

1

"I want Vienna sausages," Nate said.

"And Cheese Doodles," added Benji.

"I made sandwiches," Lucy told them. "Just the way you like them. I even wrote your name on the bag so you know which one is yours. And you have bags of chips plus a brownie. Just make sure you don't drop your trash."

Ella and Amelia sat up on their blanket, but waited for the boys to get their food and go.

"Did you bring salads?" Ella asked.

"Not to the beach," Lucy said. "A sandwich now and then won't hurt you."

Ella huffed and rolled her eyes at the mention of bread, but she still devoured her lunch.

After everyone finished eating, fed their scraps to the seagulls, tucked away their trash, and put the leftovers back in the cooler, they started walking toward the inlet—at least Lucy and the girls walked. The rambunctious boys ran and flipped and jumped their way down the beach, always in perpetual motion.

Ella and Amelia hunted for shells close to the water's edge, then ventured out onto sandbars that revealed themselves and their secret treasure at low tide just steps across shallow pools and running rivulets.

Walking the beach had always been a balm for Lucy's soul. She closed her eyes and listened to the birds. People called them laughing gulls, but to Lucy their cries sounded haunted and sad.

At low tide, the breakers lapped the shore with a whooshing sound—a heartbeat, a whisper, a promise. When the tide turned, however, waves pounded the sand in loud crashing repetition. Lucy loved to listen, but sometimes the waves sounded foreboding, their power uncontrollable.

Opening her eyes, Lucy checked the location of all her children then let her gaze wander out to sea. Even though sunset was still hours away, the sun began its descent in a cloudless sky, its rays sparkling on the water like dancing diamonds. Shrimp trawlers dotted the ocean, their riggings stretched wide, the doors lowered, nets dragging. Lucy could easily tell which ones were culling their catch, the skies around them darkened with flocks of flitting birds ready for an easy meal. Occasionally, a dolphin would break the water in an upward leap behind a trawler.

After walking a couple of miles, Lucy reluctantly called to her children. "Come on guys, time to head back. We need to get home."

With busy boys trailing behind, Lucy and the girls picked up the pace to add a little exercise to their day, making it just about perfect. Lucy couldn't keep up with the long-legged teens, but she didn't mind. It gave the girls privacy for talking and her more time to think.

Weather reports revealed a huge storm headed their way, but the sky surely didn't divulge what was still hundreds of miles out in the ocean. That was always the way with hurricanes—the weather teasingly gorgeous just before. This was their proverbial calm before the storm, and she planned to squeeze every beautiful moment out of the day.

Hurricane Florence definitely threatened, but the storm just couldn't seem to make up its mind. It would gain strength then lose it, then gain strength again. It increased all the way to a Category 4, then started decreasing again.

Last Lucy heard, Florence was just a tropical storm. But living near the coast all her life taught Lucy that these storms had minds of their own. She'd check the weather again when she got home. Right now, Florence wasn't much of a threat as it headed their way.

Most hurricanes didn't really worry Lucy—she lived through a number of them without much damage. And the house where she and the children lived with her grandmother had even withstood Hurricane Hazel—the storm by which all others in North Carolina were measured.

This one moved slowly, so Lucy had a few days to pick up and put away outside items that might be carried off in the wind, then board up the windows if the storm's wind speeds increased significantly. At tropical storm strength, it shouldn't cause too much damage to the crops, especially since many of their fields were surrounded by wooded acreage that would diminish some of the wind's effects.

The risk of flooding always loomed—especially with a rain soaked, slow moving storm—but her grandparent's home had been spared during the floods from Floyd in 1999 and Matthew in 2016. Although some of the land flooded, the buildings did not.

Unfortunately, the home Lucy shared with her husband and children wasn't so lucky. Hurricane Matthew filled it with three feet of flood water, basically destroying everything below the water line and much above it due to moisture and mold. They moved in with her grandmother after that. At least they had somewhere to go—unlike so many people who ended up living in tents. Two years later, some still did.

Lucy and her grandmother knew the drill for having plenty of non-perishable food on hand and running up pots and jugs of fresh water for drinking. They would fill the bath tubs with water to flush the toilets because the electric pump wouldn't run if the power went out, and that almost always happened for a few days. At least they had an old hand pump for backup.

She'd gathered up flashlights and new batteries plus kerosene lamps still full from preparing for the last storm that turned northeast and never made landfall or even came close enough to the coast for a heavy shower. Their crops could have used that rain.

Lucy smiled to herself at the thought of Memaw surely scurrying around the house right now checking supplies and making a list. With very little additional preparation, they would be ready to ride out the storm. Then they could do a little clean up afterwards and move on to harvesting the fall crops. Everything was growing great, and she should have plenty of fruits and vegetables to sell to the grocery stores and at the fall markets plus some to keep for the upcoming holidays.

For one last time before they gathered up their chairs, umbrella, and cooler to leave the beach, Lucy gazed back out at the ocean. She always hated the leaving. The now rising tide caused the waves to swell larger and stronger, cresting foamy white as they created rolling tunnels, closed in on themselves, and crashed onto the shore. The hurricane would intensify them exponentially, growing larger and more dangerous, creating undercurrents that could sweep even the best of swimmers out to sea. But that very size and strength and power became a siren call to surfers.

Monday, September 10

Lucy carried the case of canned tomatoes out the back door and down the steps. She placed it in the rusty red Western Flyer wagon that the boys 'let her borrow' for transporting heavy items. It worked well to carry her supplies from the house to the shed. The rambling ranch where they lived lacked adequate storage, especially for the fruits and vegetables she and Memaw grew and canned to help with the grocery budget and sell at the farmer's markets.

The wagon rolled easily over the grassy yard her granddaddy had tended so carefully. Everywhere Lucy looked, she saw and felt her granddaddy. He and Memaw had been married sixty years when he died a few years earlier.

Their family traditions included repeating family names into the next generation. She named Benjamin and Nathaniel after her father and grandfather. Lucy herself had been named after her grandmother Lucille, and Ella was named for Lucy's mama. All those family names helped Lucy feel closer to relatives—all gone now except Lucille "Memaw" Malpass. She just celebrated her 80th birthday.

Too often, Lucy relived in her mind the horrific events of September 11 when her parents died and their world turned upside down. At just sixteen, a devastated Lucy and her brother, David, moved to the farm with their grandparents. He was eighteen, in college only a couple of weeks when he vowed revenge, left college, joined the Army, and deployed to Afghanistan to fight in Operation Enduring Freedom.

Lucy shook her head to release the memories of those difficult days. Today, the sun shone brightly, she could hear her boys' laughter from high up in their treehouse, and everything felt right.

In the shed, Lucy placed the box of jars in the lift she created for hauling items up to the loft. She couldn't possibly carry them up the rickety ladder. She planned to one day build a set of steps, but the dumb waiter would still be invaluable. She couldn't help but be a bit proud of herself for creating it, including the attached system of pulleys that made transporting even heavy cargo an easy task. She climbed the ladder, walked to the corner, turned the crank, and watched her sixth case of tomatoes rise up to join the others.

Lucy took each jar out of the box and placed it on the shelves beside the other tomatoes, potatoes, peas, beans, okra, squash, pickles, peaches, and sweet corn—all from this year's harvest. They still had a couple of jars of strawberry jam from last year's crop and added dozens more this year.

Only a few jars of grape jelly remained, but their vines hung full, the abundance of scuppernongs almost ripe and ready. Even after they sold most of them, they would have enough to restock the jelly supply. Memaw was a master canner, so they also had peach jam, apricot jelly, apple butter, pear relish, and scores of jars filled with other delicacies.

Lucy walked to the end of the loft. She used her apron to wipe the grime from the small window and peered out at the land that had been her salvation after losing her parents, and her refuge each time her husband deployed when she was first a young bride, then a new mother, sometimes pregnant, always scared.

She saw the small vineyard of grapes and a few fruit trees—apples ripening and pears hanging so heavy the limbs succumbed to the weight and wept toward the ground.

Rows of field corn that her granddaddy always planted for the deer and bear to enjoy at will were now fiercely protected by their dogs so she could harvest and bag it for the hunters to buy. By the looks of it, they should have an even better harvest this year than last.

Since Memaw broke her hip a couple of years ago, she kept mostly to the house while Lucy was in charge of planting and harvesting. But Memaw's mind was not broken at all, and neither was her life-long sense of working hard to build the life she wanted. She hired some help when needed and made sure everyone ate a hot meal in the middle of the day—never without fluffy homemade biscuits to eat with her array of jams and jellies.

Lucy needed to plant the collards, but the other fall greens were growing well as were the pumpkins and peanuts. Her watermelon harvest had been a good one, too. She felt so blessed that a few of the local grocery stores carried their produce, and going to the farmer's markets at Poplar Grove Plantation, Kure Beach, and Southport proved very lucrative.

Together with the hand-sewn crafts and alteration business she and Memaw created for income between harvests, the little farm put food on the table and helped keep up with the expenses—for the most part anyway.

As she descended the ladder, Lucy heard Rex and Roxy begin barking and caught a glimpse of a black blur as they ran past the shed doorway toward the front of the house. Even before she saw the car coming down the driveway, she'd know if the visitor were friend or foe just by the tenor of their barks.

The collie/shepherd mix rescues were as docile as they could be with Lucy and the children, but equally as fierce and protective if a stranger dared travel down the long dirt driveway. Many a Jehovah's Witness learned a hard lesson and left.

Lucy reached the bottom of the ladder and relaxed when she recognized their 'everything is fine' jovial barks. She rounded the corner of the house just in time to see her brother's truck pull up. Before he could even exit his truck, the boys climbed out of the treehouse and ran past her to see him.

David saw his nephews heading his way, but he watched their mother. Lucy had changed so much—both physically and emotionally—over the years. She was a beautiful young mother with almost unbearable weight on her shoulders. When their parents died, his anger seethed. She just withdrew. He joined the Army without thinking what his leaving Lucy would do to her.

David slightly shook his head, remembering how fast and hard Lucy fell for his friend when David started bringing Charlie home with him on leave. David had worried how future deployments of both her brother and her boyfriend would affect Lucy, but she wouldn't listen to any warnings from her brother.

They had built such a beautiful family, David thought, and Lucy blossomed. David still couldn't shake the guilt he felt for not being here when Charlie died. But he was career Army, and had no choice but to go where the government sent him. Often that was the other side of the world. He knew that if not for Lucy's children needing her, though, she might not have made it through.

Lucy wore frayed cutoff jeans and a purple tank top that revealed tanned, toned limbs. She was petite like their mother with the same blonde hair and blue eyes. Sometimes she stirred up memories so vivid, his heart hurt to look at her.

She was wiping her hands on their mama's pink gingham apron she often wore. It looked stained and dirty—probably from the vegetables Lucy and Memaw were always harvesting and canning added to the years of use by their mama.

Farm life and day trips to the beach obviously agreed with Lucy. She seemed increasingly more self-assured. Sunlit highlights streaked her long blonde hair falling from a messy bun. Her eyes—the color of blueberries—no longer stayed downturned and shrouded with constant despair. Sometimes when she smiled, he caught a glimpse of the old sparkle.

She came toward him with open arms and a big smile. He gave her a bear hug and kissed the top of her head. He couldn't help but worry that beneath the outward signs of healing and strength, she was still fragile.

"Hey Uncle David, can we go fishing in the creek?" Benji asked.

"I want to swing on the rope," Nate said. "Can you take us to the creek, please?"

Watching the easy camaraderie between her boys and her brother, Lucy's mind wandered. She loved the rare times when he could come home, but she was also grateful to feel competent when he wasn't there. Memaw set the example of a strong, capable woman, and Lucy strived to be like her.

She developed a sense of independence that she hadn't wanted, but was beginning to embrace. She liked the feeling of rising before dawn and knowing the work she did that day would put food on the table and help clothe her kids. Sure she struggled, and there never seemed to be enough money, but she was managing just fine. She had no other choice.

"Earth to Lucy," David said, grinning at her. "You mind if the boys and I go to the creek for a while?"

"No, that would be great," Lucy said. "Let me straighten up my canning supplies, and I'll bring down some snacks. You boys go get your fishing gear from the shed."

David put his arm around Lucy's shoulder and pulled her close as they watched the boys head off to the shed. She soaked up the strength he offered, knowing she could draw from it on days when she needed an extra boost.

"You're doing such a great job with them," David said. "I don't know how you keep up with everything. Do you know how amazing you are?"

"Not hardly," she said. "But thanks for boosting a girl's ego."

"Before I go back to base, I want to help you and Memaw get ready for the hurricane. It's been picking up strength, and they're predicting it could be a Cat 4 when it makes landfall. The fickle things can never make up their minds where they're going, but last I saw, it was headed this way."

"I think we have everything mostly under control. But if it gets worse, and we need to cover the windows, I could use the help. I just don't want to do it until the last minute. I can't stand being closed up in the dark."

"Understood."

The boys came barreling back around the house with their cane poles, worm buckets, and life jackets.

"You listen to Uncle David," Lucy said to the boys. "And no fighting!"

She watched David's tall lean figure saunter with her boys down the dirt trail toward the creek. Nate ran up ahead, but Benji held tight to David's hand at every opportunity. He missed his daddy so much.

Lucy turned toward the porch and saw Ella standing at the screen door watching. She backed away when Lucy started up the steps.

"I'm going to take some snacks down to the creek for a little picnic," Lucy said to Ella's retreating back. "Do you want to come along?"

"No," Ella said. She walked into her room and closed the door—not quite a slam, so Lucy let it go and walked into the kitchen in time to see Memaw sliding a pan of homemade biscuits into the oven. David loved using homemade biscuits to sop up molasses and butter.

"She'll be alright," Memaw said. "You weren't very nice at that age either."

Lucy hugged her grandma.

"I just hate the way she treats her Uncle David," Lucy said. "I told her she'd regret it one day, but she just shrugged me off. I don't understand."

"Teenagers are funny creatures, that's for sure," Memaw said. "But I have a hunch it has a lot to do with the fact that her Uncle David is still alive and her daddy isn't."

"That doesn't make any sense. It wasn't David's fault," Lucy said.

"I know baby girl," Memaw said. "I know."

They put apples in a basket along with some crackers and peanut butter. She tossed in a bag of mega-stuff Oreos and grabbed one of her hurricane water jugs along with a few paper cups. She could replenish the supplies before the storm arrived. Throwing the red checked cloth over the goodies, she left the house and started down the path to the creek.

She heard happy squeals before she could see her boys. By the sound of the splashing, they were doing more swinging and swimming than fishing. Good thing she grabbed the towel bag on her way out the door.

When she reached the creek bank, Lucy spread out the checked tablecloth and sat down on it, close to where her brother stood fishing.

David pulled in his line, tossed his bait into the water, twirled the cane pole to wrap the line around it, snagged the hook into the bottom of the pole, leaned it against a tree, and sat down beside her.

"Fish aren't going to come anywhere near this commotion anyway," he said with a satisfied smile. "Hope you weren't counting on crappy for dinner."

"Not tonight," she said. "Memaw's frying chicken. How long can you stay?"

"I only have a couple of days leave," he said. "I have to head back to base day after tomorrow."

"Well, we're glad for what we can get," Lucy said, more than a little disappointed that his visit would be so short. "Memaw will be, too. She was appalled that you let the boys drag you away before you even went in to give her a hug!"

"I'll make up for it in a bit," he said. "How is she doing?"

"Remarkably well," Lucy said. "Her hip doesn't seem to bother her much unless the weather is changing—so you know it's giving her a fit right now. But most of the time, she's still doing everything she wants to do. She even walks out to the round pen to watch Ella work with the horses. I think she really misses riding."

"Well, I'm just glad she decided on her own that it was time to stop."

"Me, too." Lucy laughed. "Most people have to worry about convincing their grandparents to give up a driver's license. We had to worry about Memaw surrendering her saddle!"

Chapter 2

Wednesday, September 12

Lucy watched the morning news as she helped Memaw prepare breakfast. Hurricane Florence loomed closer with every update. It grew to a Category 4 then decreased back down to a Cat 2. The forecast predicted early morning landfall on the 14th just north of Wilmington, which placed a bullseye right on their farm. They were at least thirty miles from the coast as the crow flies, so Lucy still wasn't all that worried. But by definition, official landfall meant the eye of the storm reached land, so if the storm made landfall at 7 a.m., they would experience hours of wind and rain long before then—all through the night before.

Lucy preferred to be over-prepared, so she would make another trip to Burgaw after breakfast and pick up a few more supplies, including gallon jugs of water—something that seemed so silly to buy since she had a perfectly good well. But the grocery shelves were always laden with water just before a storm, so it must make sense on some level. She'd need to store it in the shed because there was no room in the house.

David called the previous night to tell her he made it back to the base, but his unit had received orders and was flying out first thing that morning. He was probably already in the air headed some place he could not divulge. She said a silent prayer for his safety.

"Breakfast!" Memaw called as she put a basket of hot biscuits on the table.

The boys came scrambling, but Ella didn't come out of her room.

Lucy knocked on her door. When she heard no response, she opened the door and peered inside. A big lump in the bed indicated that Ella remained curled up under her covers in the darkened room.

"Time to rise and shine," Lucy said. "I need to go to Burgaw to pick up a few things before the storm gets here. I'll need your help when I get back. The first rain bands are predicted to move in sometime tomorrow."

"Do I have to go?" Ella asked without moving.

"No, but you do have to get up. Breakfast is ready."

"I'm not hungry. Everything Memaw makes is so fattening."

"You have to eat something. Leave off the pancakes and biscuits, but eat the eggs and fruit. You can burn that off easily just tending to the horses, which is something I want you to take care of today. You need to groom both of them and give them a good workout since they may be cooped up for a while. And you'll need to clean their stalls and prepare extra hay before the storm hits. We might not be able to get back out to them for twelve or more hours during the storm."

"Please don't tell me the boys are staying here."

"No, not this time, but Memaw will be in the house if you need her. When I get back, we'll all have to pitch in and make sure we're ready. The storm is a Cat 2 now, which is dangerous enough. But you never know what will happen in the next few hours."

"They never amount to anything," Ella said. "I think it's funny watching the weatherman on television get so excited. Can Amelia spend the night?"

"Not tonight. I'm sure her mother would prefer that she be home."

Lucy loaded up the boys and headed to Burgaw, hoping the store there wouldn't be as busy as the ones in Wilmington.

When she arrived at the grocery store, finding a parking space proved difficult. She hoped she could find at least a couple more loaves of bread and a few jugs of water. She wanted to buy some more Vienna sausages, too. They might not be all that healthy, but they were easy and the kids loved them. What they didn't need for the

13

storm, they could always take to the beach.

The checkout lines bustled. Lucy never understood the raid on perishables right before a storm, though. Why buy five gallons of milk when your electricity will probably go out in even a modest hurricane, and the temperature will rise to 95 degrees with hot sunshine right after? Oh well, to each his own.

Lucy had to reign in the boys to keep them from tossing every bag of chips and cookies they could grab into the cart. She headed toward the bread aisle where she found empty shelves. She resigned herself to making do with what she had when she saw Nate down on his hands and knees.

"Hey, mom!" he said with great excitement. "I found some down here."

He climbed nearly all the way onto the bottom shelf then came out with two squished loaves of bread and one bag of hot dog buns.

"Great job!" she said, putting the bread in the cart and brushing down Nate's hair that now stood on end. "Where's your brother?"

"I don't know," Nate said. "I was under there."

Lucy had been watching Nate and took her eyes off of Benji. She didn't like to let him—or any of the kids for that matter—out of her sight in a public place. Her heart started to race, and she pushed the cart to the end of the aisle. She looked both ways trying to decide which way to go and had no idea what to do. There were just so many people. She told herself not to panic. He couldn't have gone far, and he knew not to go anywhere with strangers. They had been taught to scream if someone tried to take them. She stopped and listened. She didn't hear any screaming.

"Do not get out of my sight," she told Nate. "Help me look for him."

Thinking he might have gone in search of water, Lucy started that way, her head going back and forth trying to catch a glimpse of Benji in the crowd. She didn't see him anywhere. He wasn't in the water aisle. She picked up her pace and headed for the front of the store. She would have someone call him over the intercom system. She didn't care if they thought she was crazy. That wasn't a far stretch right that minute. Just as she reached the end of the crowded aisle, Benji turned the corner and almost ran into her.

"Where have you been?" She tried unsuccessfully not to raise her voice. Several people stopped and stared.

"I got these," Benji said, holding up two 12-can packs of Vienna sausages. "We needed them."

Lucy grabbed the packs, threw them in the cart and wrapped her arms around her son.

"Yes, we did," she said, "but don't ever scare me like that again."

"Gosh, Mom," Benji said, pulling away. "I'm not a baby. I'm eight years old. You don't got to see me every minute."

"Just stay with me," she said, turning the cart back down the aisle to get water. "Show me how big and strong you are by loading several gallons of water in the cart."

After checking out with far more than she intended to buy, Lucy loaded up the boys and drove back to the country.

When she pulled up to the house, she told the boys to start carrying the water jugs to the shed and fill the lift.

"Can I crank them up?" Nate asked. "I'm not a kid anymore."

"Ok," Lucy said, not really listening. She was mesmerized by the sight of Ella and her horse in the round pen.

What a natural horsewoman Ella had become. The solid black gelding glistened in the sun as he galloped with outstretched strides hugging the round pen fencing, his long tail and thick mane blowing behind him. Ella stood in the center giving almost imperceptible cues. One small step to the left with her training stick outstretched and he reversed directions, hardly breaking stride.

Lucy walked up to the round pen and leaned on the fence, one foot on the lower railing, just like Memaw who was already there. Ella faced in the opposite direction, so Lucy didn't say anything to startle her. She heard Ella say "trot" in almost a whisper and Ace immediately responded, slowing his pace. Ella stepped to the right and the horse reversed course again. When Ella whispered "walk," Ace reduced his gait to his slowest speed without stopping. Ella turned in place slowly, continually facing him as he circled, acknowledging Lucy

15

with a slight smile when she saw her standing there. After Ace completed a couple of times around the pen, Ella leaned her head and body toward the direction he was facing, looking into his eyes. Ace stopped and turned toward her, dropping his head slightly, but keeping his eyes on Ella, waiting for direction.

His ebony coat glistened with sweat and his chest heaved from exertion. But he didn't move or take his eyes off Ella. She walked toward him, offered a treat, and leaned in to rub his neck. The horse lowered his head onto her shoulder as if hugging her. They stood that way for a few moments, a perfect pair.

Lucy watched Ella working with Ace every day, but their wordless communication still amazed her. She never ceased to be awed by how the majestic half-ton horse responded to the tall, skinny, wisp of a teenager.

"That girl is something," Memaw said. "Best horsewoman I've ever seen."

"Yes, she is," Lucy agreed.

Ella moved to Ace's side, standing just to the left of his shoulder. She scratched his neck a few times, then dropped her hand, lifted her right foot demonstratively, and stepped forward. Ace did the same. As Ella walked forward, Ace did, too, even though he was not on a lead line. Ella turned toward her left. Ace turned, too. They walked in a zig-zag pattern around the pen. When she stopped, he stopped. When she backed up, he backed up. Ella walked forward and turned to her right, going in a complete circle. Ace did, too, never closing nor widening the distance between them. When Ella started jogging, Ace trotted. When Ella stopped, Ace stopped. Lucy heard Ella say, "Good boy," as she reached up to scratch behind his ears, then give him a treat.

Ella raised her hand in a signal to stay and walked away from Ace. Then she turned back toward him and nodded to give him permission to walk toward her. When he reached her, she stood beside him and tapped on his front leg. Ace circled once, folded his front legs, and lay flat on the ground, obviously with total trust in Ella. She sat down beside him and lay her head on his long outstretched neck. Neither

16

moved until Ella slowly stood up and signaled for Ace to do the same. Then they walked together toward Lucy and Memaw at the fence.

"What you do with that horse is amazing!" Lucy said to Ella. "I am so proud of you."

"It's not me," Ella said, smiling. "Ace is the smartest horse around. I can't believe he's mine."

"You deserved him, and he is lucky to have you," Memaw said. "You two make this old heart of mine smile."

"Thanks, Memaw," Ella said. "I know horses cost a lot of money, but Ace is the most important thing in my life."

"I know," Memaw said. "Brady was a life saver for your mom when she came to live with us, and Ace is that for you. You can't put a price tag on that kind of love."

"Can I take him on the trails for a little while?"

"Sure," Lucy said. "It may be a few days before you have a chance to ride again with the storm coming. But I don't have time to ride today, and you can't go by yourself. Nate can go with you on Brady. If the wind starts to pick up too much, get off and lead them back home. Don't take any chances of them getting spooked, ok?"

"We won't," Ella said, hugging Lucy across the fence. "Thank you. I promise to help with everything when we get back."

Lucy walked to the shed to get Nate. She was surprised to see that the boys had managed to haul all the water, the Vienna sausages, and the other items they purchased up into the loft. She hadn't planned to put everything up there, but she wasn't going to disappoint them by asking them to bring any of it back down. She had enough inside the house to make it through the actual storm, and the boys would have fun bringing food back down as they needed it afterwards.

David had helped cover the windows completely with sheets of plywood before he left—all except the ones under the porch roof. Lucy told him that she and the kids could cover them, which was true. But she decided to leave them uncovered and hope for the best. She hated not being able to see outside. Now all they needed to do was safely store anything that would blow away with the strong winds. Then they would be as ready as they could be for the approaching hurricane.

Lucy walked Memaw safely back to the house, then got busy putting away bikes and toys, wheelbarrows and lawn chairs, flower pots and anything else that the storm might turn into dangerous flying projectiles.

§ § §

David pulled up the weather channel on his phone and watched the hurricane spinning toward his family as he sat waiting to board his flight overseas. He was glad he took the chance to help Lucy cover most of the windows with plywood. Lucy insisted that she and the kids could cover the ones under the porch since she wouldn't have to lift the plywood very far. He knew she could do it, but had a sneaking suspicion that she wouldn't cover them at all.

Hurricane Florence couldn't make up its mind where it was going or how strong it would be when it got there, but the forecast looked more foreboding with every update. It was slow moving, sitting out in the Atlantic, spinning like a great white cloud with a bullseye in the center. The eye was perfectly formed, indicating that the storm could gather strength as it moved toward the east coast of the US—the southeast portion of North Carolina clearly in its direct path.

Chapter 3

Thursday, September 13

Lucy was ready. The winds started picking up a little, and she could smell the rain coming. The outer rain bands would hit most any time now, which meant that the brunt of the storm would come after dark. That was the worst time to ride out a storm, when you could see nothing and only hear what was happening outside. Darkness intensified the sound of howling winds and pouring rains. She just hoped the electricity stayed on during the night.

She watched the boys squeezing every second out of their last few minutes of freedom, riding their bikes up and down the driveway. They built a small hill of dirt, creating a launch pad that lifted them airborne like a catapult. Both successfully cleared the hill and landed safely over and over again, until Benji lost control when his bike hit the ground front tire first. Lucy started to run to his aide, but saw him scrambling up and hurrying off to go again. Even her baby was growing up.

She decided to check on Ella at the barn tending to the horses. With Rex and Roxy at her heels, Lucy walked that way, taking in the scene around her—the grapes hanging heavy, the corn tassels browning, the fruit trees filled with their not-quite-ready harvest, the pumpkins growing big and round. Some of the peanuts had been harvested, but many plants still sat untouched, especially the jumbos, their bounty hiding beneath the soil.

Her grandparents once grew a pecan grove, but Hurricane Bertha in 1996 softened the ground with so much rain that when Hurricane Fran came along not far behind, it took out all those trees. Lucy was only eleven then, but she remembered holding back tears as she watched her daddy and granddaddy cut up the trees, stack the wood, and clear the land.

She looked at the large pines—limbs swaying just a little—and the scrub oaks without deep roots to hold them steady in the wind. Leaves swirled around her feet. The birds and other wildlife had already taken cover. She wondered what kind of landscape they would wake up to in the morning, and what would be left by end of day tomorrow.

"Hi there," she said to Ella as she walked into the barn. "Let's take their halters off and latch the stall doors open when we go in tonight. They might enjoy a little bit of the rain, but they're pretty smart. They'll stay out of the storm on their own when it gets bad. We don't want them trapped in their stalls if a tree falls on the barn or lightning strikes it and starts a fire."

"I put down extra hay," Ella said, stroking Brady's neck. The aging Buckskin was a well-trained six-year-old when Lucy's grandparents gave him to her after she moved in with them. That was seventeen years ago. She was sixteen, and that horse became her lifeline.

She loved the other horses her grandparents owned then that were now gone—the two Appaloosas and the blue-eyed Paint—but her grandparents sensed Lucy's need for something special of her own to love and care for. That tan colored horse with black boots and a full flowing black mane and tail stole Lucy's heart from the minute she laid eyes on him. He had always been a safe ride with a gentle heart, and she could trust him with her boys now.

Although the boys usually just rode in the round pen and inside the pasture, Lucy and Ella often rode the trails through the family property, riding the rows between fruit trees, through the pines, and down the two-rut path to the creek. Lucy loved those special times with Ella even though they didn't talk much. The riding itself gave them a connection that needed no words.

Lucy still loved riding Brady, and the boys began to show more interest, wanting horses of their own. But no one spent as much time with the horses as Ella. She watched hours of training videos at night and practiced what she learned every single day.

She worked with Brady, showing the boys and Lucy how to gently demand respect and obedience in their ground work and in the saddle. Brady had already been a great horse, and Ella's approach made him even better. But her connection to four-year-old Ace was magical. He was hers and she was his without question.

"Looks like you've done a great job with plenty of water and hay. Let's give them a little extra grain tonight and head on back to the house. It's going to be raining soon and dark. I'm going to go round up your brothers, and we'll head in for supper. Not sure how long the power will stay on, so you might want to catch a little television or computer time while you can."

Ella didn't want to leave the barn.

"And make sure you charge your cell phone," Lucy said. "In fact, let's keep them both plugged in and turned off as long as the power stays on. We'll use the computer's surge protector plugs, so that should be safe enough. Let's go."

Ella started walking with her mom.

"Come on you two," Lucy said to the dogs. "I've fixed you an extra nice bed of straw in the shed next to your houses where you'll be safe and dry. But you've got to use enough sense to stay there."

She ruffled the thick fur on Roxie's head as she called to the boys and told them to put away their bikes and help her feed the dogs.

When Ella reached her brothers, she told them to go on inside without her.

"Ace is acting a little antsy," she said. "I'm going to stay with him a bit longer."

Then she turned back toward the barn.

"You're going to get in trouble," Nate said. "But it's your hide."

She walked toward the barn, looking back over her shoulder to see her brothers riding their bikes into the shed, then toward the barn as Brady wandered back out into the pasture.

Ella and Ace stood in the barn alone, the last rays of sunlight

21

streaming through the end door, casting shadows along the center aisle between the stalls. Ella slipped a halter on Ace and hooked him to the crossties. Taking the brush from her grooming kit, she rubbed long strokes down his neck, across his back, and around his sides.

"I would stay out here with you," she said to Ace, "but you know Mom won't let me. She'd be too worried that I might get hurt or want to come back in when the storm gets too bad, but I wouldn't. I'd rather stay out here with you so I don't have to worry that something bad has happened to you. I don't know what I'd do if I ever lost you."

Ace nodded his head up and down, acknowledging her words. Ella put her arms around his thick neck and rubbed her face into his coat. She loved the way he smelled—a little sweaty but sweet, too. Her friends at school thought she was crazy when she said she craved the smell of the barn—the hay, the horses, even the poop. It didn't repulse her at all. Cleaning stalls had never been a chore to her. She was her best self around the horses—in control and loved without question.

After supper, Lucy walked back to the barn.

"It's getting dark early from the storm, and the rain has started. We really should go back to the house," Lucy said softly.

Ella saw her mom standing in the doorway of the barn, twilight settling behind her.

"I don't want to leave him," Ella said. "He needs me."

"He's a smart horse," Lucy said. "You've taught him everything he needs to know. He'll be fine. We'll come check on him at daybreak when the eye of the storm reaches us, I promise."

As they walked back to the house, Lucy said, "The boys and Memaw have already eaten, but I waited for you. We can have a quiet supper while they watch television. I made us some salads."

"Ok," Ella said. "But I sure will be glad when morning comes and this is all over."

"Unfortunately it won't be completely over by morning. The eye is supposed to make landfall around 7 a.m., so we'll still have to deal with the backside. But it's been downgraded again, so hopefully we can be back to normal before this time tomorrow," Lucy said, putting her arm around Ella's shoulders and giving her a quick hug on the way back to the house.

§ § §

With the kids fed, the house boarded up as completely as she was willing to do, and everything that could be carried away by the wind tucked into the barn and shed, Lucy was as ready as she could be for the storm. As Ella sat in her room talking to Amelia on the phone, and the boys argued over games in their bedroom, she sat with her grandmother in front of the television watching the storm spin closer and closer to shore. The outer bands of the storm were already bringing sporadic heavy showers and the trees swayed to the force of the early winds. It would get worse. But right then, the power was still on, and for that she was grateful.

§ § §

As all the children and Memaw slept, Lucy sat on the couch in the darkened living room and listened to the storm rage. Although the electricity still held strong, it flickered a time or two so Lucy turned off the television and unplugged anything that could be hurt by an electrical surge or lightning strike. A small lamp burned on the end table.

When the lightning flashed, she could see the trees bending to the will of the wind. The rain pounded on the metal roof added after Hurricane Matthew tore the shingle roof to shreds. Her great-grandparents built the rambling ranch, and her grandparents lived in it as long as Lucy could remember. Tobacco fields were eventually replaced by other crops, but it had always been a working farm.

She lived there as a teenager, and returned when Charlie was deployed. It was the house where she brought Ella home as a newborn and where Charlie first met his daughter months later. Her grandparents were her strength, and Charlie was her soul. Although she often felt their presence, only Memaw remained. So much

23

heartache, so much loss, and she was only thirty-three years old.

A sudden crash made Lucy jump. Another followed. The trees were coming down.

"Mom?" Ella's voice was soft and fearful. "I can't sleep."

"Come on over here and snuggle up to me. Great-Granny's quilt feels good. We can share."

Lucy lifted the edge of the quilt stitched by her great-grandmother's hand as an invitation for Ella to snuggle close to her on the couch.

"Do you really think Ace is okay?"

"I do. I bet he and Brady have huddled up in the stalls by now. They might even be sharing a stall. You remember that time we went out after a thunder storm and they were standing side by side in one stall?"

"Yeah, I remember. They hardly fit. I guess they needed to snuggle, too."

Lucy tucked the quilt over Ella's legs and wrapped her arm around her shoulder. Ella laid her head against Lucy's chest like she had done as a small child. They sat that way for a while listening to the familiar sounds of a southern storm multiplied exponentially.

Eventually, Ella sat up and moved to the opposite end of the couch, turning so her legs were still under the quilt and her back leaned against the arm.

"Can we talk?" she asked.

Lucy turned and mirrored the teen's posture, her legs under the quilt and her body turned toward Ella so she could see that Lucy was giving her full attention.

"Of course." Lucy said. "What's on your mind?"

"How do you know who is good and who's not? Deep down, I mean."

"That's hard sometimes. What makes you ask?"

"The girls at school talk a lot about guys, even Amelia."

"What do they say?"

"Just stuff about kissing and making out mostly. Some of them brag about 'doing it' and how great it is. I don't like to listen.

Sometimes I walk away and then Amelia gets mad at me. Am I weird?"

"No baby, you're not weird. Sometimes girls—and boys—talk big to make someone else think they're special. You don't have to grow up too fast. You aren't even in high school yet. You won't be allowed to date for a few more years."

"I'm just not ready. I'd rather be with Ace than a dumb old boy any day."

"I'm glad to hear that. There's nothing wrong with taking things slow. In fact, it's the best thing for you to do. Enjoy the things you love to do and learn who you are before getting into a serious relationship. When you're focused on another person, you sometimes limit yourself. I want you to know that at the right time—when you're much older—and with the right person, it will all fall into place. Loving someone and sharing that love intimately can be a beautiful thing."

"Like you and dad?"

"Yes, your dad was very special. He was the love of my life for sure."

"How old were you when you met Dad?"

"I wasn't much older than you. He was in the same platoon with David and didn't have anywhere to go on leave, so your uncle brought him home. I was sixteen and thought I was all grown up. But he was older than David—twenty-one that first time he came here—and treated me like a little sister, just like David did."

"Why didn't he have anywhere to go? Where was his family? You guys never talked about them."

"Your dad had a very hard childhood," Lucy explained. "I think you're old enough to know now. His mom was a drug addict. He was in and out of foster care all his life. His mom would get clean and get him back, then start using again and the cycle would start all over. He was about your age when he learned his mom overdosed and died."

"But what about his daddy?"

"They never knew who his daddy was. When he turned eighteen, he left the system and joined the Army."

25

"Why didn't anyone adopt him so he had a family?"

"I'm not sure," Lucy said. "Your dad said he was a handful, but with those huge brown eyes and humble heart, I can't imagine him being anything but adorable."

"But when did you become boyfriend and girlfriend?"

"It was love at first sight for me, but he just saw me as his best friend's little sister. We wrote letters while he was deployed and somewhere along the line, things changed. He came home with David between deployments while they were on leave. But being that much older than me, he didn't touch me until I turned eighteen. And the rest is history."

"There's this one guy at school who's really cute. He's eighth grade like me. He looks at me different than the other guys do, and we can have long conversations about stuff. He loves horses, too. I like being around him, but then he tried to put his arm around me the other day. I pushed him away and left. I was so embarrassed. He'll probably never talk to me again."

"Do you want him to?"

"I think so, yeah. He seems nice, but how do you know?"

"You have to trust your instincts, and I'm always here when you need to talk. I'll be happy to help you think things through. Your daddy was a very good man, Ella. I'm so sorry you didn't have a chance to love him longer. He would have been a great help to both of us in knowing who the good guys are."

"I'm sorry you didn't get to love him longer, too, Mom. I really miss him."

§ § §

Before David hit the sack for the night he wanted to check on his family. He was worried about the storm that certainly raged all around them by now. When he stole a moment to call earlier, he couldn't get through. Both cell phones went straight to voice mail, and the landline stayed busy. He looked at the clock. Midnight back home. He was sure Memaw would be asleep, but was just as certain that Lucy would not be. She would stay awake and keep watch over her children all night long. He picked up the phone and dialed, hoping against hope that the phone line was not dead.

Lucy picked up on the second ring. "Hello?"

"Lucy, it's David," he said. "How are you holding up? Is everything okay?"

"Oh hi, David," Lucy said as she smiled at Ella. "We're doing fine so far. Ella and I were just sitting here talking. I think we both need to head off to bed."

Ella waved at her mom, threw her a kiss, and headed toward her room.

"I tried to call earlier, but your line was always busy."

"I'm sure it was. Ella had to get in her last conversation with Amelia, and I didn't have the heart to tell her to hang up. We turned off the cell phones to save the batteries as long as we can. Talking to her friend helps keep her mind off Ace and Brady. She's so worried about them."

"A girl and her horse. That's a pretty special bond, isn't it?"

"Yes, it is. How was your flight? I know you can't tell me where you are, but are you safe?"

Lucy curled her legs up under her on the couch and wrapped herself in the quilt while she waited for David's answers.

§ § §

Ella looked out her bedroom window. She was glad it was under the porch like the family room, so her mom agreed not to cover it. The light over the barn door cast an eerie glow, but she couldn't see the horses anywhere. The winds died down a bit and only a drizzle of rain continued to fall. Ella knew the brief calm only meant they were between rain bands, and she also knew the storm could grow even worse any minute. But she had to go. She walked back to her closed door and listened carefully. She could hear her mom still talking to Uncle David on the phone, but knew they couldn't talk long. She needed to hurry if she wanted to check on Ace.

27

Ella saw the flashlight Lucy had placed on her nightstand, like she did for her brothers, in the bathroom, and in Memaw's room. She opened her bedroom window and slipped the screen out. Then she tiptoed back to her door to make sure no one had heard. She could hear Lucy telling David she was going to check on the kids and go to bed. Ella gently closed the window and waited.

Lucy knocked on her door before opening it slightly and sticking her head in.

"Goodnight Mom," Ella said. "See you in the morning."

"Goodnight sweetheart. I probably won't be able to sleep, but I am going to my bedroom to read."

Ella waited until she heard her mother's bedroom door close, then climbed out the window and onto the porch. She flashed the light back and forth in front of her to see if she could find a clear path to the barn. Large limbs lay scattered all over the yard, and she could see that at least one scrub oak on the way to the barn had toppled. A pine looked twisted in the middle and broke in half. But she didn't think she'd have to climb over anything too big. She started picking her way through the debris.

Battered by the wind, Ella stepped carefully, shining her flashlight in front of her. She made excruciatingly slow progress, but she dare not hurry for fear of tripping over dangers she could not see. She looked toward the barn, about half a football field away. Ace stood half outside the barn door in the glow of the area light. He whinnied—a beckoning sound that Ella took as encouragement.

When Ella reached the barn, she put her arms around Ace's neck and snuggled into his coal colored coat. Relief that he was unharmed flooded through her, bringing her to tears. She walked into the barn toward the tack room and Ace followed. On the way, she checked Brady's stall, but he was nowhere to be found. He must have headed out into the pasture. He didn't like being cooped up inside any more than she and her brothers did.

Ella found the bag of apple and oat treats and offered Ace one, her palm flat, fingers bent back, thumb tucked in tight. He would never intentionally bite her, but he did get excited about his cookies. Without taking time to even put on his halter, much less cross-tie him, Ella started to brush his long neck and thick mane. She scratched behind his ears and watched his lips twitch.

He looked so gorgeous, Ella took out her phone and backed up a bit to take his picture. Sudden strong winds and pouring rain startled her. A peal of lightning streaked jagged veins across the sky and thunder rumbled so violently she could feel the ground tremble under her feet. She heard pounding hooves and knew Brady was headed her way, but she didn't have time to step aside before he rounded the corner and brushed into her, sending her flying into the stall wall.

Chapter 4

Friday, September 14

A rumbling crack of thunder shook the windows and startled Lucy awake. She was surprised to have fallen asleep—sitting up in bed with the book still in her lap. She looked at the clock but it was dark—no electricity. She reached for her cell phone and powered it up. Five a.m. She couldn't believe she had slept almost three hours.

Lucy decided to check on all the kids before she cuddled back up on the couch. She should probably just go back to bed, but her room was not central to the kids' bedrooms like the living room was, and she wanted to be able to hear if anyone awoke scared and needed her. The next couple of hours could be loud and dark.

She found her flashlight and tiptoed down the hall to the room shared by Benji and Nate. Both were sound asleep. Then she peeped into Memaw's room.

"Don't worry about waking me," Memaw said. "That thunder did it for you. I did get some sleep, though. I'll make us some coffee. Sure glad you talked me into that gas stove."

Lucy went into the kitchen to light the kerosene lamp on the large table where they all shared their meals, played board games or cards, and the kids did their homework. She opened the boys' bedroom door so the glow from the kitchen lantern would give them some light if they awoke.

She knew the house would grow increasingly stuffy and unbearably hot now that the power was out—no air conditioning and no fans. As soon as the storm subsided, she could open the front windows, but the rain was coming down so heavy and the wind blowing so hard even those windows were being pummeled. She hoped she had not misjudged Florence when she decided not to board up the whole house.

As she started toward Ella's room, Lucy smiled at the thought of their recent conversation. Ella was growing up so fast and becoming wise beyond her years. She hoped the teen still slept.

When she opened the bedroom door, she could feel the wind whipping through the room before she even flashed her light toward the window. She saw the screen lying on the floor and rushed across the room to close the window against the rain blowing sideways through the opening. She knew Ella was gone even before she shone the light on her bed. At least she had taken her flashlight and phone. Lucy had no doubt where Ella was, but didn't understand why she had not waited for the eye of the storm. Lucy promised to go with her to check on the horses then.

First Lucy was angry, then she was terrified.

Normally, the barn was within shouting distance, but with the storm raging, she doubted her voice would carry beyond the yard. She dialed Ella's cell phone. It rang and rang, then went to voicemail. She sent a text, waited a minute or two, then started to panic.

Lucy ran to the kitchen.

"Ella's gone. Her window was wide open," Lucy said.

"I bet that young'un went to the barn," Memaw said.

"That would be my guess, too," Lucy said. "I have to go find her."

She grabbed her raincoat and an extra flashlight. She didn't bother with an umbrella because the wind would strip it inside out in a second. She stuck her arms in the coat and stepped into her boots, then pushed the front screen door open against the wind and walked out onto the front porch.

Memaw started to follow her outside, but Lucy stopped her.

"Please stay here with the boys," she said. "If they wake up they'll be scared. You don't need to be out here anyway with that cough you've been fighting. And the wind might blow you away."

While Memaw stood just inside the door, holding it open with her head stuck out, Lucy walked out on the porch and looked toward the barn. With the electricity out, she could see nothing, but she could hear Rex and Roxie barking alarmingly, and Ace whinnying like she'd never heard him before. If a horse could sound a warning, he was.

"That don't sound good," Memaw said. "You be careful."

Lucy stepped off the porch into the whipping wind and pummeling rain. She swung her flashlight back and forth. The trees swayed sideways, and Lucy could hear cracks and crashes all around her. Picking her way over limbs and a few downed trees, she made excruciatingly slow progress. Two huge balls of black and brown fur met her halfway, barreling toward her so fast, she almost lost her footing and fell. Rex and Roxie danced around her, barking and running toward the barn, then back to circle her again. Even with the roaring wind and pelleting rain, she could hear Ace calling from the barn.

When Lucy finally reached the barn, she first saw Brady trotting back and forth in the aisle from one end to the other. He was obviously spooked, and she feared she would never be able to halter him. Ace stood perfectly still about halfway down the aisle, his long legs extended slightly front and back, a soldier standing guard over Ella, who lay partially sitting against the stall door.

Lucy saw blood trickling down her face, but not enough to cause the puddle of blood on the floor. She frantically called her name and prayed for a response.

"Mommy?"

A whisper Lucy hoped she heard.

Brady danced nervously back and forth. Fearing she would be trampled and unable to help Ella, Lucy made a decision she prayed was the right first thing to do. She headed toward the tack room, staying close to the walls to avoid the nervous Brady. Scooping up a large amount of grain, she made her way quickly but carefully to Brady's stall where she dumped food into his bucket attached to the front wall of the stall. He heard the food fall and trotted into his stall where Lucy quickly closed and latched the door.

Hurrying back to Ella, Lucy stripped off her raincoat and t-shirt, not caring that she was wearing nothing but her bra. She pressed the shirt to the place on Ella's head that appeared to be the source of the blood.

"Ella?" Lucy said. Then louder, "Ella?"

The teen aroused slightly with a groan.

"Ella baby, can you hear me?"

"Mommy, I'm sorry," Ella whispered.

"I'm here, Ella, I'm here. Where do you hurt?"

"Head," Ella said. "I hit my head."

"Do you hurt anywhere else?"

Ella started trying to push herself up.

"My leg."

"Wait," Lucy said. "Let me check you first."

Lucy shone the flashlight down Ella's body to her legs. One was bent under her, but the other was stretched straight out. Blood caked her ripped jeans between the knee and ankle. It continued to ooze heavily.

"Where are your scissors and towels?" Lucy asked Ella.

"Tack room, middle shelf on the left."

Lucy pressed her t-shirt to Ella's leg and told her to hold it there until she returned.

Finding the things she needed, Lucy returned to Ella quickly. When she cut the jeans up to the knee, Lucy saw a deep gash a couple of inches long on Ella's shin. It was jagged and bleeding. Lucy knew it needed stitches.

"I'm sorry about your jeans," she said to Ella as she cut the denim all the way around her leg just above the knee. "I guess you'll have a new pair of cut-offs."

Ella had always been meticulous with her supplies. Lucy removed a small white towel from the zipper bag where Ella stored freshly laundered linens. They would be as sterile as anything she'd find in the barn.

"I need to clean this up and stop the bleeding before we try to go inside," Lucy said. "I know it's going to hurt like crazy, and I'm sorry."

"It's ok," Ella whispered.

Lucy poured peroxide from the bottle directly onto the gash, hoping that the bubbling liquid would remove the shavings and other debris. She wasn't sure if it had many medicinal properties, but at least she could clean the wound before she wrapped it up and moved Ella to the house. She wiped the dried blood and peroxide off Ella's leg, then poured on more. The gash was even deeper than she first feared and continued to bleed. Lucy took a clean towel from the bag and wrapped it around Ella's leg. Then another as the first one became soaked.

"I've got to get more pressure on this cut. Hold this," she said as she pressed another towel over the wound. "Apply pressure."

Lucy went back to the tack room searching for anything that she could use to hold pressure on Ella's leg. She returned with one of Ace's traveling boots with splints down the sides, no bottoms, and Velcro straps about three inches apart all the way down. Lucy removed all the soiled towels and wrapped a clean one around Ella's leg as tightly as she could.

"Hold the towel for me," Lucy said, as she slipped the boot around Ella's leg and tightened the straps.

Lucy ran her hands all over Ella, then felt her arms, her legs, her neck, and back. The bleeding gash on her head seemed to be the only other injury, but she knew not to move her. Maybe if she could move herself?

"Try to sit up," Lucy said. "But if you feel pain anywhere, stop, ok?"

Ella slowly pushed herself to a full sitting position.

"That's my girl," Lucy said. "Let me get a good look at your head."

Lucy pushed Ella's hair aside and shone the light at the bleeding spot.

"It doesn't look too bad," she said, relieved to see only a small gash. "Head injuries always bleed profusely. They can be so scary sometimes, but don't worry about all this blood. It's really not bad at all."

Lightning streaked in continuous jagged bolts across the sky, lighting up the entrance to the barn. Immediate booms of thunder indicated that the thunderstorm sat directly upon them. Sheets of rain created a watery door at the end of the barn aisle.

"We'll wait for this thunderstorm to pass," Lucy said. "Then maybe we can make it back to the house."

Rain and wind were constants during a hurricane, but thunderstorms were not. Florence seemed to be producing more than her share, and Lucy hoped this one would pass quickly. She worried that Memaw would come looking for them.

"Can you stand?" Lucy asked. "We need to see if you can walk."

Lucy held on to Ella's arm as she tried to get to her feet. All her limbs seemed to be working alright, but she immediately became dizzy and lost her balance.

"I can't," Ella said. "My head hurts so bad."

Lucy gently ran her hand over Ella's head again and found a huge knot on the opposite side from the gash that had finally stopped bleeding.

"Do you remember getting hurt?" Lucy asked.

"Sort of," Ella said, "I backed up a little to take a picture of Ace. Then the thunder was so loud that Brady came running back into the barn. I tried to get out of his way, but I tripped and fell. Then I heard you calling my name."

"Do you remember hearing the dogs barking or Ace whinnying?"

"No, just you calling my name."

Lucy wondered how long Ella had been lying there bleeding and unconscious while she slept. She stared into the storm.

"The eye should be on us in an hour or so, but Memaw will be so worried if we don't get back. I need to call her."

Lucy reached for her phone in her back pocket, but it wasn't there.

"I ran out so fast I forgot my phone. Where's yours?"

"I was holding it when I fell," Ella said.

Lucy looked around on the barn floor and saw the phone smashed on the concrete.

"Well, so much for that," Lucy said. "Brady must have stepped on it."

"I'm sorry, Mom, really," Ella said. "I should have waited until dawn like you said. I should have waited until the eye got here, but I was so worried about Ace and the rain let up a little bit and I thought maybe the eye was coming earlier and I had time."

"I'm just glad you're not hurt worse than you are," Lucy said, sliding down to sit on the floor and pulling Ella close to her.

Memaw worried. An hour passed without Lucy and Ella returning. Ace stopped sounding his alarm and the dogs quit barking, but Memaw couldn't rest until she saw Lucy and Ella. The relentless rain and wind just would not let up.

She slipped on her rubber boots and her raincoat, then walked out onto the porch. Dawn cut slightly through the darkness, but she could still see very little. The rain fell relentlessly and the wind whipped up so strongly she held onto the porch railing to keep from being blown back against the house.

She yelled toward the barn, but knew Lucy would never be able to hear her. Still she yelled again and again until a coughing spasm tightened her chest. By the time she went back into the house, her hair was soaked, and she felt chilled to the bone. She shivered—as much from fear as anything else.

Memaw went back to the kitchen and started whipping up eggs, telling herself that Lucy and Ella would be hungry when they came back in. She pulled out the pancake mix and syrup, the butter and peanut butter, and a package of sausage. She tried to convince herself that keeping busy would keep her mind off her girls.

An hour or more passed with excruciating slothfulness. Daylight struggled, but finally lit the inside of the barn.

"Sounds like the rain has let up a little," Lucy said. "I hope it's the eye and will give us some time to make it back to the house. Do you feel any stronger?"

Ella tried very shakily to stand up again.

"My knee's messed up on my cut leg," Ella said. "I can hop on the other one, but I can't walk."

"Just rest," Lucy said, helping her back down. "I'll think of something. You're just so grown up, I know I can't carry you."

"Ace can," Ella said.

Lucy looked at Ace. He was close to sixteen hands tall. Then she looked at Ella leaning against the stall door. At thirteen, she was already at least two inches taller than Lucy, and even though Ella was pencil thin, Lucy knew she could not carry her or even lift her onto the horse. With Ella's dizziness and inability to put weight on her injured leg, Lucy struggled for ideas.

"Ace can do it," Ella said. "Put the halter and lead line on him for me."

"But how will you get on?"

"Just trust me, Mom," Ella said.

"I do," Lucy answered, knowing that she really did trust her daughter to tell her what to do next.

Lucy retrieved the halter and lead line from the hook next to Ace's stall door. He moved enough to give her room to take care of Ella, but stayed close. As Lucy lifted the halter, Ace lowered his head to make it easier for her.

"Okay, now what?" Lucy asked.

"Lead him up in front of me," Ella said, "but not too close."

"Here?"

"That's good. Now tap him on his front leg."

Lucy had watched Ella give that cue for Ace to lie down when she was working him in the round pen. She didn't know how that would help, but she did as Ella instructed.

Ace bent his legs one after another and lay down in front of Ella.

"Good boy," Ella said, pulling a cookie from her pocket and offering it to him.

"Now what?" Lucy asked.

"Just help me get my leg over so I'm on his back."

Once on, Ella rubbed Ace's long black neck, then whispered in his ear.

Twelve hundred pounds of horse rose to his feet so carefully that Ella had no trouble staying on his back. Lucy watched in amazement.

"We're ready," Ella said.

Lucy led the magnificent animal out of the barn. The thunder and lightning had moved on, and the rain lessened for the moment, but the wind still whipped the trees back and forth sending leaves and small limbs flying around them. Ace didn't flinch at all. Lucy tried to find the most direct route back to the house that would not require Ace to cross any downed trees, but it was still a circuitous route littered with limbs. She need not have worried about Ella having neither saddle nor reins—she melded onto Ace's back with her arms wrapped around his neck as if they were one.

Lucy could see Memaw on the porch with her arms wrapped around her body, pacing back and forth.

"What happened?" Memaw said. "I was so worried. I tried to call your phone but it rang in the dining room. Why didn't you take it with you? Then I tried to call Ella's and it just went to voicemail. I scrambled eggs and cooked pancakes, but it's all cold."

"I'm sorry," Lucy said as she reached the porch. "Ella's hurt and Brady smashed her phone. I didn't have a choice but to wait until the storm calmed down to get her back to the house."

"I know you did the right thing," Memaw said, "but I was just worried. It's what I do."

Lucy stepped up on the porch and hugged her grandma tightly. "I'm so sorry to worry you," she said. "Ella is pretty banged up, and we had to figure out how to get her back to the house. I'm going to need your expertise on what we need to do next."

Memaw looked at Ella. "You gave us a real scare, Ella girl. What in the world were you thinking?"

Ella started to cry.

"Oh, Ella girl," Memaw said. "That was just fear talking. You're ok now, we'll take care of you."

"Let's get her inside," Lucy said, "then I'll need to take Ace back to the barn and let Brady out of his stall."

"How are we going to do that?" Memaw asked Lucy, then turned back to Ella. "Can you walk?"

"No," Ella said, "and taking me in the house is one thing Ace can't do."

She smiled at her great-grandma.

Then without direction, Ace circled around and straddled the steps with Ella's uninjured leg closest to the edge of the porch. She slipped easily down onto her good leg. With mom on one side and Memaw on the other, she hopped into the house.

Memaw sat with Ella while Lucy took Ace back to the barn and freed Brady from his stall. Then they both checked Ella from head to toe. The lump on the back of her head was shrinking. Lucy washed the tiny gash on her forehead well and the oozing soon stopped. It didn't look nearly as bad as she feared, but they would ice it and the bump on the back of her head to keep the swelling down.

"We'll put some turmeric oil and arnica salve on this cut," Memaw said. "I made some just last week. That'll settle the blood so she doesn't have any swelling or bruising."

But the leg was a different matter. The gash on Ella's calf was deeper and longer than Lucy first thought. Lucy was certain it needed stitches, but the eye of the storm had already passed, and she knew she could go nowhere until the back side of the storm moved through as well.

"We'll just have to do the best we can with it," Memaw said. "Like in the old days."

Benji and Nate came out of their room, rubbing their eyes.

"What's wrong with Ella?" Nate asked.

"She fell in the barn and hurt her leg," Lucy said. "Can you help me out and bring the first aid kit and that big box of Band-Aids out of the hurricane box?"

Then she looked at a frightened Benji.

"Can you please bring me some clean towels from the linen closet?"

"While you two do that for your mom," Memaw said, "I'll heat up your breakfast real quick."

Lucy cleaned the gash as well as she could, pouring more peroxide into the wound to remove the last of the shavings and dirt. She still had to pick out a few stubborn pieces with the tweezers. Lucy knew it hurt, but Ella didn't make a sound. She barely even moved.

Lucy placed clean dry towels under Ella's leg and waited for Memaw to come back and help.

"We're going to have to stop this bleeding and pull the gash together in case we can't get her to the emergency room," Memaw said. "I'll need your help."

Lucy took all the largest Band-Aids out of the box and rolls of gauze and tape from the first aid kit. She started unwrapping Band-Aids.

"Do you want the Neosporin?" Lucy asked.

"No," Memaw said, "And we won't need those Band-Aids either. Let's put some lavender oil in it. Then I'm going to try something different and tape it together in case we can't get to the hospital in time for stitches. Might not even need them if I do this right."

"But it's so deep and long," Lucy said.

Memaw reached into her sweater pocket and pulled out a bottle of oil and a small tin can.

"Granny's snuff?" Lucy said incredulously.

"Nah, that's just her tin," Memaw said, taking off the lid. She gently took a pinch of orangish-yellow powder from the tin and dabbed in into the wound. The bleeding stopped almost instantly.

"That's amazing," Lucy said. "It kind of looks like Granny's snuff, but it's so yellow. What is it?"

"Ground turmeric," Memaw said. "It clots bleeding."

Memaw wiped around the wound with a clean, damp cloth, then added a few more drops of lavender oil.

"Cut me two strips off that adhesive tape," she said to Lucy. "Then help me pull this wound closed."

Memaw applied the first strip diagonally across the wound. Then, she took the second strip and applied it diagonally in the opposite direction across the first strip creating a big X that held the wound tightly closed.

Lucy looked at Ella. She was pale and grimacing, but didn't make a sound.

"I'm so sorry, baby," Lucy said.

"It stopped hurting," Ella said, looking surprised.

"You can thank the lavender oil for that," Memaw said. "We're going to leave it uncovered. We'll need to add more lavender oil several times a day. And leaving it uncovered will let it scab over—nature's bandaid."

Even though Ella said the pain was gone, Lucy still gave her some Advil and one of her own sleeping pills the doctor prescribed last year. She convinced herself that Ella's need for sleep outweighed the danger of sharing her prescription.

Nate brought Ella the pillow and comforter from his bed and helped her get settled on the couch. Benji brought her his flop-eared bunny that continued to be his constant companion since their daddy died.

"You boys are a great help to your sister," Lucy told them. "We couldn't have done it without you. You can go play in your room if you want. No electricity, so no television. There's nothing else we can do until the storm ends."

By mid-afternoon, even though the rain kept pouring, the wind subsided enough that Lucy felt like she could probably drive Ella to the emergency room. She tried to use her cell phone to call the hospital, but she could find no service. It had always been spotty, especially when the weather was bad, but she could usually get some service. She walked through every room in the house then outside, holding her phone in every position she could think of, but still no bars. She picked up the wall phone in the kitchen. The line was dead.

"I'm just going to go ahead and take her," Lucy said. "You know it has to be open. Hopefully the roads are clear enough for me to get her there."

Holding the umbrella in one hand and supporting Ella with the other, Lucy helped her daughter hobble to their SUV.

"You be good for your Memaw," Lucy said to the boys as they stood at the back door waving to her. "We'll be back as soon as we can."

"We will," they said in unison. Sometimes Lucy thought they acted more like twins than boys born two years apart.

She pulled forward cautiously, maneuvering around limbs lying in the driveway. So far, no big trees blocked her path. Lucy turned the wipers and defrost on high. She sat up straight in her seat, placed her hands at ten and two on the steering wheel, and slowly eased down the mile-long driveway.

"You look like one of those little old ladies driving like that," Ella said, laughing.

"Don't you let your Memaw hear you say that!" Lucy laughed, too.

Maneuvering slowly down the drive, Lucy stopped occasionally to move limbs too large to drive over. The almost full ditches on both sides of the drive held swiftly running water. Every time she climbed out of the car, she got drenched from the rain, but she couldn't worry about what that was doing to the seat of her car. She had to keep going.

About halfway down the drive, water ran across the road. She eased through it for a little ways until she was close enough to see where their wooden bridge across the stream had been. The railings were completely gone. Lucy got out of the car and waded through the water to the edge of the stream. She stood there in dismay, watching the decking boards being torn away from the old telephone poles used to span the water. She couldn't drive across those.

When she climbed back into the car, Lucy put her hands on the steering wheel, laid her head on her hands, and sighed. She fought back the threatening tears.

"Mom?" Ella said. "What's wrong?"

Lucy lifted her head and looked at her daughter. She could see the fear in her eyes and tried to speak calmly.

"We have to go back," she said. "The bridge is gone."

"But how will you turn around?"

"I can't," Lucy said. "I'll have to back."

"But you hate to back," Ella said. "You always said you were a horrible backer."

"Well, I guess I'll have to prove myself wrong," Lucy said. "I'll go slow."

The trip back to the house was agonizingly time-consuming. Lucy really was a terrible backer, she conceded as she kept stopping and straightening when she'd back too close to the ditches. They were deep, and she couldn't believe they were almost full already. With her backing disability and the fact that the rain picked up even more, coming down in blinding sheets, Lucy feared she'd never be able to back the half mile required to take her and Ella to the house. But eventually, she did.

When they entered the house, Memaw said, "That was fast!"

"No," Ella said, "It was slow—really slow. We never even got out of the driveway."

"But you've been gone almost two hours," Memaw said.

"Yeah," Lucy said. "I'm not so good at backing. The bridge is out. We won't be going anywhere for a while."

"Well, at least we have plenty of food and water," Memaw said. "The rain can't last much longer."

But it did. Remnants of Florence dropped rain on the farm for three days straight.

With no electricity, no phone service, pouring rain, stir-crazy boys, and a teenage daughter in pain, Lucy was exhausted. Most of the windows remained boarded up because relentless rain gave Lucy no chance to take down the plywood. The heat in the house soared, and the humidity made just breathing difficult. Lucy worried about Memaw. In spite of her home remedies, her cough worsened daily, deeper and hacking. But she didn't have a fever—at least not yet.

Each day, Lucy tried to find a time when the rain let up enough to remove some of the plywood and then take care of the animals. She took Nate and Benji with her so the boys could get out of the house and Memaw and Ella would have an hour or two of peace and quiet.

She tried to keep the boys corralled as much as possible to avoid injury from all the debris and fallen trees or being bitten by snakes that always came crawling after a storm. Lucy didn't see too many large trees down, but over a dozen smaller ones had been uprooted and toppled. Many large limbs lay strewn across the property, and she found shingles from the roof of the shed all over the ground. The metal roof on the house held tight.

Together, she and the boys fed the chickens, the barn cat, and the dogs, then took care of the horses. She didn't see any sign of injuries on any of the animals, and the barn and fences all looked fine. The crops were beaten down from the heavy wind and rain, but Lucy thought that a day or two of sunshine would have most of them standing up and happy again. If the sun would just come out.

Each time Lucy walked past the shed, the sight of her granddaddy's big red tractor flooded her heart with memories. She could see him bouncing in the seat as he rode up and down the field rows, preparing them for planting corn and beans and pumpkins and watermelons and peanuts. He always wore a great big straw hat and an even bigger grin.

She could almost smell the peanuts boiling in a cast iron pot over an open fire in early fall. She tried to recreate that experience with her children every year, but it always seemed lacking. She missed her parents. She missed her granddaddy who seemed larger than life until the day he died—a heart attack while walking between the corn rows checking for bear tracks.

Making her way through the fields, Lucy became concerned to see the rainwater between crop rows getting deeper. Maybe with a few days of sunshine, it would be dry enough to start harvesting what was ready. Some of the grapes hung sweet and ripe. The late cucumbers and squash were ready. She was glad they were on trellises and not lying directly on the soaked ground. The rest of the peanuts would rot if the ground stayed wet. The pumpkins and field corn needed to grow a few more weeks.

Lucy checked on her gourds. Last year's crop had been good, but this year's was amazing. She trained them on trellises alongside the shed, and the vines hung heavy with what Lucy knew would be future birdhouses. She and Ella worked on their art skills and watched instructional videos when they found some spare time, so she was confident that the designs they painted on this crop of gourds would be far superior to last year's. Those sold well at the summer and holiday markets, and she hoped these would sell even better.

She couldn't harvest them until after the first frost, and then they would need to dry for several months before she and Ella could prepare and paint them. Lucy loved the creative time she spent with Ella, and depended on the money from this extra source of income. Although she had managed to scrape by so far, Lucy knew she would need more annual income as the kids grew older. Just the increased amount of food for two growing boys was staggering. Ella would be going to college in five short years. And Memaw was trying to put some money away for *when she got old and needed help.*

Each day, they raided the hurricane box for unhealthy boxed, bagged, and canned food Lucy only allowed when they were camping, at the beach, or during power outages. They played games and went to bed early. She checked Ella's and Memaw's temperatures several times a day and prayed the phone and power would come back on. If the rain would just stop, maybe they could start the cleanup process and get back to some sense of normal. Each night, Lucy listened to her grandmother fight jagged uncontrollable fits of coughing that rattled deep in her chest.

Chapter 5

Monday, September 17

After three days of relentless rain, Lucy finally awoke to sunlight streaming through the cracks in her blinds. What a welcome sight! She had actually slept soundly for six hours straight and was ready to face the work ahead. She made her way to the kitchen and found Memaw already making coffee and rolling out biscuits.

"Going to have eggs, grits, country ham and red-eye gravy today," Memaw said. "Need to celebrate this sunshine and get our bellies full so we have enough strength to start cleaning up."

"Sounds and smells good," Lucy said.

She checked on Ella, who seemed to be sleeping soundly. Feeling her forehead for any sign of fever and finding none, Lucy quietly closed her door and hoped Ella would sleep for at least another couple of hours.

Neither the electricity nor the phone were yet working. Memaw cooked all the perishable food first knowing the ice in the coolers wouldn't last long. Even though they couldn't get water inside the house because the electric pump wouldn't work when the power was out, they were blessed to have fresh water from the old hand pump that Lucy's grandparents had used before indoor plumbing. So Lucy refilled their pots and jugs daily.

That first day with no rain, Lucy and the boys started dragging limbs and made a barely definable dent in the work that needed to be done. It would be a long process.

Ella spent the day on the porch swing with her leg propped up and iced. Memaw doctored her leg with homemade remedies, but kept the taped wound unbandaged to allow natural healing. While Ella sat in the swing and watched the others work, Memaw kept a close eye on her, keeping her supplied with plenty of food, snacks, drinks, and a book all day long. Nate and Benji brought Ace over a couple of times so Ella could talk to him and see that he was okay.

It was a good day.

When all the children were tucked in and sleeping, and Memaw retired to her room, Lucy ventured back outside. She sat down on the porch swing and gave a little shove with her foot. Rocking rhythmically, she breathed in the fresh moist air and listened to the night sounds—the croaking frogs, singing katydids, hooting owls. She said a little prayer of thanks that they once again weathered a storm that could have been so much worse.

The moon rose high over the towering longleaf pines. It was full this night, first orange then bright white as it climbed higher and higher, its beams casting shadows across the yard, field, and pasture. Lucy could see the horses grazing on dew laden grass, their tails swishing to bat away the flies and mosquitoes. She knew those biting insects would be much worse in the next few weeks.

Even though she and the boys emptied everything they could find that held stagnant water, the swamp and creek would be breeding grounds they couldn't control. But the bugs were just a nuisance as far as Lucy was concerned. They didn't distract from the gratifying feeling that—against so many odds and in the midst of tragedy—she and Memaw made a good life for themselves and the children, a life they all loved.

When her limbs began to feel heavy and her head started to nod, Lucy stood, took one last long and loving look around her world, then walked inside, locked the door, checked on each of the children, and went to bed. With the windows open, the night sounds sang her to sleep.

Tuesday, September 18

Lucy awoke disoriented in the dark. She sat up and swung her feet off the side of her bed, then padded around the house checking on all the kids. They were snoozing soundly. Memaw was sleeping, too, coughing only occasionally. Lucy walked toward the front door and heard the dogs barking frantically. She opened the door to see Rex and Roxy on the porch bouncing up and down and bumping into the side of the house with their big front paws. Lucy had never seen them act that way.

"What is it?" Lucy asked. "What's wrong?"

When she opened the screen door to go out, the dogs bounded inside, straight for the children's rooms. Lucy let them go and walked out onto the porch. The moon hid behind scattered clouds and the night was dark. Timidly, she started slowly down the steps. On the bottom step, her foot hit water.

The moon cleared the clouds and Lucy looked around her in horror. Water was rising. It had crested the first step and covered the yard. The pasture looked like a lake, and the horses stood at the gate. Lucy froze with fear. In her mind, she knew what was happening, but in her heart, she prayed it wasn't true.

"Make it stop," she prayed out loud. "Please stop the water."

Standing on the first step, Lucy felt the water rising higher up her legs. That set her in motion. By the time she entered the house, Rex and Roxy had awakened the kids and Memaw. They were all standing in the living room.

"What's going on?" Ella asked. "You never let them in the house, and they woke us up. All of us!"

Lucy said a silent prayer for calm amidst catastrophe. She must make critical decisions and execute them quickly.

"I need each of you to listen carefully," she said as calmly as possible. "The water is rising outside. This house has never flooded in the past, but we have to be prepared just in case. Let's think of it as another adventure."

"I'm tired of adventures," Ella said. "Can't we just go back to bed and wake up to a normal day with electricity and running water and a telephone? Please!"

"I hope we do," Lucy said. "But we can't count on that."

"What do you want us to do?" Memaw said. "You're in charge."

"I need each of you to pack your backpacks like we were going on a camping trip. Put in some comfortable clothes, a dry pair of shoes, and a jacket. Don't forget to tie your sleeping bags on them. Then I want you to empty all the trash cans in the house and help me load them with food and other things we might need. We'll float them to the tractor shed. We're all going to the loft to wait this out. Hopefully by daybreak, the water will start to recede, but we can't wait to find out. As you get everything ready, take it to the porch. The water hasn't reached it yet."

Lucy was relieved that for once the kids listened without much argument and started hustling around the house—except for Ella, who still limped badly.

"I'll help Ella," Memaw said, seeing Lucy watching her. "You do what you need to do."

Lucy packed her backpack with clothes, and as an afterthought, added her handgun and ammunition—something she swore she would never touch again. From the bathroom, she filled a trash can with bug spray, toiletries, and her first aid kit.

Memaw pulled the Saran Wrap out of the kitchen drawer and told Ella to sit on the couch. She soaked squares of gauze in lavender oil, placed them up and down the gash, then wrapped Ella's leg in the plastic wrap, and taped it down.

"Can't take any chances getting flood water in that wound," Memaw said. "None of my remedies will work on that."

After she helped Ella pack and sent her to the porch swing, Memaw worked in the kitchen, loading food and plates and utensils and napkins into trash cans and coolers. The boys took them all to the porch.

The water covered the second step. One last step before the water reached the porch.

"Ella, I want you to stay in the porch swing and keep your leg up," Lucy said. You do not need to get this water on your cut."

"But I need to help you," Ella said.

49

"We can help," Nate said. "Come on Benji, put your backpack on and grab something to float."

The water rose high on the thighs of the boys as they waded with their backpacks and sleeping bags hooked around their shoulders and pushed floating trash cans full of supplies. Nate walked in front with one flashlight and Lucy followed behind with another shining between them. She wanted to make sure she could see if anyone fell or started lagging behind. Rex and Roxy stayed on the porch with Ella and Memaw.

Lucy helped the boys lift their trash cans of supplies onto the large tool box in the corner, then instructed Nate to shine his flashlight on the ladder as Benji climbed, then to follow him up.

"I'll fill the lift and you can crank it up, then I'll go back and bring some more until we have everything up top. I need you both to stay there."

As Lucy turned back toward the house, she yelled up to the boys to turn on the battery powered camping lantern so they were not totally in the dark.

"The sun should be coming up soon," Lucy said loudly. "And the moonlight is beautiful tonight, don't you think?"

Lucy made a couple more trips with supplies and loaded them into the lift for the boys to crank up. They unloaded them up top. She would straighten everything up once they were all safe.

Lucy didn't want either Ella or Memaw to wade through the water, so she went to the pasture and got the horses. Lucy helped Ella onto Ace and Memaw onto Brady.

"Well, I never thought I'd sit a horse again," Memaw said. "It feels good."

Lucy led both horses slowly through the water. Rex and Roxy followed them to the shed, the water almost high enough that they needed to swim.

"Let the lift down only partway," Lucy yelled up to Nate. "I'll tell you when to stop so it doesn't reach the water."

By now, the water was reaching mid-thigh on Lucy. The dogs barely kept their heads above water, but Rex had somehow managed to gain a passenger. Spoof, their drenched gray barn cat, was riding on his back. Lucy helped Memaw slide from Brady's back directly into the lift. Memaw reached out for Spoof so he could ride up with her, and the cat leapt into her arms—a rare move for the skittish feline.

"I need help!" Nate cried. "I can't wind her up."

Lucy handed Brady's lead line to Ella, waded through the water to the ladder, then climbed up and helped wind the lift up. After helping Memaw out, she climbed back down to Ella.

"Your turn," she said, helping Ella into the lift.

Before her mother started winding her up, Ella rubbed Ace's long neck and wrapped her arms around him.

"What will happen to him, Mom?"

Lucy had never faced anything like this before and knew that every decision she made would be from the gut and could be totally wrong. But she must sound like she knew what she was doing to keep the children as calm as possible. Ace had a hold on Ella and her heart that was so tight and so strong it was visible in the way they looked at each other—the big black horse and the fragile teenage girl.

"The pasture gate is open and won't swing closed in this water, so they can't get trapped if they head back to the pasture," Lucy said. "I'm sure they will find higher ground. And you know Ace will come back to you just as quickly as he can."

"But what if somebody sees him and doesn't know who he belongs to and keeps him?" Ella cried.

Lucy thought fast, shining her light in the corner where she stored the paint.

"Look there," she said. "See the spray paint? I'll paint my cell phone number on the horses so anyone who finds them will know how to get up with us when this is over."

Lucy didn't know what else to do for the horses, but she knew she could not confine them inside the fence. So when she finished adding her phone number to their backs, she took off their halters and lead lines and left them on their own, hoping an instinct of survival would override Ace's sense of loyalty to Ella.

"You might have to tell him to go," Lucy said to Ella.

When she completed as much as she could do for the horses, Lucy helped the dogs—one at a time—into the lift. The boys weren't strong enough to haul them up and neither Ella nor Memaw were able to help, so Lucy climbed the ladder to crank up one dog, then back down to load the other.

The chickens made their way to the top of the coop. Lucy looked up and saw Spoof resting in the rafters of the shed. By the time she felt she had done all she could do, the water was up to her waist and still rising.

But the horses did not move. She knew that Brady would follow Ace's lead, so she slapped Ace on his rump and told him to go. He didn't budge.

"Don't hit him, Mom!" Ella screamed.

"He needs to go, Ella," Lucy said. "Tell him to go."

With tears running down her face, Ella told Ace to run—over and over and over again until he finally did.

Lucy slowly climbed the ladder as the sun began to crest, casting light on a new day of unknown challenges.

"Spread your sleeping bags out and try to get a little more sleep," Lucy told her children.

"You didn't sleep much last night. It's going to be a long day, but it will be a little shorter if you're sleeping at least part of it."

Lucy was thankful for windows at both ends of the loft that would let in some air and enough light to keep from burning up the flashlight batteries during the day—but nooks and crannies could hide danger, and she must investigate before she'd feel safe enough to rest. First she needed to put on some dry clothes. Stripping out of her jeans, she remembered that her cell phone was in her back pocket. So much for that.

Lucy walked the perimeter of their refuge shining the light in every corner of the rafters, looking for spiders and snakes and wasp nests. Since she stored her canned goods there, she tried to keep it clean, but you just never knew. And she wasn't taking any chances.

Two black widows, three wasp nests, and no snakes later, Lucy sat down and leaned against the wall, close enough to the edge of the loft that she could see the rising water. It was cresting the top of her granddaddy's tractor tires—the big ones in back that were taller than her boys. She wished she had thought to bring their life preservers up, but they were still tucked safely away in the storage box, now covered with river water.

She looked over her shoulder out the window toward the fields. Everything that so valiantly survived the hurricane's rain and winds was almost covered now—a total loss beneath the tannin darkened water of the rising Black River.

Lucy didn't have to look to know what was happening to the home her great-grandparents built—the house that survived Hurricane Hazel and escaped the floods from Floyd and Matthew when so many other homes were ravaged by the rising river. It was the house that held their legacy, their memories, their family's life for four generations.

The floodwaters would have made it inside now—the solid wood floors would be saturated, the rugs would be soaked and covered in sludge. The legs of the walnut dining table and chairs her granddaddy so painstakingly crafted by hand would be standing in water, but maybe salvageable if the river would just stop rising, then quickly recede. It had reached the halfway point of the ladder now, and she was counting rungs.

"Mom, I gotta pee," Benji said.

"Me, too," said Nate. "I can't hold it much longer."

"Ok, boys," their mother told them. "Line up at the railing and shoot it toward the tractor. See who can get the closest."

"Eeww," Ella said. "That's gross."

"Turn your head and don't watch," Lucy said. "Go over there with Rex and Roxy. Start thinking of what we can do for them before nature calls."

The boys pushed and shoved for position at the railing. Lucy was almost worried they would push each other over the side, but at least it was something to keep them busy for a few minutes. She walked over and knelt down beside Ella, who sat on the floor with her injured leg stretched out in front of her. She rubbed both furry dogs lying calmly in a corner.

"What will we do, Mom?" Ella asked quietly without turning her head.

"I guess we'll have to use a bucket," Lucy answered. "We can grab some quilts out of the cedar chest we moved up here and build us a privacy screen.

Ella looked at Lucy, giant blue eyes shimmering with tears.

"No, Mom, what will we do?"

Chapter 6

As nightfall approached, the water covered several more rungs of the ladder. It slowed late in the day to less than one rung every couple of hours. Lucy could measure the rise by inches now instead of feet. But only four rungs remained before flood waters breached the loft.

They spent their day setting up camp – sleeping bags spread on the floor, games stacked in a corner, food placed on shelves, and backpacks hung on hooks.

They used old newspapers to make a place for Rex and Roxy to relieve themselves, but so far both had been holding strong.

Benji and Nate found an old ski rope and helped Lucy string it across a corner from wall to wall. From the family cedar chest, she pulled out a couple of quilts and hung them over the rope. They created a makeshift bathroom with a bucket and lid for Lucy, Memaw, and Ella to use and for the boys during times when peeing over the rail just wasn't enough.

"I remember," Lucy said, "when I was a very little girl and came to visit my great-grandparents. The house didn't have running water back then. We had to bring it in from the pump outside like we do when the power goes out. They didn't have a bathroom inside the house either—just an outhouse in the back yard."

"What's an outhouse?" Nate asked.

"Well," Lucy said, "it was a small wooden building—taller than it was wide—with a bench to sit on and a hole cut in the bench."

"What was the hole for?" Benji said.

"Use your brain, dimwit!" Nate said to his little brother.

"Enough," Lucy said. "Apologize."

"Sorry," Nate said unconvincingly.

"People back then, who didn't have bathrooms in the house," Lucy continued, "would dig a big hole in the back yard and hope to hit water. Then they set the outhouse up over the hole."

"Wouldn't you fall in?" Benji asked.

"Oh, no," Lucy explained. "The outhouse had a floor in it so you wouldn't fall in. The only open hole was the one in the seat."

"Oh," Benji said. "Now I get it."

The boys both snickered, and Ella wore her 'how gross can you get' teenage glare.

"Anyway," Lucy said, "Granny refused to go to the outhouse after dark. So she kept what was called a chamber pot under the bed. She wore these dresses that looked like sacks and hung down several inches below her knees, but she didn't wear anything but a slip under it. When she needed to go, she'd just pull out the chamber pot and stand over it to let the stream flow."

"Sure hope she had good aim," Ella said.

"Your Uncle David and his friend Greg got in big trouble one day when they hid under Granny's bed, then stuck their heads out and tried to look up under her dress," Lucy said with a smile. "They only tried that once, that's for sure."

The kids all laughed. Lucy was glad to be able to take their minds off the flooding for a few minutes anyway.

"What about when she needed to do number two?" Nate asked.

"I guess she only did that in the daytime," Lucy said, not really knowing the answer to that question. "Maybe you should ask Memaw."

"But we don't got no outhouse," Benji said. "Where we doing that?"

"We'll make do the best we can," Lucy said. "The bucket in our corner outhouse will have to do for now."

"I can't believe this is happening to me," Ella said under her breath and limped to her sleeping bag where she picked up a book and a flashlight.

Lucy stood at the window on the end of the loft overlooking the pasture. The top of the doorway to the barn was visible barely two feet above the rising water. She neither saw nor heard any sign that the horses were still there. She hoped and prayed that they escaped to higher ground—wherever that might be.

Ella was uncharacteristically silent about Ace, and that in itself worried Lucy. Maybe Ella thought voicing her fear would make the worst case scenario become reality. Lucy tried early on to convince Ella and the boys that the horses were smart enough to save themselves, and that she was certain they would find both of them after the water subsided. Lucy was no longer confident about anything. The visions in her mind delved much darker than she dare voice.

§ § §

Not long after dark settled around the flooded farm, the children slept. Lucy could hear Memaw's labored breathing, but at least she seemed to be sleeping. Lucy propped up a pillow, wrapped herself in a quilt—not because she was cold but because she craved the comfort of familiarity—and leaned back against the wall of the loft, close to the ladder so that no one accidently stepped off the side if they awoke and started wandering. Although she was what her mama would have called bone tired, Lucy was afraid to sleep. She kept her eyes on the rising water. The moon glowing through the limbs of the longleaf pines cast light and shadows across its ripples.

Lucy's mind wandered into the house. Even though it wasn't the house she grew up in for the first fifteen years of her life, it was her refuge after her parents died, where she lived with the children when Charlie deployed, and where they moved their little family when Hurricane Matthew stole their home. Every material thing that defined generations of her family was lovingly displayed there. It was the only place where Lucy felt safe after tragedy threatened to drown them in despair—not just once or twice, but three times.

As she walked up the steps in her mind, she saw the flowers drowned and sagging. Currents could be making the porch swing sway still holding soggy cushions Memaw had made years before. She could hear the sewing machine humming as Memaw's hands guided the colorful fabric under the needle.

How many times did Lucy stand at that screen door when she was little and watch Granny or Memaw walking from the kitchen, wiping floury hands on her apron and smiling because Lucy and her mama and daddy and brother had come to visit? Not nearly enough.

Inside the living room, Granddaddy's recliner would be under water now, the lamps floating, the doilies Granny and Memaw crocheted would be washed off the tables and sinking as water soaked through the meticulously designed threads.

Family pictures dating back decades might still be hanging, or the rush of water could have torn them from the walls. Either way, they were ruined and could live on only in Lucy's memory.

Funny thing, memory. Sparked by the sight of a picture, a whole lifetime of special moments could come rushing to mind, making you smile or laugh or cry. Without the pictures, will the memories still come as vividly?

Exhausted from an unimaginable day, Lucy started to nod off, catching a last glimpse of the water still rising.

She slept in fits and starts. Sometime after what felt to Lucy like hours of tossing and turning, she stirred from a half sleep stupor, Rex and Roxy bumping her legs and barking—alarming yaps punctuated by deep rumbling growls. Lucy was instantly wide awake.

"What is it?" Memaw asked.

The dogs stood at the railing of the loft, barking incessantly at the dark, rippling water. Lucy immediately checked the ladder rungs, afraid the water had risen to threatening levels. It covered another rung, but was not yet in danger of coming over the top.

"What's wrong?" she asked her dogs. They kept barking and bouncing.

Lucy began to scan the floodwater, watching it roll and shimmer in the rays of moonlight. The water was black—black like the name of the river from which it came. She saw things floating—a piece of wood, a watering can that had not yet filled and sank, piles of yard debris, a clump of weeds or grass maybe. She reached into her pocket for her flashlight and shone it on the clump. It was moving—not just floating toward her. Definitely not grass. It was a writhing mass of something dark red that looked like fire ants.

Those pesky stinging insects had been on the farm for years. She worked so hard to destroy the hills, but they just popped up somewhere else like a game of whack-a-mole. Now a mass of them floated toward her. How could that be? She didn't see anything for them to be riding on—no wood, no grass, nothing. It was as though they had linked themselves together to form a floating mass of mayhem.

Benji was allergic. She couldn't take a chance on even one of those ants getting to her children. If they stung someone, she could put some alcohol on the bites, but that wouldn't help the pain much at all. Maybe Memaw's lavender oil would help the sting, but even that couldn't do anything about Benji's anaphylactic reaction. The vitamin C and Benadryl still sat in the kitchen cabinet. The EpiPens became so expensive Lucy did not immediately replace the last one. How could she be so stupid and careless? She owned nothing to counteract the allergic reaction that caused Benji to swell and itch and have trouble breathing. Absolutely nothing in her first aid kit prepared her for that. .

Lucy kept watching. Not stagnant, the water carried some current as it rose. She thought if she could just push the mound away from the edge of the loft and keep it far enough out, maybe it would float on through the doorway at the other end of the shed. At least a foot and a half of space remained between the water and the top of the doorframe. The massive ant structure didn't seem to be taller than that, being much wider than it was tall.

Stepping over children she could not believe still slept through all the commotion, Lucy started searching for something long enough and strong enough to alter the trajectory of the dangerous mound.

She saw her daddy's fishing rods leaning up in the corner. Most were freshwater rods that were definitely too short and flimsy. But he owned one large saltwater rod that might work. It was longer and stouter, probably strong enough not to bend if she poked and prodded at the anthill. But what if she got the end caught in their looped legs? That eye through which the fishing line ran was big. Just her luck, she'd bring the ants closer rather than pushing them away.

She shone her light back toward the water, gauging the size of the floating mound. Lucy didn't think the ant hill was tall enough to hit the side of the loft and send the ants running across the floor, but she didn't want it floating up under the loft section of the shed either. As the water continued to rise, however slowly now, the ants would be caught beneath the wood flooring. She knew those ants could come up through the cracks.

Lucy opted for an old hoe handle lying up against the wall. She wished the hoe was on it—that would make a better tool for pushing, but at this point she couldn't be picky. By the time she got back to the railings, the ant hill was less than four feet from the edge. She handed her flashlight to Memaw who stood almost trancelike at the railing, watching the water, pointing the light toward the ants.

Lucy stretched the wooden handle out and shoved hard against the mound of interlinked and floating ants. The side was spongy and gave way to her prodding, not firm enough to be much affected by the small end of the handle. She'd given herself a little time, but needed some kind of leverage.

She frantically searched for something to throw over the floating ant island. She opened the chest where they stored blankets and quilts painstakingly stitched by her great-grandmother, grandmother, and even her mother. They might work, but she just couldn't bring herself to sling her family's prized possessions over a writhing bed of ants. She quickly convinced herself they were too big anyway.

In the decoration box, she found the tablecloth Memaw always used at Christmas. Granny had used it, too, and Granny's mother before her. The poinsettia scattered oilcloth dated back generations, and Lucy couldn't imagine Christmas dinner without using it. Glancing over at Memaw, Lucy knew she couldn't just throw that cloth away over a pile of biting beasts.

Panic started to set in, and she turned in circles.

"What do you need?" Memaw asked between spells of coughing.

"Something to throw over the ants," Lucy said. "Anything to cover them up."

Lucy closed her eyes and visualized all the items she knew were in the loft.

"What about the burlap bags?" Memaw suggested.

Of course! Why hadn't Lucy thought of that? Her granddaddy always used them for lima beans that had started to dry. Filled with the beans and lying in the sun, the bags bounced as the shells finished drying, then popped open, releasing the beans. Lucy used the bags to transport her peanuts which were certainly drowned and would begin rotting and molding almost immediately. She wouldn't need the bags this year.

"They're in the corner," Lucy said, hustling to find them. She grabbed a bag and began ripping the course thread from one side and the bottom to open it up, making it rectangular and flat.

Meanwhile, Memaw watched the floating ant island.

"Hurry," she said.

Lucy saw that the ants were uncomfortably close. She would have only one shot.

Opening the bag to its full width, Lucy grabbed a back corner with her left hand and a front corner with her right. Keeping her feet planted firmly, she turned her full body slightly to the left and twisted back toward the right, releasing each corner in turn, mimicking the motions she had seen her daddy use when he threw his minnow net. Her aim was perfect, and the burlap settled in the water, covering almost all of the floating island.

Lucy placed the hoe handle on the edge of the burlap covered mass and shoved. It responded, but not enough. Spinning slightly from Lucy's off-center contact, the ant island retreated only slightly. Lucy knew she'd have to let it float closer so she'd have more leverage when she tried again. At least it moved a little further toward a possible exit—an unexpected benefit of the less than centered push.

Lucy let the mound float closer to the edge of the loft. She positioned her prod slightly off-center, pushing not only out but in the direction of the doorway. Her method seemed to be effective, but she had a lot more work to do. The mound kept drifting back toward the loft.

"Any way I can help?" Memaw asked.

"I don't think so," Lucy said. "Just pray."

"Constantly," Memaw said.

Lucy moved down a ways and repeated her process, each time sending the floating bed of pain out a little farther and closer to the doorway. But it kept coming back. Lucy maintained her assault, moving down a few feet and pushing. The mound kept coming back. She saw some ants fall free and prayed that the stragglers would drown without the support of the others.

Finally, Lucy moved as far down as she could, standing directly over the ladder. Memaw moved down, too, leaning against the railing and holding on to the waistband of Lucy's jeans to steady her. Lucy leaned against the wall to give herself more support and gave one last shove.

She lost her balance and stumbled into the water, but the extra shift of her weight and strength solved the problem. She popped back up and grabbed onto the top rung of the ladder with one hand just in time to see the burlap covered ant bed float through the shed door and away from her family.

When she couldn't see Memaw, she cried out, "Are you ok?"

"Yep," she heard Memaw say. "Just landed on my butt."

Relieved, Lucy reached for the ladder with her other hand, pulled her feet onto the lower rungs and climbed back up. She collapsed on the floor and sobbed with relief while two big tongues licked her face.

Chapter 7

Wednesday, September 19

On the second day in the loft, the water rose more slowly and the current created by the flood decreased in speed and strength. But only two rungs could be seen on the ladder by the end of the day. If the water didn't stop rising soon, Lucy's family would be in grave danger. They had nowhere else to climb and no way to call for help.

That day presented other challenges, too. They still had plenty to eat and enough fresh water to last for many days to come. But the temperatures rose into the mid-nineties and the oppressive humidity stifled every breath. Misery compounded irritability.

Lucy washed Ella's leg wound with soap and bottled water three times a day, then applied drops of lavender oil right in the wound. The small gash on her head had practically healed, but Lucy continued to wash it and apply lavender oil there, too. She checked for fever. So far, so good.

But Memaw's cough became deeper and louder and more persistent. That day, when Lucy checked Memaw's temperature, it was almost 102, so she gave her more Tylenol. Lucy wished she could create a eucalyptus steam, but had no way to safely heat water and nothing for making a poultice either. She settled for Vicks Vaporub and convinced Memaw it was better than nothing. Lucy took the cough syrup from her supplies and poured Memaw a slightly larger than recommended dose from the almost empty bottle.

Mosquitoes swarmed and bit, causing itchy welts on arms and

legs.

Humidity hung heavy and the heat soared. No one was immune to the growing tension and impossibly irritating atmosphere. The boys would play together for a few minutes, then fight for hours, and yell at each other to shut up. Lucy had never allowed anyone in the family to say those words, but she was almost too tired to care.

Worst of all, the stench from body functions of five humans and two gigantic dogs filled the loft. They began to see dead animals floating in the water—a few of their chickens, somebody's dog, a cat or two, a raccoon—some following the slow moving current through the front and out the back of the shed, others visible outside the two small windows of their refuge.

Ella withdrew more than Lucy could remember since right after her daddy's death. She kept a book in her hand any time she sat down on her sleeping bag, but Lucy could tell she wasn't reading. When Lucy tried to engage her in conversation, Ella shut down completely. She spent most of her time standing at the window overlooking the barn, where the water covered the top of the doorway. But she never asked about the horses. She hadn't spoken in hours.

Lucy wanted to reassure Ella that Ace was fine, but she tried never to lie to her children. As much as she wanted to trust that horse, wise and ingenious beyond comprehension, she just didn't see how he and Brady could have survived. With the water as high as it was on the farm, Lucy couldn't think of any place nearby where dry ground could be found. And with Ella in danger at home, Lucy just didn't know how far Ace would go—even to save his own life.

Late in the day, Lucy decided she needed to do something to improve their living conditions. She rolled up the dogs' newspaper bathroom and tossed it out the window on the back side of the loft where the current flowed away from them. Then she took the bucket the humans used and tossed the contents out the same window as she prayed forgiveness for damaging the environment. She feared her granddaddy, who always taught them to respect nature and never do harm to any living thing, would roll over in his grave. Using some of their precious stash of water, she rinsed the bucket then squirted in some disinfectant they packed. She placed clean newspapers on the floor for the dogs.

Lucy opened the box of potpourri sachets she created to sell with her fall produce and hung several of the cinnamon scented sacks around the loft.

"Mom! Mom!" she heard the boys yelling in unison.

What now? Lucy wondered. She scanned the water. There, between a large log and a dead possum, a small bunny swam frantically.

"Nate, bring the fishing net," Lucy said. "It's in your corner with the rods. Hurry!"

Nate hurried to retrieve the net while Lucy and Benji kept close watch on the bunny. Memaw came over, too, but Ella still stood staring at the barn.

"Scoop him up," Lucy said, grabbing the back of Nate's shirt while he leaned over.

The log bumped up against the bottom of the loft floor just as Nate reached the net out and under the small, scared animal, then lifted him up into the loft.

"Empty one of the supply boxes," Lucy told Benji. "I don't care which one as long as it's deep so he can't get out. We'll make a bed for him. Poor thing is exhausted."

Caught in the net, the drenched ball of fur breathed heavily as the family gazed down at him. Even Ella limped over to see, bringing a large towel with her.

"Will this work in the box?" she asked.

"It will be perfect," Lucy said, happy to hear her daughter's voice. "Wrap him in it first so he will dry out and maybe you can calm him down a bit. He's frantic."

The boys helped untangle the bunny from the net and Ella wrapped him up in the towel, cooing to him as she snuggled him close. Ella never ceased to astonish Lucy with her uncanny connection to animals—from the gigantic horses to the tiniest creatures, she could communicate with them like no one else Lucy had ever seen. With the horses, she didn't even use words most of the time. She was already working her magic on the small bunny. His little long ears perked up now and his nose wiggled as he stared up at Ella.

"What can we feed him?" Benji asked.

"We have some lettuce and cabbages in the basket in the back corner by the shelves," Lucy said. "Tear off a few leaves and put them in his box. See what you can find to pour some water in, too."

"He needs a name," Nate said.

"But she might be a girl," Ella said. "I really think she is a girl. Look, she's already asleep. She was so exhausted."

"How about a name that could work for a boy or a girl," Lucy said. "Any ideas?"

"How about Fluffy," Benji said. "Boy bunnies and girl bunnies are fluffy."

"She is now that she's dry," Ella said. "She sure wasn't fluffy before."

"True," Lucy said, smiling and relieved to hear her children laugh, glad they found something to take their minds off their situation, even if only for a few minutes.

"That's a good one," Lucy said. "Any other ideas?"

"My stuffed bunny is named Floppy 'cause of his ears," Benji said. "He's a boy 'cause he's mine, but he could be a girl with that name, too. If he was Ella's bunny, he would be a she."

"We could use Flopsy, Mopsy, or Cottontail," said Ella.

"But they're all girls," Benji said. "And Peter is the boy."

"We are not going to name her Peter," Ella said emphatically. "We could name her after the hurricane."

"Florence?" Benji said. "No way! That's not a boy's name."

"Yuck!" Nate said. "That's a terrible name!"

"How about Lucky?" Ella said. "She's lucky we found her, and we're lucky she came our way."

"Family vote?" Lucy said.

"Sure," Ella said. "I'll count. All in favor of naming her Lucky, raise your hand."

The boys looked at each other and shrugged, then raised their hands along with Ella, Memaw, and Lucy.

"You are officially named Lucky," Ella said, touching the bunny between the ears like a knight being dubbed. "Now bring us some luck."

"Ok, guys," Lucy said. "Let's wash up and get ready to eat some supper. Sorry I can't cook anything, but we can have peanut butter and jelly sandwiches with chips and a cookie. That's about the best we can do tonight."

After they ate, Lucy kept a close watch on the water while the boys paired off to play cards and Ella held the bunny. She knew she'd have a struggle convincing Ella to put Lucky in the box at bedtime. She'd surely hop away if left unattended—even if Ella snuggled her close. Lucy estimated the ball of fur to be a baby—weaned but not nearly half grown. She didn't like to even consider what happened to its mother and siblings.

The debris laden water nearly reached the top rung of the ladder by nightfall. Anything floating would soon breach the floor of the loft. Lucy sent the kids to bed to conserve battery power from their flashlights and oil in the lanterns, but she knew she'd not close her eyes—even though nightmares could be preferable to their current reality.

§ § §

Lucy listened to the soft sounds of sleeping children—the rhythmic breathing, an occasional snort or snore, an indistinguishable word here or there spoken from the depths of dreams. She listened to Memaw's labored breathing and fits of coughing. Her fever hadn't spiked any higher, but did not diminish either. As hot as it was in the loft, Memaw snuggled beneath heavy covers.

But Ella remained awake. She had found a soft baby blanket in the cedar chest and swaddled Lucky in it so that even her ears were tucked in tight. Lucy unsuccessfully tried to convince Ella to put the bunny in the box.

"But she'll be all alone—and scared," Ella said. "She's lost everything. I can't do that to her."

Lucy acquiesced easily. Seeing Ella concentrating on something other than the horses relieved Lucy's fears that she would regress into silent brooding.

Lucy sat, leaned back against the wall near the top of the ladder as she had the night before. Even though she was already hot, she wrapped herself in the quilt Mama made for her when she was fourteen years old. It was a birthday present—the back a dark blue field for thousands of tiny gold sunflowers scattered across it. For the front, Mama cut squares from a fabric filled with large sunflowers. Each square held the full face of a flower. Around each square, she sewed strips of green, then pieced all the squares together.

Lucy loved watching Mama place the quilt in the same quilting frame that her mother and grandmother had used—a rickety wooden frame that allowed her to layer the top, the interior batting, and the back together with most of it lying on the floor at her feet. She stretched the first section tightly between the top rails less than an arm's length apart. As she completed each meticulously finger-stitched section, she would roll the back rod, winding the quilt through and bringing up a new section to stitch through all three layers.

Granny and Memaw stitched their quilts in circular patterns, but Mama always used arches—kind of like interlocking rainbows. Even as a child, Lucy thought of those rainbows as promises from her mama—promises of love and protection. She needed that right now more than she ever needed it in her life. And she needed the reminder to pray.

So, for the next few hours, that's what she did. Lucy prayed that God would stop the rising waters. She prayed that God would protect her family. She prayed that Memaw would get better. Lucy feared pneumonia and knew that could be deadly. She prayed that God would give her strength and wisdom and patience—although she started to take that last prayer back.

She'd always heard that praying for patience was dangerous because God could send adversity to teach patience. But she decided adversity had already arrived, and she really needed patience right now. Hers was onion-skin thin.

And she prayed for the ability to trust, not only in God's promise but in other people. She had the ominous feeling that if they were going to survive, she would soon be faced with the need to trust somebody—anybody—like she never had before. Even strangers. Lucy knew that she might have to release the total control she held onto so tightly, even if it were only perceived control. Trust was no longer something Lucy succumbed to easily. She fought daily to hold on to faith.

Dawn couldn't possibly be too far off, Lucy thought, as she fought to stay awake. Her head kept nodding and she'd jerk it back up, determined not to let her guard down. She scanned the water back and forth, readying herself for whatever might float by. The water had almost stilled—no more rushing current—and it seemed to have stopped rising. She leaned over to assess the height of the water in reference to the rungs of the ladder. The top rung was completely submersed, but the water didn't appear to be any deeper than it had been at dusk. Thank God.

Movement in the water caught her eye. Lucy stared but could not make out what it was. At first she thought she might be seeing a large stick or tree limb, but the object was moving in the still, stagnant floodwaters. Her heart raced as she reached for the flashlight by her side. When she shone the beam toward the movement, her worst fears became reality. She saw a snake—and not just any snake. A harmless water snake would have been bad enough, but this was a monster moccasin—a cottonmouth—deadly and heading straight toward her. With the water at the level it was, the snake could easily enter the loft.

Lucy quietly retrieved the .38 caliber handgun hidden in her backpack. She knew how to use it because she and Charlie often went target shooting in the woods, but she had not touched it in over a year—except to bring it to the loft. Her hands shook and her heart hurt at the sight of it. She had forced herself to grab the gun and ammunition at the last minute when the flood waters started rising. Now, she loaded it.

The water had risen so high that when Lucy placed the flashlight on the loft floor beside her, it illuminated the top of the water. The snake swam close enough now that she could see the slitted pupils of its eyes. She had time for one shot. Lucy steadied her arms and hands, pulled the hammer back with her right thumb, took aim, and squeezed the trigger.

The shot rang out in echoes around the shed, and the children started screaming. Memaw sprang from her pallet. Rex and Roxie yelped and growled. Lucy picked up the flashlight and shone it down into the water. She watched the snake—its head practically blown off—float under the loft floor. Trepidation quickly replaced relief. She knew that where there was one, more probably lurked.

Chapter 8

Thursday, September 20

When the sun rose on the third day in the loft, Lucy sat trancelike staring into the water. She hadn't slept and barely moved since shooting the snake. She still held the revolver in her right hand.

"Mom, the boys are awake," Ella said. "They're hungry, but they were scared to bother you. Are you alright?"

Lucy didn't respond. She just stared into the water.

"Mom," Ella said a little louder. "Are you ok?"

When Lucy still didn't answer, Ella gently touched her shoulder. "Mom?"

No response.

"Mom!" Ella said loudly. "We need you!"

The dogs started barking and Lucy swung around toward the noise, raising the gun in her hand.

"Mom! Don't!" Ella screamed. Her brothers echoed her cry.

Rex and Roxie surrounded Lucy—effectively blocking her from the children—and started licking her face. She finally responded. Carefully laying the gun down, she put her arms around Roxie's neck and started to cry.

The boys and Ella gathered around Lucy hugging her and the dogs. Memaw carefully slipped the gun off the floor and placed it high on a shelf where the boys couldn't reach it. Then she joined her family.

"Lucy," Memaw said, touching her shoulder until Lucy raised her head and looked at her. "Ella and I can take care of everything for a little while. You have to get some sleep. You haven't slept in days."

"I'll fix Pop Tarts for breakfast," Nate said.

"I can help, too," Benji said.

"Memaw is right," Nate said. "You coulda shot us."

Ella gave Nate a look that would melt steel.

"I mean you gotta rest," Nate said. "We been sleeping and you ain't slept none 'cause you been looking out for us. We're big enough to handle things for a while so you can sleep."

"But the snakes," Lucy said. "More will come."

"We'll take turns being lookouts," Ella said. "And if we see anything at all, we can wake you up. Besides, I know how to use the gun if I need to."

"Do not touch that thing!" Lucy said. "None of you. You promise right now!"

"We promise, right kids?" Memaw said, staring them down.

They all nodded in agreement.

"We need you to be rested and strong, Mom," Ella said, knowing that if she made everything about what they needed, her mom would be more likely to respond. "Please take a nap. We'll be safe in the daylight. Rex and Roxie would never let anything happen to us. You know that."

"You're right," Lucy said after a long silence. "I'll try."

While Lucy slept and Memaw sat in an old wooden rocker crocheting, Ella stood at the window overlooking the pasture—or at least where the pasture was supposed to be. Nothing but an extension of the river now, with only the top of the barn visible.

Her mom had fallen asleep a couple of hours earlier, and surprisingly seemed to be sleeping soundly even though the boys argued loudly over games and who was winning and who cheated and who was just plain mean. At least they did not resort to physically fighting, not yet. Given the circumstances, Ella considered that a feat in itself. She wanted so badly to just hit something.

Ella held Lucky in her arms. The little bunny liked the soft blanket—as long as Ella didn't try to swaddle her with her ears down.

They stuck up like little antennae, only fuzzy like bedroom slippers.

"You're my sweet girl," Ella said, rubbing Lucky's head from her ears, down between her eyes, to her tiny twitching nose. "I won't let anything happen to you, I promise."

Then she felt guilty. She had promised Ace the same thing many times—that she would never let anything bad happen to him. And what did she do? Yelled at him and left him to fend for himself while the water just came rushing in and covered everything. What was he supposed to do, fly? A terrifying picture had formed itself in her mind that first night, and she couldn't shake it no matter how hard she tried—Ace standing nearby with the water rising up his legs, covering his back, soaking his mane. Beautiful ebony Ace, with his proud head held high until water covered it, too.

Above the ruckus the boys were making, Ella heard a new sound, sort of like a lawnmower, but that was crazy.

"Shush, guys, listen!" Ella said. "Do you hear that? Memaw, did you hear it?"

"What?" Benji said. "I don't hear nothing."

"Yeah, there ain't even any birds or crickets or squirrels or nothing making noise," Nate said.

"Just listen," Ella said.

"I hear it," Memaw said. "Sounds like an outboard motor. We better wake your mom up."

"Let's wait just a little," Ella said. "I don't want to wake her up if it's nothing to worry about. We told her we could handle it."

But two very rambunctious dogs thought otherwise. Rex and Roxie heard it, too, and started barking and growling. They rushed to the railing as close to the front opening of the shed as possible in the direction of the noise, barking non-stop.

"What's going on?" Lucy said. "How long have I been asleep?"

"Just a few hours, Mom," Ella said. "Everybody is fine, but we might need you now. We think there's a boat coming."

"Where's my gun?" Lucy said without hesitation.

"I put it on the top shelf over the tomatoes," Memaw said.

"You kids get back as far as you can. Stay out of sight," Lucy said.

"Memaw, try not to cough."

The sound grew increasingly louder, and in the distance Lucy could see a small dot moving toward them in the water. As it came closer, she could make out a jonboat with two passengers—one in the back steering the motor by the tiller, and one in the front with binoculars. Both were men.

Lucy simultaneously wanted to holler for help and hide in the shadows with her family. She gripped the cold metal of the handgun and stepped into the sunlight streaming through the loft window. There was no way the boat would fit under the small space left between floodwaters and the header of the door. She made herself seen in the window and raised her gun.

"Hey, lady. Put that thing down!"

The person in the front was nothing more than a teenage boy, she realized, but didn't lower her gun. He wore a camouflaged t-shirt and jeans with heavy rubber boots that reached up to his knees. His ball cap sported what Lucy recognized as the garnet and gold of Ashley High School in Wilmington—the brand new school she had to leave in 2001 when she moved in with her grandparents. Shaggy dark hair curled around the edges.

"We thought you might want some help," the boy said, "But we aren't coming any closer until you get rid of that gun. We're not here to hurt anybody."

"Ma'am," said the older gentleman, who Lucy realized wasn't old at all when he puttered the boat a little closer. "We're just out looking for survivors, people we can help. You and your neighbors are having it bad right now, and me and my boy are just trying to help out. We took your neighbor out to the church. Mr. Rigsby? He said we might better check on you and your grandma and your kids just in case you were still here."

"What church?" Lucy asked, recognizing her neighbor's name even though they had never been close.

"The one about ten miles north of here up on that hill that always looked out of place. Mount Calvary? You know that one? Anyhow, seems God might have put it there years ago knowing what was coming. Kinda like Noah's Ark before the flood. It's the only place for miles in every direction that's not under water. They have huge generators for electricity, but the landlines don't work. Cell service is spotty.

"We go to the First Baptist Church in Wilmington and when my pastor got a message from the pastor at Mt. Calvary saying they were trying to rescue people and bring them to the church, we figured we could help since we have a boat. It's not big, but we can haul a few people at a time. Wilmington's pretty much cut off from everything, too. All the roads coming in are either flooded or washed out, so we put the boat in almost before we got out of town."

The man's soft southern drawl and easy-going mannerisms calmed Lucy enough that she lowered the gun, but she didn't let go.

"The name's Sam Matthews, ma'am, and this is my son, Ryan. I'm going to come a little closer now so we can tie off, ok?"

"Alright, but don't make any wake. The water's already about to swamp us."

Sam slowly maneuvered the jonboat up just below the window. He tossed a line to Lucy, and she wrapped it around a nail in the window casing.

"Now ma'am, tell us how we can help you."

Sam looked to be about forty if Lucy were guessing right, with eyes the color of molasses. Eyes like Charlie. Honest eyes. He looked like he spent a lot of time outdoors—tanned and a bit wrinkled. Like his son, he wore camouflage, but only his pants. His black t-shirt stretched tightly across a muscular chest and arms. He wore an Operation Enduring Freedom Veteran ball cap. Lucy waffled between fear, respect, gratitude, and admiration. When he smiled at her silent stare, she wavered.

"I don't know you," she said. "Your boat won't hold all of us, and I surely cannot send my children away with strangers."

"Holds more than you think, ma'am," Ryan said. "How many people you talking about?"

"Five," Lucy said, not happy that the children and Memaw had gathered behind her.

"And two big dogs," Ella said. "We can't leave them here alone."

Rex and Roxy barked on cue, pushing their way to the window and hanging their huge shaggy heads out.

"Well, unless any of you weighs more than 200 pounds, I believe we can get you there," Sam said. "But we can't take the dogs."

"We're not leaving them," Ella said. "Mom, we can't leave them! If we try, they'll jump in the water and try to follow us. They'll drown!"

"She's right," Lucy said to Sam. "I think we'll just take our chances. The water looks like it stopped rising. It can't be long before it goes down, and we can get on with our lives. In the meantime, we have plenty of food and fresh water, and we're dry up here."

"The rivers have not crested and probably won't until Saturday at the earliest," Sam said. "That's two more days. And even then, I wouldn't be so sure about any of this water going down any time soon, especially if one of the dams up river breaks or worse yet—and you know they do it—somebody opens the dams in those lakes so as to protect the big cities and fancy houses in the middle of the state. They got a lot of rain from this storm, too, and they will sacrifice us downriver to keep dry up there. You know it as well as I do."

Lucy stood silent for a few moments, taking in what Sam said. She knew he was right. And when the flood waters did go down, what would she have? Certainly no house they could live in, no vehicle that would run. They couldn't live in the loft forever. The heat and humidity were suffocating. And the bugs were getting worse. The mold would start growing and make them sick. The dead animals made the water dangerous, and there was no telling what kind of toxins washed into the water from all the farms and factories. The mud would be dangerous, too. And what if the horses hadn't left? What if they drowned, were under all that water, just lying there rotting? Ella would never live through seeing that.

"I don't mean to rush you ma'am, but if we're going to save your family before it gets dark, we got to get going," Sam said. "We don't risk life and limb after dark. It's just too dangerous."

Lucy looked down at the boat as though she had forgotten they were there.

"But I don't know you," she said. "How am I supposed to send my kids off with strangers? How do I know you two aren't some hoodlums who will kidnap my kids and kill me and take what little bit I have left? I can assure you that I have no cash—well maybe just a little bit, but certainly not enough to kill me over."

Ryan turned his face toward the bottom of the boat to hide his smile. He had seen the pretty blonde teen hovering behind her mama, taking a stand for the animals. He liked that about her almost as much as he liked the way she looked. But her mama was some kind of lunatic.

They had saved three families already that day. Other boats were out rescuing people, too. But he and his dad got this assignment. Go figure. He was ready to go home, take a shower, eat, and watch TV. At least the power was still on in their part of Wilmington. Well, it was when they left before dawn. No telling what they might find when they got back home.

Memaw started coughing—a ragged hacking cough from deep inside her chest. Lucy looked back at her. She was flushed and shaking. Her fever must be higher.

"My grandmother is sick," Lucy said. "She needs a doctor."

Sam simply smiled at Lucy and said, "Ma'am, there's times in our lives when we just got to pray and thank God for whatever blessing he sends us, even if it don't look like we think it ought to look. You can't stand there and tell me honest that you haven't prayed for God to save you and your children."

He stopped and waited for Lucy to answer, but she didn't say anything. Memaw just kept coughing.

"Well, ma'am," Sam said. "Ryan and I here in this boat are the answer to your prayers whether we look like your idea of an answer or not. Sometimes you just gotta trust people. Sometimes that's all we got. And I just happen to be a doctor."

"You are?" Lucy said, astonished.

"Yes, ma'am, I am," Sam said. "I don't always look like this, but it's been a long day already. If you'll let me come up, I'll check on your grandma. Sounds like she might need some help."

Ella pulled on her mom's arm and motioned for her to move away from the window.

"Mom, I need to talk to you. Now!" Ella said.

Lucy took Ella's hand and led her away from the others.

"I'm scared, Mom," Ella said. "We don't know them. How can we trust them? I wish Daddy were here."

"I don't know," Lucy said. "I don't know. But what choice do we have? We can't live up here forever, and what if he's right? What if the rivers haven't crested? What if they do open the dams? What if the water keeps rising and comes into the loft? We have no higher place to go. I've done all I know to do, Ella. Sometimes we just have to trust in people—even people we don't know—especially when the alternative is probably worse. And that young man doesn't look much older than you. He lives in Wilmington. He doesn't have to be out here in the sticks. He could be home watching television, but he's out here doing good things for strangers. And Memaw is really sick. We don't have a choice. We have to trust them."

"Ma'am?" Sam yelled. "We got to be going. Are you coming with us or not?"

Lucy looked at her daughter, and Ella nodded.

"Yes!" Lucy hollered back. "We're coming."

"Do you have a rope you can throw down to me?" Sam asked. "I'll grab my bag and come up to check on your grandma while you get your stuff together—not much stuff, now mind you."

Lucy gathered the children together and told them to start packing their backpacks.

"Pack fast—only what you need, but don't forget clean underwear, your sleeping bag, and your toothbrush," Lucy said.

She went to the window and tossed a rope down to Sam, who easily climbed up and into the loft.

Memaw sat in her rocker, wrapped in a quilt.

"My name's Sam, ma'am," he said kneeling in front of her. "Sounds like you need a little help."

She barely acknowledged him.

78

Sam opened his bag and began examining Memaw.

"Your fever is 103.5," he said. "I'm afraid you might have pneumonia. We need to get you to the hospital ASAP."

"How will we do that?" Lucy asked.

"There's an EMS station not too far from where I left my truck on Hwy 421," Sam said. "If I can get her there, the paramedics will be able to put her on some oxygen and monitor her on the way to the hospital in Wilmington. The whole downtown is flooded, but they can go the long way around and get her to the hospital."

"But I can't send my grandma off with someone I don't know!" Lucy argued.

"I need a word with you—in private," Sam answered, trying his best to be patient. He took Lucy by the elbow and led her to farthest corner in the loft. She let him.

"Your grandmother is very sick," Sam said. "I won't lie to you. She could die if we don't get her some help fast. I can take her to the EMS station and still have time to come back here and take you and your children to the church. But you can't dilly-dally anymore. Either you trust me or you don't, but don't endanger your grandma's life because you're scared. Hell, everybody's scared right now."

"Why can't we go with you now? Can't you take us somewhere in Wilmington?" Lucy asked.

"No, the shelters are filling up fast there, too, and we have instructions to take you and the other people in your area to the church. Those are my marching orders, and I learned long ago when to follow orders without question."

"Ok," Lucy said, dropping her head. "I understand."

Sam touched her shoulder, and Lucy didn't pull away.

"She'll get the care she needs there," Sam said, "and I'll check on her personally when I get back to town."

"How will you get her in the boat?" Lucy asked. "Normally she's a very strong woman and could probably shimmy right down that rope, but she's so weak now."

"The water is high enough that it's not far down to the boat," Sam said. "Bring me a bed sheet if you've got one, and we'll make a sling so I can lower her slowly down to Ryan."

Lucy and the boys gave Memaw hugs and kisses and told her they would see her soon.

"Get better, Memaw," Ella whispered, leaning down close. "We can't lose you, too."

Memaw hugged Ella as tightly as she could.

"Don't worry yourself about me Ella girl," she said. "I'm going to dance at your wedding—but not for at least a dozen years!"

"I'll be back for you and the kids as quick as I can," Sam told Lucy. "Be ready."

"We will," Lucy said. "Please take care of her."

"I'll make sure she gets the care she needs," Sam said. "And I'll be back soon."

"Ms. Lucy?" Ryan said tentatively. When Lucy didn't respond, he spoke louder.

"Ms. Lucy?"

Lucy leaned out the window and looked down into the boat where Ryan sat with his arm around her grandmother.

"Yes?" Lucy answered.

"I know you're worried about your dogs and all. And I'm sure you're right about them trying to follow you because they don't know us either, and they'll want to protect you."

"Well, I think they've decided you're good people. They're not barking or growling at you."

"True, but I have an idea," Ryan said. "There's some other people out trying to rescue animals and taking them to the shelters and vets' offices and other places in Wilmington where it's not flooded. I can call them up when I get close enough to Wilmington for my phone to work and send them out here to pick up your dogs if you want. I believe I can give them good enough directions."

"That would be wonderful," Ella said, leaning out from behind her mom. "They have our phone number and address on their tags. But I don't guess either one of those matter anymore."

Lucy put her arm around Ella and said, "We'll figure it out."

"Thank you," Ella said to Ryan, then leaned in and whispered to

80

her mother. "I think he might be one of the good guys."

Lucy hugged her daughter. "I think you might be right."

They stood that way for several minutes watching the boat—with Memaw inside—disappear around the bend.

Chapter 9

Lucy thought about what Sam said—the rivers would not crest for at least two more days. Although it was rising more slowly now, that probably meant the water would breach the loft. And if the lock and dams in the river broke or they released the dams in the lakes...

"We have a lot to do before they get back to pick us up," Lucy said. "Put your backpacks next to the window and let's get everything else up as high as we can put it."

Since Lucy and Memaw had not completed canning for the season, many of the shelves sat partially filled, organized by what the jars held. That didn't matter much anymore. The children helped Lucy move all the jars to highest shelves, filling each shelf to capacity and leaving the lower ones empty.

They folded the quilts they had been using, and Lucy laid them across the jars on the top shelf. The cedar chest still contained more quilts and family heirlooms. Lucy looked around for anything they could use to move it up higher.

A set of Grandpa's saw horses stood stacked on each other in the corner—moved to the loft when they were no longer sturdy enough to use. Throwing them away was out of the question. Maybe, if she could secure the sawhorses to the shelving that would keep them steady enough in slowly rising water.

The boys moved the sawhorses in front of the shelves and Lucy tied everything together. Ella helped her lift the cedar chest and sit it on top of the sawhorses.

"What about the Christmas decorations?" Ella asked, pointing to the plastic containers stacked against the wall. "And the paper products."

"Let's put them all on top of the cedar chest," Lucy said. "Hopefully, the water won't get high enough to float anything off."

Looking around the loft, Lucy decided they'd done about as much as they could. A couple of feet of water inside the loft wouldn't reach anything she couldn't bear to lose.

"Ok," Lucy said, turning to her children. "Let's figure out what to do with the dogs and make sure we have the bare essentials in our backpacks so we're ready when they get back.

"Where is Spoof?" Ella asked.

"I don't know," Lucy said. She looked around but did not see the cat.

They kept busy for what seemed like hours, but the boat had not yet returned. With nothing else to keep her occupied, Lucy started to worry. Deep down she felt that Sam and Ryan were as Ella said—some of the good guys—but she couldn't help question her decision to send her very sick grandmother off with strangers. People were always taking advantage of senior citizens these days.

Lucy stopped pacing and looked at Benji, Nate, and Ella playing Uno. She could see concern on Ella's face, but the boys were nonchalant about the drama unfolding around them. Their backpacks sat ready by the window.

Rex and Roxie lay quietly in their corner of the loft. Lucy found old ski ropes and prepared them to tie the dogs up—something she had never done before. But she knew that if she didn't restrain them in some way, they would try to follow and protect her and the kids and would die in the attempt. She just hoped that Ryan would be able to contact the animal rescuers he mentioned in time to save her dogs.

Lucy heard the hum of the outboard motor in the distance and moved to the window so she could watch Sam and Ryan approach.

"Pack up your cards and grab your backpacks," she said. "The boat is coming."

Then she tied up the dogs and hugged them desperately, squeezing herself between their big heads. When she lifted her head, she spotted Spoof sitting on a limb in the oak tree closest to the loft. As free spirited as that cat was, she knew there was nothing she could do to help him.

She turned her attention back to the dogs and whispered reassuringly but firmly, "Stay."

Lucy heard Sam's congenial voice calling, "Ahoy there, maties! Time to board the rescue ship."

"That's not a ship," Benji laughed. "It's too little."

"But it is our rescue vessel," Lucy said to him. She looked out the window at Sam and Ryan in the jonboat. It seemed even closer to the height of the window than when Sam left with Memaw.

"The water is still rising," Lucy said. "Did they release the dams?"

"Not yet," Sam said. "But there's talk of it, so we need to get you guys to safety."

Lucy caught the line and tied it off so she could help the kids out the window and into the boat.

"How are we going to do this?" Lucy asked.

"We're not too far below the window," Sam said. "We'll just have to ease everybody down one at a time. You want to go first young lady?"

"Yes," Ella said, "and you can call me Ella."

"Ella, it is," Sam said. "Toss me your bag."

"How about I come down and then Mom can hand my bag to me. Will that work?"

"Suit yourself," Ryan said, reaching out to help her down.

Ella handed her bag to her mother and said, "Gently, ok?"

"You didn't," Lucy said, and Ella just smiled.

Benji went next, then Nate. When they were all settled in, the boat sat low in the water, and Lucy's concern apparently showed on her face.

"We'll be fine," Sam assured her as he held the rope steady and reached up to help her climb down into the boat.

With one final goodbye to the dogs, Lucy took a last look at all the shelves full of food. She thought about the past work and future promise they represented. Her heart caught at the thought of losing that, too, if the water continued to rise. She tossed her bag to Ryan, grabbed hold of Sam's hand, and climbed through the window.

Rex and Roxie started howling.

Benji called dibs on the back seat. He wanted to help steer, but Sam let him down easy, saying he knew he was capable under better circumstances, but there was just too much debris in the water to chance it this time.

"Why don't you let your mom sit back here and you go up front with Ryan so you can see better," Sam said.

Ella sat down on the center seat when she loaded, but Benji and Nate insisted they needed to sit together in the middle. Ella was too embarrassed to argue with her brothers. They could be such brats.

"Come on, Ella," Ryan said. "You can sit up front with me. I could use your help watching for debris in the water and making sure we go the right way."

"How can you tell where you're going?" Ella asked, looking around. She saw nothing but water, the tops of trees, rooftops, and occasional windows of two-story houses. It was so eerie.

"We're using a compass and a GPS," Ryan said. "The church is due north. And there's still a few landmarks to help us know where we've been so we can get back—a building here or there on a rise, or some very tall trees or telephone and power poles."

"Make sure you keep your hands inside the boat," Sam said to his passengers. "No telling what's in the water."

They skimmed along steadily, but not fast. The boys became uncharacteristically silent, and Ella turned back to make sure they were still there. She held her backpack steady between her feet, careful not to jostle or squeeze it. She wasn't sure what she'd do when they arrived, but she'd figure it out.

"I'm 18," Ryan said. "I'm a senior at Ashley High School."

"I'm 13," Ella said. "I just started my last year of middle school at Cape Fear. I play volleyball. Or at least I did. I don't even know where we'll live or where we'll go to school now."

"Yeah, I heard a lot of schools in the county are flooded or damaged," Ryan said. "And all the roads are messed up—so I'm hearing nobody will be going to school here any time soon."

"That's just great," Ella said.

"Maybe you could move to Wilmington."

"Yeah, maybe," Ella said. "But I don't know where I'd keep my horses there."

"Horses?" Ryan said. "Where are they now?"

Ella felt her throat knot up and her eyes fill. She looked away as she fought back the tears.

"Ella?" Ryan asked tentatively. "I didn't mean to make you sad."

"I don't know where they are," she said with a sob. "I yelled at Ace to make him leave and Brady followed him. We made them take care of themselves. I don't know what happened to them."

"Tell me about your horses," Ryan said.

As Sam slowly navigated the boat through flood waters filled with debris, Ella brought Ryan into her world and talked about the horses—especially Ace. Ella lost herself in memories from the day she first met and fell in love with Ace, through the times he saved her emotionally and physically, to the last time she saw him after he carried her to the tractor shed so her wounded leg would not get wet in the polluted floodwaters. She knew she saw hurt in Ace's eyes when she yelled at him and told him to leave. She deserted him.

"He's the best thing that ever happened to me," Ella said. "I don't know how I could even live without him."

"Ace sounds super special," Ryan said. "I'd be willing to bet that he figured out a way to save himself and Brady, too."

Ella looked up at Ryan and offered a small smile.

Sitting on the back seat next to Sam, Lucy fought the tears that threatened to fall. She had struggled successfully over the past few months to lift herself out of the depths of that dark place she descended after Charlie died. She feared that this disaster would swallow her up like the flood waters engulfed her farm, but for right now at least, she held her tears at bay.

Lucy watched Ryan and Ella talking and listened to Sam engaging her boys in conversation, pointing out the tops of places no longer recognizable amidst the devastation.

"Look at that!" she heard Nate yell. "It's a deer on top of a house!"

Lucy looked where her son pointed, and sure enough, a deer stood on the peak of a housetop, the only part of the house visible above the water. She thought about all the other animals—wild and domestic—that surely died as the flood waters rose. And she prayed that through some miraculous force of nature and divine intervention, Ace and Brady found dry land.

Her mind became a movie reel she couldn't control. From visions of neighbors and animals drowning and water swallowing up every material thing they owned to all the work they put into the farm and all the vegetables left to harvest and sell and all the kids' toys and clothes and her dogs and her horses and her whole life being sucked under the mud. She couldn't hold it in any longer. Tears fell in torrents and her body began to shake.

Ryan and Ella both noticed, then Ryan began engaging the boys in conversation, pointing out anything he could find to keep them from looking at their mom—giving her a moment to compose herself.

Sam put his arm around Lucy and she sank into his broad chest, drawing strength from his reassurances and the steady cadence of his voice as he told her to just let it go.

"Mommy?" Benji said. "Are you okay?"

"Your mom will be just fine," Sam told him. "She just needs a minute to get all that sadness out. I bet she's been real strong for you kids and your grandma the last few days and she's real tired. But she'll be just fine—probably by the time we reach the church. Look ahead. See which one of you can spot it on the horizon first."

Look ahead, Lucy heard Sam say to her boys and feared what the future held. As her tears ebbed to a trickle and her sobbing slowed to snubs, Lucy knew she should pull away. But Sam's warmth and strength and the soothing motion of his hand rubbing her shoulder tethered her to him for just a little while longer. She was barely aware when Sam shifted so that her head rested in his lap, and she drifted off to sleep.

"There!" Nate said after more than half an hour of watching passed. "I see a church over there. Is that where we're going?"

"Great eye," Ryan said. "That's exactly where we're going—only dry land around for miles."

The boys' excited whooping and hollering startled Lucy out of a sleep deeper than any she had experienced since before the hurricane. She sat upright, looked around to get her bearings, and settled her gaze on Sam's smiling face.

"I'm so sorry," she said, embarrassment tinting her cheeks.

"No problem," Sam said reassuringly. "I'm sure you haven't slept in days, and I'm afraid the conditions at the church won't be conducive to sound sleep either. You needed that few minutes, and I was happy to oblige."

Lucy let herself be warmed by his words.

"Hold on," Sam said. "We might bump a bit when the boat slides onto the hill. You guys man your backpacks."

Ella had seen the church many times before—they sometimes rode by it on their way to Burgaw—but it looked so different sitting on the hill surrounded by water. It was on an island unto itself with a few vehicles parked around that must have been driven there before the flood. They surely couldn't go anywhere now without adding pontoons and an outboard motor.

The late afternoon sun lit the large white building like a beacon and reflected off the stained-glass windows, casting color into the air. Atop the steeple, a white cross rose upward into a sky so clear and blue that its beauty denied the devastation swallowing up everything for miles around.

In the midst of all that incongruent beauty, Ella thrilled at an area of brush and trees off to the side of the unflooded area—a place where she could possibly keep Lucky. She clutched her backpack in front of her, careful not to squeeze too tightly. She vowed to keep the precious bundle of fur with her as long as possible.

Sam eased the jonboat gently onshore. The boys jumped out of the boat and ran up the hill. Ryan threw the boys' forgotten bags onto the grass, then reached back to offer his hand to help Lucy out. Ella had never known a boy his age who was so gallant.

"Are you okay?" Ella asked her mother.

"I'll be fine," Lucy said.

"Let me introduce you to Sally Warren," Sam said to Lucy. "She's the pastor's wife and she's in charge. She'll help you settle in as best you can."

"Can you keep an eye on the boys?" Lucy said to Ella.

"Sure," she replied, looking over at her brothers who already headed toward the playground.

"I'll help you," Ryan said, "But it's not like they can go anywhere unless they swim."

"Let's sit there," Ryan said, pointing to a picnic table near the playground.

Ella slipped her hand inside her backpack and touched Lucky's soft fur. She knew the bunny needed food and water, but she couldn't bring herself to reveal her—not yet. The bunny sniffed Ella's hand, tickling it with her whiskers—proof that she was alive.

When Sam and Lucy entered the church, he raised his hand at a middle-aged woman coming toward them—a welcoming smile barely masking exhaustion. Her strawberry blonde hair was piled on top of her head with escaped curls cascading around her face.

"Mrs. Warren, this is Lucy Brown. She and her three children will be staying a while."

"Welcome," Mrs. Warren said. "We're a little crowded in here right now, but we hope to disperse folks around the church building as the day wears on. A lot of good people like Sam and his son are literally saving people all over the county."

"Good people indeed," Lucy said, looking around.

Sam touched Lucy on her shoulder, and she jumped.

"Sorry," he said. "Just wanted you to know I'm going to check on a few things, then head on out."

Lucy smiled tentatively and nodded slightly. She didn't want him to leave—they stood in a sea of sad strangers.

"Let me help you find a room," Mrs. Warren said, touching her elbow and directing her down a hallway.

Ella caught a glimpse of Sam jogging across the grounds toward a couple of men in boats that had just arrived.

"Your dad seems really nice," Ella said. "Do you have other family?"

"Just my little sister," Ryan said. "She's three."

"And your mom?" Ella asked, immediately regretting her question when she saw the tortured expression darken Ryan's face. "I'm sorry. None of my business."

"Nah, it's okay," Ryan said. "She died when Faith was born. I should be able to handle it by now, but it's hard, you know?"

"I do know," Ella said. "My daddy died a little over a year ago."

She didn't tell him how.

"I'm sorry," Ryan said, pausing only momentarily before continuing. "Being an only child for so long spoiled me, I guess. But they were so excited when they found out mom was pregnant. They had been wanting more children ever since I was a toddler. Mom and dad both said it wasn't because having me wasn't enough, but that because having me was so amazing that they wanted more children. They said they wanted me to have siblings. I was fine just like I was."

"I'm glad I have my brothers," Ella said, "even though they can aggravate the fool out of me sometimes."

"I'm glad I have my sister, too," Ryan said. "At least I am now. But back then, I didn't want things to change. And then when mom died having her, I was mad at Faith. Imagine being mad at a baby. But if she hadn't been born, I'd still have a mom."

"How did your dad handle it?" Ella asked. "I can't imagine a macho guy like your dad knows much about taking care of little girls."

"You'd be surprised," Ryan said. "He even knows how to French braid hair. And Faith looks just like my mom did—same blonde curls, same blue eyes. I took after my dad, but Faith is all mom."

"I guess that helped," Ella said. "Or maybe it made missing her worse. Why does life have to be so hard?"

"I don't know," Ryan said. "Why do you keep your hand in your bag? You don't have a gun or knife or something in there, do you? I'm really a nice guy."

90

"No argument there," Ella said. "You are the nicest guy I know. Can I trust you with a secret? I need some help."

"Sure," Ryan said. "I'm good for it."

Ella slowly unzipped her bag, revealing the bunny hidden inside.

"She was swimming in the flood waters, and we rescued her with the fishing net," Ella said. "I couldn't leave her behind to die."

"Of course you couldn't," Ryan said, "but I know they won't let you keep her here."

"I was wondering if you thought she'd stay in the bushes if I put her there," Ella said. "I have some cabbage leaves and stuff in my bag to feed her, but I don't have a cage or anything."

"Well, she can't go too far unless she swims," Ryan said, "and I bet she's had enough of that."

"But what if something hurts her?" Ella asked.

"I haven't seen any dogs around," Ryan said. "But there are a lot of kids, and I'd be afraid some of them might chase her and scare her enough that she'd try to run away."

"What should I do then?"

"Maybe you could let her out for a few minutes to eat and do whatever else she probably needs to do, then put her back in your bag for the night. She might be too scared to run away right now."

"What then?"

"I've got a cage at home," Ryan said. "Maybe I could bring it tomorrow, and we could hide it in the bushes so she can't run away."

"Will you help me now?"

Ryan glanced up the hill and saw his dad trotting their way.

"Doesn't look like I can stay," Ryan said. "Dad's in a hurry and we have to get back before dark. Faith's been with the neighbor every day, and we need to pick her up and spend some time with her before bed. She's too little to know what's going on."

"Ok," Ella said, understanding, but not wanting him to leave.

"I'm pretty sure we'll be back tomorrow. Hang in there, ok?"

"Yeah, sure," Ella said. "Thanks."

"Come on champ," Sam said to Ryan as he passed. "Gotta get a move on."

Ryan caught up with his dad and helped shove the boat back into the flood waters. He had something on his mind he wanted to ask, but was sure it would probably go over like a lead balloon. They rode in silence for what seemed like miles. If he didn't speak up soon, it would be too late.

"What's on your mind, son?" Sam asked, leaving Ryan no choice but to answer.

"I was thinking about Ella and her family," Ryan said. "Did you know they owned horses?"

"No, I didn't."

"Ella said they opened the gates and shooed the horses away when the flood waters started rising. Her horse's name was Ace. He was her best friend. She's had a pretty tough life the last year or so and that horse helped her cope. They have so much to deal with now, I just can't imagine how hard it is. Do you think those horses could have survived?"

"I don't know, son," Sam said. "I just don't know how or where."

"But we do know where their dogs are," Ryan said. "And we could do something about them."

"I'm not so sure we can," Sam said.

"Come on dad," Ryan said. "You saw how upset Ms. Lucy was at leaving them. They've lost so much already. We can do something about those dogs. Can't we?"

Sam thought about Lucy's breakdown and how right it felt to comfort her. Ryan wasn't asking for all that much. They did have a fenced yard where they could keep the dogs for a little while. And it would be amazing to give Lucy the news that her dogs were safe. That was something they could do—such a little thing they could do.

"Do you remember their names?" Sam asked Ryan. "They might not tear us to bits if we call them by their names."

"All right!" Ryan said, pumping his fist in the air. "Their names are Rex and Roxie. Ella told me her family rescued them when they were just pups and that they had protected the family and their farm ever since. They even saved them from a water moccasin swimming in the flood waters toward the loft—the dogs and her mom's dead

92

aim with a .38."

"Why does that not surprise me," Sam said, chuckling. He sped up the motor and headed toward the farm.

Chapter 10

Ella tucked Lucky safely back into her bag following a brief but successful romp in the bushes. Lucy wasn't thrilled about keeping the bunny and trying to sneak it inside, but she didn't have the heart to tell Ella no. She gathered her children up for a pep talk before heading back inside.

"We will be in tight quarters for a while," Lucy told them, "But Ms. Warren was able to find us a small classroom that we could share as a family—just us. They have a fair amount of food right now, but don't be greedy. I'll expect you to take what you need at meal times, but don't you dare let me see you wasting food. And I expect all of you to be on your best behavior. Everybody is tense and upset and scared and worried and the last thing we need to hear is children squabbling. Do you understand?"

They all responded affirmatively by either nodding or saying, "Yes, ma'am."

"How long will we be here?" Nate asked.

"I wish I knew the answer to that," Lucy said. "It all depends on the flood waters."

"But where will we go when we leave?" Benji asked.

"Nobody can answer that question," Ella said. "Right, Mom?"

"Unfortunately, I do not have an answer to that right now," Lucy acknowledged, "but we'll figure it out as we go. The most important thing is that we're all safe and all together again."

"Not everybody," Nate said. "Not Rex and Roxie."

"And not Ace or Brady," Ella said. "Or Spoof."

"And not our chickens," Benji said. "Or our toys or our clothes or our bikes or nothing."

"And not Memaw," Lucy said. "But she's where she needs to be to get better."

"I hope she'll be alright," Ella said.

"I'm sure she will be," Lucy said. "She's one tough lady. And the other three people I love most in the whole wide world are safe and right here with me. Grab your bags. Let's get our room set up and see if there's any way we can help with supper."

They started up the hill to the church just as another boat pulled in full of more refugees from the flood.

§ § §

David found little opportunity to call Lucy, and the couple of times he tried, he couldn't get through. He hadn't worried too much since the last he saw before Florence hit was that she had decreased to tropical storm strength.

But then his buddy Brian got an email from back home in Tennessee.

"Hey, Randolph," Brian said to David. "Don't you have family down on the coast in North Carolina?"

"Yep," David said. "My grandmother, my sister, and her three kids."

"Have you heard about the flooding?"

"What flooding?"

"From Hurricane Florence," Brian said. "That storm slowed down and dropped over thirty inches of rain in just a couple or three days. They say all the rivers have overflowed and flooded out thousands of people. Mama's been keeping a close eye on it since she has family down there, too. Phones and power are out, roads are either flooded or washed out—even the main ones like Hwy 74, Hwy 421, and I-40. It's a real mess."

"I haven't been able to reach my sister," David said, worry settling heavy in his chest. "I thought everything was going to be fine. It had

95

been downgraded when I left the states, so I wasn't worried until I couldn't reach her on the house phone or her cell phone. Tried calling Ella, too, and couldn't get through. Teenagers always have their cell phones."

"Yeah, man," Brian said. "Maybe the service is just spotty because of the water."

"I'll email her before we head out tonight," David said. "But no telling when we'll get to check email again."

"Just gonna have to pray, brother," Brian said. "For them and for us."

§ § §

Lucy had never been comfortable around crowds, and living with solitude and serenity on the farm certainly did not prepare her for their current situation. People stood shoulder to shoulder waiting in line for food. Babies cried, children fought, and adults argued. She shepherded her children through the line for hot dogs and chips then out the side door to sit in the grass. In spite of the mosquitoes, being outside was preferable to the chaos inside. The moon crested the tops of the pines and stars started to flicker. Lucy clung to the night splendor as a promise that everything would ultimately be alright.

Back inside, they navigated their way through the people, down the hall, and into the small classroom that would serve as their sanctuary during their stay. The children lined their sleeping bags along the wall then sat with their mom in the middle of the room playing cards until Lucy called for lights out. Long after she could hear the rhythmic sounds of sleep emanating from her children, Lucy sat on the one cot brought to their room, leaned against the wall, and wondered what in the world she was going to do now. Eventually, she drifted into a disturbed sleep.

Lucy awoke early to the sounds of activity in the makeshift refuge. She had become such a loner, shutting herself away from everyone but family since Charlie died. She was a little hesitant to get involved, but she knew she couldn't just take and not give back. Her parents and Memaw raised her better than that.

She woke her children and told them to come to the kitchen after they dressed and rolled up their sleeping bags. Then she made her way to find Ms. Warren.

"Good morning, Mrs. Warren. How can I help?" Lucy asked after finding the smiling woman bustling around the fellowship hall where tables were set up with a breakfast buffet.

"Start by calling me Sally," she said. "And remind me who you are. I'm so sorry that I'm not doing a very good job of keeping up with names."

"Lucy," she said. "And I have three children with me. Sometimes even I have trouble keeping their names straight!"

The women both chuckled. The warmth of Sally's congenial smile melted Lucy's reservations.

"Well, let's see," Sally said. "If you want to stand in the serving line this morning that would be great. You can man the scrambled eggs. We have folks in the kitchen cooking who will bring food out as it's prepared."

"This is amazing," Lucy said. "Where did all the food come from?"

"Oh, people delivered it before everything flooded. Some folks sheltered here even before the storm because their houses weren't real secure against the winds. Then we've had people bringing it in by boat since the flooding began—from Wilmington and Burgaw. But with so many main roads either flooded or washed out completely, the grocery stores are cut off from deliveries. We'll be alright for a few days, but I'm not sure what we'll do after that. We'll be praying over loaves and fishes for sure."

"I'll get to work," Lucy said.

They fell into a routine of helping each other. In addition to three meals a day, the refugees helped sort donated clothes on tables set up along the wall. Anyone could take what they needed.

The teenagers, including Ella, created activities for the children and helped care for them during the day. Ella especially loved spending time with the babies and toddlers. Individual families slowly became one big family—all with the same plight and uncertainty about their future, all pitching in to help each other with physical and emotional support.

Folks in Wilmington and Burgaw donated food and clothing to shelters set up in less affected parts of their towns with some supplies being shipped off to areas isolated by flood waters. Boats arrived at the church daily, but Ella and Lucy were always happiest to see Sam and Ryan putter up to shore.

Sam checked on Memaw every day. She had improved a little bit, he told Lucy, but remained on oxygen and antibiotics. As Sam feared, Memaw did have pneumonia. Lucy could only pray that her spunky eighty-year-old grandma could beat the odds—because the odds of survival at her age were not good.

Wednesday, September 26

Almost a week after being rescued, Lucy and her family were outside enjoying the sunshine and fresh air when Sam and Ryan arrived mid-morning.

"How are the dogs doing?" Lucy asked after they shared greetings and the teenagers carried fresh cabbage leaves toward the edge of the woods where Lucky lived safely stored away in a cage.

"Loving life," Sam said. "Ryan is spoiling them, though, so I hope they aren't too much to handle when you get them back."

"I can't thank you enough for rescuing them," Lucy said, "and us, of course. But the dogs became your burden to bear. You didn't have to do that, and I'm so grateful."

"No burden at all," Sam said. "It was actually Ryan's idea. He took up the cause saying you guys had lost far too much already, and he was right. He worried that he couldn't get the cat to cooperate, though. It was sitting in the rafters of the shed, so he did dump him out some food and fill the water bowl."

"You've raised a mighty fine son," Lucy said. "I'm sure you and your wife are very proud of him, and rightfully so."

"I am indeed," Sam said. "And he was the apple of his mother's eye."

"Was?" Lucy asked.

Sam looked up at the sky, then over to the kids playing, and finally back at Lucy.

"She died a few years ago," he said.

"Oh, I'm so sorry," Lucy said. "I shouldn't have pried."

"No, it's fine," Sam said. "I'm getting used to the idea, but sometimes I miss her so much my mind and body ache. She was an amazing woman and a terrific mom. We were married for almost twenty years before I lost her. I was gone a lot after 9/11, but all our years were amazing. Ryan was such a joy that we wanted more children. It took a long time, and we thought Faith would be the miracle that completed our family. But Karina died in childbirth."

Sam looked off into the distance obviously deep in memories. Lucy didn't interrupt.

"I guess I'll get used to the hole in my heart at some point in time, but it's so hard," Sam said. "Listen to me rambling on. I don't usually do that. You lost your husband more recently than I lost my wife, right? How do you do it?"

"Well, the children and the farm keep me and Memaw busy," Lucy said. "My husband was in the army, too, and my brother still is. He deployed right before the storm. They both served in Afghanistan and Iraq, but I don't know where my brother is now."

"Oh, Lucy, I had no idea," Sam said, wondering how her husband died, but not asking.

"Of course you didn't, and now I'm just rambling on. I worry about my brother, though."

"I know you do," Sam said, wishing he could find words to comfort her. "We'll keep your brother in our prayers."

"Thank you," Lucy said. "Right now, I have to figure out what I'm going to do about my children, where we're going to live, and how I'm going to support them with no home, no farm, and no income. I have to go."

Lucy turned and hurried up the hill to the church.

"Wait, Lucy," Sam called after her. "I didn't mean to upset you."

"Where's Mom off to in such a hurry?" Ella asked when she and Ryan approached Sam.

"I'm not sure," Sam said. "I guess she had some work to do. Come on, son, let's unload the boat and be on our way."

"Sure thing," Ryan said.

"I'll get the boys so we can help, too," Ella said.

Once they unloaded all the supplies, Sam searched the crowd of people trying to spot Lucy. She was nowhere to be seen.

He did see Sally Warren and headed over to share some information with her that would affect the shelter in the upcoming days.

"Sally," Sam said. "Can we talk?"

"Serious talk?" Sally said.

Sam nodded.

"Well, maybe we should go down to the office so you can hear yourself think, and I can hear what you say."

When Sally closed the door and the din of scores of people was drowned out enough that they could hear each other, Sam began.

"Black River crested a few days ago. And as you can see, the flood waters are starting to recede," he said. "That's good, of course, but it also creates some dilemmas. The boats are not going to be able to keep coming when the flood waters get much lower. And at the rate it's going now, that could happen as early as tomorrow. Hwy 421 was our main route to this part of the county before the storm, but it washed out completely. Right now, we're parking on the other side of the washout and putting the boat in there, but we won't be able to do that when the flood waters recede past that point."

"I understand," Sally said. "The guys coming in from Burgaw told me pretty much the same thing. One of the roads between here and Burgaw might be passable soon by some of those jacked up hunting trucks, but the grocery store is empty. All the main supply routes are cut off, and the trucks can't get in to deliver anything. The grocery store there lost all its perishables because the electricity stayed out so long, and the generators didn't work. The power and phones are back on now, I think, but they can't get new supplies."

"How much do you have?" Sam asked.

"With what you brought today, we can probably make it through tomorrow, breakfast the next day at the latest." Sally said. "Maybe if the floodwaters recede enough, some folks can go stay with friends and relatives whose homes are on this side of the washouts and didn't flood, but I just don't know how many people that might be. We're way over capacity right now, but we just didn't have a choice. I sure wasn't going to turn anybody away."

"I'll try to make at least one more trip if I can find some more supplies," Sam said. "Guess I better hustle on out of here and see if I can make it back today."

"Thanks for all you've done, Sam," Sally said. "You and your boy have been our guardian angels. God will bless you, I just know it."

"Can always use another blessing," Sam said. "But I know how blessed I already am."

Sam left Sally in the office and started down the hallway, his head bent in contemplation. He walked right into someone when he rounded the corner.

"Oh, I'm so sorry," Sam said, looking into Lucy's red-rimmed eyes. She stepped back so quickly, she lost her balance and he grabbed her by the elbow to steady her.

"Are you ok?" he asked gently. "Did I hurt you?"

"No," Lucy said. "I'm fine. I should have been watching where I was going. I just need to check on the kids."

"May I walk with you?" Sam asked.

Lucy shrugged. "Sure," she said softly.

"May I ask you a question?" Sam said.

"Yes," Lucy answered.

"I don't mean to pry, but do you and your children have anywhere you can go when the floodwaters are gone? Any family close by whose house didn't flood?"

"No," Lucy said. "We're pretty much on our own. My parents died on 9/11 and Memaw took me and my brother in. The farm was all any of us had left."

"I am so sorry."

Lucy didn't respond. Sam sensed she didn't really want to be talking to him. He wanted to ask her about her husband, about her parents, about her life, but knew this was absolutely not the right time to do that. He was afraid he might not see her again once she left the shelter, and he really wanted to spend more time with her under better circumstances.

There was just something so intriguing about Lucy. He told himself it had nothing to do with the blonde hair and blue eyes—so much like his late wife and their little girl. No, that wasn't the reason. But once he left and couldn't get back, he wouldn't even know how to reach her. Except he did have her dogs. He needed to give her his phone number so she could reach him when she was ready.

"Sally just told me that she's almost out of food, and I probably can't get back here even as early as tomorrow because the flood waters are receding pretty fast now."

Lucy still didn't respond. They walked in silence, stopping close to where the boys were playing fort with some other kids stranded just like them. They piled up old limbs and tires that had washed up during the flood and were left behind when the waters started to recede. Most definitely germ laden, but at that point, Lucy was hard pressed to keep them from playing with anything they could find that wasn't deadly.

"Can you still get back to my house?" Lucy asked after several minutes of silence.

"I'm pretty sure I can," Sam said. "But I know the floodwaters haven't receded enough for you to go back there yet."

"No, but do you know if it ever reached the loft?"

"Maybe just a little," Sam said, "judging by how much it rose after we rescued the dogs. But definitely not much."

"I have food," Lucy said. "Lots of canned food that I put up to feed us and to sell at the farmer's markets—beans and corn and vegetable soup and chili and tomatoes and even homemade chicken noodle soup. And there's a lot of sweet potatoes and some other stuff, too. And cases of bottled water."

"But won't your family need that?" Sam asked.

102

Lucy shrugged again. She looked so defeated that Sam wanted to console her. But he didn't try.

"My family needs it now," Lucy said. "And so do all the other families here. Can you get it?"

"I can surely try," Sam said, "but if it's as much as you say, my boat won't hold it all, and I really believe that today may be my last chance to cross the washed-out road. I think the waters will be down too much by tomorrow for me to get here."

"Other boats have been coming," Lucy said. "Maybe they can help you."

"You're right, of course," Sam said. "I'll go talk to Sally."

"I'm coming with you," Lucy said.

They hurried back up the hill toward the church just as another boat pulled in from the opposite direction.

"I'll go talk to them," Sam said, hurrying toward the boat. "You talk to Sally and see if she expects anyone else."

An hour later, Sam and Ryan had finished helping unload three boats and organized a trip to Lucy's house to pick up the supplies in her loft.

"I'm going with you," Lucy said.

"To your house?" Sam asked. "Ryan can help me."

"I'm going with you," Lucy repeated. "If you don't let me ride with you, I'll get in somebody else's boat. But I'm going."

Sam couldn't help but smile at the spunk emanating from the woman who seemed so defeated just an hour earlier. She was on a mission now. Who was he to stand in her way?

"Your chariot awaits," he said, holding out his hand to help Lucy into the boat.

"Ryan," Sam said. "Do you mind hanging out with Ella and the boys?"

"No, sir," Ryan said with a wink. "Have a safe trip."

Lucy sat in the front so she wouldn't feel the need to carry on a conversation. With Sam steering the tiller from the back seat, he couldn't have heard her anyway. She had shown so much emotion in front of him the past few days, she was embarrassed. After talking about Charlie and David earlier, she hid in her room at the church until she felt sure Sam had left. She never expected to run headfirst into him. But now she was glad that she did.

Everyone from across the state and beyond had been giving and giving since the storm—to people most of them didn't know and would never meet. Lucy and her children had only been on the receiving end. High time to be a giver instead. She hated feeling so helpless day after day. At least now she could actually do something.

Chapter 11

Everything looked so different than it did days earlier when Sam and Ryan rescued Lucy and her family. Houses and barns now rose halfway or more out of the dark waters. A few on higher ground had emerged completely. They were covered in mud, windows broken out, trash up against the sides. Vehicles sat in the sludge—trucks, tractors, cars. Toys lay strewn in the mud. All the foliage was dead or dying.

Occasionally, the roadway would rise up out of the water and the boaters would have to find a detour around high ground. In some places where the water was shallow, they sped up to make the boats ride higher in the water and plane out so the motors wouldn't hit bottom. But most of the time, they cruised along slowly enough to watch for debris—including dead animals.

Lucy kept an eye out for horses, praying that she wouldn't see Ace or Brady among the carcasses. She could think of nowhere they might have gone to survive, but she held onto hope and prayed for a miracle.

Sooner than Lucy expected, she could see her farm in the distance—the barn rising partially out of the water, the shed and house still halfway submerged. The crops she could see protruding from the floodwaters sagged muddy and mangled. Most were still drowning. She felt her chest tighten and her hands begin to shake. With slow rhythmic breaths, Lucy fought to control her panic and tears.

"You okay?" Sam asked as he slowed the boat and turned directly toward the shed.

"I'll be fine," Lucy said softly. "I don't have a choice."

"I think if we duck down, we can maneuver right into the shed," Sam said. "What's in there for us to avoid?"

"Granddaddy's tractor is in the middle," Lucy said. "Nothing tall anywhere else."

Sam motioned for the other boats to hold up outside the shed while he and Lucy slid inside. He puttered up to the ladder and kept the boat steady while Lucy climbed onto the lowest visible rung.

"I have a lift we can use to drop the food down closer to the boats," Lucy said. "But it would be faster if I had some help loading it."

"Of course," Sam said. "Looks like we have room for at least one more boat in here. Call out the window for Randy and Bobby to come inside. Once we fill these boats, we'll switch places with Arnie and Bud."

Lucy concentrated on the task at hand, struggling to avoid looking at her home or crops or anything else she had lost. More than an hour later, all the boats were loaded to capacity and her shed sat virtually empty of food, water, and paper goods.

"Let's go," she said, climbing back into the boat. "Sally may need some of this for supper tonight."

"Yes, ma'am," Sam said, saluting her. "You sure you're ok?"

"What choice do I have?" Lucy asked, turning in her seat so she effectively cut off the conversation.

The trip back took longer—the boats sitting low in the water from the weight of the supplies and the water levels decreasing at an alarming rate. Sam wasn't sure he'd be able to maneuver the boat back to his truck after they unloaded the supplies. He wasn't even sure how close they could get to the church to unload.

Since the water continued receding, they parked the boats a good distance from the church. Sam jogged up the hill where he found Pastor Jerry outside talking to other rescuers.

"Some of the roads are passable now," Pastor Jerry said to Sam. "People can get to Burgaw in their trucks."

"That's good to hear. You think a couple of you could drive over the hill to our boats back there?" Sam said, pointing. "They're loaded with supplies that would be a bear to try to bring up by hand."

They unloaded the boats and moved supplies into the church in short order—directed by Lucy at the boats and Sally in the church.

"Those ladies would make good drill sergeants," Ryan joked as Sam backed their boat up and eased away from the church, praying they could get back to his truck one last time.

"I can't believe you brought all this food!" Sally said to Lucy as the women put jar after jar of vegetables, soups, and jams onto the nearly empty shelves. "And water and paper products. You are a blessing indeed."

"Well, it certainly wasn't doing us any good sitting in the shed," Lucy said. "And my kids have put a hurting on all the food others have donated. I'm just glad to be giving instead of taking for a change."

"You and your family have given a lot," Sally said. "Don't think you haven't. You're always pitching in, Ella is fantastic with the children, and even your youngest ones have helped clean the tables and put away the toys. You've done a great job with your children, Lucy. We're fortunate to have met you. I just wish it could have been under better circumstances."

"Me, too."

"When all of this is over, we'd love for your family to be a part of our church family," Sally said. "You're always welcome."

Lucy turned toward the window so Sally could not see the tears welling up in her eyes. She spent a few moments blinking them away and swiped her cheeks with her sleeve. Sally didn't interrupt.

"I really don't know where we'll be," Lucy said without turning back to face Sally.

She walked away abruptly, escaped outside, and sat down at the picnic table to watch the children play. Lucy thought about the services she attended since being a refugee at the church—filled with beautiful music and prayer and people in the same predicament as she was. Many of those people talked about their abundant blessings.

Lucy knew she should be more grateful, but right now she just wasn't. Memaw would be so disappointed in her.

§ § §

Sam steered the boat through shallow water, hitting ground, backing up, and redirecting. He and Ryan should have reached the truck an hour ago, but the water fell faster than he expected and their route dried up again and again.

Now he tried making his way to Moores Creek which would take him to Black River. He hoped that from there he could reach his truck parked on the other side of the washout. If not, he'd have to stay in the river until it ran into the Cape Fear and go all the way to Wilmington.

Nearing the creek, Sam saw tall bald cypresses rising up toward the sky. Many of those trees, he knew, were over a thousand years old. Some twice that. Scientists tested a few of them recently and proved that those ancient trees predated Christ.

Limbs from hardwoods and creek-side growth dangled in water that still needed to fall a long way to get back to normal. Slowing the boat, Sam took out his cell phone and tried to call his neighbor to let her know he would be late.

Again.

Mrs. Darcy had been helping out with Faith while Sam worked and volunteered, but he always tried to arrive home before dinner and bedtime. That would not happen tonight. The sun hung low in its descent—a couple of hours at most before dark.

Sam tried to call, holding his phone in the air, pointing it in different directions, knowing all along that really didn't help. His service had always been spotty in this part of the county, and with the storm destruction and high water, trying to call was hopeless.

"I'll keep trying," Ryan said. "Let's go. I don't like the looks of this place."

"I'm going to have to steer us through those limbs," Sam said. "You may have to push some out of the way. Watch for snakes."

He eased the boat through the limbs and bushes and into the creek, hoping for a clear path toward the river, but seeing little.

Fog began to settle in around them.

From a high bank on the opposite side of the creek, Sam watched an alligator slide into the water, his eyes barely visible as he swam. Turtles rode the length of a log floating along beside them. A splash behind the boat made both men turn and look.

"Was it a fish?" Ryan asked.

"Most likely a snake," Sam said. "Keep your eyes open. The last thing we need is one dropping into the boat."

§ § §

Ella pushed one of the toddlers in the baby swing, but watched her mother sitting at the picnic table alone. She seemed to be looking at her, so Ella waved. Her mother didn't respond. She continued to watch as she pushed the curly haired little girl and listened to her giggle.

"Higher," she cried. "Higher."

"Just a few more minutes," Ella said, not taking her eyes off her mother. She sat so still, staring into space, not responding.

"Let's take a walk," Ella said to the child, slowing the swing, then lifting her free. She took her by the hand and walked toward Lucy. Ella touched her mother on the shoulder before Lucy even realized she was standing beside her.

"Are you ok, Mom?" Ella asked. "You look so distracted and sad."

"You don't need to worry about me," Lucy said. "Have you made any friends since we've been here?"

"Just the babies," Ella said. "There aren't many people here my age, and they don't want anything to do with me. They were friends already and don't need me. I wish Amelia were here. And I need my phone so I could at least call her. I don't even know if she flooded, too. She could be dead for all I know."

"Don't be so dramatic, Ella," Lucy admonished.

"I'm sorry," Ella said. "It's just so hard being here not knowing anything—not where my friends are, not where we're going to live, not if Ace is alive or drowned somewhere rotting, or if he's hurt and needs me, or even stolen. What if he made it away from the flood and somebody took him? What if I never get him back?"

Lucy brushed Ella's hair back from her face, and touched her cheek.

"I wish I could tell you everything is going to be alright," Lucy said. "But you know I never lie to you."

"What are we going to do, Mom?"

"I wish I knew," Lucy said. "I wish I knew."

§ § §

Ryan spotted at least half a dozen snakes curled around limbs as his dad eased the boat through debris and hanging foliage in the narrow creek. Spanish moss bearded many trees. Through the soupy fog, he spotted another alligator lying on the bank and two deer standing in the swamp on the other side of the creek. He wondered how many deer and turkey and other wildlife died in the flood. And how many horses.

"We should be close to the river," Sam said. "Keep your fingers crossed that we can get to the truck."

"What if we can't?" Ryan said. "Will we have to go back?"

"No, we can't go back," Sam said. "We'd get stranded for sure. Only option would be to follow the Black River to the Cape Fear, take that all the way to Wilmington, then dock downtown. We'd have to call a cab to take us home."

"Watch out," Ryan yelled. "Snake on starboard!"

Sam turned the tiller quickly, barely avoiding a snake as it dropped from a limb into the water alongside the boat.

"That was close," Ryan said.

"Yeah," Sam said. "Too close. Keep watching. I'm sure that's not the last one we'll see."

Sam steered the boat slowly toward a large downed tree hanging in the water. Assessing the situation, he hoped he could maneuver between the large limbs of the downed tree and the edge of the bank where roots jutted out and limbs hung overhead.

"This is going to be a tight one," he told Ryan. "Keep an eye out."

The boat scraped up against the bank, roots scratching its side creating an eerie screech that caused Sam to shudder. He and Ryan ducked low in the boat to avoid being knocked overboard by the hanging limbs.

Around a sharp bend, the creek forked into the river, and the water widened slightly. It ran swiftly, debris floating past and bumping into the boat.

"Tide's falling," Sam said. "Should make our trip faster if I can avoid running into anything."

"I'll watch for logs," Ryan said. "How much further do you think?"

"Not sure," Sam said, "and it's going to be hard to see where that little creek comes in. I don't think it's much wider than a big ditch."

"Gonna be dark soon," Ryan said. "I hope that creek's close."

"I just hope we can get to the truck," Sam said. "Still a long way to Wilmington by water, and I don't want to have to go that route. We need to get home to Faith before Mrs. Darcy decides she can't keep her anymore. I know I'm going to have to do something different soon. I can't keep taking advantage of her generosity. She didn't sign up to replace the nanny, and that's what I need."

"I think she likes having her around," Ryan said.

"I think you're right," Sam said. "But I don't want to push my luck."

"Yeah, I guess so," Ryan said. "Hey look, over there on the left. Is that the creek?"

Sam slowed the boat and peered through the fog to a spot where the foliage separated slightly.

"I think it might be," Sam said. "Only one way to find out."
Turning the tiller, he steered the boat into the small creek and eased his way toward where he hoped to see a washed out road and his truck. About fifteen minutes later, Ryan whooped with glee.

Sam carefully backed his truck off the shoulder of the road at an angle that dropped the trailer off toward the water. Dragging the boat close enough to load exhausted both of them. After strapping the boat to the trailer, Sam put the truck in four-wheel drive and eased up the bank.

"I will not want to go fishing in the river for a long time," Ryan said. "I don't even want to see fresh water again anytime soon. Give me saltwater any day."

"I know the feeling," Sam said. "The waterway will be a welcome sight when we get home."

"I feel sorry for the people who don't have a home anymore," Ryan said. "What will they do? There's so many shelters and so many people. Where will they all go?"

"I wish I knew," Sam said. "I wish I knew."

§ § §

Lucy, Ella, and the boys sat in the grass watching Lucky hop around within the circle they created with outstretched legs. Some of the other children joined them, and the circle grew large enough that the bunny had room to play. They took turns tossing bits of lettuce and cabbage into the circle and watching her find it.

"It's getting dark," Lucy said to the children. "Y'all better go inside and find your moms. It'll be bedtime soon, but I'm sure Ms. Sally will have Bible story time if you want to go listen."

"I'll put Lucky in her cage," Ella said. "I sure wish I could bring her inside."

"You say that every day," Lucy said. "And every day I tell you that's not possible."

"I know," Ella said. "But I still wish."

"I wish a lot of things, too, Ella," Lucy said.

Mother and daughter walked side by side back toward the church, watching the boys romp and play all the way.

"They act like they don't have a care in the world," Ella said. "What's wrong with them anyway?"

"Oh, Ella," Lucy said. "Maybe we both need to be more like them. Worrying and wishing surely isn't making anything better."

"Have you given up, Mom?"

Those words stung more than any Lucy had heard in weeks. She wrapped her arms around her daughter and buried her face in the teen's soft, coconut-shampooed hair.

"Oh, baby, no," Lucy said. "I'm so sorry I made you think that. I will never give up. You and your brothers and Memaw depend on me. I can't just give up. I'll figure something out. I've done it before, and I'll do it again. It just seems a little harder this time."

"I trust you, Mom," Ella said. "You'll figure something out."

"Tell you what," Lucy said. "Let's get the boys to bed, then ask Ms. Sally if we can use her computer. You can email Amelia since you haven't been able to reach her on the phone, and I'll email Uncle David.

Chapter 12

Memaw sat in her hospital bed staring out the window at the sparkling September sunshine. She pulled the covers up closer to her chin. Why could she never get warm enough? The oxygen cannula in her nose aggravated her, and she lacked a good night's sleep since she arrived—everybody coming in at all hours of the night checking her blood pressure and temperature. Then about the time she'd drift back to sleep, the blasted alarm would go off on one machine or the other. And the relentless hacking. The coughing made her whole body hurt. She kept telling them she needed pineapple juice, but they kept bringing cough medicine instead.

That cute Dr. Sam came in to see her almost every day. He brought news from Lucy and the kids when he could, said they were fine. Memaw knew better. Lucy didn't like being around a lot of people, and she didn't like asking for favors. That's probably why she hadn't called more than a couple of times from that shelter—not her home, not her phone, not her style to impose.

"Good morning Mrs. Malpass," the nurse said. "Are you about ready to go home?"

"Today?" Memaw asked.

"Your doctor is pleased with your progress," the nurse replied. "Maybe not today, but you'll probably be released tomorrow at the latest."

"Oh," Memaw said.

"You don't seem very happy about that," the nurse said. "I thought you might be ready to dance a jig."

"My dance floor is a bit soggy these days," Memaw said.

114

"Excuse me?"

"Never mind," Memaw said. "I think I need some sleep."

§ § §

After straightening their little corner of the church and helping serve breakfast, Lucy walked outside. She answered David's email last night, but didn't know how long it would be before he would see her reply. At least he wouldn't have to worry about them anymore. She told him everything was fine, and that they should be leaving the shelter and going back home within the next couple of days. The floodwaters were receding quickly, she'd said. Everything was fine.

She hadn't talked to Memaw in three days. Maybe she would call her today, but it was just so darned hard talking to Memaw without making her worry—and worry wouldn't help her get well. Memaw had always seen right through any front that Lucy tried to put up, so she was certain Memaw would just as easily hear despair in her voice. The phone number at the church was in Memaw's file and no one had called, so Lucy knew that Memaw must be on the mend.

People left the shelter every day—some back to their own homes, some to stay with family or friends, some to motel rooms established as extended shelter for those who lost their homes. But those weren't free.

Jerry and Sally set up one room in the church for folks to get help with their insurance claims and talk to FEMA representatives. But Lucy and Memaw didn't have any flood insurance—why would they when their home had been spared during the 500-year flood following Hurricane Floyd and what NOAA called a 1,000-year flood after Hurricane Matthew just two years ago?

So Lucy stood in line to enter the room where she could talk to a FEMA representative. The room was small, with several people sitting side-by-side at one table talking to strangers about their situation, sharing private information within hearing distance of people sitting just an arm's length away. Lucy felt like she had no alternative other than to start the process. She left the room heavy-hearted and discouraged, but with FEMA paperwork to complete.

Charlie had tried dealing with FEMA when their home flooded after Hurricane Matthew. But the process was so frustrating, he eventually gave up and started trying to do the work himself with whatever money they could scrape up while they lived with Memaw, whose home was high and dry then.

She'd heard the horror stories about other people trying to get help from FEMA after Hurricane Matthew. Too many of them received absolutely nothing from FEMA, so Lucy didn't hold out much hope. The home she and Charlie shared was not habitable, and only about three feet of water rose inside the house then. Seemed most of the ones who moved back into their homes after that flood were helped by the Baptist Men or other volunteer organizations that came to their rescue.

Lucy shivered despite the warm September sunshine baking down on her back. She had not only lost their home, but their livelihood, too. She didn't know anything other than farm work—making a living using her hands and hard work, taking care of her children, tending to the animals and the land, keeping the books for the farm. She didn't have a college degree, no job experience. She had never even created a resume.

"You look mighty deep in thought," Sam said, walking up behind Lucy, making her jump.

"I haven't seen you in days," Lucy said. "Have you seen my grandmother? Is she okay?"

"Yeah, well, it's been a struggle trying to find a route," Sam said. "But yes, your grandmother is doing much better. I just checked on her last night."

"Thank you," Lucy said. "I just wish I could get there to see her. But I don't have anything to drive."

"That's what I wanted to talk to you about," Sam said. "I think it would do your grandmother a lot of good to see all of you. Now that I've found a route here from Wilmington—albeit a long way around roads that are either washed out or still flooded—I wanted to take you and the children to see her."

"Are you serious?" Lucy said. "Yes, we would love to go. Now?"

"Yes, right now," Sam said. "You round up your kids while I get some help unloading supplies that I brought for Sally. People just keep donating, and the centers are getting full."

"Thank you," Lucy said.

"Be prepared," Sam said. "It's going to be an all-day excursion. You want me to let Sally know you and the kids will be gone most of the day?"

"Yeah, sure," Lucy said, turning toward the group of playing children to locate her boys. As early as it was, they were already dirty, so she sent them inside to wash up and change clothes.

Lucy found Ella sitting on the ground snuggling with her bunny.

"Hey," she said to Ella. "Sam has a surprise for us today."

"What?" Ella asked, looking up with eyes so sad they made Lucy want to cry.

"How would you like to get away from here for the day?"

"What do you mean?"

"Sam offered to take us to the hospital in Wilmington to see Memaw," Lucy said. "Maybe while we're out, we could go by Chick-fil-a. I sure could use some chicken nuggets that aren't out of a freezer bag."

"And waffle fries?" Ella said. "That would be amazing."

"And lemonade," Lucy said. "We just have to pretend that everything is fine when we see Memaw. We don't want to worry her because we need her to get well, and stress doesn't help."

"I understand," Ella said. "And the boys are clueless, so you don't have to worry about them spilling the beans."

"Oh, to be young and innocent," Lucy said. "I'm sorry you had to grow up so fast, Ella girl, but I sure am proud of the young woman you've become."

"Thanks, Mom," Ella said. "I need to go change."

"Me, too," Lucy said. "Let's make it a celebration."

They saw Sam on their way into the church, and he pointed toward a dark blue Suburban being unloaded by volunteers.

"This shouldn't take too much longer," he said. "Meet me over there when you're ready to go."

"We'll be fast," Lucy said.

Sam nodded and walked back to help unload more supplies. The outpouring of help in the form of supplies and funds and time from folks not devastated by the storm and subsequent flooding was nothing short of amazing. But there was just so much any of them could do in the midst of unimaginable loss and need. Some days Sam felt like they were fighting a losing battle, but the alternative was unthinkable.

"We're ready," Lucy said as she reached the truck followed by Ella and the boys.

"Great timing," Sam said. "Load up and let's go."

They drove down a narrow road toward Burgaw with flood waters running rapidly in ditches alongside and sometimes shallowly across the road. Yards held huge amounts of water, some still completely submerged blocking access to homes and vehicles that rose up out of the waters.

"Water still has a long way to fall for some folks to get back home," Sam said. "And most of those houses won't be habitable. With all that moisture and all this heat, mold will be growing uncontrollably."

"Have you been by our farm?" Ella asked. "Has the water gone away?"

"No, Ella, I haven't had a chance to go that way," Sam said. "Some of the roadways are washed out and some still under water from what I hear. I can't get back home that way. Hwy 421 is still impassable and I-40 just opened back up between here and Wilmington, so that's how I could come around this long way to bring supplies over to you guys and a couple of other shelters."

"It's been more than two weeks since the hurricane," Lucy said. "Seems like a lifetime some days."

"Well I know your grandmother is going to be so happy to see all of you," Sam said, trying to lighten the mood. "It was touch and go at first, I gotta tell you, but she has improved so much in the last couple of days."

"Thank you for checking on her so often," Lucy said. "With your patient load and family and volunteer work, I know you have been beyond busy."

"Glad to do it," Sam said. "She's a spunky lady."

That made Lucy smile. Spunky was a perfect word for Memaw.

"There's a black horse!" Ella exclaimed. "Pull over. Please, pull over."

Sam slowed the truck, then backed up and pulled into a two-rut road beside a pasture with several horses standing near the back fence. Before he could stop completely, Ella was out of the truck and running toward the fence. Ella climbed through the railings and ran across the pasture. The horses lifted their heads, but none made their way toward Ella. Lucy's heart sank.

Ella slowed and walked toward the horses. She knew none of them was hers, but she just wanted to touch one of them, smell the special scent she missed so much. They looked at her briefly, then dropped their heads back down to graze. She was no threat.

Ella reached out, and the black mare nuzzled her palm. The horse was smaller than Ace with a white star between her eyes and one white sock on her left hind leg. She was beautiful, but she was not Ace. Ella laid her head against the horse's neck and breathed deeply. Then she turned and walked back toward the truck.

"I'm muddy," Ella said to Sam when he and Lucy met her beside the truck. "I don't want to get your truck dirty."

"No problem," Sam said. "I have a few towels in the back. I'll get you one."

Lucy helped Ella clean up as best she could, but her jeans remained splotched, stained by the mud, and her favorite flowy tee was speckled with dirt. At least she wore her boots instead of her white Vans she started to slip on.

"I can't go see Memaw like this," Ella said.

"Of course you can," Lucy said. "Memaw, of all people, will understand."

"I'm sorry, Mom. I just wanted so bad for it to be Ace."

Lucy hugged her daughter, standing there beside the road, and let her cry.

When they arrived at the hospital, Sam told Lucy he needed to check on his patients and would meet her in Memaw's room in about an hour. Lucy and the children rode up on the elevator and walked down the hall. Pushing the door open slowly, Lucy peered inside the darkened room. She saw a small lump underneath a pile of covers.

"Quietly," she told the children, motioning for them to enter.

They gathered around the bed and waited.

"She looks so little," Benji said. "Did she shrink?"

"I think she's just snuggled up to stay warm," Lucy said.

"But it's so hot in here," Nate whispered.

Memaw moved under the covers.

"I think she's waking up," Ella said.

Lucy leaned over and kissed her grandmother on the forehead. Memaw opened her eyes.

"Well, jumping Jehosaphat," Memaw said, pushing herself up to a sitting position. "Aren't you a sight for sore eyes."

"We're here, too," Benji said. "What's a Jehosasat?"

"Heck if I know," Memaw said, laughing. "But my daddy said it all the time. I wasn't smart enough to ask like you."

"How are you feeling?" Ella asked.

"Better every day," Memaw said. "But I want to hear about you guys. What have you been up to?"

They spent the next hour talking about the shelter and the people and what they did to pass their time. Memaw told them about her nurses and how terrible the food was and how she couldn't wait to get back to the farm in her own kitchen so she could make some hot biscuits and eat them with some decent jam. Lucy bit her lip to fight back tears.

"The nurse said I will be released in the next day or two," Memaw said. "Can we get back home by then?"

Lucy hesitated, not knowing how to respond.

"So you're about to fly this coop," Sam said, walking through the door and saving Lucy from having to choose between lying to her grandmother and breaking her heart.

"Well, if it ain't the handsome doc," Memaw said, winking at Lucy.

"Your doctor ready to let you go?" Sam asked.

"That's what I hear," Memaw said.

"Well, if you don't mind me butting in a bit, I have a suggestion," Sam said.

"I guess you did save my life," Memaw said. "So, I owe you one."

"Pneumonia can make you mighty weak, and can come back real quick if you're not careful. Since you've been in the hospital more than three days, Medicare will pay for you to go to rehab," Sam said. "That would be an excellent choice since Lucy and the kids are still in the shelter. It'll give her a little bit of time to get everything ready for you."

"We can't go home?" Memaw said, looking at Lucy.

"Not yet," Lucy said. "I think rehab is a great idea. I'll need you to be your strong, spunky self as soon as possible."

"Is the food there any better than it is here?"

"Memaw is the best cook ever," Ella said, making her great-grandma smile.

"Well, I can't guarantee it," Sam said, "but your family can sneak some good stuff in. And you won't be confined to your bed, so you can sit outside in the fresh air if you want."

"That will be an improvement," Memaw said. "I reckon I don't have much choice 'til I can get back home."

"I'll get the ball rolling on that," Sam said. "Now I have to whisk your family away."

They took turns hugging Memaw before they left. When Lucy leaned over the bed, Memaw whispered, "It's all going to be alright, baby girl. Just hang in there."

As they walked toward the elevator, Sam asked, "Where to for lunch?"

"Chick-fil-a," Ella said without hesitation, and the boys piped in their agreement.

When they finished eating, Sam said, "You want to go see your dogs?"

"Can we?" Benji said. "For real?"

"I don't want to impose any more than we already have," Lucy said.

"No problem at all," Sam said. "I don't live all that far from here, and I really need to check on Ryan and Faith before we head back. He's good with her, but sometimes a three-year-old can be a handful."

"Ok, sure," Lucy said. "Whatever you need to do."

Less than half an hour later, Sam turned onto a tree-lined private drive into a subdivision of large homes with larger yards offering shade beneath huge oaks dripping with Spanish moss. Large bushes—azaleas and oleander Lucy thought—were grouped in artful displays throughout the lawns with taller camellia bushes rising amidst them. Sam drove for about half a mile before turning into a narrow paved drive, reaching for the remote on his visor, and opening black wrought iron gates. They had barely driven inside the gates, when two big black and brown bundles of fur came barreling toward them. The boys jumped out of the truck and tumbled to the ground with Rex and Roxie licking their faces.

"I'm sorry they didn't wait for you to stop," Lucy said. "They really do know better."

"Yes, we do," Ella said. "May I get out now?"

"Of course," Sam said. "Do you want me to wait for you to get back in or are you okay walking the rest of the way?"

"I'll walk," Ella said. "And I'll watch the boys, too."

Sam eased the truck down the drive bordered by large Bradford pear trees, crepe myrtles, and azaleas. At the end of the drive sat a Southern Plantation style home with white columns, floor length windows, wide porches on both levels, and two centered staircases curving toward each other to a brick portico at ground level.

"Your home is lovely," Lucy said, trying to hide her awe.

"We were blessed," Sam said. "My practice has been good, but Karina's parents gave us the land and a down payment as a wedding present."

"Your wife?" Lucy said.

"Yes," Sam said. "This was her dream home. She oversaw every detail when we were building—inside and out. Living on the water was everything we ever wanted for our family."

"I know you miss her terribly," Lucy said.

"Yes," Sam said. "I do."

The drive circled around the end of the home, and Sam drove into one bay of a four-car garage. A charcoal colored Toyota Tundra sat in one bay, a silver BMW sedan in another, and the jonboat and trailer in the fourth. They exited the Suburban and walked out into the yard. Lucy's breath caught at the view—a large swimming pool sat directly behind an expansive deck with a beautiful white shingled bungalow beyond the pool. The immaculately landscaped yard sloped toward sparkling water with a long dock ending in a gazebo. Live oak trees bordered the property with limbs larger than the trunks of most trees dipping toward the ground forming perfect places for a treehouse within and picnics underneath. A black wrought iron fence enclosed the yard with a gate to the dock without blocking any of the view.

Lucy heard a child's laughter and swept her eyes to the other side of the lawn. A wisp of a child—blonde curls bouncing—came running toward them. From where she ran, Lucy saw a treehouse in the limbs of an oak with a swing hanging below, still swaying from the child's exit. Sam caught the pixie in mid-jump and tossed her high into the air.

"This is our Faith," Sam said to Lucy, smiling with obvious pride as he settled her on his hip.

"Hello, Faith," Lucy said.

The child hid her face on her daddy's shoulder.

Ryan walked up more slowly and extended his hand to shake Lucy's.

"Nice to see you again, Ms. Lucy," Ryan said. "I'm glad you could come by and see Rex and Roxie. We surely do like having them around. Faith thinks they're horses, and they don't seem to mind."

"They look great," Lucy said. "I can't thank you enough for saving them—and us."

Lucy reached inside the purse slung on her shoulder and pulled out several twenty dollar bills.

"I know it's not much, but please take this to help pay for their food."

"No, ma'am," Ryan said at the same time that Sam reached over to stop him from taking the money. "You might need that for something else. I feel like we should be paying you rent on the dogs. I've been wanting one for a long time, but Dad thought we didn't need one—especially big hairy ones. I think Rex and Roxie might have changed his mind, and for that, I owe you."

"In that case," Lucy said, putting the money back in her purse.

Rex and Roxie came bounding around the house followed by Ella and the boys.

"Horsey, horsey," Faith said, reaching toward the dogs as she climbed out of her daddy's arms.

"Let's walk down to the water and sit for a moment," Sam said. "There's something I want to talk to you about."

"Ok," Lucy said.

They walked down the slope, onto the dock, and sat down in a swing hanging from the roof of the gazebo. In the marsh across the Intracoastal Waterway, Lucy saw two snowy egrets foraging for food. A half dozen seagulls flew by, their bright white bodies in stark contrast to a cloudless Carolina blue sky.

"It would be easy to forget things here," Lucy said. "At least for a moment."

"I know how lucky we were with this storm," Sam said. "I wanted to ask you something, and you can tell me to butt out if you want."

"Ok," Lucy said. "You've done a lot for my family. I think that entitles you to ask a question."

"Have you thought about what you're going to do?" Sam asked.

"It's all I've been thinking about," Lucy said. "I know we can't stay at the church forever, but I can't even get back to the farm to see what I'm dealing with."

"I want to help," Sam said.

"You already have helped us and so many other people," Lucy said.

"But I want to do more," Sam said.

"Why us?"

"I don't know exactly," Sam said, "but out of all the people we rescued, Ryan and I both feel a special connection to your family—all of you."

"You've been helping us all day," Lucy said. "You brought us to Wilmington to see Memaw, you took us to lunch and wouldn't let me pay, you brought us to see the dogs, you even stopped in the middle of nowhere for Ella to look at a horse that I'm sure you knew couldn't be hers. And I had no idea what I would do if the doctor released Memaw. I have no place to take her, and I wouldn't have known what to do. But you did. I didn't know Medicare would pay for rehab. But you did. That's a perfect solution—for now."

A large yacht eased by with an American flag flying from its mast. The woman standing on the stern looked up and waved. Dark-headed ducks floated up and down on the wake before diving for fish and reappearing yards away. Lucy didn't know their scientific name, but remembered Charlie calling them die-dappers.

"Your grandmother will need you to come visit now that there's a road open," Sam said. "And I'm not sure how often I'll be able to get out that way to bring you into town."

"I wouldn't impose on you to drive us around," Lucy said.

"No, that's not how I meant it," Sam said, struggling for the right words to say to the most independent and defiant woman he had ever met. "I just have a suggestion."

"You seem to be full of those today," Lucy said, sounding haughtier than she intended. "I'm sorry, that was rude."

"No, you're right. I have made a lot of suggestions today," Sam said. "It's just that I know you'll need a way to get around, and I have a car sitting in my garage that's hardly been driven in over three years, and I want you to take it. Just until you're on your feet, of course—a loaner, not a gift."

"Your wife's car?" Lucy said incredulously.

"Well, yes," Sam said. "But it was the family car, too. I just drive the Suburban most of the time, and Ryan drives the truck, and the car just sits there."

"Absolutely not," Lucy said, standing.

"But..."

"But nothing," Lucy said. "I won't do that."

She turned and started walking.

"But you need something to drive," Sam said, following Lucy down the dock back toward the house. He kept talking to her retreating back.

"You need something to drive to come see your grandmother, to go check on your farm, to find a place to live, to look for a job, to take the kids to school. Heck, you can't do anything if you don't have something to drive. You surely can't call a taxi!"

"Ok," Lucy said, turning around so abruptly that Sam almost ran into her. "All those things are true. If you really want to help, take me by Hertz so I can rent one. Then you won't even have to drive us back to the church."

She turned around and marched up the hill to where the three younger children were playing with the dogs while Ryan and Ella sat in the lush grass with their legs stretched out in front of them. Faith sat on Roxie's back while Benji led her around and Nate walked beside her in case Faith fell off.

"Let's go," Lucy said.

"But we're having fun," Benji said.

"It's time to go. Now."

"Yes, ma'am," Nate said.

"Are you ok, Mom?" Ella asked.

"I'm fine. Sam is going to take us to rent a car. Then we're going by US Cellular to get some phones before we head back to the church. I want to get back before dark."

§ § §

Lucy felt a little bit of her independence returning as she put the rented car in reverse then headed out of the parking lot. Fortunately, they kept comprehensive insurance on her car for fear of hitting deer while driving in the country, and that covered flood damage as well. Her insurance would only pay a low daily rental rate, so she couldn't afford a very big car, but the Ford Fiesta would work just fine until the adjuster could reach her car, give her an estimate, and then send her money she could use toward buying one. She wasn't expecting much, and her bank account was always low right before harvest, so she didn't know what she'd be able to buy.

But that was a worry for another day.

She drove straight to U.S. Cellular and bought new phones for herself and Ella—not replacing the iPhone Ella loved and lost, but buying economical androids that would get the job done. At least she could make calls and send emails without mooching off of Sally. She could check her bank balance, and she could search for jobs—what kind of job she had no idea, but she couldn't be too choosy. Even if they could move back to the farm, this year's harvest was ruined, and she could think of no way to make money off the land short of selling it all.

Chapter 13

The next few days passed slowly for Ella—the same sad people, the same boring routine, the same so-so food. Many people left to go somewhere—home maybe, she wasn't sure where—and that included her favorite dark-haired toddler who called her "Ewa."

At least she could talk to Amelia. Her house didn't flood, but the creek beside it came close. Amelia hadn't spent any time with their friends because everybody was too busy cleaning up the disaster and trying to get back to normal. At least she hadn't missed out on anything, Ella thought, then reprimanded herself for being what Mom would certainly call self-centered. Amelia told Ella that her mama said their school was so messed up no one knew when it would reopen. Amelia's mama would know since she taught there.

Ella didn't know what her own mom would do now. She was searching the internet for jobs, but she never worked anywhere except the farm. She wasn't a teacher or a nurse or even a secretary. Mom never said anything about money, but Ella knew she was worried. She glanced over Mom's shoulder yesterday when she was checking her bank account on her phone. Ella couldn't see how much money they had or would even know if it was enough if she did see it, but she could tell by Mom's reaction that it wasn't good. She saw her shoulders slump and her head shake ever so slightly.

And Mom asked Ms. Sally if she could use the computer. Ella knew she didn't like doing that. She heard her tell Ms. Sally that she needed to create a resume so she could apply for some jobs she found online. Ella had learned about resumes at school. She wondered what her mom would even put on a resume.

§ § §

Lucy searched through the piles and racks of donated clothes trying to find a suit that would fit. After submitting her resume to almost every job she could find online, she received only one call for an interview. Responses from some of the others were swift rejections. They were sorry, they said, but other candidates' qualifications better matched what they were seeking. That made sense, but she didn't like it.

She didn't receive responses from most of them. But it had been less than two weeks, so maybe? Who was she kidding? Even if they called her later, she couldn't wait forever. She needed money now. She wasn't even sure she should burn the gas and waste the money to go to this interview. She didn't have any receptionist experience. But it was close to Memaw's rehab, so she'd just visit while she was in town.

Lucy would have been happy to wait tables or flip burgers, but so many restaurants shut down because of the flood—some temporarily and some permanently—that the market was flooded with experienced wait staff and burger flippers. She didn't have a chance.

She found a white blouse she thought would fit, a purple skirt and a black blazer. Taking them to her family's room, she did her best to look professional and confident. She would leave Ella in charge of the boys with Sally as back-up.

"I won't be late," Lucy said to Sally as she left. "Wish me luck."

"I'll pray for good results," Sally said. "You look beautiful."

Three hours later, a dejected Lucy walked into the rehab center. She knew she wouldn't be able to hide her disappointment from Memaw no matter how hard she tried. Besides, Memaw would know right away that something was up because Lucy simply never wore suits. She walked down the hallway to Memaw's room, but found it empty. She stood in the doorway and looked down the hall in both directions.

"Are you looking for Mrs. Malpass?" a nurse aide asked.

"Yes, I am," Lucy said.

"Oh, she's not spending much time inside these days," the aide said. "You'll find her in the garden right down that way, turn left, and then go through the double doors."

Lucy followed directions and found Memaw sitting on a bench in the midst of a plethora of colorful blossoms—the flowers were blooming, the bushes were blooming, the trees were blooming. Daffodils created a carpet of bright yellow in the beds. The garden looked like spring instead of October.

"What is all this?" Lucy asked.

"Well, I'm not really sure," Memaw said. "But everything has decided to bloom. I'm sure there's some kind of scientific explanation, but who am I to question all this beauty?"

Lucy walked over to touch the white Bradford pear blossoms.

"These always stink," she said.

"Like cat pee," Memaw agreed. "But there's enough of the good smelling ones to drown them out."

"It's beautiful," Lucy said.

"Speaking of beautiful," Memaw said. "You look like a spring blossom yourself. What's the occasion?"

"I had a job interview," Lucy said. "Just to make a little bit of money until the crops come in."

"I'm not as naïve as you think, baby girl," Memaw said. "I know we won't have any crops this year. I've been watching the news for weeks. Not much else to do when you're confined to a bed."

"I'm sorry," Lucy said.

"Well, maybe you'll get some good news," Memaw said.

"No," Lucy said. "I don't think so. They told me they'd let me know something when they finished up interviews this week, but I could tell just by their questions and the looks they exchanged between each other. I was wasting my time and theirs."

"Well, we've got a little bit saved up," Memaw said. "We can just dip into that if we have to."

"No," Lucy said defiantly. "I'm not going to touch the kids' college funds—there's not much money there anyway, and I'd lose too much in penalties if I pulled any out early. And we're not going to touch your emergency savings. We got lucky this time, and you got better. But if you need help I can't give you in the future, we'll need that money."

"How are things looking at home?" Memaw asked.

"I don't know," Lucy said. "I've been trying to get there every day since I rented the car, but there's still at least one place where the road is too flooded for my little car to get through. I'll try again this afternoon."

"Would a big four-wheel drive truck get through?" Memaw asked.

"Probably," Lucy said, "but I don't have one of those."

"I bet you know a dark-haired doctor who does," Memaw said. "And if you don't have his phone number, I do."

"I can't ask him to do that," Lucy said.

"Why not?" Memaw asked. "He comes by to see me every now and then, and he's always asking if I've heard from you and the kids. I think he's sorta sweet on you, Lucy."

"Oh, Memaw, no. He's still grieving his wife, and even if he were interested, I'm not."

"Charlie's been gone over a year, Lucy. All he ever wanted was for you and the kids to be safe and happy."

"I'm not ready, Memaw. And I don't know if I ever will be again. It hurts too much."

"Don't close your heart to happiness, Lucy," Memaw said, taking Lucy's hand in hers and lifting it to her lips. "Don't ever close your heart."

§ § §

Lucy made a quick stop by the grocery store before returning to the church. Sally needed a few things to make what they had stretch farther, so Lucy offered to pick it up. She didn't have to pay for it out of pocket, though, because Sally gave her a Food Lion gift card someone donated to help out. The donations just kept coming, but Sam wasn't delivering them. Lucy had not seen him since the day they all went to his house.

Lucy didn't know how she hadn't noticed on her way to town, but everything was in bloom—Bradford pears, crepe myrtles, azaleas. Now that she was actually looking, she saw their flood ravaged world bursting in blossoms. Beauty in the midst of devastation.

When Lucy pulled into the church parking lot, she saw a familiar blue Suburban backed up to the door. As she stepped out of the car, Sam saw her and waved—like he hadn't made an unreasonable offer, like she hadn't been rude in her refusal, like nothing bad happened, like he wasn't avoiding her after all.

She lifted the few grocery bags from the back seat and walked toward the same door where Sam was unloading supplies.

"How's it going?" Sam asked. "Sorry I haven't been around lately, but Faith contracted a stomach bug, then Ryan got it, then I did, so we've been cooped up a while."

"Glad you're feeling better," Lucy said. "And doubly glad you didn't bring that bug here. I can only imagine how fast it would spread with this many people in close quarters. Although, as you can see, we've thinned out a lot."

"I noticed," Sam said. "Sally told me a lot of people moved back home because even though the flood waters drove them out, it never rose inside their houses."

"Well, I know that's not the case at my house because it was already to the ceilings when we left, but I sure would like to see if anything's salvageable."

"You haven't been able to get there yet?"

"No, I tried," Lucy said. "Every day since I rented the car, but there's still too much water on the road in some places."

"Would you like for me to see if I can get through when I leave here?"

"No," Lucy said. "You already know you can't go home that way and you'd have to double back."

"I don't mind," Sam said.

"No," Lucy said. "I was going to try again this afternoon, but it's getting so late, I'm going to wait and try tomorrow morning."

"Well, if you change your mind, let me know," Sam said. "I can give you my cell phone number."

"No, that's okay," Lucy said.

"Sally has it if you change your mind."

"I better get these bags inside," Lucy said. "I'm sure Sally is ready to cook supper, and she needed some spices and potatoes."

"Yeah, I've finished unloading and should get back home. I need to pick Faith up at the neighbor's house. I don't like leaving her there too long."

"Well, bye," Lucy said, turning to go through the door.

"Bye," Sam replied.

He pulled out of the church parking lot and turned left instead of right toward home. Lucy's farm was less than ten miles away, so checking on the flooding wouldn't put him home too late. For most of the way, the floodwaters had receded off the road completely, but what he estimated to be a couple of miles before her farm, water ran shallowly across the road for about fifty yards. He eased the Suburban forward. He could easily see the centerline under the weak-tea colored water, so it couldn't be very deep.

The road remained clear the rest of the way to Lucy's drive. Sam turned into the muddy driveway and eased the Suburban along the two-rut road. Large puddles still held water, but he thought Lucy could probably get that little car she rented between the worst of them.

Then he saw the real problem. Where a bridge had obviously been, water rushed under creosote pole crossbeams at least three feet apart with no decking. He was pretty sure that wouldn't stop Lucy, though. She'd probably just use one of them like a balance beam and scurry across. He just hoped she wouldn't lose her balance and fall.

He could see the buildings about half a mile further in, but Sam didn't have time to figure out a way to get there. Ryan was volunteering in Wilmington today, so Sam knew that if he didn't arrive at Mrs. Darcy's house soon to pick up Faith, she would start to fret. He'd been gone so much lately, and she was too young to understand. Mrs. Darcy had been such a godsend since his nanny quit abruptly, but he needed to find a more permanent solution soon.

Wednesday, October 10

Lucy swiped her phone screen to wake it up. She wanted to check her email and see if she received any responses from potential employers. But a weather alert stared back at her. Hurricane Michael—just what they needed. She hadn't paid much attention to the news or weather lately. She knew the hurricane had formed, but she thought it was going into the Gulf. She checked the time, then walked down the hall to the classroom where Pastor Jerry set up a television someone donated. Most of the kids who usually watched movies were still playing outside in the afternoon sun. Lucy turned on the television and found the local news channel.

A few minutes later, she clicked the television off and walked outside. Hurricane Michael was devastating the Gulf Coast of Florida and expected to track inland toward Georgia and the Carolinas. At least it would only be a tropical storm by then, not the monster Cat 4 it had been when it made landfall in Florida. She would definitely need to go to the farm tomorrow if she hoped for any chance of getting in. When the hurricane arrived in a couple of days, it would be packed with rain, and the floodwaters would rise again.

Lucy walked outside, sat at a picnic table near where her boys played, and pulled up her email. Three rejection letters including one from her only interview. Not really a surprise, but still.

The only thing that worried her more was the lack of response from David. He always contacted her when he could. He warned her though, that this time those opportunities might be few and far between. She couldn't know where he was or what he was doing, but at least he wouldn't worry about them and could concentrate on staying alive. She emailed him several times since the storm to reassure him they were fine. She hated lying to him, but if that were the only way she could help him, she would—and did.

"Hi, Mom," Ella said, walking up behind her.

"Hi yourself," Lucy said, patting the seat for Ella to sit beside her.

"Do you think we might could go to Burgaw tomorrow? I'd really like to see Amelia, and she said her mom told her she could have a friend over tomorrow."

"I can't tomorrow," Lucy said.

"Why not?"

"I'm going to go check on the farm."

"Can I go?"

"No, I don't think so," Lucy said. "I wouldn't want to take any chances of you reinjuring your leg."

"It's fine, Mom," Ella said. "Even Dr. Sam said so. You know he's been checking it ever since that first day they rescued us. He said you should be a doctor or a nurse or something because he had never seen a wound heal that good."

"That's Memaw's doing with all her tinctures and salves. It looks even better than if you had stitches. But I need you to stay here with the boys," Lucy said.

"Ok," Ella said. "But you shouldn't go alone either. Maybe you should ask Dr. Sam to go with you."

"Not you, too," Lucy said.

"Not me too what?"

"Matchmaking like Memaw."

"She is?"

"Yes, and you can both just forget it."

"I'm not matchmaking, Mom," Ella said. "Trust me. He's nice and all, but I don't want a new dad. Can I go to Amelia's the day after tomorrow?"

"We'll see," Lucy said, smiling at how quickly her teenage daughter could turn a conversation back to what mattered to her most in that moment.

Thursday, October 11

Clouds began to gather as Lucy left the church and headed toward the farm. No sunshine made for a dreary day, but according to the weather, rain would not move in until late that night or early the next morning. She planned to make the most of her time. Sally gave her some gloves and a few boxes for things she could salvage. Sally insisted that Pastor Jerry go with her, but Lucy convinced them he was needed at the church, especially since she might not even get past that flooded part of the road that stopped her every day for the past week.

If she could get through, she'd call her auto insurance company and set a time for the adjuster to come out. Her covered rental car period was quickly coming to an end, and she could not afford to pay daily rent on the car. Nor could she afford to go buy one.

Lucy tried to concentrate on the road in front of her instead of the devastation around her as she drove. She needed to stay focused and upbeat. Who was she kidding? She rolled down the window and turned the radio up high, singing along with her favorite songs while the wind whipped her hair from its clasp. Focused and upbeat.

Lucy saw standing water in the road with plenty of time to slow down. She was pretty sure it had receded some since yesterday. Seeing no other vehicles in front of or behind her, she eased the car to the middle of the road and drove slowly forward, straddling the centerline now visible above the water. She made it through, breathed a sigh of relief, and picked up speed.

Turning into her driveway, Lucy knew where most of the deep puddles would be. She had avoided those holes for weeks, and now regretted not taking time before the storm to scrape the driveway with the tractor and blade, filling in the holes. Add that regret to the growing list.

Halfway down the drive she stopped. Of course Lucy knew the bridge had washed out, but she'd somehow let that little bit of knowledge bury itself in her brain. The boxes wouldn't do her much good today, yet she was not going to get this far and stop now. Standing at the edge of the creek, Lucy spoke encouragement aloud to herself, then stepped out onto one of the telephone poles. One slow step at a time, she made her way across, listening to the rushing water below her. The driveway was filled with debris and she stopped again and again to drag a limb to the side.

More than once, Lucy stood still as a snake slithered away. Most were harmless, but she kept her eyes peeled for copperheads, cottonmouths, and rattlesnakes. With water still high in the creeks and rivers, their habitat had diminished, too. She pulled her cell phone from her back pocket and checked for service. Three bars—that was good enough. If something happened, she should be able to call for help.

The flood waters had receded from inside the house, but the porch and yard were a wet, muddy mess. Scores of rotting fish lay stranded in the yard. Lucy could see the flood line inches above the top of the window casings. She walked slowly to the front steps, took a deep breath, then stopped and turned away. Bypassing the house, Lucy cleared a path to the barn, stepping or climbing over the larger limbs and fallen trees. She knew the horses wouldn't be there—they couldn't be there—but she still couldn't help but look.

Halters and lead lines lay strewn across the aisle, muddy and molded. She looked into the tack room and saw their saddles—somehow still on the racks, but soaked, stained, and growing profuse amounts of mold. Saddle blankets were crumpled on the floor in the same, sad, molded mess. She had no idea if she would be able to salvage any of it. Or if they'd even need them anymore.

Stepping out into the light, Lucy saw buzzards circling high above the pasture near the back fence. She'd need to see what drew them. But she turned toward the shed instead. Lucy saw what was left of her chickens pushed up against the side of the shed. Their coop had been washed away from its location and destroyed by the force of the flooding, now lying splintered and twisted just feet away. The tree where the boys' treehouse once created a lookout for pirate play had fallen, splintering the treehouse and crushing their picnic table in its wake.

Always watching for snakes, Lucy walked inside the shed and stopped while her eyes adjusted to the darkness. She heard a rustling above her, then ducked as a barn owl flew across her to the other side of the shed.

The kids' bikes appeared demolished. All her tools were scattered around the shed, some broken, others simply caked in rotten mud.

137

Granddaddy's tractor had already begun to rust. She worked so hard the last few years since his death to keep the Massey Ferguson not only running well, but shiny and red like he had done. He was so proud that day he came home with a brand new tractor after using his father's old Ford until he just couldn't piece it together anymore. He saw the purchase of a tractor—a brand new tractor—as a sign that their hard work on the farm had paid off. They were successful, and he was so very proud of that.

Memaw, Charlie, and Lucy did their best to continue that success after Granddaddy's death—and they were succeeding, too. Then Charlie died. And now this.

Lucy climbed the ladder to the loft. The shelves stood empty now, and the food that was once there had already been consumed at the shelter. She owned nothing else to offer. Lucy walked over to the cedar chest that contained some of their family heirlooms—quilts her mother, grandmother, and great-grandmother hand-stitched plus baby clothes from each generation, including hers and her children's. The water had not reached the chest, perched up on the sawhorses, but the dampness surely did. She hoped she could salvage something.

She climbed back down and walked out into the fields, knowing nothing survived. A black bear stood far down the corn row, then lumbered away when it spotted Lucy. She wondered where it had spent the last few weeks. The corn stalks—full and tall before the storm—lie flat on the ground. Lucy pulled an ear of corn out of the mud and stripped back the shuck, knowing what she would find inside.

The grapes were destroyed, the peanuts rotting, the pumpkins black and mushy, the gourds that would have made beautifully hand-painted bird houses ruined. She knew she would salvage nothing in the acres and acres of fields that held their fortune for the future each year.

The only thing she saw still standing as though no storm had come through were the acres of long-leaf pines granddaddy planted when Lucy was just a toddler. She always looked forward to walking through the rows of trees with him when she visited as a child, loved riding Brady beneath them as a teenager, and thrilled at introducing Ella to the paths they created when she started riding Ace. The land was low and water still covered the ground from what Ella could see, but at least the trees still stood.

Lucy watched the buzzards circle and land, then lift off and land again. She didn't want to see what they were feasting on, but knew she had no choice. Today she searched for answers—even if they were not the answers she wanted.

Watching each step carefully, Lucy made her way to the back of the pasture. As she neared, she could glimpse what was left of two large animals covered in buzzards that fought for position and tore at the exposed meat. She couldn't tell from where she stopped what color the animals might have been, and she couldn't seem to make her feet move anymore.

Lucy wasn't sure how long she stood frozen in the pasture, but when the sun partially broke through the clouds sending shafts of light across the grass, she gathered her courage and walked forward. Some of the buzzards took flight as she neared. Others held their ground, hopping a bit, but not leaving. Lucy walked slowly forward. All the hide had been torn away, but at this distance she could tell they were never large enough to be horses. Deer probably, or maybe a bear. But not horses.

Relieved, Lucy walked back toward the house, but was distracted by men's voices in the distance. She took one last glance at the house on her way by, then started down the drive toward the noise. She checked her back pocket for her phone and regretted not bringing the gun she had given to Pastor Jerry to store in the safe. Walking past the curve in the drive, she could make out more than one truck parked behind her car. Several men walked back and forth, carrying lumber. She didn't recognize any of them at first, but getting a little bit closer, she could make out her neighbor Mr. Rigsby and Pastor Jerry. She didn't know the others.

"I don't know if you remember me or not," Mr. Rigsby said when Lucy was close enough to hear, "but I was real close to your granddaddy. I tried to check on your place a few days ago when I checked on mine, and figured you wouldn't get much done if you couldn't get down the drive."

"Thank you," Lucy said. "But you didn't have to do this. I really can't afford to pay you right now."

"Wouldn't accept it if you could," Mr. Rigsby said.

"You've been a great help at the shelter," Pastor Jerry said. "Just think of it as a small thank you for all the food you gave us and all your hard work helping Sally out."

"By the way," Mr. Rigsby said, "you missing a grey cat?"

"Yes, why?" Lucy said.

"One took up at the house with my three tabbies," Mr. Rigsby said.

"That would be Spoof," Lucy said. "Is he ok?"

"Fine and dandy," Mr. Rigsby said.

"I was afraid he had drowned," Lucy said. "The day we were rescued, he climbed out the window of the loft into a tree and wouldn't come down. He never has been very friendly."

"Well, he seems right happy with my cats. He can stay as long as you want," Mr. Rigsby said. "I come by and feed them every day and make sure they have fresh water. Mine aren't much for handling either."

"Thank you," Lucy said. "I'm not sure what I would do with him right now."

"Let me lay these last few boards down and you can walk over," one of the other men said. "I'm Ralph, a member of the church."

"Nice to meet you," Lucy said. She looked back over her shoulder toward the house.

"I'm not one to tell you what to do," Pastor Jerry said, "but it's getting late in the day and that Hurricane Michael is bearing down on us. You look right exhausted. Sally tells me you came out early in the day. A body can't take but just so much. Why don't you head on back to the church? We'll finish up here nailing these boards down then put up a cable so nobody can drive across. I'll bring you back the key."

Lucy looked back again, but didn't speak.

"We can come back and help you after this next storm is over if you'd like," another man said. "We're trying to help out the neighbors."

"Thank you," Lucy said, suddenly feeling the weight of the day on her shoulders. "But I did want to at least look in the house. I haven't had a chance to do that yet."

"Suit yourself," Pastor Jerry said. "We'll just finish up here. If you need us, let us know. And you might want to call your daughter. She was getting worried about you when I left. Heard her talking to Sally."

"Thank you," Lucy said, pulling her phone out of her pocket. "I'll call Ella to let her know I'm ok."

When she reached the house, Lucy took a deep breath to boost her courage. She could hear the men hammering in the distance. Somehow their presence calmed her. She took each step slowly, bracing herself for what she would surely find.

Chapter 14

"How are you doing today, Ms. Malpass?" Sam asked, stepping into the garden where Memaw spent most of her days. "You're looking as bright as all these brilliant blossoms."

"Ah, shaw," she said. "You don't have to sweet talk me. They sure are something, ain't they?"

"Looks like nature forgot it was fall," he said. "I saw on the news last night that the hurricane could cause plants to bloom out of season. I never saw it happen before. But plants go into survival mode after that kind of damage, and that's their way of making it through."

"Learn something new every day," Memaw said.

"That's what keeps us young," he said. "You really are looking and sounding great. Has your doctor said anything about sending you home?"

"I sure as heck hope he ain't planning on doing that," Memaw said. "Not that I love it here, but I don't think we have any place to go, and Lucy already has the weight of the world on her shoulders. She don't need nothing else to worry about. At least while I'm here and the Medicare is paying, she don't have to worry about me."

"That's what I wanted to talk to you about," Sam said. "I've seen how independent Lucy is, but I have a guest house that's empty since my nanny and groundskeeper left. I sure wish she and the kids would move in there."

"That sounds real nice," Memaw said. "But if you think she'll take that kind of handout, you don't know my Lucy at all. And until she

142

finds a job, we won't have any income to pay rent—not with the crops all ruined."

"And I have an in-law suite right off the kitchen in my house that would be perfect for you," Sam continued as though he did not hear what Memaw said. "It has a bedroom and a sitting room and a private bath. And you'd be right off the kitchen so you could use it like it was your own."

"Like I said, it sounds real nice," Memaw said. "But we couldn't impose on you like that. It's not the kind of thing we could do and sleep at night."

"Are you a good cook?" Sam said, undeterred.

"Of course I am," Memaw said. "Unless I forgot how since I've been laid up with pneumonia."

"That's not likely," Sam said, smiling. "Here's the thing. My nanny who left was also my cook. Ryan and I do alright, but neither of us is Paula Deen. I want you to think about something while you wait for your doc to kick you out of here."

"I'm listening," Memaw said.

"So, things aren't great with my childcare arrangements, but we're making do with the help of the neighbor. Meals are another thing altogether."

"Go on," Memaw said.

"Would you consider moving into my in-law suite and cooking for us? I wouldn't expect you to do any childcare or housekeeping or anything else. Just cook. I can give you room and board and a small stipend."

"I don't know how Lucy would feel about that."

"Well, you don't have to give me an answer yet. Just think about it. Seems it would be a pretty good solution for both of us. And one thing I do know about your granddaughter is that she puts everybody else first. If this arrangement is good for you, I can't imagine her being against it."

"She is a selfless one," Memaw said. "Too much so most of the time."

"And another thing I can't imagine," Sam said, "is that you let many people tell you what you can and cannot do."

Memaw just laughed.

§ § §

Lucy turned the doorknob and pushed, but the door wouldn't open. Leaning her shoulder against it, she used the weight of her body to make it move. Her feet slid in the inches of mud on the porch, and she almost lost her balance, but then the door gave way a little at a time.

She stepped inside and waited for her eyes to adjust. Scanning the room, she felt her heart race and her chest tighten. She struggled to breathe in the thick humid stench. Sweat beaded up on her brow as heat flushed through her body. Her legs began to tremble, and she leaned against the door casing to keep from crumbling. Steadying herself, Lucy started stepping carefully through what had once been their life. She walked from room to room in the sprawling ranch that housed her family for generations.

The flood spared nothing.

She wandered back and forth, stepping over the remnants of their lives, talking to herself, trying to figure out the next step.

What would she do?

Where would she start?

When should she tell Memaw?

How could she do this alone?

Lucy's knees buckled and she slid down to the floor. She leaned against the muddy leg of a dining room chair and tilted her head back, trying to draw air into her lungs. She felt like she was drowning.

Lucy didn't know how much time passed before she dared to open her eyes, but when she did, she spotted the edge of something atop the tall china cabinet, just inches above the high water mark on the wall. She thought she recognized it. Pulling herself up off the floor, Lucy slid a dirty dining room chair over to the china cabinet. When she climbed up, she still wasn't tall enough to reach it, but she stood on her tiptoes and reached as high as she could.

"Hold on there," she heard a male voice say. "You're going to topple over and break a bone."

Lucy swung around, almost losing her balance. A strong hand reached out to steady her.

"Let me help you down," Pastor Jerry said. "We're all finished up on your bridge, and it's getting late. Gonna be dark before long, and the rain could start anytime. Let me follow you back to the church."

"But I need that," Lucy said.

"Let me get it for you," Pastor Jerry said, reaching his long arm up and retrieving the photo album without hardly stretching. "Being tall pays off sometimes."

"Thank you," Lucy said, clinging to the album labeled *1st Family Halloween.*

"Let's go see what Sally has cooked up for supper," Pastor Jerry said.

§ § §

Ella saw the severe weather alert on her phone. How in the world was it fair for them to have another hurricane coming? Two to three inches of rain? Thunderstorms? Tornadoes? And where was her mom? She had been gone all day, and Ella was tired of her fighting brothers. They argued all the time. Today, Benji even threw a punch when Nate was trying to keep the ball away from him. It was a pitiful punch, and Nate just laughed. That made Benji cry. She wished they would grow up. She knew they both did it on purpose just to aggravate her.

Lucy saw her children among the few remaining at the shelter when she turned into the church parking lot. She glanced at the photo album in the seat next to her every few minutes as she drove—just to make sure she wasn't imagining it. She didn't know why the album was on top of the cabinet or why she had not seen it in years, but tonight after supper, she would share it with her children. Ella was old enough to remember that Halloween six years ago. Maybe Nate would even remember, but Benji had only been two.

"Mom," Ella said the second Lucy stepped out of the car. "I am so glad you're finally back. The boys have been awful, and I need a break."

"We have not been awful," Nate said. "You've been bossy."

"Yeah," Benji said. "And Nate made me cry."

"You hit me," Nate said.

"But you wouldn't give me the ball."

Ella rolled her eyes at Lucy. "See what I mean?"

"Ok, boys, go inside and wash your hands. I'm sure Ms. Sally has supper about ready."

"What was it like, Mom?" Ella asked as the boys ran ahead. "You're filthy."

"It's been a long day, Ella," Lucy responded. "Let me get cleaned up, and we'll talk later. It's going to be raining all day tomorrow, so we'll have plenty of time."

"About that," Ella said. "What am I going to do with Lucky? I can't leave her out in a hurricane."

"Run get her cage. We'll ask if we can keep her inside just through the storm. There aren't that many people here anymore, so maybe they'll bend the rules a little bit just for tonight."

"And tomorrow," Ella said.

"And tomorrow," Lucy agreed.

§ § §

Clouds and a steady drizzle drove Memaw back inside. She refused to use the wheelchair when she went to the garden even though the aide always wanted her to. She kept telling them she was quite capable of walking. This place was nice as rehab centers go, but it was closing in on her. She hadn't ask her doctor about leaving because she had nowhere to go, and she didn't want to worry Lucy any more than she already was. But things were different now. Funny how your future could change course in just one conversation.

She'd been thinking about what Sam offered her—a place to live, a job, a way to feel useful again. Her hands itched just thinking about rolling out some fresh biscuit dough and sliding the pan in the oven. Or frying chicken and making fresh creamed potatoes to go with it. She bet Sam, Ryan, and that little girl would love it. She felt bad for the child who was motherless her whole life.

Should she talk to Lucy before making that decision? Nah, Lucy would tell her she'd take care of things, and that her grandmother didn't need a job. But sometimes even Lucy didn't understand. There was one thing she needed to ask Sam though. What in the world would make his nanny and her groundskeeper husband up and leave without notice? Sam hadn't explained that part, and deep down Memaw felt like it was something she really needed to know.

§ § §

While the children were changing into their PJs and rolling out their sleeping bags, Lucy walked to the car to get the photo album. Dark clouds hung heavy and a damp drizzle began to fall. In the distance, she saw streaks of lightning. A heavy wind gust slammed the car door against her legs as she leaned toward the seat.

Here we go again, Lucy thought.

She entered the small room and looked at her children—clean and dry and warm. She was grateful for a safe place to weather this storm with no flooding, no fire ants, and no snakes. And Memaw was safe—in a rehab center with medical help if she needed it. Lucy knew she could have lost her.

"Mom?" Ella said. "Are you ok? You look like you're a thousand miles away."

"Yes, of course," Lucy said, shaking her head to clear the thoughts. "I was just thinking how much I love you guys. And how much your daddy loved you, too."

"What's that book?" Benji said.

"This?" Lucy said, holding up the small photo album. "This is a treasure I found today. It's a miracle that it wasn't ruined. Let's pile our pillows up against the wall and snuggle so all of you can see."

Lightning flashed outside their window and thunder rumbled

deeply.

With the children snuggled close, Lucy opened the book. The first picture showed their family dressed for Halloween. Ella was seven, Nate four, and Benji two.

"I remember that!" Ella said.

"I don't," Nate said.

"Which one is me?" Benji asked.

"The youngest one, knothead," Nate said. "You are that baby."

"Oh yeah," Benji said. "I sleep with that blanket."

"You do," Lucy said. "But it's a bit more ragged now."

"Why are we dressed like that?" Nate asked. "I didn't know you and daddy dressed up for Halloween, too."

"That might have been the only year we did," Lucy said. "We entered a contest."

"We won, too," Ella said. "I remember we got to go to Dollywood because we won."

"Yes, we did," Lucy said.

"I was a good Snoopy," Nate said.

"That was the first year your daddy was home for Halloween since you boys were born," Lucy explained. "We weren't able to afford any vacation trips, and when I saw the advertisement, we both agreed to enter the contest and knew exactly how to win."

"Where did you get the costumes?" Ella asked.

"Memaw helped me make them."

"They're really dope," Ella said.

"When your daddy was growing up, the other kids bullied him a lot because of his name," Lucy said. "They picked on him relentlessly—until he grew so tall and muscular that nobody dared try."

"Daddy was very tall," Ella said. "I love how he threw me up in the air when I was little. I felt like I was flying."

"Me, too," Nate said.

"Me, three," Benji said.

"Well, just think how much worse it was when he and I got together." Lucy said. "His buddies in the army were as big and strong as he was, and they all ribbed each other—good naturedly, of course. So your daddy was an easy target."

"Oh, yeah," Ella said, "Charlie Brown and Lucy!"

"That was us," Lucy said, smiling at the memory of the first time she realized what their names would sound like as a couple.

"Oh," Nate said. "So that's why we dressed up like that!"

"Perfect, wasn't it," Lucy said.

"No wonder we won," Nate said.

"I'm Linus," Benji said.

"And I'm a real good Snoopy," Nate said. "But you can't even see my face."

"And I'm Sally Brown," Ella said. "I love that dress! You and Memaw really did a great job on the costumes. I wish I could sew like that."

"When we get settled again," Lucy said. "Memaw and I can teach you."

"How come I got no hair?" Benji said.

"Linus only has sprigs of hair, remember? So we made a skull cap for you and made you look just like Linus," Lucy said. "We struggled getting you to keep it on, though."

"Did my daddy have a skull cap, too?" Benji asked. "Or was he bald already?"

"No, your daddy had beautiful hair—although the Army made him keep it short. We made him a skull cap, too—just like yours except with curls in the front like the real Charlie Brown instead of spiky hair like Linus. See?"

"Is that a wig or did you dye your hair black?" Ella asked.

"I thought about dying it," Lucy said, "but I was afraid I'd never get it normal again. So we splurged on a wig."

"Memaw should have been Peppermint Patty," Ella said.

Their chatter and laughter warmed a part of Lucy's heart she had guarded far too long. They flipped through the rest of the album—more photos of them dressed in their costumes, winning the contest, receiving their free passes to Dollywood, then photos of their trip. Fun family memories carried them late into the night as tropical storm winds and rains battered the window of their room.

"I miss my daddy," Benji said as Lucy tucked him into his sleeping bag.

"I miss him, too," Lucy said, kissing her son on the forehead and hugging him just a little longer than normal.

An hour later, both boys were sound asleep, but Lucy and Ella were not.

"I'm going to check on Lucky," Ella said.

"Want me to walk with you?"

"Sure, Mom."

They walked quietly down the hallway where most of the rooms were closed off and dark even though some of the families who had returned home came back before Michael hit. The forecast called for flash flooding, which meant low lying areas could be perilous. And damaged roofs covered with tarps were subject to leaking again. People just couldn't feel safe in their homes and didn't want to take the risk of needing to be rescued again.

In the fellowship hall where Lucky's cage sat in a back corner, Pastor Jerry stood looking out the window into the dark. An area light revealed heavy rain blowing sideways in the wind.

"How are you tonight?" Lucy asked him. "I wanted to thank you again for my bridge. I'll be able to get to the house with the boxes now."

"I'm worried about what this rain is going to do," he said. "They're calling for flash flooding, and the rivers can't recede anymore as long as the rain levels rise. You might not be able to get back there for a while."

This was the first time Lucy heard him sound so dejected. Even at the farm, his tone had been encouraging.

"We just wanted to check on Lucky," Ella said.

"Cute bunny," the pastor said, then turned and left the room.

Ella sat down on the floor and took the bunny from its cage, snuggling her face into its soft fur.

"Mom?" Ella said, causing Lucy to turn from the window and face her daughter. "Where do you think Ace and Brady are?"

"I just don't know," Lucy said.

"What did we do that was so wrong?" Ella asked.

"You haven't done anything wrong, Ella. What do you mean?"

"What did we do wrong to make all these bad things happen to us? I miss my daddy. I miss my friends. I miss Memaw. I miss Ace. I just want to wake up in my own bed with my daddy tickling me awake like he used to do. I want it all to be a bad dream."

Chapter 15

David was exhausted, but he had not found an opportunity to check his email in weeks to see if Lucy replied. He sat down in front of the computer, logged on, and opened his email account. Scanning past the unimportant ones, he spotted Lucy's reply and clicked it.

Hi David,

Good to hear from you. I hope you are staying safe and will be able to come home to us soon. I know you're worried about the storm and flooding and all, but you don't have to be.

We lost electricity and you know the internet never works very well anyway, so it just took a while for me to answer. Everybody is fine here, so just take good care of yourself and hurry home to us.

Memaw and Ella and the boys said to tell you hi and that we all love you. Memaw will make hot biscuits and fried chicken when you get home. We all hope that is soon!

Love ya big brother!
Lucy

Dear Lucy,

You can't know how happy that makes me. I knew the farm never flooded before, but some of the guys have family back there, and they heard awful stuff. That's why I was so worried when I sent the last email.

You know I can't tell you anything about what I'm doing or where I am or even when I'll be home, but just know that I'll do my best to get back home in one piece. Looking forward to fried chicken and hot biscuits. Memaw knows me well.

Tell everybody I said hello and send my love. Pretty exhausted tonight so I'm going to hit the sack.

Goodnight little sister.

Love you bunches.
David

Relieved, David sat on the side of his bed and unlaced his boots. He worried so much about his family, and that was never a good thing. He couldn't afford to be less than fully focused on the mission at hand. The next one would not be easy. None of them were, but this one made him more anxious than most. Not that he'd ever admit that to anyone. At least he could put the worries about his family behind him and concentrate one hundred percent on completing the mission and keeping his men and himself alive.

As he drifted off to sleep, David smiled at the thought of his nephews up in their treehouse, Memaw in the kitchen with her hands covered in flour, Lucy picking the last of the grapes, and his spunky niece galloping through the trees on that big black horse of hers, her long blonde hair flying in the wind.

Friday, October 12

Lucy woke up to pouring rain that didn't stop all day. With the shelter almost full again, she and Ella helped Sally prepare and serve three meals to a large number of people. Once again, the cupboards looked almost bare. She hoped the roads would be clear enough the next day for someone to deliver more supplies.

Even though Michael decreased to a tropical storm, the wind and rain made going outside impossible. It was an excruciatingly long day—just like every other one when her boys and other kids in the shelter couldn't get outside to release their pent up energy. Frustrations ran high and even the adults argued.

By the time she put the boys to bed, Lucy was exhausted. But she couldn't sleep from thinking about Ella's question. She knew the old adage that 'bad things happen to good people' but she didn't want to patronize Ella by saying that to her. She had heard it too many times in the past seventeen years. That, and 'everything happens for a reason.' She didn't understand how either one was supposed to make you feel better while your world disintegrated around you.

She thought back to the day her parents left for their two-week driving celebration up the east coast, including New York City. They saved for years to take that trip for their twenty-fifth wedding anniversary.

Unlike Lucy, her mother loved to shop and looked forward to going to the original Macy's and other iconic stores. Her daddy didn't care much for shopping, but would tag along with his wife to make her happy. In turn, she would indulge daddy in stops at any historical site he wanted to visit. They both loved museums and art galleries, so their plan included as many of those as they could—especially in Washington, DC.

Lucy remembered her mama calling and telling her about their stop at Gettysburg. They had toured the battleground on horseback, and Lucy's mama seemed as excited about it as her history-loving daddy did.

Mama called every night to tell Lucy and David about their day—

riding the Blue Ridge Parkway from North Carolina through Virginia and stopping at little shops, fruit stands, and restaurants on the side of curvy connecting backroads; falling in love with the horse-drawn carriages, the food, and the crafts in the Amish country; being surprised by the beauty of western New York state on their way to Niagara Falls and how much more commercialized yet still beautiful the falls were on the Canadian side where they made a reservation for the night of their actual anniversary.

Mama told Lucy how many pictures she took and how nice strangers were to offer to take pictures of her and Daddy together. She was enjoying every minute, but was also excited to get home, send the photos to the printer, and create a photo album of the trip of a lifetime.

"We'll take you with us next time," Mama said. "I felt a little guilty riding the coasters at Busch Gardens knowing how much you would love them."

They headed back home via the Big Apple and tried to get on the Today Show. Even though they woke up super early carrying their special "Celebrating our 25th Anniversary in The Big Apple" sign, the camera never caught them in its lens. Memaw and Lucy sat watching and waiting.

They took in two Broadway shows—*42nd Street* and *If you ever leave me...I'm going with you!*

Once they left New York City, they planned to drive down the coast, making stops along the way, with their last weekend spent in the Outer Banks. Mama was so excited about the possibility of seeing wild horses.

But before they headed out that September morning, Mama wanted to visit her childhood friend who worked in the north tower of the World Trade Center. She would be in her office at 8 a.m., and Mama couldn't wait to see the view from her office. Mama—who never lived anywhere but southeastern North Carolina—was so proud of her friend's accomplishments and the exciting life she had created for herself in New York City.

Lucy quietly sobbed herself to sleep.

Sunday, October 14

The rains from Michael caused the waters to rise and the road to Lucy's farm to become impassable again. On Sunday, she loaded up the children and headed to Wilmington to visit Memaw.

"Can we please go to Chick-fil-a or McDonald's or somewhere?" Benji asked. "Ms. Sally's nice and all, but I sure am tired of her cooking."

"Of course, we can," Lucy said. "But Chick-fil-a is closed on Sundays. How about PT's Grille? We haven't been there in a while. You boys love their burgers and fries, and I could use a good grilled chicken sandwich with sautéed mushrooms.

"Their salads are ok," Ella said. "But not great."

Ignoring the teenager sulking in the seat beside her, Lucy eyed her youngest son in the rearview mirror.

"Remember to be nice, Benji," Lucy warned. "We need to thank Ms. Sally every day. I can't imagine cooking day in and day out for so many people."

"When can we go home?" Nate asked.

"I don't know," Lucy said.

"When will we go back to school?" Ella asked. "I need to go shopping for clothes. My backpack didn't hold but one pair of shorts, my favorite pair of jeans, and two shirts. And I can't wear those hand-me-downs from the shelter to school."

"You can and you will," Lucy said. "Be grateful. Anyway, some of those jeans and tops are really nice name-brand clothes. They were much more expensive new than anything I was ever able to buy for you."

"Yes, ma'am," Ella said, crossing her arms and leaning back in the seat with her eyes closed.

Lucy was grateful for the rebuff rather than a contracted argument. Life with a teenager could be challenging in the best of circumstances.

She had seen the news about the schools in Pender County and it wasn't good. So many were damaged and so many roads washed out or flooded. But they might start back later that week—October 18 at the earliest. That would be six weeks since schools closed in expectation of Hurricane Florence. How would they ever make that up?

She pulled into the rehab center and the children piled out quickly, seeing Memaw sitting in a rocker on the front porch.

"I've been waiting and waiting for you!" Memaw said. "Have you been good for your mom?"

"I have," Benji said. "But not Nate or Ella."

"I have too been good," Nate said.

"Oh, come on now boys," Memaw said. "Just give me a hug and tell me what you been up to. I have some news, but I want to hear yours first."

The boys rattled on and on about their new friends and the games they made up and how great it was not to have to go to school and how they hoped they never had to go back.

"How about you, Ella?" Memaw said.

"Not much to do," Ella said. "I did get a phone so I can talk to Amelia. And I've been taking care of Lucky and helping in the kitchen. I'm so over it all."

"You will never guess what I found when I went to the house," Lucy said.

"You went to the farm?" Memaw asked, surprised. "How was it?"

"We can talk about that later," Lucy said nodding toward the kids. "But you remember that photo album of the Halloween we dressed up as the Charlie Brown gang? I found it on top of the china cabinet. It didn't even get wet."

"How did it get up there?"

"I have no idea, but I'm sure glad it did," Lucy said. "We spent hours the other night looking at the pictures and remembering our trip to Dollywood."

"That sounds real good," Memaw said.

"Now, what kind of news do you have?" Lucy asked.

"Ella, take the boys inside and go down to my room," Memaw said. "There's some cookies and some drinks in there you can have.

157

Watch a little television."

"But I wanted to hear your news," Ella said.

"Do as you're told," Lucy said in a tone that even Ella knew not to challenge.

After the children went inside the building, Lucy asked, "What kind of news can't you tell me in front of the kids? What's wrong?"

"Nothing's wrong," Memaw said. "I'm getting sprung. Doc says I'm as good as I'm gonna get for an old codger like me."

"But can't they keep you a little longer?" Lucy asked. "I know you want to get out of here, but the shelter just won't be a good place for you, and we can't go home."

"No," Memaw said firmly, then softened her voice. "He's a funny fellow, my doctor. He told me I was well, and he can't recommend keeping me any longer without committing Medicare fraud—and as much as he likes me, I'm just not worth going to jail for."

"I'm sorry," Lucy said, near tears. "But we just can't go home, and I don't know when or if we'll ever be able to go home."

"Don't fret, child," Memaw said. "I've got it all worked out."

"How?"

"Well, I got me a new job that includes room and board."

"What?"

"Dr. Sam needs a cook, and he offered me the job," Memaw said. "And he has an in-law suite right off his kitchen where I'll have my own sitting room, bedroom, and bathroom."

"No, Memaw," Lucy said. "I can't let you do that."

"Let me?"

"You know what I mean," Lucy said. "You shouldn't have to work. You took care of me all those years, and now it's time for me to take care of you."

"I don't mean to hurt your feelings, Lucy," Memaw said. "But how are you going to do that? Did you find a job?"

"No," Lucy said. "Not yet."

"Well, I have," Memaw said. "It doesn't solve the problem for you and the kids even though I can pitch in some money, but it's a perfect solution for me. The only thing I'm asking you to do is take me out

158

there to his house so I can check it out before I give him my final yes. But I'm being released tomorrow whether I have a place to go or not. So, will you take me or do I have to call a cab?"

"Now?" Lucy said.

"Yes, now," Memaw said. "He'll be home this afternoon with that little sprite of his. I can just tell the staff I'm taking a field trip since the sun is finally shining after all that rain."

"I'll take you," Lucy said. "But I don't have to like it."

"This isn't about you, baby girl," Memaw said. "But I do wish you'd try to be a little bit happy for me. I get to put my hands in some flour again, and I can't tell you how much I'm looking forward to some steaming hot biscuits instead of those frozen fake things they been trying to make me eat here."

Ella and the boys came out carrying cookies and cokes.

"Get in the car," Lucy said. "All of you in the back seat."

"But Mom, there's not enough room," Ella said.

"Well, I'm sure not putting your Memaw back there," Lucy said.

"Where are we going?" Benji said. "Memaw's going with us?"

"Just get in the car," Lucy said.

"Alright, already," Nate said, scuffing his feet as he walked. "I don't know why you're mad at us. We didn't do anything."

"Your mom's not mad," Memaw said. "She's just got a lot on her mind. You gotta give her a little slack. You're going to like this field trip."

Memaw held the address and a map in her lap. She told Lucy when and where to turn although Lucy was sure she had not forgotten. Once Memaw saw that house and the yard and the waterway, she'd be caught hook, line, and sinker. Lucy could never compete with what Sam offered.

Lucy turned into the neighborhood, and the beauty made her breathless. No flooded homes or muddy cars or broken trees or storm debris. Everything was lush and green and in full bloom—pinks and whites and yellows and purples glistening in the afternoon sun.

"Oh, my," Memaw said.

"This is nothing," Ella said. "Wait until you see where Dr. Sam

159

lives."

"Will we get to see Rex and Roxie?" Benji asked.

"You know we will knothead," Nate said. "We're going to Dr. Sam's house, and that's where they are."

"Don't call me that," Benji whined. "Mom, Nate's calling me names."

"Be nice boys," Memaw warned. "You don't want me to make you stay in the car."

"Yes, ma'am," Nate said, elbowing his brother. Benji didn't make a sound.

Lucy turned into Sam's driveway.

"I don't know how we'll get through the gate," she said.

"I'll just let him know we're here," Memaw said. "Hand me your phone."

"I don't know his number," Lucy said.

"Well, I do," Memaw said. "I have it right here. You can just save it in your contacts when I'm done."

Seconds after she called, the gate swung open. Rex and Roxie came running down the tree-lined drive.

"Roll your window up kids," Memaw said. "That many Bradford pear trees in full bloom are going to stink to high heaven."

The boys were out of the car before Lucy could come to a full stop. Sam came around from the back of the house with Faith sitting high on his shoulders, her hands clasped firmly on his forehead.

"Welcome ladies," Sam said, opening Memaw's door.

"This is quite the place you have here," Memaw said. "You have any garden space back there?"

"Well, no," Sam said. "But I don't see why we couldn't create one."

"If I decide to take this gig, we'll talk about it for spring," Memaw said, winking at him.

"You got to see what is back there," Benji said. "It's so cool. There's a yard big enough to play football and a treehouse and water."

"And a boat," Nate said. "A great big boat."

"I'll check that out later," Memaw said. "But first, I want to see my my new digs."

"What are you talking about, Memaw?" Ella asked.

"Come on in, and we'll show you," Sam said, pointing the way for Lucy, Memaw, and Ella to go up the back steps and onto the porch.

"Stay far away from the water," Lucy said, raising her voice so the boys could hear her as they wrestled in the grass with the dogs. "Do not go through that gate."

"Hi, Ms. Lucy," Ryan said, coming out the door. "I'll watch them for you."

He caught Faith as she slid off their daddy's shoulders, then lifted her to his.

"I'd appreciate that," Lucy said, overwhelmed by how fast everything was changing—totally out of her control.

They entered the door Ryan left ajar.

"Woah," Ella said, voicing Lucy's amazement.

A huge bright kitchen opened out before them with sparkling oak floors, bright white cabinets that rose toward a ten-foot ceiling, and stainless appliances that gleamed in the sunlight streaming in through walls of windows. Light grey granite countertops glistened with specks of silver.

A breakfast nook with floor-to-ceiling windows jutted out toward blooming crepe myrtle trees. It held an oval white table with placemats that matched the flowers outside and a centerpiece of at least a dozen fresh roses in various shades of pink.

Lucy watched Memaw walk around the room, sliding her hand across the island countertop, bending down to look in the oven, opening the double-door refrigerator and peering inside. She stood in front of the sink and gazed out the window that gave her a perfect view of the sloping yard, the waterway, and a shrimp boat gliding past.

"I can cook some mighty fine meals in here," she said. "If I can keep my mind on my cooking."

"It is quite a view," Sam said. "My wife made sure the architect created a perfect place for the family to start the day. She loved this kitchen."

Lucy tried to catch Memaw's attention. She wanted to tell her, "I told you so."

"Well, she did a mighty fine job," Memaw said. "Now show me where I'll be living."

"You're going to live here?" Ella asked.

"If she accepts my offer," Sam said.

"What offer?"

"Your old Memaw has a job, Ella girl," Memaw said. "Dr. Sam here hired me as his cook."

"Well, that's not fair," Ella said. "Who's going to cook for us?"

"I'll cook for us," Lucy said defiantly.

"Come this way," Sam said, pointing to a door down a short hallway off the kitchen. "Karina wanted a private retreat for her mother when she visited."

"Does she still visit the children?" Memaw asked. "She won't like having someone taking up the space her daughter built for her."

"No," Sam said. "She died before Karina did. She never met Faith."

Sam opened the door and Memaw walked directly into the sitting room—small but comfortable with a wall of floor-length windows and a French door opening onto a screened porch that overlooked the pool, the manicured lawn, and the waterway. Oak floors gleamed around the edges of a multi-colored rug with turtles and seaweed woven in. The furniture—nothing like anything Memaw ever owned—created a welcoming space.

Living on a farm, she always chose solid, dark-colored, heavy duty couches and chairs. Her one big splurge had been a plush recliner that fit her small frame. But even it was brown. This furniture was soft but not bulky, pale blue instead of dark brown. Throw pillows splashed with color in flowers, shells, and flamingos tied together the design of the rug, the butter yellow walls, and the coral-colored recliner—just her size. It should have been too busy, too frou-frou, too untouchable, but it wasn't.

"This is perfect," Memaw said.

"I love it," Ella said.

Lucy remained quiet, but gazed out the windows and felt her heart sink further. Why would Memaw not want to do this? It really was perfect.

The pale coral-colored bedroom was carpeted with light beige plush, both colors alternating in wide stripes on the drapes. A queen-size bed, centered under a large painting of sunset at the beach, held a beige quilt with a stitched star-fish design. Pleated and quilted throw pillows echoed the soft yellows, oranges, pinks, corals and teals in the painting. The dressers and headboard were solid wood, off-white, a little antiqued. An upholstered tangerine colored swivel rocker sat in the corner, one arm draped with a teal chenille comforter.

"There's a walk-in closet," Sam said, "and the bathroom is over here."

Memaw wasn't surprised by the time she walked into the bathroom. She expected luxury and that's what she found—dark beige tile on the floor extended to the large walk-in shower highlighted with a wide horizontal stripe of sunset colored glass tiles. The large seat in the shower would make it easy to sit down and wash her feet. But if she wanted to take a bath, Memaw could sink into the soaking tub. Coral and teal towels hung side-by-side, pictures of sea life decorated the walls, and a tall jar of seashells sat on the vanity. The bathroom window even captured a view of the water.

"Wow!" Ella said. "Can I move in here with you?"

"No, of course not," Lucy said.

"I was just kidding, Mom," Ella said, rolling her eyes.

They followed Memaw and Sam back to the sitting room.

"Well, I've seen all I need to see," Memaw said. "When do I start?"

"As soon as your doctor releases you," Sam said. "Make me a grocery list before you leave, and I guarantee the refrigerator and pantry will be stocked to your liking."

"They sure are empty," Memaw laughed. "You'd be surprised what I can whip up when supplies are low, but a stocked refrigerator and pantry would be a dream come true."

"Would you like to see the rest of the house?" Sam asked.

"Yes!" Ella said.

"We need to go," Lucy said.

"Not today," Memaw said to Sam, then turned to Lucy. "I need to go shopping for some clothes and personal items. Will you take me?"

"Today?" Lucy asked.

"Yes, today. If I could buy a few things and put them in your trunk today, that would be helpful," Memaw said, sounding more than a little exasperated with her granddaughter. "We can do a little more shopping tomorrow before I move in. The doctor is releasing me in the morning. You are going to pick me up, right?"

"Of course I am," Lucy said. "I just didn't know anything about any of this until today and everything is moving so fast."

"I'm sure Ryan would be happy to watch the boys if you ladies want to shop in peace this afternoon," Sam said.

"But they haven't even eaten lunch yet," Lucy said.

"We'll order pizza," Sam said. "Your boys do like pizza, don't they?

"All boys like pizza," Lucy said grudgingly.

"You deserve an afternoon off," Sam said. "Enjoy a relaxing lunch with your grandma and daughter, do a little shopping, and don't worry about the boys. They can run around and get exhausted before you take them back home."

"Alright," Lucy said. "I don't seem to have a lot of say in this anyway."

"You can bring some things back here today and will have less to do tomorrow," Sam said. "Unless you're getting tired, Ms. Malpass."

"Haven't felt this good or been this energized in a long time, Doc," Memaw said. "And no more of that Ms. Malpass stuff. If you can't call me Memaw, at least call me Lucille."

"Lucille it is," Sam said. "But Ryan already calls you Memaw when he talks about you, so I'm sure Faith will, too."

Lucy felt her world shift on its axis.

Chapter 16

Wednesday, October 17

Lucy tried every day to drive back to the farm, but after Michael drenched them with an additional five inches of rain, water crossing the road ran too deep for the little car to pass through. School would start back the next day, so she checked her bank account and took the children shopping, giving them each a limit for what they could spend.

Even though the clothes were still used, Ella wasn't as averse to buying from Plato's Closet as she was choosing from the vast selection of donations at the church. Lucy gave her a two outfit limit. They still needed to buy school supplies, too.

The boys didn't care, so Lucy selected an entire school wardrobe for them from the donations, complete with an extra pair of tennis shoes. They did enjoy picking out new notebooks and backpacks at Walmart. And Lucy felt better buying all three children new socks and underwear.

They had not visited Memaw since she moved into Sam's house, and Memaw insisted that they swing by and eat lunch there today. She wanted to cook for them as a 'going back to school' celebration.

Apparently, Lucy did not hide well the fact that she didn't want to go.

"Why are you jealous of Memaw?" Ella asked as they drove toward the doctor's house.

"I'm not jealous," Lucy said. "That's ridiculous."

"Just saying," Ella said, leaning back in her seat and putting the inexpensive earbuds they found at Walmart in her ears.

"I miss Rex and Roxie," Benji said. "When can we get them back?"

"As soon as I find us a place to live," Lucy said. "But at least you can play with them today."

Lucy had already met with FEMA three times, and every time, she talked to someone different. She repeated the same facts every time—no forward progress. No one seemed to know the results of the forms she had already completed or when she would have any answers. She filled out more forms each time. She asked about FEMA housing thinking that maybe she could put one of those trailers at the farm, but every time, they told her that their area had not been approved.

"What's Memaw cooking today?" Nate asked.

"I'm not really sure," Lucy said, "but as much as you boys like her country style steak and creamed potatoes or her fried chicken and mac 'n cheese, I think either of those would be a good bet."

"And biscuits with molasses and butter?" Benji asked.

"I would definitely say hot biscuits," Lucy said. "Has Memaw ever made a meal without hot biscuits?

"I miss her," Benji said.

"We all do," Lucy said.

"Ryan said nobody lives in the pool house," Nate said. "Why can't we move there? Then we could see Memaw every day and eat her food."

"Because the house doesn't belong to us," Lucy said. "And neither does the food Memaw is cooking. It all belongs to Dr. Sam. I'm doing the best I can, boys. Just give me a little more time, okay?"

Lucy thought about the little house on the outskirts of the farm that she and Charlie built for their family. The VA loan had been a godsend—the only way they could have built the house even though Granddaddy and Memaw gave them the ten acres where it sat. After Hurricane Matthew flooded it with three feet of water, they moved out.

Even though it hadn't been habitable since, and they had no flood insurance nor received any assistance from FEMA, living with Memaw allowed them to keep up the mortgage payments. Charlie insisted that they would not default. It might be cheaper to repair than the big old farm house. But even if she could ever bring herself to go back in that house, could she really move her family back there? Could she sleep at night?

"Are you going to call Memaw to open the gate," Ella asked, "or are we just going to sit here all day? You've been sitting there staring out the window like forever."

Rex and Roxie bounced and barked on the other side.

Before Lucy could call, the gates swung open.

"I've been so excited about you coming!" Memaw said, meeting them at the car when Lucy pulled up to the garage doors. "I looked out the window and saw you just sitting there. Why didn't you call and let me know you were here?"

"We just got here," Lucy said, hugging her grandmother. "How are you? You look like you've been out in the sun."

"Oh I have," Memaw said. "I sit on the dock between meals and watch the boats and birds."

"Must be nice," Ella said.

"Are you kids excited about going back to school?" Memaw asked, ignoring the teenager's sarcastic tone.

"At least I will finally get to see my friends," Ella said. "I've only seen Amelia once during this whole disaster of a life, and I haven't seen any of my other friends at all."

"Come on in and let's eat," Memaw said. "Boys, the dogs will still be here after lunch. Follow your sister to my bathroom and wash your hands."

"Stay in this part of the house," Lucy said to her children. "Just the kitchen and Memaw's rooms."

When they finished lunch and cleaned up the kitchen, they all headed outside. The day was overcast, but streaks of sun sometimes seeped through the clouds.

"More rain in the forecast," Memaw said. "Rainfall already

breaking records this year."

"I'm so sick of rain," Lucy said, watching her boys and Ella throw Frisbees for the dogs.

"The sun will shine again," Memaw said, "and I don't just mean today. Things will get better, baby girl."

"I want to believe that, Memaw," Lucy said. "I really do. But every which way I turn, all I see are roadblocks in my way, unsurmountable mountains of problems, and soul-sucking mud. The only answers I get are no – no to jobs, no from FEMA, no from trying to find a place for us to live—not just a decent place that I can afford, but any place at all."

"A lot of people are displaced," Memaw said. "I reckon they're all trying to find the same things you are."

"Well, not all of them lost their livelihood, too," Lucy said. "At least if I worked a regular job, we'd have money coming in every month."

"I have an idea," Memaw said. "Let's go sit on the dock and talk. It's so pretty down there and just the sounds of the birds can help relieve stress. Yesterday I saw a pod of dolphins."

"You sound happy," Lucy said.

"As happy as I can be when the people I love are not," Memaw said. "But this was a blessing for me—and for you, too, if you think about it. One less thing to worry about."

Lucy looked over at the white shingled cottage as they walked by. Nate called it a 'pool house' but it wasn't directly adjacent to the pool. It sat sheltered under huge live oaks at the edge of the property about halfway between the main house and the waterway with a full-length covered front porch facing the lawn—complete with cushioned rockers—and a screened porch on the end facing the water. A cobblestone pathway wound its way toward the slate pool patio, then around the pool fence to the back deck of the house. Although perfectly landscaped, Lucy noticed the yard and gardens looked a little ragged in places. Everything needed tending.

"Let's sit here," Memaw said, pointing to the swing suspended from the dock gazebo. "It's my favorite place, although I've been taking my afternoon nap on the screened porch. "You'd be surprised how comfortable that wicker furniture is."

"You talk like you've lived here for months," Lucy said. "It hasn't even been three full days yet."

"It already feels like home," Memaw said.

Lucy looked out over the water at the impossibly perfect scene and felt her eyes begin to fill. She was sick and tired of being so emotional all the time. Memaw put her arm around Lucy's shoulder and pulled her in for a hug.

"I have an idea about how you can make some quick money," Memaw said. "I'm not sure how much, but any little bit will help."

"How?" Lucy said. "I've tried everything I can think of short of selling off part of the land, and even though you deeded it to me and Charlie, I'm not going to do that. Who would want that flooded mess anyway?"

"The timber," Memaw said. "Your granddaddy planted it with your future in mind. It's been there thirty years—more than enough time for it to be ready to harvest. There's about fifty acres of full-grown pines. It should bring in enough to keep you solvent until you figure things out."

"I don't want to cut Granddaddy's trees," Lucy said.

"Why not?" Memaw asked. "That's the very reason he planted them—not for us, but for you. That land we deeded David has timber, too, but it's not as old. He'd be better off to let his grow another ten years. It should be ready to cut when he retires from the Army. And he doesn't need the money right now. You do."

"But won't it make the land look awful?" Lucy said.

"Sure," Memaw said. "It won't be a pretty sight to start with, but when you get back on your feet, you can replant, and it won't be long before it's beautiful again. Then you'll be making an investment in your own children's and grandchildren's future."

"I hadn't thought of it that way," Lucy said. "In fact, I hadn't thought of it at all. How much money do you think it would bring in?"

"I'm not sure," Memaw said, "but all you have to do is contact some timber companies and pick the one you like who offers you the most money."

"But we'll lose the income from the pine straw if I have all the trees cut down."

"That's true, but the timber is worth more to you now if you cut it. And you'll still have the ten acres around the house you and Charlie built that has the younger pines where you can continue harvesting straw. They're producing pretty good already."

"But what if the pines were damaged in the storm?" Lucy said. "I haven't checked any of the timberland."

"I was doing some reading," Memaw said. "And even the ones that were damaged can be harvested for pulpwood. They made it through thirty years of hurricanes without much damage at all, so I'm thinking you're probably in good shape to sell it for lumber and get the most money."

"I need to check it all out, but I haven't been able to get back to the farm since Michael dropped all that rain, and now we have more rain coming," Lucy said. "I don't know if the four-wheeler will run, but I might can fix it. I don't think I'll be able to get granddaddy's tractor running again without dumping some hefty money into it. It looks like a big rust bucket already."

"But now you have a plan," Memaw said. "And this pathway won't be a dead end."

"Thanks, Memaw," Lucy said, hugging her grandma. "I'm sorry it took two days for me to visit after I just dropped you off on Monday and left so fast."

"It's ok, baby girl. I know you don't feel comfortable here. But Dr. Sam is a good man. He can't help it if he's handsome and rich, too."

Memaw laughed, and Lucy rolled her eyes.

"Cut him a little slack," Memaw said. "We need all the friends we can get right now."

"You're right," Lucy said. "I know you are, but there's just something bugging me about how he latched on to our family out of all the people he saved during the storm."

Thursday, October 18

After dropping the kids off at their schools for the first time in six weeks, Lucy headed to the local ATV shop. She had spent hours on the computer after the children went to bed researching how to repair a flooded ATV engine. She watched numerous videos and, with Sally's permission, printed out instructions on what she needed and the steps she would have to take to get the engine running again.

Lucy made minor adjustments and repairs to the four-wheeler and even the tractor in the past, but never anything this major. Her bank account, however, mandated that she at least try to fix it herself.

Lucy stayed awake most of the night with her mind reeling over the solution Memaw suggested. She researched how much she could expect to earn by selling fifty acres of prime timber, and if what she thought she read was true, this could be the answer to her immediate financial problems. She would call some companies later, but first, she needed to drive back to the farm and check out the condition of her trees. She just hoped the roads were clear enough for her to make it through today. The weather report forecast more rain by the weekend.

Lucy knew her tools would, at the very least, be too rusty to use today, so rather than spend time she didn't have cleaning them up, she pulled out her credit card and bought the ones she knew she would need to work on the engine along with carburetor cleaner, spark plugs, cleaning rags, a plastic gas can, and some engine oil. Looking back at the directions for engine repair, she double checked her supplies. She would need a fan and wondered if the electricity was working.

As she drove toward the farm, Lucy made a mental list of things she wanted to do. She only had a few hours, though, before she needed to drive back to school to get the kids. Working on the four-wheeler took precedence over everything else. She did need to see how bad her Expedition looked and call an auto insurance adjuster. She remembered a tree leaning close when they started cleaning between the hurricane and the flood, but she didn't even walk behind the house to check on it last time she was there.

And granddaddy's truck. Lucy hadn't thought about it in a while, locked inside the little garage behind the house. He bought it new, that 1953 F-100 Ford Pickup, and drove it right up until the day he died. That would have to wait, she decided, because she didn't know where the key to the deadbolt on the garage was. Lost probably.

Luckily, Lucy had no trouble getting to the farm. She could see the centerline under the water standing on the road, so she drove down the middle, staying far from either edge. She parked at the cable the men installed after repairing her bridge, hopped out, and used her key to open the lock. She drove across the cable and bridge continuing toward the house, then backed up and relocked the cable. She didn't want to be disturbed. Neither did she want to be surprised by anyone—good intentions or bad.

Lucy underestimated how hard staying focused would be. The destruction felt apocalyptic. Bones from decayed fish lay scattered in the yard like a dinosaur dig. Other bone piles picked clean by scavengers were unidentifiable.

She walked up the steps to the house, then talked herself out of opening the front door. Descending the steps, she strode right past the shed where the tractor and four-wheeler sat and continued to the barn—just in case. Of course, the horses were not there, so she went to the car and unloaded her tools.

Dragging an old piece of plywood out of the shed and laying it flat on the ground, she was able to keep all the things she purchased out of the mud and have a place to work so she wasn't sitting in mud either. The shed was dark and the electricity was not working, so she put the four-wheeler in neutral and pushed it out into the light of day.

Lucy drained the fuel tank, the fuel lines, and the oil into a metal bucket she located in the shed. The instructions told her to put a fan on the wiring and dry it out. Since she didn't have electricity, she hoped the sunshine would stay out from behind the brewing storm clouds long enough to do the job. The more she tore into the job, however, she didn't have much hope for finishing in one day.

She removed the carburetor and cleaned out all the oil and water and debris. That took almost two hours. She was nothing if not slow.

Granddaddy always taught her to do the job right the first time no matter how long it took. She knew he never anticipated the turtle-paced speed she'd need to do it right, but even though she could see the laughter in his eyes, he was patient and let her do the work—no matter how long it took. She could make minor adjustments and repairs on most of the farm machinery, large and small, but she never even tried to work on the bush-hog after one of her granddaddy's lifelong friends died working on his.

Being back on the farm, especially by herself, Lucy felt the onslaught of memories flood her mind as surely as the waters flooded her farm. But she must keep her head above water and concentrate on the job at hand.

The next step said: "Take the plugs out of the engine and turn the motor over to force any water in the cylinder out."

But she knew the wiring was still wet, so maybe she should wait on that step. She tried to think of anything else she owned that might dry it out. Maybe the leaf blower? But it would be waterlogged, too. Nevertheless, she went back into the shed, opened the little room where she kept her smaller yard tools and found the blower. Sure enough, it looked as bad as everything else. She carried it to the car with intentions of trying to fix it before she returned the next day. Not wanting to do anything to damage the four-wheeler engine further, Lucy rolled it back in the shed and carried her tools and supplies in as well.

Checking her watch, Lucy couldn't believe how little time remained before she had to pick the boys up from school. Ella didn't know whether or not she would have volleyball practice, so Lucy told her to go to the office and call when she knew. Lucy checked her phone, but no messages yet.

Lucy looked with longing at the stand of timber on the other side of the corn fields, but knew she didn't have time to even walk any of it today. She should have just enough time to check on her Expedition and take a few pictures. She stopped by the car and retrieved the Expedition keys, glad that in the terror of that night she remembered to grab her purse. She checked the back pocket of her jeans to make sure her phone was still there and started around to the back of the farmhouse.

The big fig tree at the end of the house lie uprooted and toppled. It produced a huge crop before the storm, and Memaw put up dozens of jars of fig jam. When Lucy helped the men gather all the food from the shed and take it to the church, she filled one box full of various varieties of jam to save. She needed to take that box to Memaw now.

The red hand-pump sitting on that end of the house for generations looked a little rustier, but not that much worse for wear. The same could not be said for the flower beds or the rose garden or the swing that had hung from an old metal swing set frame, now twisted and crumpled beyond repair, the old wooden swing splintered and strewn.

Lucy remembered as a child, riding down the long drive to the farmhouse and seeing her great-grandma and great-granddaddy sitting in that swing holding hands, knowing the grandkids were coming, and waiting for them to jump out of the car and offer bear hugs. She and David knew that their great-granddaddy, Grandpa as they called him, would have two packs of Juicy Fruit gum for Lucy and her brother in the front pocket of his plaid flannel shirt and their great-grandma, better known as Granny, would have a Hershey bar for each tucked away in her apron pocket.

Standing there lost in thought, Lucy could smell Granny's rosewater perfume competing with Johnson's baby powder, and Grandpa's Old Spice—mixed more often than not with the sweet spicy smoke of his pipe.

She stepped over limbs and debris, always on the lookout for snakes. Constantly looking down, Lucy walked right into a cobweb that clung to her hair and clothes. She pulled at the silky strands and brushed at her hair hoping the spider wasn't there. She disliked spiders almost as much as she hated snakes—except for the beautiful yellow and black garden spiders that spun sparkly circular webs overnight. They were special, but she didn't want one of them on her either.

Lucy saw her black Expedition crumpled beneath a large turkey oak—the one that had been leaning—now fallen across her car on the driver's side. She pulled out her phone and started taking pictures. Walking to the passenger side, she unlocked and opened the door. Even after all that time, water spilled out and splattered mud on her jeans. Lucy took pictures inside and out so she could email them to her insurance adjuster. She was sure he would still have to come out to investigate, but maybe the pictures would give him a head start. One limb punctured the roof just above the back seat on the passenger side. The driver's side between the front and back seats was crunched in from the weight of the tree.

Lucy knew it was beyond repair. She hadn't been automobile shopping in six years, and couldn't begin to imagine how much anything decent would cost. She just made the last car payment a couple of months ago. The Expedition had been a big splurge, but Charlie wanted to make sure the kids were safe. He felt better with a big SUV, and it was useful around the farm. If she wasn't farming, though, she didn't need a large four-wheel drive anything. But what would she do if she wasn't farming?

Lucy tucked her phone back in her pocket and headed to the car. She needed to pick up the children and help Sally with supper. She and her children were the only ones left at the shelter except for two other families. People still came by daily for food and bottled water, cleaning supplies and other household needs, as well as clothes and shoes and blankets and pillows. But most of them had been able to find another place to live—with relatives or friends or back in their own homes.

After supper, Lucy pulled the blower out of the trunk of the car along with the few tools she purchased earlier. She took it to a picnic table under a shelter next to the church and started tearing it down. After working on it for an hour and a half, she still couldn't crank it.

"You've been out here a long time," Pastor Jerry said. "Are you sure I can't give you a hand?" He had asked earlier, too, but Lucy declined.

"I think it's a hopeless cause," Lucy said. "I'll just have to buy another one, but they're so expensive."

"May I ask why you need a leaf blower right now?" Pastor Jerry asked, looking perplexed.

"Well, it definitely won't clean up the mess at my house," Lucy said, smiling at him. "But I'm trying to get the four-wheeler running. I've pulled it apart and cleaned the carburetor, but I need to dry out the wiring before I try to crank it. A fan would work best, but I don't have a fan and there's no electricity, so I thought this might work."

"It might," Pastor Jerry said, "if you don't blow it so hard that it tears the wires loose."

"I thought about that," Lucy said, "so I'll have to be careful. But I can't blow it at all if I can't get this thing working."

"I'm sure you're overwhelmed right now," Pastor Jerry said.

He paused before continuing. Lucy just kept working on the blower.

"May I ask you why repairing the four-wheeler is at the top of your list right now? It just seems a little odd to me with everything else going on in your life."

Ordinarily, Lucy would be quite perturbed by anyone questioning her judgment, but she could tell that Pastor Jerry's concern was sincere. He and Sally had been their lifeline for weeks. What could it hurt to explain her motives to him?

"I'm not losing my mind," Lucy said. "Not yet anyway."

"Oh, I never thought you were," Pastor Jerry said. "Forgive me if I've overstepped my bounds."

"No," Lucy said. "It's okay. I wanted to get the four-wheeler running so I could check out the timber on the back fifty acres. Memaw said I should sell the timber, but I wanted to know how badly it was damaged before I called anyone about cutting it. Walking up and down all those rows of trees on fifty acres just seemed too overwhelming—and a little dangerous with the snakes still crawling."

"Oh," Pastor Jerry said. "Tell you what. I was going to offer to loan you my blower, but I have a better idea if you don't mind my help."

"I'm listening," Lucy said.

"Stop back by here after you drop the kids off at school tomorrow, and I'll go with you," Pastor Jerry said. "I'll load the Gator on the trailer and hook it up to the truck while you're taking the kids to school. Then we can head right out to your place."

"I can't ask you to do that," Lucy said.

"You're not asking," Pastor Jerry said. "I'm offering."

Lucy thought for a few moments. What would it hurt to accept his offer? The sooner she was able to check out the timber, the sooner she'd be able to sell it. That would help Pastor Jerry and Sally. She knew they must be ready for everyone to be out from under foot so they could set the church classrooms and fellowship hall back to normal.

"Sure," Lucy said. "I'd appreciate that. Thank you."

Chapter 17

Sam was late getting home again. He knew Ryan would pick Faith up at Mrs. Darcy's house after football practice, and with Lucille there now, at least his children didn't have to eat takeout or fast food or pizza. They would have a healthy hot meal waiting for them and a warm smiling face to greet them. A plate of food most likely waited for him in a kitchen that would otherwise be spotless by now.

He pulled into the garage, petted the dogs who met him when the door opened, and sent them to their beds in the corner. They enjoyed free reign of the yard during the day with shelter if they needed it, but he preferred them being in the garage at night.

The house was quiet when he entered the mud room. Faith's sparkly little rain boots lay on the floor next to Ryan's football cleats. Sam ran his fingers through his thick black hair and sighed. He still missed their mother so much his heart ached.

Stepping into the kitchen, Sam saw Lucille standing at the refrigerator with the door open. She turned when she heard him come in.

"I'm hungry or thirsty or something tonight," she said. "I can't decide which or what I want. I tried to keep your plate hot, but it was getting so late, I didn't want to leave it out any longer. Have a seat and I'll warm it up for you. You look exhausted. Do you want some coffee?"

"It was a hard night," Sam said. "And yes, coffee would be great."

Memaw busied herself warming Sam's food and fixing his coffee.

"You really don't have to wait on me," Sam said. "It's way past the

178

time of night when you should be working."

"No problem at all," Memaw said. "I'll sit with you and have some ice cream if that's okay."

"Of course," Sam said. "This is your kitchen now."

"And I'm enjoying it. I've never seen such a nice kitchen or such a big pantry."

Memaw set a plate of pork chops, butter beans, okra, rice and gravy, and fresh biscuits in front of Sam with a cup of coffee and a glass of ice water.

She dipped herself a bowl of vanilla ice cream, added chocolate syrup on top, poured herself a glass of milk, and sat down at the table.

"I don't want to worry you none," Memaw began, "but Alice brought Faith home today before Ryan could go pick her up. She said she needed to do some shopping for her big trip and couldn't wait any later. Something about having dinner with a friend and then going shopping together. I called Ryan on his cell so he wouldn't worry when he went by to get her and she wasn't there."

"I'm sorry," Sam said. "Babysitting isn't part of your job description. I hope she was good for you until Ryan got home."

"She was a little angel," Memaw said. "Ryan came home with a lot of homework to do, so after supper Faith and I played princesses before I read her some books and tucked her in."

"I can't thank you enough for that," Sam said.

"Alice and I drank coffee and chatted a bit," Memaw said. "She said she sure hoped you had not forgotten about her trip to Australia to spend the holidays with her kids and grandkids. She said she leaves in two weeks and will be gone until January. That's some trip! And she said that you knew about it, but to remind you anyway."

"Oh, no," Sam said. "I did forget. She told me when she first started taking care of Faith that she couldn't do it for long. I was just so busy at the hospital and helping out with the flood victims that the time slipped up on me."

"What happened to your nanny?" Memaw asked.

"Too many hurricanes," Sam said. "She and her husband had been working for us about a year when Faith was born. Betty helped Karina with the cooking and cleaning, and Drew was my groundskeeper and handyman. Betty was a lifesaver when the doctor put Karina on bed rest the last two months of her pregnancy. And she was indispensable after Karina died. She was the only one who ever helped take care of Faith, right from the day I brought her home."

"When did they leave?"

"Right about the time Hurricane Florence became a Cat 5," Sam said. "They had lived near the coast for years and been through a number of hurricanes. When Hurricane Matthew came through, Faith was only a little over a year old. I got called to the hospital, and they came to ride the storm out with Faith and Ryan. While they were here taking care of my family, a tree fell on their house, damaging it pretty bad and letting the rain in. Before they could get that repaired, the flood waters rose, and they lost most everything."

"How awful," Memaw said. "I sure know how that feels."

"They wanted to leave then, but I talked them into staying," Sam said. "They moved into the in-law suite while the guest house was being built. I thought they were happy. But when Hurricane Maria tore the Virgin Islands and Puerto Rico to shreds the next year, she threatened to leave again."

"Why didn't they?" Memaw asked

"She said Faith's sweet little face kept her here, especially when the storm looked like it wasn't going to do anything but bring us a lot of rain. They seemed content, and Faith blossomed under her care. But the morning Hurricane Florence started battering Haiti, Betty just walked in and said they'd had enough. They were moving back to the mountains of Tennessee where she grew up and hoped they never saw a hurricane again."

"And Alice stepped in to help?" Memaw asked.

"I was desperate," Sam said. "Faith's in preschool two mornings a week, and Mrs. Darcy keeps her when she's not in school. Most days, I can get away from the office on time, but when I have an emergency, I have to go to the hospital. Ryan has been watching out for Faith at night when I have to leave, but if she wakes up, he loses sleep and still has to go to school the next day. I really need to find a new nanny, but I can't trust just anybody with her."

"I can help out some," Memaw said. "But I don't think I could keep up on a permanent basis."

"And I would never ask you to do that," Sam said. "But I really appreciate what you did tonight."

Memaw finished off her ice cream and put her bowl in the dishwasher.

"Can I get you anything else?" she asked Sam, taking his empty plate. Even an intense conversation didn't prevent him from eating everything. "I made a pound cake today."

"No, I'm stuffed. But that meal was delicious as usual," he said. "You can't know how happy we are to have you here."

Memaw walked back to the table just as Sam was rising from his chair. He looked so tired, she felt bad for him. What a weight he carried.

"You know when you mentioned Lucy and the kids moving into your guest house?" Memaw said.

"Yes, and you shut me down fast on that one," Sam said. "I've seen that independent stubborn streak enough now that I understand exactly what you meant."

"But," Memaw said slowly. "If she felt needed... if she felt like she were pulling her weight... if you offered her a job and not just a handout... maybe she'd say yes. You won't find a finer person to teach Faith the things she needs to know. And I sure would love having them close by."

Friday, October 19

Lucy enjoyed talking to Pastor Jerry as he drove to her farm. He seemed to understand that she held her secrets close. He didn't pry and didn't give advice. He told her about growing up on a farm in Upstate South Carolina where rolling hills promised nearby mountains and lush pastures with miles of white fencing bordered winding roads and intersecting interstate highways. It was horse country, he said, with a system of trails that crossed from farm to farm in North and South Carolina.

"Ella would love living there," Lucy said.

"Any horse lover would," Pastor Jerry said. "Have you heard anything about your horses?"

"No," Lucy said. "Ella is so afraid that someone found them and decided to keep them. I hope she's not right."

"I truly believe that most people do the right thing," Pastor Jerry said. "But in times of disaster, what they think is the right thing often isn't."

"I know. I've heard people say that if someone didn't protect their animals that they don't deserve them. I had to save my family. I just couldn't come up with a solution for the horses."

"I'll pray that you find them safe and sound," he said.

"Thank you," Lucy responded.

He turned the truck into the long driveway and stopped at the cable for Lucy to unlock it.

"I can't thank you enough for helping repair the bridge," Lucy said, hopping back in the truck. "I couldn't do anything without the bridge."

"One step at a time," he said. "Never doubt that you can have help with anything you need here from the men and the women in the church. All you have to do is ask."

"I have no doubt," she said. "But sometimes I just don't know how to ask for help."

"Do you know which lumber company you're going to hire to cut the trees?"

"No," Lucy said. "I need to do some research first. I plan to do that tonight."

"Well, I've never sold any timber, but I know a few men in the church who have. Would you like for me to ask them?"

Lucy hesitated. Just because someone made suggestions didn't mean she would have to do what they said. And that would give her a place to start.

"Sure," she said. "I'd appreciate that."

The green Gator sported two bright yellow seats and a dump back. It sat higher off the ground than her four-wheeler did and should be able to clear any remaining water. Lucy wondered why a church owned such an unusual and expensive ATV, but she didn't ask.

"This Gator's been a real godsend," Pastor Jerry said, apparently reading her mind. "One of our members donated it after her husband died not long before Hurricane Matthew. I can't tell you how handy it was in helping people clean up after that flood. And we've kept it busy since Florence."

"That was a real nice gift," Lucy said.

"It truly was," he said. "Point the way."

They traveled around the house and down the edge of the cornfield, riding over everything except the largest limbs and fallen trees. The rain-soaked ground was muddy everywhere, but when they reached the edge of the timberland, Lucy gasped. Water still stood as far as she could see.

"I think we can clear it if it doesn't get over a couple feet deep," Pastor Jerry said. "At least you can get an idea of what you're dealing with."

He drove along the edge and chose the highest point to turn into the rows of towering pines. A few limbs lie broken at their base here and there, but for the most part, the trees seemed to have fared well. When they encountered water too deep to drive through, he turned and drove across the rows until he found one with less water. They crisscrossed the property for about an hour before heading back to the house.

"I think the trees look great," Pastor Jerry said, "and I don't know much about cutting timber, but they might not be able to get in there for a while."

"I think you might be right," Lucy said. "And this year's crop of pine straw is buried in water and mud. Don't guess I can count on that income either. The crops are a total loss."

Lucy thought about the ten acres of pines surrounding the house she had shared with Charlie. She couldn't imagine that it looked any better than this did, and she wasn't ready to go there yet.

"FEMA reps will be at the church one last time on Monday. Have you experienced any luck with them?"

"None," Lucy said. "They don't seem very organized or interested in helping. At least the three different ones I talked to haven't been."

"I've heard that from other people, too," Pastor Jerry said. "I figure they are pretty overwhelmed right now and may be having to train new people."

"Well, they can't be any more overwhelmed than the people they're supposed to be helping."

Lucy realized too late how angry she sounded. She tried so hard not to let her frustration turn into rage, and Pastor Jerry certainly did not deserve to take the brunt of it.

"I'm sorry," she said. "I'm just having a hard time not being so angry these days. But I shouldn't take it out on you."

"Not to worry," Pastor Jerry said. "Show me what else you need help with while I'm here."

"I need to go back in the house," Lucy said. "But I've seen enough to know that I won't be able to salvage any of the furniture and probably none of the clothes or pictures or books or anything water and mold could claim. I don't think a few more days will make much difference to the dishes and pots and pans I might be able to rescue and scrub."

"Do you want to work on that today?"

"No," Lucy said. "I'm not ready. As long as I don't go in, I can pretend it's not all gone."

"What about in the shed or the barn?"

"The tractor is rusted," Lucy said. "And the implements and tools, too."

"What about the kids' toys?" he asked. "Do you have anything out here we could load up in the back of the truck or on the trailer?"

"The bikes looked ruined to me," Lucy said. "And the most important thing for Ella would be the saddles and tack. I don't know what to do about them."

"Do you think taking them back for her to clean would make

things better or worse while she waits to find out what happened to her horses?"

"I honestly have no idea," Lucy said.

"Tell you what," Pastor Jerry said. "Let's load up the bikes, the saddles, and the tack, and take them back with us today. You don't have to show the saddles to Ella until you get a better feel for how they will affect her."

"That sounds like a good idea to me," Lucy said. "Thanks for your help—and advice."

"Not advice," he said. "Just a suggestion from a friend."

§ § §

While Sam made his rounds at the hospital and saw patients in his office, he thought about what Lucille said last night. Hiring Lucy to take care of Faith and moving her family into the guest house sounded like a perfect solution for her family and his. But he'd taken too many missteps with Lucy already. He had never met anyone quite like her—strong and stubborn for sure, but vulnerable, too, with a wide wall around her that screamed 'not too close'.

But he had a problem to solve and not much time to do it, so he needed to pull himself up by the bootstraps and just ask her. Why should he cower in front of a five-foot-two ball of fire? He'd been to Iraq and Afghanistan for heaven's sake. Surely, he could offer Lucy Brown a job.

He pulled his cellphone from his pocket and searched his contacts for the number Lucille had given him. Poised with his finger above the phone, he hesitated long enough to convince himself he had a better idea. He scrolled some more until he found Lucille's number.

"What's up Doc?" Lucille said, laughing at her own joke. Man, he loved that woman.

"I have an idea," he said. "The weather looks great tomorrow. Since it's Saturday, why don't you invite Lucy and the kids over for lunch, and we'll take a ride in the boat."

"Need some backup?" she asked.

"No, I just thought you'd enjoy spending time with the kids, that's all."

"Liar, liar, pants on fire."

"Ok, I do want to talk to Lucy about what you suggested," he said. "But I don't need help."

"Sure you don't," Memaw said. "But I could watch the boys while you two talk. I believe Ella is spending the weekend with her friend."

"Yeah, that would be good," Sam said. "I can grill something if you'd like, or we can take the boat to a restaurant down the way. You deserve some time off."

"Yeah, right," Memaw said. "You can't do without my cooking and you know it."

Sam marveled at the easy camaraderie that developed so quickly between his little family and this feisty eighty-year-old lady. He knew she'd faced her share of hardships in life, but she came out on the other side seemingly unscathed with an attitude of gratitude and a sense of humor like none he'd ever encountered. He wanted to learn from her, needed to learn from her, as he tried to move forward from Karina's death.

§ § §

Lucy helped unload the bikes, her tools, the saddles and tack, plus a few other things they rescued from the shed and barn. She needed to pick the boys up from school soon. Ella convinced Lucy to let her go home with Amelia after school and spend the weekend, so she had a couple of days to decide whether or not to show Ella the saddles and tack—and do a little research on whether or not they could be salvaged. Presenting Ella with anything that couldn't be saved would be disastrous.

"We can store the saddles in my garage," Pastor Jerry said. "That way we won't risk Ella seeing them until you decide what to do."

"Thank you," Lucy said. "Could we put the bikes under the picnic shelter? The boys and I can try to do something with them."

"Sure," he said. "And I might have some spare bike parts in my personal shed if you need them. I usually do a little bike restoration and donations for Christmas."

"Why am I not surprised," she said.

Lucy felt her cell phone vibrate in her back pocket and pulled it out, looking at a number she didn't recognize. She hated answering numbers like that, but with her children and grandmother scattered, she felt she had no choice.

"Hello?"

"Hey, baby girl."

"Memaw?"

"Yeah, it's me. Anybody else call you baby girl?"

"Nobody. Whose cell phone are you using? I almost didn't answer because I didn't recognize the number."

"Well, you better put me in your contacts then."

"You? Since when did you get a cell phone?"

"Since the handsome doc gave me one. Perc of the job."

"I never knew you wanted a cell phone. I would have bought you one."

"I never did. But I spend a lot of time out at the dock when I'm here by myself, and he wanted to make sure I could reach somebody if I needed anything."

"That was nice of him, I guess."

"He's a nice man."

"What's wrong?" Lucy said. "Are you okay?"

"Don't always assume something's wrong, Lucy," Memaw said. "Everything is as good as it's going to get until we're living in the same place—or at least close enough to see each other every day. I miss you and the kids."

"I'm doing the best I can, Memaw."

"I know you are. I just wanted to invite you to lunch tomorrow. Doc said he wants to take us all out in the boat since it's going to be a pretty day."

"I don't know."

"Oh, come on, Lucy. I want to go on the boat, and I'd feel a lot better if you and the kids came with me."

"Are you trying to guilt me into coming?"

"If that's what it takes. And you probably need a break. I can't imagine that what you've been doing the last few days has been easy."

"You're right about that," Lucy said. "Everything is a total disaster. Except the pine trees. They look good, but there's still a lot of standing water back there. I'm going to do some research on timber companies tonight, and Pastor Jerry is going to talk to some of the church members who've had timber cut and see if they can recommend somebody."

"Sounds good. Now, are you coming tomorrow or not?"

"Yes, we'll come. But just me and the boys. Ella is spending the weekend with Amelia."

"Be here by eleven. We'll eat an early lunch then have the whole afternoon to play during the warmest part of the day."

"Ok, Memaw," Lucy said. "I have to run pick up the boys now. We'll see you tomorrow."

Memaw smiled as she put the phone in her sweater pocket and walked down to the dock to watch the shrimp boats returning from their morning trawls.

Chapter 18

Sam paced back and forth in the grass. Lucy and her children would arrive in less than an hour. He had one shot at convincing her to become Faith's nanny. Ms. Darcy would leave in a couple of weeks, whether he was ready or not. He didn't have a backup plan. He watched Faith climbing up into the treehouse and sliding down. *Help me, Karina*, he whispered. *I've got to get this right.*

"Hey, Dad," Ryan said, walking across the lawn. "Would it be okay if I don't hang out with you guys today? I've got this project, and I have a new lead."

"Wanna share?" Sam asked.

"Nah, I don't want to jinx it."

"Sure," Sam said. "I would have second thoughts if Ella were coming. She'd appreciate having someone here that's closer to her own age, but she's at a friend's house for the weekend."

"I'm not really that close to her age, Dad," Ryan said. "She's still in middle school."

"I know, but you remember being that age don't you? You felt like anybody six months younger than you was just a kid. And that parents were ancient."

"Yeah, I remember," Ryan said. "Sorry I gave you and mom such a hard time."

"You weren't that bad," Sam said. "Go on, but keep your head about you, ok? Nothing crazy."

"You know it," Ryan said. "Good luck. Hope she says yes."

"Thanks," Sam said.

He watched his almost grown-up son walk across the yard, and saw Lucy's car pull up to the garage door. She must have called Lucille to open the gate. He needed to give her the code so she could come and go as she pleased.

The boys jumped out of the car and ran toward the treehouse, both dogs yapping and jumping around them. What would it be like to have them here all the time? Good, he thought. With Ryan off to college in less than a year, some energetic boys could keep things interesting.

"It's so good to see you," he heard Memaw say to Lucy. He watched her walk across the deck, wiping her hands on her apron. Must be making biscuits again. He was going to have to be more careful how much he ate, or he'd be fat as a butterball and rolling down the hospital halls instead of walking. But he wasn't going to complain to Lucille about all that country style cooking. It was delicious.

"Hey, Memaw," Lucy said. "Are you making biscuits for lunch? I thought we'd have something light and easy. You didn't have to make a full meal."

"Thought you might want some to take back to the church," Memaw said. "We're having salad for lunch—egg salad, chicken salad, broccoli salad, tuna salad, garden salad, fruit salad. And I fixed some hot dogs, macaroni and cheese, and tater tots for the boys and little Faith."

"That sounds wonderful, Lucille," Sam said, walking up the steps to the deck. "But way more than we need. Maybe Lucy will want to take some back with her."

Lucy shot a glare straight at him. Had he done something wrong already?

"My thoughts exactly," Memaw said. "Come on in, baby girl, and help me pour the tea. Sam, you get the kids and tell them to wash their hands."

"Yes, ma'am," Sam said, saluting her.

"I see you have things under control," Lucy said.

"My kitchen, my rules," Memaw said. "Boss said so."

"I'll have to admit you snagged yourself a pretty good set-up,"

Lucy said.

"It's nice here," Memaw said. "Real nice. Maybe you'll snag a good set-up, too."

"I keep hoping," Lucy said, "but so far no job, no response from FEMA, and no available housing. At least I'll have some money when they cut the timber."

"Did you learn anything last night?"

"Yes, I have four companies I'm going to call on Monday."

"Well, I hope you find the right one, and they can get started right away."

The boys came bustling into the room followed by a laughing Faith and her dad.

"I'm gonna sit side Nate," Faith said. "And Benbi."

"Ben-gee," Benji said, correcting her.

As they held hands around the table and Faith stumbled through her extended version of the 'God is Great' prayer, Memaw peeked and looked around the table. This is a perfect little family, she thought, plus two teenagers. They might have to find a couple more chairs or move to the bigger table in the dining room when they all ate together.

They spent the afternoon on the water, riding fast with the warm autumn wind blowing their hair, then stopping to fish for speckled trout. Sam helped the boys fish while Memaw, Lucy, and Faith named all the birds they could see and looked for dolphins and alligators. The girls tossed crumbs to the seagulls off the front of the Grady White while the guys fished off the back.

"I'm sorry Ella is missing this," Lucy said. "She would have loved it."

"How is she doing?" Memaw asked. "Any word on the horses?"

"She's ok, I think," Lucy said, "With a teenager it's hard to tell under the best of circumstances. But no word on the horses. I've called around to the local rescues. One of them had a black horse, and I rode out to check, but it wasn't Ace."

"Maybe going back to school will help keep her focused on something else for a while. How about volleyball?"

"Middle school volleyball season is always short," Lucy said. "And they missed so much being out six weeks, they just canceled it for this year."

"I know she wasn't happy about that," Memaw said. "She loves volleyball almost as much as she loves horses."

"Well, that's an exaggeration," Lucy said. "But she does love it. I need to ask you something."

"Anything," Memaw said.

"I brought her saddles back to the church with me yesterday. They're a mess, but I was reading up last night, and I think we can clean them and oil them and maybe save them. But I don't know if it would make Ella feel better or worse if she had the saddles and no horses."

"Oh, I definitely think you should let her work on them," Memaw said. "That would show her that you haven't given up on finding Ace and Brady."

"Yeah," Lucy said, looking down at the sleeping child in her arms and brushing the strands of blonde hair from Faith's face.

"Looks like you wore her out," Sam said. "The boys caught enough trout for supper. Let's head on back to the house."

He revved up the engine and cruised back toward the house. Both boys fell asleep on the back seat while Lucy sat in one of the captain's chairs holding Faith, and Memaw sat on the bench seat in front of the center console wrapped up in a warm thick afghan she brought along.

A perfect family indeed, Memaw thought as she dozed off.

Lucy and Sam rode in silence. Less than half an hour later, Lucy recognized his dock in the distance.

"Do you need me to carry her up to the house?" Sam asked Lucy after he eased the boat up to the dock and tied it off so they could climb out.

"I think I can handle it," Lucy said. "She's light as a little fairy."

"You can lay her down in my room," Memaw said, "that way you can come back outside while I listen out for her."

"Ok," Lucy said. "We'll need to leave soon."

"Come on, boys," Memaw said, giving them a little shake to wake

192

them up. "I'll fix you a snack and start a movie in my room."

After they settled the children, Memaw asked Lucy to go back to the boat and get the afghan she left lying on the seat.

"We need to leave now," Lucy said to Sam. "I just came back to get the afghan for Memaw. Thank you for a wonderful day."

"Are you sure you can't stay for supper? I can clean these fish up in no time. I've tasted Lucille's fried fish and cornbread. I know I don't have to tell you how amazing they are."

"No, you don't." Lucy said, "We've eaten plenty of fish in my lifetime—saltwater and freshwater both. I don't think there's anything Memaw can't make taste good."

"So you'll stay?" Sam asked expectantly. "The boys were hoping you would."

"You're as bad as Memaw using my kids to make me go against my better judgement."

"Do you need to rush back?"

"No, I don't guess we do," Lucy said. "I'll call Sally and let her know not to expect us. She worries like a mama."

Lucy turned to head back to the house.

"Lucy?" Sam said. "Wait."

She turned back to face him. "Do you need help?"

"No, I've got this," he said. "Could we talk?"

"Sure," she said, "Is something wrong?"

"No, I was just wondering."

He stayed silent for several seconds.

"Wondering what?" Lucy asked, sitting down on the dock. Even in October, the weather was warm enough that Sam wore shorts and a t-shirt. He scrubbed the boat and said nothing.

"Wondering what?" Lucy asked again.

Sam turned to face her. "Wondering how you're doing," he said.

"You want the pat answer or an honest answer?"

"Honest, of course," Sam said.

He put down the long-handled scrub brush and water hose, then sat down beside her, their legs hanging over the side of the floating dock.

"I don't want to sound overly dramatic, but losing the farm feels like another death in the family," Lucy said. "Especially since it was our whole life—not just where we lived, but how we made a living. Now it's all gone. Everything my family spent generations building drowned in that water."

"I know how it feels to lose someone you love," Sam said. "I can't even imagine what it would be like to lose our home and all the connections to Karina that go with it."

"It might sound silly," Lucy said, "but that old house was like a living, breathing member of the family and the only place I always felt safe. I just want my life back."

"Not silly at all," Sam said.

"I've been through a lot of tragedies in my life," Lucy said, "and most of them were totally out of my control. But looking back on a few of them, I feel like I could have done something different to affect the outcome. I feel that now."

"But you couldn't stop the storm or the flood," Sam said.

"Maybe not, but every single decision I make now will affect what it does to my family going forward forever."

"That's an awfully heavy weight on your shoulders," Sam said. "But from what I've seen, your shoulders are pretty darn strong."

"I don't feel very strong, and so the honest answer to your question is that I'm not doing very well right now," Lucy said. "But, that's enough whining. I'll go tell Memaw we're staying for supper and see what I can do to help. Unless you need me to clean the fish?"

"No," Sam said. "I have that under control."

He watched Lucy walk back up the hill to the house.

"You and Sam have a nice talk?" Memaw asked from the kitchen sink.

"Were you watching us?" Lucy said.

"Nah, I just came in here to start supper. Faith and the boys are watching a movie. They let her pick, so it's *Tinkerbell*."

"How can I help?" Lucy asked. "We're staying. Sam thinks he convinced me, but it was really the thought of your fried fish and cornbread fritters that did that."

"That's wonderful," Memaw said. "Did he say anything else?"

"Not really, why?"

"Oh, nothing," Memaw said. "Can you grate some cabbage for slaw?"

"Sure," Lucy said.

Sam scaled the fish with so much frustration that he practically took the skin off, too.

"Hey dad," Ryan said, walking onto the dock. "Looks like you had some luck with the fishing poles. How did the rest of the day go? Did she say yes?"

"I haven't asked her yet," he said, throwing one scaled fish into the sink and pulling another out of the cooler.

"It's not the fish's fault," Ryan said. "What happened? Why didn't you ask her?"

"It just wasn't the right time," Sam said.

"No time better than the present is what you always tell me," Ryan said. "You want me to do it?"

"Of course not," Sam said. "I'll do it. They're staying for supper."

"Well, you don't have much time," Ryan said. "Mrs. Darcy is leaving in two weeks."

"I know that, big shot," Sam said. "How was your day? Any progress on this mysterious project of yours?"

"Yes," Ryan said. "I've been online and on the phone checking all the animal rescues, especially the ones that specialized in large animals. You wouldn't believe how much livestock needed to be rescued."

"You're looking for their horses, aren't you?" Sam said.

"I have been, yes," Ryan said. "And I'm pretty sure I might have found them. There's a rescue about two hours north of here where a lot of the horses were taken after being rescued. People in boats led them through the water to safety, then other people used their trailers to transport them to different rescues. This one place has three black horses and one buckskin in the mix, so I drove up there to check today. I'm almost positive one of the black horses is Ace and the Buckskin is Brady. I don't know a lot about horses, but those two were hanging out together, and they responded when I called them by name."

"That's amazing, son," Sam said.

"I just don't want to get Ella's hopes up if they're not her horses. She's really torn up about them."

"Why don't we talk to Lucy about it," Sam said. "She'll know the best way to handle it."

"I took pictures," Ryan said.

"I'm sure she'll recognize them if they're her horses," Sam said. "Great job, son."

"I'll go get her," Ryan shouted over his shoulder, already running up the hill toward the house.

"Ms. Lucy," Ryan said, the second he opened the door. "Can you come down to the dock?"

"What's wrong?" Lucy asked, dropping the colander and partial head of cabbage into the bowl.

"Nothing's wrong," Ryan said. "Dad and I just need to talk to you for a minute. Something might actually be right for a change!"

Even though they ran downhill, Lucy had a hard time keeping up with the excited, long-legged teenager.

"Did you cut yourself?" she asked Sam.

"No, of course not," Sam said. "Why do you always expect something bad?"

"Look, Ms. Lucy," Ryan said, pulling out his phone. "Do you recognize these horses?"

Lucy took the phone. With shaking hands, she scrolled through Ryan's pictures. Her knees buckled, and she sat down on the dock.

"Where did you get these pictures?" she asked.

"Is it Ace and Brady?" Ryan asked.

"Yes," Lucy whispered. "Absolutely."

"I found them!" Ryan said, raising his fist in the air and dancing in a circle.

"Where?" Lucy said. "How?"

"I've just been looking online and talking to some other guys I know," Ryan said. "One of my buddies talked to another guy whose cousin helped rescue animals instead of people."

"Are they ok?" Lucy asked. "They look good."

"I think so," Ryan said. "But I don't know much about horses."

"Where are they?" Lucy asked.

"About two hours north of here," Ryan said. "On a farm that took in a lot of rescued horses and cows and other livestock."

"Have you told Ella?" she asked.

"No," Ryan said. "I didn't even tell her I was looking. And I wanted to talk to you first because if they weren't your horses and I told her I found Ace and it wasn't true, she'd never forgive me. I wouldn't want to hurt her that way."

"You're right," Lucy said. "Thank you."

"So you're sure?" Ryan asked.

"Oh, yes," Lucy said. "Without a doubt."

"Can I call Ella?" Ryan asked.

"We need to go get them," Lucy said. "But my trailer is a disaster, and I don't have anything to pull it with anymore."

"The truck will pull it," Ryan said. "And so would the Suburban. You want me to go to your house and get it? I'll clean it up tonight, and we can go tomorrow."

"I can't ask you to do that," Lucy said.

"Oh yes, ma'am," Ryan said. "You have to let me. I've been working on this a long time, and I want to see Ella's face when she sees Ace."

"Why don't you and the kids stay in the guest house tonight," Sam said. "That way, Ryan can get the trailer ready, and we can leave in the morning. We could pick Ella up on the way."

"I couldn't impose on you that way," Lucy said. "We'll just go back to the church."

"Do you always have to be so stubborn?" Sam said. "It's a perfect solution. You'll be here to help Ryan clean up the trailer, and we can leave the kids with Memaw in the morning. The guest house is empty and the sheets are clean."

"But we don't have a change of clothes or toothbrushes or anything," Lucy said.

"Don't create roadblocks where they don't have to be," Sam said. "You brought a change of clothes because we were going out on the boat, didn't you? The bathrooms are already stocked with toothbrushes and toothpaste. Go buy you some clean underwear at Walmart. It's not even three miles from here."

"I could do that," Lucy said. "But I don't have anywhere to take the horses. They can't go to the farm. It's too dangerous and the barn is full of mold."

"What else do you need for the horses?" Ryan asked. "There's a Tractor Supply not too far from here."

"We'll need halters and lead lines," Lucy said. "But I have no place to take them."

"I've already figured that out," Ryan said. "One of the guys on my football team lives on a farm not far from here. It's practically just across the road, but a few miles the long way around. They board horses. They don't have any stalls available right now because so many people needed a place for their horses to go, but they can pasture board two more horses, and all the pastures have open sheds so they can get out of the rain or the sun if they want."

"You are an amazing young man," Lucy said, reaching up to hug Ryan. She wasn't sure how she would pay to board the horses, but it was a non-negotiable necessity as far as she was concerned, and she'd just have to figure it out.

"Ok, so we have a plan," Sam said. "You go to Walmart and Tractor Supply while Ryan and I go to the farm and get the trailer. I'll take an air compressor just in case the tires are flat."

"What about Ella?" Ryan asked.

"I'll call her tonight," Lucy said, "and tell her I have to pick her up early. You can explain when we get to Amelia's house."

"Ok," Sam said. "Let's go tell Lucille the fish will have to wait until tomorrow. I'm sure she won't mind a bit."

"Oh, Ms. Lucy," Ryan said. "I almost forgot. They said you gotta have proof that the horses are yours if you come get them."

"I don't know how anybody could doubt ownership when those horses see Ella," Lucy said.

198

"That's probably true, but do you have anything just in case?" Ryan asked.

"Unless it was ruined in the flood, I have paperwork in the barn," Lucy said. "Their colic insurance papers have all my info, their info, and identifying markings."

"Where can I find it?" Ryan asked.

"When you go in the barn, the tack room is on the left," Lucy said. "There's a fireproof box sitting on top of the cabinet in the corner. Let's just hope it was waterproof, too."

Hours later, they were ready. They all sat around the kitchen table discussing their plans for the next day while eating hot apple pie and ice cream.

Although Benji and Nate begged to go with their mom to get the horses, Lucy convinced the boys they should stay and play with Rex and Roxie as much as they could before leaving them at the end of the day. Lucy reminded the boys how much their dogs needed and missed them.

And Memaw went on and on about how much she needed the boys to help with Faith, while convincing Lucy and Sam that she was perfectly capable of taking care of a three-year-old for a day.

The trailer was as clean as they could get it and hooked up to the Suburban. Lucy purchased a couple of bales of hay, some apple treats, a bag of feed, halters and lead lines for the horses, as well as clean underwear, socks, and toiletries for her and the boys. Ryan even found Lucy's and Ella's muck boots in the barn and brought them to her. They now stood on the corner of the deck washed and drying.

Lucy called Ella and listened to the belligerent teenager complain about how unfair it was for her mother to pick her up almost a whole day early when she didn't ever get to spend the weekend with Amelia anymore. Lucy just smiled and told Ella that if she kept arguing, she'd come get her right then that night. No way would Lucy ruin Ryan's surprise. He had earned the right to see Ella's face when he told her. Sam and his wife had done an amazing job raising their son.

"When you're ready, I'll take you over and show you around the guest house," Sam said.

"I'm ready any time," Lucy said. "It's been quite a day, and I'm exhausted."

"Come on, little one," Sam said to Faith, lifting her out of the chair and settling her on his hip. "Let's show Benji and Nate where they can sleep."

"The bwue room," Faith said.

"That's a good choice," Sam said.

Lucy and the boys hugged Memaw and told her goodnight.

"See you in the morning," Memaw said. "I'll have a big hot breakfast ready for you before you leave. It's going to be some kind of day!"

"Yes, it is," Lucy said.

"I'll help you clean up, Memaw," Ryan said.

Hearing the familial name spoken by someone else didn't bother Lucy the way she expected it would.

Sam opened the door, then waited to follow behind Lucy. She looked down at the dock, mesmerized by the lights strung inside the roof of the gazebo. Moonlight sparkled on the water. Underwater lights in the pool rotated rainbow colors, and small low solar lights lined the cobblestone walk toward the cottage.

"It looks like something out of a fairytale," Lucy said. "Everything is so beautiful."

"Thank you," Sam said. "We are blessed."

When Sam put her down, Faith ran over to the porch swing, climbed up on the shell motif covered cushions and said, "Swing wif me Nate."

Sam unlocked the door and Lucy stepped inside. Soft light glowed from lamps at either end of a dark blue sofa, their glass bases filled with seashells. An open floor plan discreetly decorated with ocean colors spread out before her. Every piece of furniture and every item of décor was obviously chosen and carefully placed. But the room didn't look untouchable. It looked comfortable and lived-in. Floor-length windows on every outside wall promised lots of sunlight during the day.

Lucy glanced to her left at a kitchen of white cabinets and dark blue countertops with a large sink window overlooking the screened porch with the water beyond.

"The master bedroom is over there behind the kitchen," Sam said. "It has a door to the screened porch so you can easily sit out there at night if you like."

"I'll probably just go to bed," Lucy said. "But it's lovely, I'm sure."

"And the other two bedrooms are down the hall to your right," Sam said. "Each of them has a private bath as well."

"Thank you," Lucy said. "Shall I strip the beds in the morning and bring the sheets to the house or is there a laundry room where I can wash them before we leave?"

"There's a laundry room down that hall with the other bedrooms," Sam said. "But no need to strip the beds. No one else will be coming."

Faith came in the front door dragging a boy by the hand on each side of her.

"Games in there," she said, pointing to a large cabinet on the wall. "And the TV's over there."

Lucy looked where the child pointed and saw a large television hanging over a corner fireplace.

"And your room is down there," Faith said, pointing down the hall. "It's bwue and it has boats."

"Man, this is great," Nate said, sitting down on the couch with his arms folded behind his head and his tennis shoe clad feet up on the coffee table.

"Take your feet down and your shoes off," Lucy said. "Put your shoes on the porch."

"I'm sorry," Lucy said to Sam. "Sometimes they act like they were raised in a barn."

"No harm done," Sam said. "It was built to live in."

"I promise we'll leave it the way we found it," Lucy said. "We'll be out early."

"Well, I guess I better get the little princess up to bed," Sam said. "It's way past her bedtime."

Lucy walked with him to the front door so she could lock it behind him.

"Call if you need anything," Sam said as Lucy started to close the door.

"I will," she said, "but I'm sure we'll be fine. Thank you, again—for everything."

Lucy walked down the hall to find the boys. The room was aquamarine with sailboats painted on one wall. White wooden bunk beds sported wide striped comforters of navy and white. The boys had already put on the pajamas Lucy purchased at Walmart and climbed in the beds—Benji on the bottom and Nate on top.

"Did you brush your teeth?" Lucy asked.

"Do we have to?" Benji whined.

"Don't you always have to?" Lucy whined back.

The boys clambered out of their beds and into the adjoining bathroom with navy walls; white cabinets, countertops, and shower curtain; white and navy checked tile; and a large mirror.

"This is so cool," Nate said. "I wish we could live here."

"We're just visiting," Lucy said. "One night, that's all."

After Lucy tucked the boys into bed, she walked back into the kitchen, made herself a cup of coffee, and walked out onto the screened porch. In the quiet of night, she thought she could hear the ocean waves crashing in the distance.

When Sam entered the house, Memaw and Ryan both started in on him.

"Well, did you ask her?" Memaw said.

"What did she say?" Ryan asked.

"No, it wasn't the right time," Sam said. "But she liked the house."

Chapter 19

Sunday, October 21

After packing her bags grudgingly, Ella sat with Amelia on her bed. Ella wore an ugly pair of baggy jeans rolled up at the bottom and a ragged sweatshirt with paint stains on it that they found in some donated clothes not good enough for Amelia's mom to take to the shelter. She didn't brush her long blonde hair, but pulled it up in a messy bun. She knew her mom would comment on her appearance, especially if they were going anywhere besides back to the shelter, but she didn't care.

"Did she tell you why you have to leave?" Amelia asked, scrolling through Instagram on her phone.

"No," Ella said. "But you know my mom. She thinks I'm a baby and she can just boss me around. She won't even let me have Facebook or Instagram or anything, and she reads my texts and emails every single night. That's the only way she'll even let me have my own phone."

"Well, you'll just have to use my phone when you need privacy."

"Yeah, I guess."

"Do you know anyone who drives a big blue Suburban?" Amelia asked, looking out her bedroom window. "And owns horses?"

Ella looked out the window and saw Dr. Sam's Suburban pulling up to the curb with what looked like her horse trailer behind it.

"Oooo, he's fine," Amelia said. "Do you know him?"

Ella saw Ryan walking up the sidewalk.

"He's the one who saved us," she said over her shoulder, already

203

running down the hall. She opened the door and ran into Ryan mid-knock.

"What's going on?" Ella shouted. "Where's Ace?"

"Woah," Ryan said, reaching out to keep her from running into him full force. He put his hands on her shoulders and stepped back, smiling as he took in her appearance.

"Nice look," he said.

Ella's face reddened as she glanced down at herself, but that didn't matter now.

"Why do you have my trailer? Did you find Ace? Is he in there? Let me go! Move out of my way!"

Ryan let go of her shoulders. Ella ran around him to the trailer and slung open the back door.

"It's empty," she said.

Ryan walked up behind her.

"Not for long," he said, pulling out his phone. "Do you recognize this big boy?"

Ella stared at the phone, then scrolled through the pictures, teardrops falling on the screen.

"It's Ace," she cried. "And Brady. Where are they?"

"We're going to get them now," Lucy said, wrapping her arms around her sobbing daughter. "Ryan has been searching since you told him about Ace, and he found them yesterday."

"How?" Ella said. "Where?"

"Ryan can explain that to you on the way," Lucy said. "But do you really want to wear that? Might be easier to ride in your own skinny jeans."

"I'll be right back," Ella said.

Less than five minutes later, Ella climbed into the back seat beside Ryan, wearing her favorite jeans, a soft yellow t-shirt, a flannel plaid over-shirt tied at the waist, and her boots. Her brushed and braided hair hung over one shoulder.

"I recognize that girl," Ryan said.

"Yeah, well," Ella said. "Tell me everything."

For the next two hours, Ella and Ryan talked non-stop. He told her about how he located the horses and everything he had done since then to make sure they were really her horses and find a new place for them to live. Ella educated Ryan on training and riding and how Ace was the best friend she ever had. She told him she'd teach him how to ride if he wanted to learn.

Lucy loved listening to this Ella. She heard none of the teenage angst that so often haunted her daughter. Even when Lucy or Sam broke into the conversation with a question or comment, Ella responded without sarcasm or disgust. Lucy delighted in listening to Ella and Ryan joking and talking like old friends. Although most of the conversation centered around the horses, a little bit of volleyball and football sneaked in, too.

Sam glanced at Lucy occasionally, and she actually smiled if she caught him looking. Maybe she would be open to his offer. The last couple of days had shown him—and her, too, he hoped—that their fractured families could work and play together. He couldn't remember the last time he enjoyed a weekend that much.

"Almost there," Sam said as he followed directions from his GPS. "Two miles on the right."

Ella looked across Ryan and out the window at the rolling pastures with wooden rail fencing along the road. Electro-braid attached to symmetrical rows of wooden posts ran along the sides and between pastures. She strained to see if she could locate Ace and Brady among the dozens of horses grazing in the pastures and paddocks.

"We'll have to talk to the owner before we go looking for Ace," Lucy said, turning in her seat to face Ella. "So be patient."

"He knows we're coming," Ryan said. "I called this morning so he'd be expecting us." He said he'd keep them in a paddock close to the barn instead of turning them out in the pasture."

A short, tanned man in jeans, a flannel shirt, and a cowboy hat strode toward them, his legs bowed and his boots muddy. When Sam stopped the vehicle, Ella jumped out and ran up to him.

"Where are they? How are they? When can I see them?" Ella asked.

"You must be Ella," he said. "Ryan told me all about you."

"Yes, I'm Ella," she said. "Ace and Brady are mine. Can I see them?"

"Patience," Lucy whispered, putting her arm around Ella's shoulder.

"Billy Walls, ma'am," he said to Lucy, offering his hand. "Nice to meet you and your daughter."

"Lucy Brown," Lucy said, shaking the proffered hand. "I have the paperwork you asked for Mr. Walls. It's a little messed up from the flood, but I think you can make it out enough to prove ownership."

"Just Billy, ma'am," he said. "I have a feeling the paperwork might not be necessary, but I'm required to ask for it. Pretty sure the horses will tell me all I need to know."

"Are you ready, young lady?" Billy asked, turning toward Ella.

Sam and Ryan joined the ladies as they followed Billy around the barn to a rather large paddock where two horses grazed—one black and one buckskin.

"Oh, my god," Ella whispered climbing up and over the wood rail fencing. Lucy didn't correct her language. Not this time.

Ace lifted his head and came galloping toward her, stopping within inches and laying his big black head on her shoulder. Ella wrapped her arms around his neck and sobbed into his shiny coat. Brady came, too, slower and limping.

"How are they?" Lucy asked. "Brady's limping."

"They're doing remarkably well," Billy said. "The buckskin had a laceration on his leg, but the vet has been tending to it. She's a smart one—uses lavender oil like my grandma taught me to do. Been putting a clean sock on it every day to keep the dirt and flies out. He's on antibiotics to ward off infection and a little bit of bute to tamp down the pain so he doesn't colic. The swelling has gone down a lot. Always touch and go with those bacteria infested flood waters, but the vet thinks he'll fully recover."

"And Ace?"

"Not a scratch or anything," Billy said. "But we decontaminated them like we do all the horses rescued from flood waters. Our volunteers scrubbed them down with some antibacterial Dawn to wash away the toxins and debris."

"So if it works for oil-soaked birds, it works for horses, too?" Sam asked.

"Exactly," Billy said. "And with most of the horses, we have to address some hoof problems from walking through the mud or even being stuck in the mud for days on end. But those two didn't even have much mud in their hooves. Rescuers found them in the middle of the road in belly deep water. I'll be damned if I don't think that black horse was smart enough to stay on the road, and the buckskin just followed along."

"Wouldn't surprise me a bit," Lucy said. "Ace is brilliant, and Brady is a follower."

"Well-trained, too," Billy said. "Most of the horses are stressed beyond being manageable and sometimes we have to sedate them enough to lead them and load them on the trailer. But they didn't have any trouble harnessing these two, leading them beside the boat until they were out of the water, or trailering them. Yes, siree, they're well-trained horses."

"That's all Ella's doing," Lucy said. "She's amazing."

"I can see that," Billy said, watching the sprite of a girl with more than a ton of horse flesh doing her bidding.

"I was hoping someone would call me if they found them," Lucy said. "I spray painted our phone numbers on their backs."

"Not sure what kind of paint you used, ma'am, but it didn't hold. I could tell there were some numbers there, but not enough left to give us a good lead."

"I don't know how I can ever repay you," Lucy said, "but if you'll work up a bill, I'll do my best to send a little along until I pay it off if that's okay. But can we still take them with us today?"

"Absolutely," Billy said. "And don't worry about the money. We do this because we love the animals. We have a lot of great volunteers and some businesses and vets that donate goods and services. I'm expecting you have a lot of other things to worry about right now."

"That's too true," Lucy said, "but we don't expect anything for nothing."

"I'll tell you what," Billy said. "If you want to send a donation when you get back on your feet that would be great. And we've got a big fundraiser coming up in the spring with a horse show, and a battle of the bands, and a barbecue dinner. You and your family are welcome to join us and bring the horses, too. There's some flyers in the barn that you can take with you."

"Thank you," Lucy said. "I'll put it on our calendar."

They stood for a few moments watching Ella trot Ace bareback around the paddock, holding on to strands of his long black mane. Brady walked over to the railing, and Lucy ran her fingers through his shaggy black forelock.

"She's a natural for sure," Billy said. "Every day that we see a horse improve makes the work worthwhile, but days like this make the best memories."

"Our family is whole again," Lucy said. "There are no words to tell you how forever grateful we are."

"My pleasure, ma'am," Billy said, tipping his hat.

"Are you ready to head back?" Sam asked. "We'll get the horses settled and see if Memaw can fry up those fish for supper."

"Sounds great to me," Lucy said. "But I doubt if I'll be able to tear Ella away from Ace before dark."

While Lucy and the teens loaded the horses, Sam motioned Billy over to the side out of view. He placed three one hundred-dollar bills in Billy's hand.

"It's all the cash I have with me today," Sam said. "But I'll be making a big donation to the rescue before the end of the year. I needed a tax write-off anyway, and I can't think of a more deserving place to send my money."

"That's real generous of you, doc," Billy said. "And we'll put it to good use."

"You already have," Sam said. "And I know you will."

They had been riding about fifteen minutes when the conversation in the back seat stopped. Lucy glanced over her shoulder to see Ella sound asleep with her head up against the window. Ryan apparently took off his sweatshirt and made a pillow for her.

"She just passed right out," Ryan said.

"I don't think she's slept well a single night since Ace went missing," Lucy said. "Now she doesn't have to worry about him anymore, thanks to you."

§ § §

Lucy and the kids headed back to the shelter much later than she planned, but she just couldn't bring herself to pull Ella away from Ace until after dark. Memaw fried the fish for a late supper and insisted that they stay and eat. Although the boys would be going to bed far too late and wake up grumpy in the morning, Ella was beaming.

Such were the decisions of motherhood, Lucy thought, smiling to herself and realizing she had smiled often throughout the weekend. That surely felt good for a change. She knew, though, that it had been a brief escape into a fairytale existence. Reality would demand much from her this week, but she decided to worry about that in the morning.

"Can we go back to see Ace after school tomorrow?" Ella asked.

"We'll see," Lucy said. "It will depend on how much I get done before I pick you up from school."

"We'll see always means no," Ella said. "Don't forget that we have to doctor Brady's leg every day."

"You're right," Lucy said. "I guess we'll have to go every day for the next two weeks, but after that, we can't go that often. I just can't afford the gas or the time."

"If we lived in that house, it would be easy," Nate said.

"I told you it's not our house," Lucy said. "And you have to go to school."

The boys spent the rest of the ride back to the church telling Ella about their weekend, about going fishing on the boat, and about spending the night in the blue bedroom with boats painted on the wall.

Maybe, just maybe, Lucy thought, she could get enough money from the timber to find them a place to live. And she would paint

209

boats on the wall. But she also needed a job, and that didn't look promising.

After sleeping in that big bed surrounded by fluffy pillows and covered with a cozy comforter, Lucy's little cot didn't offer a very good night's sleep. And the kids were back in their sleeping bags. They deserved better than that. Lucy needed to do something, and soon.

Monday, October 22

Lucy spent the morning making phone calls to timber companies—some she found online and a list Pastor Jerry created from the recommendations he received from church members. Some of the companies were so busy, they didn't offer her any hope of helping soon. The storm and flooding put them way behind, they said. Some gave her estimates far below what her research indicated that her timber was worth, although they all said they'd need to cruise the timber first to make an educated offer.

Only one company made her feel truly comfortable after their conversation. Both Mama and Memaw always told Lucy to follow her instincts. Trust her gut. That company also came highly recommended by more than one of Pastor Jerry's friends. So Lucy chose it above the others. One decision down.

But the standing water would be a problem. They could come out and give her an estimate in the next couple of weeks, but they were already so booked up that they wouldn't be able to start on her timber until after Christmas—and then it would depend on standing water and mud. Their equipment was heavy, he explained, and he wouldn't start a job that risked getting it stuck when there was timber on high and dry land that he could cut first. She understood, even though she didn't like it much.

By the time Lucy finished that job, she didn't have enough time before picking up the children to go out to the farm, so she spent the next couple of hours on the computer searching for jobs. She found several more rejections in her inbox, and virtually no open positions that didn't require at least an associate degree or specialized certification, let alone the ones that required a bachelor degree or higher.

Sally knocked on the door and opened it to peer in. "Can we talk?"

"Sure," Lucy said, closing out the open windows and putting the computer to sleep. She turned to face Sally who had taken a chair next to Lucy.

"Jerry told me you found the horses," Sally said. "I know that was a relief."

"Yes, it was," Lucy said. "And Ella is a different person now that she knows Ace is okay."

"I can't imagine how hard this has been on all of you," Sally said. "Especially Ella. Being a teenager is hard enough when everything else is perfect."

"That's true," Lucy said. "But I'm sure you didn't want to talk to me about the horses. What's up?"

"I dreaded this day," Sally said, "but knew it would come sooner than later. I hoped you would find a job and a place to live before we decided to close the shelter."

"You're closing the shelter?" Lucy said, her heart starting to race.

"I'm sorry," Sally said. "But with just the three families left, the deacons held a special meeting last night. They decided it was time to close the shelter and set the classrooms back up for the congregation to use as they were intended. We'll still be a place where donations can be dropped off and people can come get what they need, but we will no longer have anybody living here."

"I understand," Lucy said, although she didn't know how they could just throw her and the other families out on the street.

"We won't do anything until near the end of the month," Sally said, "but they want the fellowship hall ready for our Harvest Festival on October 31."

"But that's next Wednesday," Lucy said. "A week and a half."

"I'm sorry," Sally said. "I wish I could do more to help you."

Chapter 20

Lucy drove to school in a daze. Just when she thought she was making progress the bottom fell out. She berated herself for thinking she could stay at the church indefinitely. How dumb could she be? They had been living there almost five weeks already. Of course, the church needed its space back.

The boys threw their backpacks in the trunk and piled in the backseat.

"Can we go see Rex and Roxie today?" Benji asked. "Ella said she was going to see Ace."

"You don't want to go see the horses?" Lucy asked them.

"Nah, we talked about it while we were waiting for you," Nate said. "We just want to play with the dogs.'

"As long as Memaw doesn't mind watching out for you, I guess it will be alright."

Lucy didn't know how she was going to tell Memaw that in just a few days her family would have no place to live, no job, no timber money for at least two more months, and maybe no car. The rental agreement ran out in ten days, too. She couldn't afford the daily rent, couldn't afford to buy a new one, and hadn't heard from the insurance adjuster. Nothing from FEMA either. And how in the world could she justify boarding horses when she couldn't even house her children? Lucy felt herself being sucked under a wave of despair just like the day Charlie died.

"You ok, Mom?" Ella asked when she climbed in the front seat.

"I'm fine," Lucy lied. "Just a little tired today."

"I'm not tired at all," Ella said. "I was so excited all day I could hardly concentrate in class. I can't believe Ryan went to all that trouble to find my horses and they didn't drown and nobody stole them and I finally have them back."

Lucy drew strength from her daughter's excitement.

"In all the craziness this weekend I forgot to tell you," Lucy said. "Pastor Jerry and I brought your saddles and tack back to the church last week. I did some research, and I think you might be able to clean them up and oil them well enough that you won't need new ones."

"That's awesome, Mom," Ella said. "How about my helmet?"

"The inside foam was too molded," Lucy said, "Even if we could clean them up, I wouldn't want that so close to your face. I think we'll have to buy new helmets."

"Ryan said the farm has saddles and helmets I can use until I get mine," Ella said. "I'm going to teach him how to ride."

"That should be fun," Lucy said. "But I don't know how long it will be before Brady is sound enough to ride again."

"Oh, I wouldn't teach him on Brady," Lucy said. "I'd use Ace. And it will be a while before Ryan can go on a trail ride and we need both horses. He might be a football jock and all, but he doesn't know a thing about horses."

"The boys want to stay at the house and play with the dogs, so I need to drop them off on the way to the farm," Lucy said. "Will you give Memaw a call and make sure we can swing by there now?"

"Sure."

"Can we go fishing off the dock?" Nate asked.

"No," Lucy said. "I don't want you anywhere near that water when I'm not there. You promise me or you won't be able to stay."

"I promise," Benji said.

"I'm not a baby, and I know how to swim," Nate said.

"Promise," Lucy said more firmly.

"Ok," Nate said. "I promise."

"Memaw said it was fine," Ella said after she hung up the phone. "And she said that she was making chicken and pastry for supper and that we had to stay and eat. She won't take no for an answer."

Lucy had neither the strength to argue, the money to pick up fast food, nor the desire to eat at the church tonight. She wouldn't feel comfortable there anymore. And she must find time to tell Memaw.

The laceration on Brady's leg had not completely healed, so when they first arrived at the barn, Lucy had cleaned it well, treated it with lavender oil, and then put on a new clean sock. Ella gave Brady his penicillin shot and a small dose of bute. His leg was looking so much better, but he still limped a little.

Tony, who owned the farm, told Lucy his vet would be by for her regular monthly visit in two weeks, and he'd have her check Brady then if she'd like. Another bill Lucy didn't have money to pay, but she told him yes, then climbed up on a set of bleachers next to the arena to watch Ella ride Ace.

"You're deep in thought," Sam said as he climbed up to sit next to Lucy. "I've been standing there at least five minutes, and you never even noticed."

"I'm sorry," Lucy said, not facing him. She knew her eyes were red, and she didn't want him to ask why. "I didn't mean to be rude. Just a lot on my mind, I guess."

"I know what you mean," Sam said. "Lucille said I'd find you here. Faith was excited to see the boys, and she roped them into watching a movie with her. It was another one of those princess ones. *Brave*, I think."

"They actually like that one," Lucy said, "They like the horse and the bear and a girl who can ride and shoot a bow and arrow at the same time."

They sat in deafening silence for at least five minutes before Sam spoke again.

"Lucy?" he said.

"Yes?" She still didn't look at him.

"I have a problem, and I'm hoping you can help me out."

"I'm not sure how I can help anybody right now," Lucy said, her eyes welling up again. "I'm doing a lousy job of helping myself."

"Lucy," Sam said. "Look at me, please."

She turned and faced him. She saw reaction on his face, but he didn't say anything.

"I'm sorry," she said. "Just having a pity-party today."

"Well maybe we can help each other," he said.

"How?"

"My babysitter is going on an extended vacation in less than two weeks, and I need somebody to take care of Faith. At least until she gets back after Christmas—or longer if you want to stay."

Nervous energy kept him talking without giving Lucy a chance to respond.

"You see, my nanny left before Florence hit because she didn't want to be around hurricanes anymore and my neighbor Mrs. Darcy was just helping me until I found another nanny but she's going to Australia for two months and I don't have anybody to watch Faith. And I love how you are raising your kids—they're really good kids—and I know you would do a great job with Faith and you can live in the guest house and drive the Suburban."

"Wait, what?" Lucy said.

"I'm offering you a job," Sam said more slowly. "It pays well and comes with a place to live. Sometimes I get called to the hospital at night so it wouldn't just be a nine-to-five job. I need someone who lives on the property so they can stay with Faith on a moment's notice if I get called to the hospital. I built the guest house specifically for my nanny and groundskeeper. You like the house don't you?"

"Who wouldn't like that house," Lucy said. "It's perfect. But I've never been a nanny before. Why me?"

"You've been more than a nanny," Sam said. "You've been a mother—and a good one by the looks of your children."

"Two months?" Lucy said.

"Well, yes, that's how long Mrs. Darcy will be gone. But I wouldn't run you off if you wanted to stay. Mrs. Darcy is just a temporary arrangement, and it hasn't been a perfect one by any means. But if you don't want to stay, if you get a better job offer, then at least this will give me time to make other arrangements. I'm just in a pickle, and I really need your help."

"But I couldn't do that. My kids just started back to school, and I can't take them out again or move them to a new school for two months. That's not fair to them."

"I thought about that," Sam said. "Faith is in preschool two mornings a week. I already go into the office late those days so I can take her to school. And if I don't wake her up early on the mornings she doesn't go to school, she sleeps until nearly nine. Maybe Lucille would listen out for her those days. Then you could take your kids to school every day. And she still takes an afternoon nap, so maybe Lucille will watch her while you go pick them up."

"You've already talked to Memaw about this, haven't you?" Lucy said vehemently. "Have you two been in cahoots all this time?"

"Well, not exactly," Sam said. "But we did talk about it a little bit."

"I don't like being manipulated," Lucy said. "Is that why you invited us to your house on Saturday, so you could butter us up and make us fall in love with the place so I'd say yes? For all I know, you told Sally to tell me they're closing the shelter so I'd have no place else to go."

"What?" Sam said. "They're closing the shelter? I didn't know that, I swear."

Lucy had to admit he looked like he was telling the truth. But she didn't like him talking to Memaw behind her back. She could just hear them now—poor Lucy. No telling what Memaw told him about her. And Charlie. Oh, god, no.

"Honest, Lucy," Sam said. "Here's what happened. Mrs. Darcy had coffee with Lucille one afternoon last week and told her to remind me that she was leaving in less than two weeks. She did tell me before, but I forgot. Lucille suggested that I should offer you the job, but it's not like I hadn't already thought about that. I didn't invite you here last weekend to butter you up. I invited you so I could offer you the job, but I chickened out."

"Why?"

"You can be very intimidating, Lucy Brown," Sam said. "And I'm not as self-confident as I might seem."

Lucy couldn't help but smile.

"Anyway, I was afraid you might say no if I didn't ask you the right way, and then I would really be in a jam. And Faith deserves the best."

"I'll think about it," Lucy said. "But I'll have to talk to the kids. And I won't drive the Suburban. I'll drive my car."

"No," Sam said. "That's not negotiable."

"What's not negotiable—me talking to my kids?"

"No, not driving the Suburban," Sam said.

"But I have a car," Lucy said.

"And I have a bigger one," Sam said.

"What?" Lucy said, raising her voice. "Are we really playing my car is bigger than yours?"

"No, that's not what I meant," Sam said. "But just like I built the house for the nanny, I bought the Suburban to keep Faith safe. You've got to understand, Lucy. I already lost her mother, and I'm not going to lose her, too."

Lucy sat silent.

"I'm sorry," Sam said, all the bluster gone from his voice. "That was thoughtless."

"No," Lucy said. "I understand more than you can imagine."

"Will you talk to your kids?" Sam said. "Will you consider taking the job?"

"How much do you pay?" Lucy asked.

"Now that is negotiable," Sam said. "But I promise it will be worth your while. And I'll keep the Suburban filled with gas and pay all the utilities on the cottage. You have full reign of the property and can eat Lucille's cooking with us anytime you want."

"You drive a hard bargain," Lucy said, her heart a little lighter than it had been since before the hurricane.

"See you back at the house?" Sam said. "I hear Lucille is making chicken and pastry."

"So I hear," Lucy said. "And if you haven't eaten it yet, it's divine."

Lucy watched him drive away, then tried to catch Ella's attention on her next round.

"Time to go," Lucy said. "Go ahead and cool him down."

"Can I work him in the round pen just a bit?" Ella asked. "I'll take it easy so he cools down, but he needs some freshening up on his ground skills. It's been a long time, and he wants to be a little bossy."

"Fifteen minutes," Lucy said. "Then you need to brush him down and tell him goodnight. You'll see him again tomorrow."

Lucy had no doubt what Ella would say about living so close to Ace. And Nate was already begging to move into that little cottage. They could sleep in real beds and put their clothes in dressers instead of plastic containers. She would have a paycheck—at least for two months, or longer if she did a good job and wanted to stay. In two months, she might have money from the timber.

She would see Memaw every day, and get paid to snuggle that sweet smelling blonde haired beauty of a child. She could listen for the ocean waves before she went to bed at night and wake up every morning to that view. It sounded too good to be true, and the timing felt too perfect.

Chapter 21

After supper, Lucy and Sam drew up a two-month contract with an addendum for an extension at the end of the year. He offered her far more than she expected, plus medical benefits. She didn't even try to negotiate her pay. Sam said they would revisit that in two months with the promise of a raise if she decided to stay.

Sam told her she didn't need to start working until Monday, October 29, but that they could move their things into the cottage and call it home the next day. That would give her almost a week to take care of some of the things she needed to do at the farm while her children were in school. She wouldn't have to drive back to the church in the evenings after visiting the horses. And they could sleep in real beds every night.

"Ryan said he could take me to the church tomorrow in his truck and get the saddles and tack," Ella said on the drive back to the shelter. "He can just pick me up at school so you don't have to. He said he could pick up the boys, too, so you can spend more time at the farm. He's on early release, but we're not."

"I don't know," Lucy said.

"You can trust him, Mom," Ella said, "and it's almost like he's going to be my big brother now."

"No," Lucy said. "His father is going to be my employer."

"You know what I mean," Ella said. "We'll be living right next to each other."

"And his truck has a back seat," Nate said, "so we can hook our seat belts."

"It's a very nice offer," Lucy said. "But I need to talk to him myself."

"I'll call him and put him on speaker phone," Ella said.

They made a plan on the phone. Ryan would pick the kids up at their side-by-side schools—boys first at exactly 2:30 so they didn't have to wait, then Ella at 2:45. He would bring them to the church, saving Lucy a twenty-five mile round trip and almost an hour of time. He would help them load the saddles, tack, and battered bikes in his truck, and she would load their clothes in her car. When they left that Tuesday, they wouldn't return to the shelter.

"We'll have to thank Ms. Sally and Pastor Jerry for all their help and hard work since we've been at the shelter," Lucy said. "I know it hasn't been easy or much fun, but we had a roof over our heads and food in our bellies for five weeks because of them. Even if you did have to sleep on the floor."

"I can't wait to leave that place," Nate said. "But I'll say thank you."

"Me, too," Benji said.

"I can't believe how beautiful my new bedroom is," Ella said. "Can I invite Amelia over to spend the night?"

"Yes, but not anytime soon," Lucy said. "We need to get settled first and see how things go. And remember, this is only for two months."

"Where will we go then?" Ella asked.

"I don't know," Lucy said. "We'll cross that bridge when we come to it. Let's just be grateful for what we have and enjoy these two months—one day at a time. We'll have a beautiful place to live through the holidays, and I'll have a good job so I can buy you kiddos some Christmas presents."

Sally had hidden a key for Lucy since they would be getting back so late. Darkness enveloped the church, save one light over the door where they entered and nightlights along the interior corridor. She admonished the children to be very quiet as they tiptoed down the hall to their room for the last night.

Lucy set her alarm for much earlier than usual. She knew Sally would be up and wanted to talk to her while they were alone.

Tuesday, October 23

Lucy found Sally in the kitchen at 5 a.m.

"You're up extra early this morning," Sally said.

"I wanted to help you prepare breakfast," Lucy said, "and apologize."

"Whatever for?"

"I didn't react to your news about closing the shelter very graciously," Lucy said. "And I wanted to tell you how grateful we are for the weeks we have been here. I don't know what we would have done otherwise. My children and I have been safe and warm and well-fed when we could have been living in a tent."

"You and your family have been a blessing to us," Sally said. "I just feel so bad about making you leave."

"Don't," Lucy said. "Knowing we would have to leave probably gave me the courage to accept a job offer I otherwise might have resisted. We'll be moving out today."

"However did you turn things around that quickly?" Sally asked. "And where will you go?"

"Sam needs a nanny for his three-year-old daughter while his babysitter is on an extended vacation," Lucy said. "It's not permanent, but it gives me a paycheck and a beautiful place to live, at least through the holidays."

"You're moving into his home?" Sally asked.

"No. He has a guest house on the property," Lucy said. "The children and I will live there. But my grandmother does live in the in-law suite in his home. He hired her as his cook when she left rehab after her pneumonia."

"You didn't tell me about your grandmother," Sally said.

"She was very sick when Sam rescued us," Lucy said. "He made sure she got to the hospital for the treatment she needed. Otherwise, I'm sure she would have died."

"He's a good man," Sally said. "I had never met him before, but he certainly proved that over and over again."

"Anyway," Lucy said. "After I take the kids to school this morning, I'm going to pick up some plastic containers at Dollar General and go over to the farm to start retrieving what I can from the house. I have less than a week before I start working. But we'll be moving our stuff out this afternoon. Sam's son is coming with his truck to pick up the bikes and the saddles."

"Would you like some company at the farm today?" Sally asked.

"I'm sure I won't be able to salvage much," Lucy said. "So I should be able to handle it."

"Let me rephrase that," Sally said. "May I go with you? For moral support if nothing else. I can't imagine how difficult this will be for you. We can talk about the kids or the horses or good books or television shows or trips we took or whatever—just to keep your mind above water."

"That would be nice," Lucy said. "Thank you."

"I believe there are some large empty plastic containers in the back that came packed with donations, and I know I can round up some work gloves and face masks and other things we might need. Swing by here after you drop the kids off, and I'll have everything ready to go."

Lucy had devised a schedule that would allow her to finish up at the farm on Saturday and spend Sunday with her children before starting her job on Monday. With only five days left to find anything salvageable in the farmhouse, she'd conquer certain rooms each day.

When Sally offered to come with her, Lucy decided to start with the kitchen and dining room. She could handle her emotions better in those rooms, she thought, since they probably held the least personal items. And she did not want to break down in front of Sally. Besides, the kitchen and china cabinet probably contained the most salvageable items in the house and would take her longer without help. If Sally wrapped the dishes, put them in boxes, and helped Lucy carry them to the car, they should be finished before time to meet Ryan and the kids back at the church.

Tomorrow, she'd tackle the family room and bathrooms, then that would leave three days to take care of all four bedrooms. If she finished faster, she'd have more time with her children on Saturday. Armed with a plan, Lucy was ready to get it done and move on.

Lucy opened the front door with Sally following behind. The musky odor slammed into her the moment she stepped inside. Her home smelled rotten and made her gag. She turned and ran off the porch, breathing the fresh air deeply into her lungs.

"Let's open all the windows and doors," Sally suggested, "and let it air out a little while before we go inside."

"But I need to get it done," Lucy said. "I only have a few days."

"Is there anything we can do outside while it airs out?" Sally asked. "Maybe something in the barn or the shed?"

Lucy thought about the cedar chest in the loft of the shed, filled with family heirlooms. They could start there.

"Yes," Lucy said. "In the shed."

"Ok," Sally said. "Let's put these masks on and open windows and doors as fast as we can. Then we'll head to the shed."

Some of the windows were swollen and hard to open. They raised the ones they could, then Lucy went to the shed for a crowbar. Eventually, all the windows and doors stood open, welcoming the warm fall breezes.

"That should help," Sally said. "I packed a cooler. Let's get some iced tea before we move on."

"Sounds good," Lucy said. She hadn't thought she wanted help, but having Sally with her today truly was a godsend.

"There's a cedar chest in the tractor shed," Lucy told Sally, "filled with quilts my mother and grandmother and great-grandmother hand-stitched."

"Such treasures," Sally said. "I bet they are beautiful. Did the water reach them?"

"No," Lucy said. "But I don't know how the moisture affected them—all those days with water standing just inches below."

"Well, I guess it's time to find out," Sally said. "Lead the way."

When they reached the shed, Lucy cringed at the sight of the rusted tractor.

"Do you think Pastor Jerry could use a tractor?" Lucy asked. "I doubt that we will ever farm again, and I don't really have the money to repair it. If you think he'd be interested in having it for the church, I'll talk to Memaw about it."

"Oh, we couldn't do that," Sally said. "But I'm sure he'd be happy to find someone to take a look and give you an estimate on repairs. And paint—it definitely needs a fresh coat of paint."

"Maybe," Lucy said. "Let me think about it."

She passed the four-wheeler—torn apart but not repaired—and reminded herself to try to get it running. The wiring should be dry by now. She surely couldn't sell it if it didn't run. And the money would help pay boarding expenses for the horses. Lucy made a mental list of all the farm tools she might be able to sell.

"I'll climb up and lower stuff down on the lift," Lucy said. "I'm sure the cedar chest won't fit, but I can take the quilts out and stack them on it."

"I brought a container if you need it," Sally said.

"That was smart," Lucy said. "My family on my mother's side saved one baby outfit from each child since my great-great-grandma, so I'm sure I'll need it."

"What treasures," Sally said. "I hope they are alright."

"Me, too," Lucy said, slowly opening the cedar chest.

Relief flooded Lucy when she saw her mother's wedding ring quilt undamaged. She'd quilted it in shades of blue and green. Lucy thought how beautiful it would be on the back of the couch in the cottage. Without unfolding it, she lay the quilt on the plastic Sally had placed on the lift. Sally thought of everything.

Layered between that quilt and the next, Lucy found Ella's ruffled yellow dress from the Easter before her first birthday. Charlie was overseas then, and didn't have a chance to hold his daughter until several months later. By then, the dress was too small, but he showed Lucy the picture he'd kept in his pocket—Lucy in her spring green suit holding Ella wearing her frilly yellow dress, white lace-trimmed socks, and black patent leather shoes. Her blonde curls were still so short, twisted in little ringlets on her head.

Looking at this picture of my favorite girls kept me going every day, Charlie had told her. *And banished the bad dreams at night.*

Lucy placed the dress in the bottom of the plastic container and lifted another quilt from the chest. This one was a lap quilt in butter yellow and sage—perfect to drape over the chair in Ella's new room. She was getting older and might appreciate the handiwork of her great-great-great grandmother.

With every quilt Lucy lifted from the chest, she thought of a perfect place in the cottage to display them. She found Benji's little sailor suit, and Nate's favorite ball cap with the dirty bill bent just so. Near the bottom of the chest, she found the christening gown that she had worn and her mother and grandmother before her, along with moth-eaten baby sweaters, caps, and booties worn by generations before.

Lastly, she reached on the top shelf to retrieve the quilts and blankets they used during their refuge in the loft and placed them on the lift.

"The quilts don't look damaged," Sally called up to Lucy as she transferred them from the lift to the containers sitting on the ground.

"I hope not," Lucy said. "But I'm sure they need washing—or at least airing out. I have two boxes of Christmas ornaments, then we'll be done up here."

"Let's put these containers in your trunk, take out some empty ones, and try the house again," Sally said. "We can work an hour or so, then come back outside to eat the lunch I packed, and work a little more before heading back."

"Sounds good," Lucy said, jumping off the bottom step of the ladder and brushing the dirt and grime off her jeans. "I'll get the newspaper for wrapping dishes."

They started in the china cabinet. Lucy climbed on the stool and handed dirty dishes down to Sally, who wrapped them and stacked them in the container. They were filthy and a few were broken, but for the most part everything could be washed and sterilized. She didn't expect that they would ever use them again, but they had belonged to Granny so she wanted to at least display them again someday. When they finished in there, they took a break for lunch and fresh air, then moved on to the kitchen.

Lucy wasn't trying to save any of the food—even the canned items that looked perfectly fine seemed like too big a risk. Mice infested the cabinets, and she cleaned away nests in an attempt to reach the pots and pans. Many of them were stainless, and she packed those. Her great-great-grandma's cast iron frying pans in varying sizes were rusted and looked ruined, but Lucy couldn't bring herself to leave them behind. Maybe Memaw would know how to make them useable again. Just yesterday, she complained about having to fry fish in one of those new-fangled non-stick pans.

They were making great progress, and Lucy's thoughts about sentimental snares being fewer in the kitchen proved true. But then she found the sifter. It was white with red flowers painted on the front between the crank on one side and the handle on the other. The wire bottom allowed the flour to sift through into a bowl. Lucy felt faint as her mind traveled like a tornado back thirty years to her third birthday.

§ § §

June 13, 1988

Lucy could hardly wait to get to the farm and talk to the animals. She fidgeted as Daddy drove slowly down the long driveway. When he finally stopped, Lucy jumped out of the back seat of her parents' station wagon and ran up the steps to the porch where Memaw sat on the swing crocheting a pink and white blanket.

It's for your baby doll, Memaw said. *That one you call Suzy.* She lowered her needles and leaned over to accept a kiss.

Lucy wore navy blue shorts, a pink and white flowered t-shirt with ruffles on the bottom, and her favorite red tennis shoes. Granddaddy stepped out the front door and let the screen slam shut behind him. That always made Memaw mad. Lucy laughed, knowing Granddaddy would get in trouble, but before Memaw said a word, he

226

lifted Lucy up and hugged her tight.

Happy Birthday, baby girl, he said. *We got a surprise for you the best you ever saw.*

Where is it? Lucy asked. *I wanna see it now!*

Not yet, Granddaddy said. *Run on in the house and see your Granny and Grandpa.*

Lucy climbed up in Grandpa's lap on her way to the kitchen. He reached in his pocket and pulled out a pack of Juicy Fruit gum.

Are you big enough for this?

I'm three, Lucy said, doing her best to hold down her pinky finger with her thumb.

That makes you a big girl, Grandpa said. *But let your mama help you, ok?*

I will, Lucy said, kissing him on the cheek before sliding out of his lap and running toward the kitchen. Her great-grandmother stood with cake-making ingredients spread out in front of her. She was busy measuring flour into the white sifter with the pretty red flowers painted on the side.

Can I help? Lucy asked, tugging on Granny's red-checked apron.

Of course you can help make your birthday cake, she said, lifting Lucy up and sitting her on the counter. *Just turn this crank right here and watch the flour snow down.*

§ § §

Sally watched Lucy, but didn't say a word. She wondered how long Lucy could immerse herself in all those family memories—now lying in ruin—and not let her guard down. For almost five weeks, Lucy had been stronger than Sally ever thought anyone could be during this whole ordeal—at least in public. Sally had not once seen her cry, and she rarely seemed rattled or angry. But a person could only hold it in so long. She watched as Lucy's shoulders began to tremble and her knees gave way.

Sinking to the floor, Lucy stared into the bottom of the sifter. It had been a little rusty here and there for years, but Memaw used it all the time. Lucy could hear Memaw telling her how she'd learned to bake cakes and make biscuits using that sifter. She owned a shiny new one now, but Memaw said the biscuits didn't taste the same. Of all the things Lucy knew were in that kitchen, the cast iron frying pans and the sifter were the things she hoped most to salvage. She had imagined seeing Memaw's face when she handed the sifter to her. But looking into it now, Lucy knew that Memaw would never use it again. The wire bottom rusted completely through, a big hole gaping in the middle.

Lucy hugged the sifter against her and let the torrent of tears she blocked for five weeks flow down her face. She felt Sally's strong arms surround her and accepted the embrace, leaning her head on Sally's strong shoulder and crying until the flood of feelings stopped flowing.

When nothing remained but the snubs, Sally whispered against Lucy's hair.

"Let's go get you packed up to move to your new home," she said. "You've done enough for today."

Lucy nodded and slowly rose to her feet, still clinging to the sifter.

"Let's leave the windows open," Sally said. "I don't think it's supposed to rain."

When they returned to the church, Lucy took time to take all the backpacks and sleeping bags to her car before the children arrived in Ryan's truck. They owned more clothes now than when they fled the flood, thanks to the generosity of the community. She emptied the plastic containers of clothes into a large garbage bag. The bag would be easier to stuff into the car, and she was sure Sally could use the containers since they'd taken most of her stock to the farm.

Lucy slammed the trunk just as Ryan pulled into the parking lot. The boys piled out of the back and ran to greet her, Benji wrapping his arms around her waist and squeezing.

"Ryan's truck is really rad," Nate said. "It has Bluetooth and everything so he can play music from his phone, and it comes out the radio."

"Where should I park to load the saddles, Ms. Lucy?" Ryan asked, walking over with Ella.

"They're in the garage at the parsonage," she said. "You'll probably need to drive around, but the kids and I can walk across the yard."

Pastor Jerry met them at the garage.

"Just back the truck up right here," he said, directing Ryan as he backed up.

"We'll take the bikes off your hands, too," Lucy said. "I'm sorry we didn't get around to fixing them up."

"That's ok," Pastor Jerry said. "You've been pretty busy."

"I can't wait to see my saddles," Ella said.

"They don't look great right now," Lucy warned her. "But we'll work on them."

Pastor Jerry lifted the garage door and led them inside.

Three shiny bikes sat in a row. They looked new, but Lucy knew they weren't. Benji's now shone neon green, Nate's bright orange, and Ella's was a sleek, shiny black.

"Wow!" Benji shouted. "Is that my bike? It looks like the Hulk."

"You did all this?" Lucy asked.

"I had some help," Pastor Jerry said. "A couple of the men who worked on your bridge hang out sometimes and help me refurbish the bikes. We found all the parts we needed. Just bought some paint."

"How can we ever repay you?" Lucy said. "You've all done so much."

"Just pay it forward," he said. "Give me a hand here, Ryan. Let's load the bikes up first, then the saddles."

Ella knelt next to her saddles lying on the cement. The metal was rusty, the leather dirty, molded, and misshapen.

"Do you really think we can clean them and make the leather soft again?" she asked her Mom, looking up with hope in her eyes.

"All we can do is try," Lucy said, reaching down to take her hand and help her up. "Let's get them loaded and go home."

"I'll help you work on them," Ryan said, lifting one saddle after the other into the back of the truck. "I'm sure you can store them in the tack room at the barn where the horses are. Tony said you get a saddle rack and shelf for each horse, even with pasture boarding."

"But they look awful," Ella said, near tears.

"I read some articles online," Lucy said. "Directions for how to take care of saddles and other tack after a flood. Just study up on what it says and do your best. If anyone can do it, I'm sure you can."

"Mom?" Ella said. "What am I going to do about Lucky?"

Lucy had forgotten all about the rabbit.

"I think you should set her free," Lucy said.

"But she needs me," Ella said. "I can't desert her. She won't know where I went."

"Why don't we take her to the house?" Ryan said. "There's lots of bushes and places for her to hide. That way you can set her free, but still see her."

"Are you sure your dad won't mind?" Ella asked.

"What's one more rabbit?" Ryan laughed. "They're all over the place already."

So they loaded the rabbit cage in the back seat of the truck, forcing the younger boys to unhappily climb in the car with Lucy.

"I'll take Ella by the barn to see the horses and drop off the saddles if that's okay with you, Ms. Lucy," Ryan said. "I'll bring her on home after she rides."

"You don't have to do that," Lucy said. "I'm sure you have other things you'd like to do."

"I like watching her ride," Ryan said. "Besides, my buddy Barry from the football team—the one whose daddy owns the farm—said he'd be there this afternoon, and we're going to toss the ball around a bit before practice."

"Ok," Lucy said. "Drive carefully."

"Yes, ma'am," Ryan said. "You can count on it."

"Can we go to McDonalds?" Benji asked. "I need some food."

"Sure," Lucy said. "Fast food coming right up."

When they arrived at the cottage, Lucy unpacked the containers, carrying their meager belongings to the right rooms. Then she took the rusted frying pans and holey sifter to the big house for Memaw.

"I'm sorry about the sifter," she said. "I really wanted you to be able to use it again."

"Not to worry," Memaw said. "My new one works fine. I just like to complain and blame something other than myself if I don't get my biscuits just right. Not the sifter's fault."

"And the frying pans?" Lucy said. "Can you do anything with them?"

"No problem," Memaw said. "I'll just scrub 'em up and get all this rust and grime off, then rub 'em down real good with some Crisco. Sit them in the oven turned on real low and let them season. Would you do some of your research on it, though, to see if using them would be dangerous? Even if I can't use them anymore, I sure am glad to have them back."

"I smell chicken pot pies," Lucy said.

"That you do, baby girl. Made a plenty so we could all eat together. They've only been baking about half an hour, so supper should be ready by the time the doc gets home with Faith."

"I'm going to go home and get cleaned up," Lucy said. "I'll make sure the boys stay inside with me so you don't have to keep an eye on them. I haven't needed a shower this badly since the day we were rescued from the loft."

"Going home," Memaw said. "That sounds real good."

"It does," Lucy said. "But it's only temporary, so don't get too used to it."

"I hear you," Memaw said.

Chapter 22

Wednesday, October 24

Lucy dropped the kids off at school and headed to the farm. When she arrived, she found Sally sitting in her car at the locked gate. Lucy didn't want help, especially not Sally. Embarrassment from yesterday's breakdown colored her cheeks as she walked up to Sally's car on her way to unlock the gate.

"I hope you don't mind," Sally said, "but I thought I'd help out again today."

"I'm sure you have better things to do," Lucy said. "You've already spent an entire day here helping with the heaviest things. I've got it from here."

"I really don't mind helping," Sally said, the hurt not quite hidden behind her brown eyes.

Lucy berated herself for being ungrateful, swallowed her independent arrogance, and forced a smile.

"Sure," she said. "Let me unlock the gate. You pull on through. I'll follow then hop out and lock the gate behind me."

"That's a great idea," Sally said. "No need for unexpected visitors."

That's the truth, Lucy thought, turning the key in the lock, and dropping the cable so they could drive across it.

Following Lucy's plan for the day, Sally offered to go through the bathrooms and see if anything could be saved. Lucy told her she wasn't worried about bagging anything to throw away just yet—that would have to wait for another day—but if the shower curtains or any of the towels could be washed and saved, she wanted them.

Lucy started in the family room. Leaving the windows open all night had made the house bearable, but the stench still overwhelmed her at times, especially if she picked up something like the pillows they used to cozy up on the couch or the comforter from the recliner. A thick black line ran all the way around the room less than a foot from the ceiling. Mold bloomed on the walls, the front of the television, the glass in the picture frames hanging on the wall, and every other surface.

Lucy pulled photograph albums from the shelf, flipped through them briefly, and threw them on the floor. She opened the ottoman, peered inside, then closed it, slamming the lid harder than she intended.

She locked her hands on top of her head and turned a full circle, taking in the entire room. Nothing could be saved—not the throws or pillows or pictures or books or anything else in that room. She was wasting her time.

"Are you alright?" Sally asked, walking out of the hall bath. "I heard a loud noise."

"I dropped a couple of things," Lucy said. "We're wasting our time here. Are you ready to go?"

"I couldn't find anything worth saving in either of the bathrooms or the linen closet in the hall," Sally said. "Once towels and sheets and blankets sour and mold like that, there's really nothing you can do. What about the bedrooms? Do you want to do those while I'm here to help?"

"No," Lucy said. "I've got to get out of here."

"Alright," Sally said. "Are you coming back tomorrow?"

"I don't know," Lucy said. "It's nothing but a waste of time. I just need to have the whole place and everything in it bulldozed to the ground or set on fire and burned up."

Sally sensed that Lucy didn't need or want a response. She was glad that she had come, even though unwelcome. Whether Lucy knew it or not, having someone close by who could absorb the vitriol emanating from every pore in her body was better than being by herself. Sally knew it wasn't directed at her personally, so she just took Lucy by the hand and led her out of the house.

"Call me if you need help tomorrow," Sally said when she reached her car. "Or any other day. People care about you, Lucy."

"Thanks," she whispered, just loudly enough that Sally could hear her.

Lucy led the way, unlocked the gate, then pulled out onto the highway, driving slowly enough that Sally passed her. When Sally was out of sight, Lucy turned her car around, drove back to her house, and tried to follow the two-rut road behind the farmhouse to the home she and Charlie built on the opposite side of the farm. She wanted to check on the timber, too.

Water still stood around the trees as far as she could see. And more rain loomed in the forecast. Large limbs in her path created a maze she navigated slowly. Fifty yards or less down the drive to the home she had not entered in over a year, a large fallen oak blocked the drive. She would have to back up and go the long way around—four miles on paved roads.

The house she and Charlie built—much of it by their own labor—was supposed to be where they raised their children and grew old together. Three feet of water inside ruined it after Hurricane Matthew, but Charlie had been working to repair it so they could move back in. They would have to buy new furniture, but with a little bit of warning as the flood waters rose during daylight, they were able to save pictures and clothes and personal treasures—everything that Hurricane Florence just stole from her.

Lucy pulled into the drive, but she didn't get out. She could tell—sitting there staring at the modest robin's egg blue house with the red front door—that the water rose much higher this time, probably drowning the entire house right up to the tip of the roofline. It had been their dream home, and now it only housed nightmares. She backed out of the drive and headed to pick up her children at school, even though she would be two hours early.

Thursday, October 25

Lucy stood at the kitchen sink drinking a cup of coffee, watching a large sailboat glide down the waterway. Its mast stood tall, but the sail wasn't extended, the boat moving instead under motored power.

"Mom," Ella said, "are you going to the farm today?"

Lucy turned to look at her daughter, sitting at the counter finishing off her yogurt and blueberries. She was growing up so fast, Lucy thought, and Charlie would miss the milestones in her life—high school sports, prom, college, marriage, babies. Who would walk her down the aisle?

"Well, are you Mom?" Ella said louder.

Lucy shook her head to clear the 'what ifs' away.

"Yes, I am," Lucy said, "right after I drop you off at school. You boys run brush your teeth if you've finished your cereal. We need to leave in five minutes."

The boys jumped off their stools and jostled their way down the hall. Lucy was glad their vanity had two sinks.

"Can you look for my locket?" Ella asked. "The one daddy gave me. Do you think it still might be ok?"

"I'll find it," Lucy said. "I doubt if the pictures can be saved, but we can print new ones."

Lucy never thought much about the value of digital photography or social media or Google photos or the Cloud until she tried to go to sleep the previous night, tossing and turning, grieving all the things that created her family's memories. Ruined. Unsalvageable. Gone.

She remembered her mama always said that if their house ever caught on fire, the thing she would work hardest to save—after the children, of course—would be the pictures. Because pictures captured a moment in time that they'd never experience again. Once any day in their lives had passed, she said, you can't relive it—so make the most of every day and take lots of pictures, too. Mama always said that pictures could never be replaced.

But now many of them could. Every picture Lucy took of their children was digital, and she scanned and saved most of the earlier pictures of her and Charlie so she could email them—one each day—to Charlie when he was overseas. A pictorial record of their life as a couple and then as a family lived in the Cloud.

"We're ready, Mom," Ella said.

Still standing on the kitchen side of the island counter, Lucy looked up from her coffee cup—no longer warm, but held between both hands—into the faces of her three children. They stood at the door with their backpacks slung across their shoulders, staring at her like she had sprouted two heads.

"Let's go, Mom," Ella said. "I can't be late for math. I have a test."

§ § §

Lucy was relieved to see that she did not have help waiting when she pulled up to the bridge and unlocked the cable. She should have been more grateful, but she needed time by herself to process each depressing discovery. At least with no one else around, she didn't have to pretend that she held everything under control. Nothing was further from the truth.

Since Ella made a specific request, Lucy decided to start in her room. She wasn't ready to go in the room she had shared with Charlie anyway. Maybe she could get the boys' room done, too, then tackle Memaw's room tomorrow. She needed to talk to her tonight about anything specific she wanted Lucy to try to find.

With the windows still open, odors in the house had subsided some. The mold blossomed more each day, so Lucy donned plastic gloves and a face mask to protect herself. She was a bit surprised not to find a snake curled up somewhere inside the house and always kept watch for snakes and black widow spiders, but so far, she had not seen any.

Only slivers of Ella's walls peeked out from behind her posters. Once pink, the walls now grew black mold, and the posters were covered in sludge and mold. Ella hadn't asked about them, so Lucy left the boy-band posters hanging on the wall. She removed any laminated ones with horses or volleyball, rolled them up, and set them aside. She would take them out when she needed a break and wash them at the pump, then leave them in the sun to dry. More rain would move in on Saturday leaving only two dry days to do the work.

Lucy paused at the bulletin board and mourned her daughter's simple teenage treasures. Pictures of her friends and her team and doodads telling the girls to 'Beat the Rams' or 'Bump, Set, Spike – Win!' bled colors on rippled paper. She decided that seeing those would hurt Ella more than just leaving them there. So the bulletin board stayed screwed to the wall.

Lucy didn't even touch the bedclothes or curtains—they were covered in mold and mud. Ella hadn't loved them anyway since she became a teenager, so they weren't a great loss. She opened each drawer of Ella's dresser, lifting the still soggy, mold-laden mess enough to see if she could try to save anything at all. Nothing.

Ella owned two favorite pairs of jeans and two favorite shirts—one set she wore and one set she packed in her backpack when they fled the rising water, and she'd saved her favorite riding boots. Ella wouldn't mind going shopping for new clothes. Lucy didn't even try to close the swollen drawers. The laminated wood had already begun to separate, so she didn't contemplate trying to save any of the bedroom furniture either.

She opened the closet, held her breath against the overwhelming soured stench, and looked at Ella's dresses, her coats, several pairs of shoes, her volleyball, and her rollerblades. All ruined. Even the papers and games and boxes of keepsakes on the top shelf had been soaked and now bloomed with mold. She closed the closet door and turned toward Ella's desk.

Lucy didn't need to waste her time on the computer or the printer or the books or the lava lamp or even the art supplies. Standing there staring at the computer, she could hear Ella's protestations at all the blocks placed on her internet access. Lucy didn't even like the idea of Ella having her own laptop, but the school started using specific sites for some of her studies, and with two loud brothers in the house, Ella needed privacy when doing her homework. The cottage came complete with a computer and printer and internet access, but Lucy would buy a computer of their own soon. She and Ella would just have to share.

Lucy picked up the jewelry box Charlie had given Ella for her birthday. It was square with mirrored glass on the top and sides. Lucy scrubbed at the mold growing on the sparkly pink heart inlaid beside Ella's engraved name. In big loopy letters, the gift encouraged Ella to *Be your own kind of beautiful* and was signed *Love, Daddy*.

Charlie ordered the gift with direct shipment home while he was in Iraq, both he and the gift arriving the day before Ella's fifth birthday. She had snuggled in his lap for hours, first looking up at him then down at the tiny dancer spinning while the tinkling sounds of *The Dance of the Sugar Plum Fairy* drifted up around them. Lucy smiled at the memory and opened the lid to silence. The ballerina didn't dance.

She took the jewelry box outside and sat down on the porch swing. The chains, crusted with rust, still held strong. The silky pink lining of the little box was soggy and molding, but Lucy reached in and started lifting out the pieces. Ella didn't own a lot of jewelry—she hadn't even wanted her ears pierced yet, so the box held more valentines and pictures and notes than necklaces and bracelets.

Ella's half of two matching friendship bracelets she and Amelia braided and shared was nearly black with mold. Lucy doubted she could clean it without completely fading the bright golds and oranges and greens and reds it once boasted. They would just have to make more.

The other pieces of jewelry were tarnished and grimy, but Lucy hoped she could clean them. She had researched that, too, and was surprised to read that soaking flooded jewelry in Coke could clean it. What could it hurt to try?

Ella's silver charm bracelet held horses and hearts and hats, boots and saddles and a lasso. She didn't wear her birthstone ring anymore because she had outgrown it, but they did talk about having it resized or putting it on a chain, so she would save that, too. Lucy lifted the golden chain that held the heart-shaped locket Charlie gave Ella when she turned ten. *Double-digits calls for something special*, he'd said. He had opened the large locket to reveal double pictures—him on one side and Ella on the other.

I'll always be with you, he had told her. *I promise.*

Ella was so angry with her daddy when he died that she took off the locket and hadn't worn it since. But now it was the only thing she'd ask her mother to find. Lucy closed the jewelry box and carried it to the car.

She cleaned the posters and laid them in the sun to dry, then moved on to the boys' bedroom. Looking around the room at stuffed animals that could never be snuggled again and toys that would never bring laughter, she was relieved that Benji stuffed his Linus blanket and flop-eared rabbit in his backpack when they escaped to the loft of the shed. He couldn't sleep without them.

She didn't spend much time in the boys' room. They had moved on—selecting a new basketball and football along with some games from the mountain of donations at the shelter. Now with their bikes repaired, they seemed satisfied. They did not mention anything they really missed or wanted her to try to find. And the clothes didn't matter to them. They were perfectly happy choosing comfy clothes from the selection of donations.

Sally encouraged Lucy to come back anytime she needed anything. New donations arrived every day, she said, and people were already donating brand new toys for Christmas. Lucy couldn't wrap her head around the generosity of strangers—from all over the state and beyond—caring so much and giving selflessly to people they didn't know and would never meet.

But Lucy had a job now—even though it was temporary—and didn't plan to take handouts when someone else might need it more. She knew the boys wanted to play baseball. But by the time spring practice began for Little League, she should be able to buy new gloves and bats and helmets for them both. And for Ella—if she wanted to play softball.

But only if she found a permanent job and a place to live back in Pender County. And if the timber could be harvested, netting the $1200 per acre she read was possible. And if the auto insurance paid

239

enough for her to buy a decent car.

Or if she decided to stay at Sam's.

But then the kids would have to change schools. The arrangement for driving them back and forth only covered the two months of the temporary contract. She had been making that drive for a few days, and the gas ate heavily into her budget even though she was still driving her small rental car. Sam said he'd pay for gas when she started driving the Suburban, but she couldn't expect him to foot the bill to transport her children back and forth to a school district in another county. He would already be making concessions with childcare for her to do that—and childcare was what he hired her to do.

Her children always came first. They had survived so much upheaval and change in their young lives. Could she really make them change schools in the middle of the year and leave all their friends, too?

She took one last look around the boys' room and walked out. She'd be sure to ask them tonight if they wanted her to try to find anything specific when she came back the next day. Lucy walked right past Memaw's room and looked inside the space she had shared with Charlie. Just one glance glued her outside the doorway. Her heart raced. Sweat beaded on her forehead. Her fingers began to tingle.

She needed fresh air.

Escaping outside, Lucy sat down on the porch steps and looked around at the devastation. She folded her arms on her knees, lowered her head, and let the tears flow. When some of the pressure on her chest had finally eased, Lucy stood, gathered Ella's posters, rolled them up, and put them in the car.

With about an hour to spare before picking up her children, Lucy drove away, locking the cable behind her—not sure why she even bothered. She found herself headed toward the house on the edge of the farm. She didn't intend to turn that way. Pulling in the driveway, she sat and stared at the dirty red door.

She wanted so badly to talk to Charlie, for him to remind her how strong she was, how he knew she could handle anything, what an amazing mother she was, how she and the children were his whole life, encourage her as he always did, be the strength she saw slowly slipping away. But she struggled most days to feel Charlie's presence.

Lucy put the car in reverse and backed out.

§ § §

Lucy dropped Ella off at the barn on their way home. She felt comfortable with the staff there, and Ella had made a new friend—a girl named Susie who owned an Appaloosa. They wanted to go riding together on the trails around the farm, but Lucy told Ella she would have to wait until Brady was better and Lucy could ride with them—at least the first time.

With the boys riding their bikes up and down Sam's long driveway, Lucy took the time to sit at the table with Memaw, sipping a cup of coffee and eating fresh pound cake.

The antique, rusted-bottom sifter sat in the middle of the table. Memaw had slipped it over a short glass vase that fit perfectly in the hole, then filled it with red camellias from the yard that had just begun to bloom.

"That is gorgeous." Lucy said. "I never would have thought of that."

"Better than being able to use it," Memaw said. "This way I get to see it every day and think about my Ma."

"Doesn't that make you sad?" Lucy said. "Thinking about her and not being able to talk to her anymore."

"Ma lived a long happy life Lucy," Memaw said. "There's only joy in remembering somebody who lived a full life, still working in her flower bed late into her eighties, with a mind as sharp as a tack."

"I guess," Lucy said.

"How are things going at the farm?" Memaw asked. "I want to go out there with you one day."

"Oh, Memaw, I don't think that's a good idea," Lucy said. "You need to hold onto your good memories. And besides, I don't want you in all that mold and mud, what with you just getting over pneumonia.

I don't want you sick again."

"I reckon you're right," Memaw said. "But I don't like it."

"Is there anything in particular you want me to try to find in your room?" Lucy asked. "I haven't been able to salvage much, but I did bring Ella's jewelry box home. I'm going to try to clean up her favorite pieces."

"That's good," Memaw said. "You really think you can?"

"I have to try," Lucy said. "She asked for her locket."

"The one her daddy gave her?" Memaw asked.

"Yes," Lucy said. "I was surprised."

"One step at a time," Memaw said. "Maybe the child will finally forgive him for leaving her."

"I hope one day I can forgive him, too," Lucy said.

§ § §

Lucy sat down on the bleachers and watched the two teenagers riding slowly around the arena—side-by-side. They were talking non-stop. Ella waved as they passed. She was beaming.

"The vet will be here tomorrow," Tony said, walking up beside Lucy. "Do the horses need any shots or anything while she's here? I'll be sure she takes a good look at Brady's leg, but he seems to be recovering quickly—especially for a horse his age."

"No shots," Lucy said. "I made sure they were up-to-date on everything before the storm. Do you know how much she'll charge for the check-up?"

"I don't know exactly," Tony said, "but since she sees a lot of horses while she's here and many of them are mine, I cover the farm call fee. So, it'll just be whatever she needs to do for Brady."

"Ok," Lucy said. "Do you also have a farrier who comes and gives a discount for seeing multiple horses?"

"I do," Tony said. "He'll be here next week. Both your horses need trimming, but I was real surprised they didn't have some hoof problems from being in the floodwater."

"We were lucky," Lucy said. "In more ways than one. How much does the farrier charge?"

"It'll be way less than a hundred for both horses," Tony said. "Unless you want to shoe them. I noticed they're barefoot."

"No shoes," Lucy said. "They never have worn them, and they've done just fine."

"I'm glad I had a spot to board them for you," Tony said. "That daughter of yours is quite the horseman. That's my daughter riding with her. They took to each other real quick."

"I'm happy she's making friends," Lucy said. "She doesn't do that easily."

"I wanted to mention something to you," Tony said, "but I don't want you to take it the wrong way."

"What is it?" Lucy asked.

"Well, I figure it couldn't have been easy for you—the flooding and all—especially financially," Tony said.

"I have a job," Lucy said defensively. "I will pay our boarding fee on time."

"Now see, you done took it the wrong way."

"What did you think I'd do?" Lucy asked.

"I just wanted to tell you, ma'am," Tony said, sounding exasperated. "That if Ella wanted to do her own feeding and help Susie clean some stalls in the afternoons, I can give you a big discount on your boarding fee."

"I'm sorry," Lucy said. "That really is a great offer, and Ella will jump at the chance to spend more time here. I've never paid a boarding fee before, so it is a strain on my budget."

"Well, she can start tomorrow. And there's a path right across from Ryan's neighborhood that leads to the back of the farm. It's less than a mile that way and a good bike trail. Ryan and Barry rode it all the time. Just have her text Susie when she leaves home, and Susie can meet her halfway."

"Thank you," Lucy said. "But after the first of the year, we'll probably be moving back to Pender County. As soon as I find a job and a place to live that is."

"I got a few friends up that way," Tony said. "And one of them

243

is looking for some bookkeeping help for his farm. You ever done any of that?"

"Just for our own farm," Lucy said. "I don't have a degree or anything, but I did do all our budgeting and bill paying and payroll and kept the farm in the black most years."

"Well, he's offering a good salary and health insurance," Tony said. "I'll give him your contact information if you want me to. But I'd sure be sorry to see you leave and move your horses. Susie doesn't make friends all that easy either—no problem with the horses, just humans. And I been real surprised and happy to see how fast those two got to be friends."

"I know," Lucy said. "This week has moved like molasses. It's only been four days since we brought the horses here. And the way our girls are talking and laughing, you'd think they've been friends all their lives."

"It's something, ain't it," Tony said.

Chapter 23

Friday, October 26

Friday morning, Lucy walked into the farmhouse and headed straight for Memaw's room. She had asked Lucy to bring home the box of family photos and letters that she kept under the bed. Lucy didn't even have to look to know how badly damaged they would be, but Memaw thought they'd be fine since she moved them all to a plastic container a couple of years ago.

Lucy threw the side of the navy chenille bedspread up over the bed and knelt down on her knees to look under the bed. Seeing nothing suspicious, she grabbed hold of the clear plastic container and started pulling it out. A snake slithered out from behind the box. Lucy gasped, fell back on her heels, then jumped up and screamed as the black snake raced away.

But where there was one…

Lucy plundered in the glove box and console of the car, but could not find a flashlight. No way was she going back in that room without being able to see clearly under the bed. Her skin crawled at the thought of what might have been hiding under the other beds she decided not to disturb. She slammed the car door closed, then walked to the shed, watching every step she took.

Lucy looked at the tractor and the four-wheeler and the implements and all the other items she needed to salvage to sell. She had not yet discussed the future with Memaw, but decided that she would never farm again. She simply could not face all the repairs and recovery that must take place to ever become profitable again. She didn't have the money. Even if she could get a farm loan—at a discounted rate because of the flood—she didn't trust herself enough to try.

Maybe they should plant it all in pines. It wouldn't help her or Memaw except for the straw they could sell in a few years, but it would be there for her children and grandchildren. Or maybe she could lease the land to hunters or someone else who wanted to farm it. The pastures sported a solid stand of Bermuda—if the flood didn't kill it all. Maybe she could pay somebody to bale the hay, and she could sell what she didn't need for her horses.

Or maybe David would want to farm it when he left the Army. He could retire in just a few years if he wanted to. Lucy feared he would stay in longer. But if he added her acreage to his, he'd have a big spread and even be able to expand into cattle if he wanted. He mentioned that many years ago.

She wondered where her brother was and how much danger he faced every day. She hadn't heard from him in a while. With all the upheaval, time lost its meaning, so she wasn't even sure how much time had passed since the last email. She always worried when she didn't hear anything, even though he explained repeatedly that not writing or calling didn't automatically mean anything was wrong.

Lucy climbed the ladder to the loft and found several flashlights there along with the oil lanterns—including a couple that had been passed down from her great-great-grandparents. Memaw would be happy to have them. Lucy found a box to put them all in, wrapping the lanterns in burlap sacks so the glass globes wouldn't break. She set the box on the lift and cranked it down. Balancing the box on one hip and securing it under her arm, she grabbed a hoe to take back in the house with her—that snake might share space with his brothers.

She put the box in the trunk and took out two flashlights in case the battery power was low in either one. Using the hoe, Lucy slowly pulled the box the rest of the way out from under the bed. She waited a few minutes, then knelt down and shone the light under the bed.

Seeing no other guests, she stood up and turned her attention to the box of pictures. Latches on each end snapped the lid shut and gaskets sealed it. From what Lucy could see, she didn't think the water filled it, but some probably seeped in. They might actually be able to salvage something inside. But rather than deal with that then, she carried the box to the car and added it to the others in her trunk. She'd help Memaw go through it tomorrow.

Tonight they were all going to Ryan's football game. It was senior night, and he asked them all to please come—even Memaw. Ella and the boys were excited, even though they would not know a single person there. All their friends from Cape Fear Elementary and Cape Fear Middle attended the football games at Trask High School to watch older siblings play. Friday night football was just one more thing that Hurricane Florence and the flood stole from them.

Trying to refocus, Lucy looked around Memaw's room. Her Bible had fallen off the nightstand and sat in sludge. Lucy didn't trust any of the lamps that floated in water for weeks so she didn't take those. She couldn't save her clothes, couldn't save her shoes, couldn't save her coats or sweaters or blankets or the box of books in the bottom of her closet.

Maybe if the flood waters had receded faster. Maybe if she could have reached the house as soon as the worst of the flood water was gone. Maybe if she had done something differently, been stronger, been smarter, been better. Maybe then her family would not have lost everything.

She didn't go down the hall to her own bedroom—she couldn't face that today. Lucy climbed in the car and headed to pick up the kids, but not before driving back to the other house and staring at the red door, wondering how long it would be before she could muster the courage to turn the knob and go inside.

§ § §

Lucy had to admit that Sam looked handsome in his navy blue suit and gold tie, proudly standing in center field at half time with Ryan in his uniform of garnet and gold. Most of the senior football players and cheerleaders walked out with a mother on one side and father on the other. This was just one of a myriad rites of passage that Karina would miss with her son. Lucy didn't require much imagination to know how much both father and son felt her absence.

Faith bounced on the bleacher in front of Lucy, calling to her daddy and brother. Lucy held onto her tightly, helping her bounce high to see over the heads in front of her. Sam had French braided her hair in two pigtails and attached huge gold bows where the braids stopped. She wore an Ashley Screaming Eagles sweater, skinny jeans, and the cutest little black boots with fur around the top. Lucy thought she was the most adorable child she knew—at least since Ella was that age. In many ways, Faith reminded her of Ella. They looked enough alike to be sisters. And the boys shared the same dark hair and eyes as Sam and Ryan—and Charlie.

Lucy couldn't help but notice the stares and shared looks among some of the women when they climbed up into the bleachers looking more like a family than an employer and employee. She could just hear the rumor mill grinding.

At the end of the game, when a last second play gave Ryan and his team the victory, the home bleachers erupted in cheers. Lucy and Sam and the kids all jumped up and down, yelling and screaming with excitement.

Even Memaw hollered out, "Yay, Ryan! That's my boy!"

In all the excitement, Sam turned to Lucy and hugged her, lifted her off her feet, and planted a quick kiss on her lips. When he set her back down, Lucy looked up at him, wondering if the surprise she saw in his eyes were reflected in hers.

After the game, they all went out for pizza to celebrate. Ryan and at least half his teammates showed up not much later. They pushed tables together, eating and laughing and talking until almost closing time. Faith fell asleep in Lucy's lap, and she snuggled the child close, breathing in the strawberry scent of her soft hair. Lucy looked across the table at Sam, and he quickly averted his eyes.

Sam knew she caught him staring, but how could he not? Seeing her with Faith like that. He had stepped over the line tonight, and he didn't know what to do about it. He just hoped she didn't change her mind about working for him. She was the perfect person to care for Faith, and he needed to be more careful not to do anything to jeopardize their agreement.

He wanted nothing more than for her to fall in love with living in the cottage, fall in love with Faith, fall in love with being so close to her grandmother, fall in love so that when the end of the year drew close, she couldn't fathom the thought of leaving. He wanted her to agree to stay—at least until Faith started kindergarten. That would be his next pitch if he needed one to keep her here. Just two more years.

Saturday, October 27

Lucy sent the boys to the big house for breakfast with Memaw by themselves. She left a note for Ella, still sound asleep, and told her where she'd be. Before leaving for the farm, Lucy texted Memaw and told her she'd be back early afternoon, hopefully before the rain started. One more room remained—the one she shared with Charlie.

Lucy drove more slowly this morning, dreading what she would find. She wasn't worried about snakes or spiders, just memories. Drowned and destroyed. Charlie's scent would no longer cling to his dress shirts she never washed until he wore them to several Sunday services. While they were closed up in the closet, the scent of his Polo lightly lingered on those shirts, and if she buried her face in them, she could still spark a memory. She would never again be able to pull out one of his sweaters and wrap herself in its warmth while she sat in her bed long past midnight mourning his memory.

And she knew she would not be able to salvage the wedding ring quilt her mother made specifically for the time in the future when Lucy got married and created her own family. Her mother started stitching it when Lucy was just a child and saved it in the cedar chest she'd called a hope chest—a place she stored special items handmade or collected along the way, hoping happiness would fill Lucy's life for as long as she lived. That's what her mother had said, and Lucy had foolishly believed it would happen.

She pulled up in front of the house and noticed the door was ajar. She must not have pulled it completely closed when she left the day before. With the windows still open, a brisk breeze could have caused the door to drift open, couldn't it?

Lucy grabbed her flashlight and climbed the front steps. She pushed the door open and stepped inside, standing still and listening. As much as she hated guns, she almost wished she brought hers with her instead of locking it in the safe inside her closet at the cottage.

Hearing nothing, Lucy started toward her bedroom, but stopped instantly when she heard a large crash coming from the kitchen. She ran down the hall to Memaw's room and retrieved the hoe, ready to swing it at anybody who dared enter her home. She stalked stealthfully back toward the kitchen, fully aware that she made enough noise to scare off any intruder who didn't want to be caught.

She thought about the phone in her back pocket, but opted to check things out first before calling the cops. They'd think she was crazy if she told them somebody was trying to steal any of that molded mess. She'd just peek around the corner and run if she must. With her back to the wall, the hoe in one hand and flashlight in the other, Lucy sneaked as quietly as she could toward the kitchen. Whoever was in there didn't seem to care how much noise they made. She heard scratching and crashing and scuffling. Lucy took a deep breath and leaned around the door casing.

She wasn't quiet enough and the intruders looked up, eyes peering through black masked faces, their hands holding food from the pantry, their fat bodies furry, and their whiskers twitching as they chewed. At least she thought they were twitching. Maybe she was just laughing too hard at herself and the three raccoons raiding her kitchen cabinets.

"Shoo," she said, waving the hoe in front of her. "Get out of here."

She followed the scavengers to the front door and closed it behind them, flipping the deadbolt to make sure it stayed closed. Then she checked the other rooms for any of their family or other critters that might have wandered in and finding none, locked the back door, too.

The interlude lightened her heart just a bit, so it wasn't quite as heavy when she walked into her bedroom. *Ok,* she thought, *I can do this.*

Then she saw the quilt—soggy and molded and muddy—lying across the bed she once shared with Charlie. She turned away and headed for the closet. But she couldn't bring herself to open it. She knew what the closets looked like in the other rooms, and hers would be no different. She preferred to remember the scent of his Sunday shirts still hanging together with his polos, sorted by color and sleeve length.

She turned back to her desk under the window overlooking the grapevines. She had spent so many hours sitting there working on the finances for the farm, watching the leaves bud out in spring, the fruit grow in summer then ripen dark and sweet in early fall. She knew her computer couldn't be saved nor could any of the folders filled with paperwork.

Lucy cared little more for jewelry than Ella did—farm life and jewelry didn't work well together for her. She only dressed up on rare occasions, so jewelry was unnecessary, but she would take the small box home with her and sort through the costume jewelry, the few pieces that Charlie gave her, and what her mother left behind. The only thing that really mattered to her was the simple gold wedding band that Charlie slipped on her finger, and she had never taken it off.

She sat down in her desk chair, felt water seep from the seams and soak her jeans. Absentmindedly, she tugged on each of the desk drawers. All her supplies were ruined—paper clips rusted and post-it notes rippled. She lost the ability to care about any of it. Then she opened the large bottom drawer on the right and lifted out the hand-carved cherry box that Charlie bought overseas. It was coming apart at the joints, the wood swollen and splitting from staying in standing water so long.

Lucy opened the lid, knowing what she would find inside—letters from Charlie. When they had become so numerous she could no longer fit folded ones inside the box, she removed the envelopes and stacked the letters flat one on top of the other. The box had been the perfect size. Although she could occasionally talk to Charlie via phone or even video chat when he was deployed, and they sent emails back and forth as often as possible, the hand written letters were more intimate, almost magical.

Countless nights while he was deployed—even more often after he died—she sat in their bed, wrapped herself in Charlie's shirt or sweater, and gently fingered paper he had actually touched, read words he painstakingly penned, and stared at every detail in the pictures he shared. Now the ink was smeared beyond recognition, and the paper was mushy and fragile, but these she would not discard. She could close her eyes and read every word.

Lucy lifted the soggy stack of letters completely out of the box and gently laid them on the desk. She could feel her chest clench and her heart begin to beat unfettered. Fingers trembled as she lifted the tarnished heart out of the box, its purple ribbon blackened with mold. She touched the crusted bronze star still lying in the bottom of the box, its ribbon's red, white, and blue barely distinguishable beneath the growing mold. She couldn't breathe.

Lucy ran from the room and out the door, leaning against the porch post and sucking in deep breaths of moisture filled air.

"I'm sorry," she screamed. Then gasping for breath, she whispered, "I should have taken better care of your medals. I should have taken better care of you. I'm so, so, sorry."

Lucy felt Charlie's memory slowly slipping away, and she struggled to hold onto some shred of it. Calmer now, she turned and walked back inside the house, to her room, and stood in front of the closet. Lucy longed to find him again. She stripped the mask from her face and opened the closet door. She pulled a shirt off its hanger and buried her face in its folds. The stench made her gag. Throwing that one on the floor, she took another, then another, and another, concentrating on the inside of the collar on each shirt—the spot where his scent lingered longest. She breathed deeply into each one, repeatedly gagging and coughing, then slinging soiled shirts across the room. Trying to catch her breath, Lucy escaped outside, still clinging to the last shirt.

She ran down the steps, around the house, and toward the dirt road. She climbed across the fallen tree and stumbled over large limbs, but kept running. At the bottom of the steps to the front porch of the little blue house, she stopped and stared at the red door while her chest heaved and her heart pounded. She clung to Charlie's shirt, pulling it close to her chest. Clouds let loose and the rain soaked her to the skin, but she couldn't make her feet move any closer.

Lucy had avoided entering that house for fifteen months, three weeks, and twenty-four days. Now, time became inconsequential. She didn't know how long she stood there in the torrents of rain, but slowly the need to enter overcame the desire to escape. Lucy ascended the steps, stopping again at the door. Moments later, she tilted the concrete planter that sat beside the door and retrieved the spare key.

She leaned against the door and shoved to force the swollen wood to swing open. The house was void of furniture and the walls completely covered in mold—both the older painted sheetrock at the top and the newer sheetrock on the bottom half that Charlie had replaced after Hurricane Matthew. The floors were stripped bare and a web of electrical wires snaked through studs where Charlie had yet to replace the wallboard. His table saw stood in the middle of the living room and his chop saw sat on the kitchen counter.

Unhung sheetrock, now soaked and soggy, lie stacked on the floor. Everywhere Lucy looked, she saw some sign of Charlie—his tools, his handiwork, his flannel shirt tossed aside because he started sweating while he worked. His orange water cooler with a white lid and tap must have been full and heavy enough to stay put on the countertop, but his Yeti coffee cup had floated off and now lay mud-caked on the floor.

Rainwater dripped from Lucy's clothes and hair as she walked across the plywood subflooring. It didn't matter. Everything was already molded. She clung to Charlie's shirt and walked from room to room—seeing not the bare rooms and molded walls, but a little girl's pink polka dots, a yellow nursery with a white crib, rocking horses, stuffed animals, books. She listened to the sounds—not the rain pounding on the metal roof, but the laughter of her children, the songs Charlie sang as he danced her around the kitchen, little feet padding down the hallway in the middle of the night.

Lucy slowly entered the room that she and Charlie had shared and stared at the spot where she last saw him. She walked across the room, ran her hands over the stains on the wall, and sank to the floor, clinging to Charlie's sour molded shirt.

Chapter 24

Memaw fed lunch to the youngest children and set them up in front of the television to watch a movie. Ella was working at the farm, and Ryan had gone to a Carolina football game with some of his teammates. Lucy should be home by now.

Pacing the kitchen floor, Memaw stopped to look out the window. She opened the door to the garage, hoping to see Sam's car pull in. He had been called into the hospital hours earlier. She couldn't call him. She dialed Lucy's number and it went to voicemail—again. Lucy promised to be home early, before the storm started. She said she would have lunch with them.

Memaw usually didn't worry much about Lucy because she was strong and independent. But she felt like this week—going back and forth to the farm—might have been the last straw for Lucy after all the weeks of upheaval. She seemed lighthearted and happy last night at the game, but then everything changed. She didn't even stop by for Saturday breakfast or just to say goodbye. Lucy sent her a text—even though Lucy knew she hated those things—and didn't respond to her reply, not even with the heart-eyed smiley face that Memaw now knew meant the conversation was over.

She checked in on the kids again.

"Memaw," Nate whispered, pointing at Faith sound asleep with her head in his lap. "Can we change to something different? I really don't like *Cinderella*."

"Sure," Memaw said. "You know how to find something, right?"

"Yes, ma'am," Nate said.

"You want me to move her?"

"Nah, she's ok."

Memaw walked to the front window and watched the rain. It was pouring so hard, she couldn't even see the gate.

She tried calling Lucy again. Still no answer. She kept trying every few minutes for the next hour. She had just walked into the kitchen to get the boys a snack when she heard the alarm beep once, indicating that the gate was opening. She met Sam in the garage.

"I need you to find Lucy," Memaw said before Sam could even get out of the car.

"What's wrong?" he asked.

"I don't know, but she should have been home hours ago like she promised. She won't answer her phone, and that's not like her. She always answers so I won't worry. But I am worried, Sam. Really worried."

"Did she go to the farm?"

"Yes, early, but something was wrong even then. You know she didn't come to Saturday breakfast, and she didn't even say goodbye. She sent me a stupid text. She knows I hate those things."

"I'll find her," Sam said. Going straight from his car to the Suburban. "And I'll call you as soon as I can to let you know she's alright."

Sam backed out of the garage and headed down the driveway, berating himself again for getting carried away last night. He knew what was wrong with Lucy this morning. She didn't want to face him. For all he knew, she could be finding another place to live so she didn't have to be around him anymore.

When he pulled up to the farmhouse, he was relieved to see Lucy's car there, but the front door stood open and that didn't feel right. He grabbed his umbrella to ward off the deluge but didn't take time to open it. Clearing all four steps at once, Sam entered the house. It was a heart-stopping sight. How had Lucy spent so many hours here by herself the last few days?

He walked from room to room trying to find her, calling her name. Everything looked as normal as it could, he guessed, except for the kitchen cabinets which appeared to have been ransacked. He looked in what must be the children's bedrooms and continued down the hall to the next one which he assumed was Memaw's. Then he found the last bedroom.

Unlike the other rooms where everything seemed relatively in place although ruined, this one looked like a tornado had blown through. Clothes lay strewn around the room, and the closet doors stood open. An elaborately carved wooden box caught his eye. Sam walked across the chaos to the desk where it sat. He touched the stack of soggy letters and stared into the box at tarnished and molded medals.

Sam left the house, grabbing the umbrella on his way. He ran out to the tractor shed, still calling Lucy's name, but couldn't find her there. He climbed the ladder to the loft to make sure she was not up there hurt and unable to answer him. Then he ran to the barn, calling Lucy's name, checking the tack room and every stall. She was nowhere to be seen. Standing in the center aisle of the barn, he took out his phone.

Memaw jumped when she heard her phone ring, glad to see Sam's name come up.

"Did you find her? Is she ok?" Memaw asked without saying hello.

"No," Sam said. "Her car is here, but I can't find her anywhere. And it's pouring. She's not in the house or the shed or the barn, and she won't answer when I yell for her. Where else could she go without her car?"

Memaw thought for a moment, certain that surely Lucy wasn't ready to go there, and wondering if she should send Sam to that house. But it was the only place she could think that Lucy might go.

"Her house," Memaw said.

"But I thought she lived here." Sam was confused.

"She did," Memaw said, "but there's another house on the outside of the property. One she and Charlie built. They all moved in with me after Hurricane Matthew flooded it."

"Tell me how to get there," Sam said, already running through the rain toward the Suburban.

In moments he pulled up in front of the home where Lucy had

lived with her husband. He could see her bright personality in the colors now partially hidden by mud and mold. It suited her. This front door stood open, too.

Sam stepped out and went inside. The house was obviously under reconstruction when Florence flooded it again. Lucy did not tell him that. He called her name, but she didn't answer. He walked from room to room, calling for her. Come on, Lucy, he thought, where are you?

At the end of the hallway, he entered the last room and looked around. He saw Lucy, sitting slumped against the wall with her head hanging to her chest, soaking wet, clinging to a dirty old shirt. Obvious blood splatter sprayed out above her head. But he didn't panic. It was old—dark and now molded.

"Lucy?" Sam said softly. "Are you ok?"

She lifted her head and his heart broke. He had never seen her look so distraught, so totally lost, broken, and dejected. He feared she was in shock, but then she blinked at him and started to cry. He walked over, slid down to sit on the floor, wrapped his arm around her shaking shoulders, and drew her close. With his left hand, he laid his phone on the floor and sent a short text to Lucille.

"Found her safe. Info later."

Sam sat with Lucy until she cried herself out. Then he drew her to her feet and walked her to the Suburban, helping her in and hooking her seatbelt. Finding Faith's large soft fleece traveling blanket next to her car seat in the back, he wrapped the kitten covered blanket around Lucy, then turned the heater up high. She remained silent, and he didn't push.

He dialed Lucille's number and asked her to meet him at the cottage in about thirty minutes. He told her Lucy got caught in the rain and could use a hot shower. Lucy still had not spoken to him. She leaned her head against the side window. He hoped she had fallen asleep.

When he arrived home, Sam drove the Suburban all the way up to the front door of the cottage. Memaw came off the front porch holding an umbrella even before he stopped the car.

"I put the kids in front of the television at your house with another movie," Memaw said. "It should keep them occupied for a few minutes."

"I'll take care of them," Sam said. "Lucy needs you."

"Can you go to the barn and pick Ella up in about an hour?" Lucille asked him.

"Of course," Sam said. "You just concentrate on Lucy."

Memaw held the umbrella while Sam guided Lucy to the steps. Lucy turned and looked up at him.

"Can we talk tomorrow?" she asked. "I guess I have a lot of explaining to do."

"Of course," Sam said. "Get cleaned up and just rest. The boys and Ella can stay at my house tonight."

"Thank you, Sam," Lucille mouthed, looking over her shoulder as they entered the house.

§ § §

Memaw stood at the French door in Lucy's room watching the rain drizzle down in the glow of the outdoor lights. After Lucy showered, she climbed right in her bed. She didn't say anything and Memaw didn't push, knowing Lucy would talk when she was ready. Memaw tucked her in like she had when her granddaughter was younger. Lucy had been asleep for hours when Ella entered the house.

"Memaw," she whispered, standing in the doorway to her mother's room. "I was worried."

Memaw walked out of the bedroom, closing Lucy's door behind her. She guided Ella to the island counter and told her to climb up on a stool while she made them both a cup of hot chocolate.

"Your mom is going to be fine," Memaw assured Ella. "But she's really sad right now."

"She's been working too hard at the farm," Ella said. "I should have helped her."

"No," Memaw said. "You should have gone to school and ridden

259

your horse and spent time with your friends and done the things teenagers do."

"But she always tries to do everything by herself," Ella said. "What happened?"

"I don't know much," Memaw said. "She hasn't talked to me yet, but Sam said he found her at that house."

"But hasn't she been going to the house every day?"

"Not the farm house," Memaw said. "That house."

"You mean our house?" Ella asked.

"Yes," Memaw said. "That house."

"Oh," Ella said.

They sat on the bar stools drinking their hot chocolate for a few minutes without conversation.

"I want to stay with her tonight," Ella eventually said. "You can go on back to your room and get some sleep. Maybe she'll be ready for Sunday breakfast."

"Maybe," Memaw said. "But I don't know."

"I'll call you if I need you," Ella said. "I promise."

"She might have nightmares again," Memaw said.

"I'll sleep with her," Ella answered.

"You're a good daughter, Ella Brown," Memaw said. "I'll keep the boys with me and see you at breakfast."

"Thanks, Memaw," Ella said. "See you in the morning."

Ella thought she should stay up a while and listen out for her mom, so she switched on the gas logs, wrapped herself in her grandmother's blue and green quilt Mom rescued from the flood, and turned on the television. She flipped through the channels until she found a Christmas movie on the Hallmark channel. They sure did start early, she thought.

When the couple finally kissed and snowflakes started floating softly down around them, Ella switched off the television and the fireplace, checked the locks on all the doors, and went to her room to put on her pajamas. She loved her room—it looked so much more mature than the pink one back at the farmhouse. And she couldn't believe she had her own bathroom that she didn't have to share with her brothers. She wished they could live here forever. Ella tried to slip quietly in the bed beside her mom, but Lucy woke up anyway.

"Hi there," Lucy said, rolling over and propping up on her elbow. "Did you have a bad dream?"

"No," Ella said. "I thought you might need me. Memaw went home after you fell asleep, and the boys are spending the night at Dr. Sam's house, too. I wanted to take care of you."

"Oh, Ella, that's my job," Lucy said. "To take care of you, and your brothers, and Memaw, too."

"But you had a really bad day, Mom," Ella said.

"I did," Lucy admitted. "Tell you what. How about we take care of each other?"

"Ok," Ella said.

Lucy slid up and propped her pillows against the headboard.

"Are you really sleepy or do you want to talk? I feel like we haven't had much time since you're back in school all day and spend your afternoons at the barn with Ace."

"Yeah," Ella said. "It's really different with so many people around, too. Doing things with Dr. Sam and Ryan and Faith. But I like it. The football game was crazy fun."

Lucy thought about the end of the game.

"Yes, it was exciting," she said. "But that was a special occasion, not something we'll do every week."

"It was like we were one big happy family," Ella said.

"But we're not a family, Ella," Lucy reminded her. "I work for Dr. Sam. And we must always remember that."

"I know," Ella said. "But we can still be friends, and friends do stuff together."

Lucy was ready to move the discussion away from Sam and his family, worried that after the way he found her today, she might have already lost her job before she even started.

"Speaking of friends," she said. "Tell me about Susie. You looked like two peas in a pod."

"She is so awesome, Mom," Ella said. "We think alike and dress alike and talk alike and sometimes we even say the same thing at the same time."

They spent the next hour snuggled under the covers, leaning against the headboard, talking about Ella's friends and horses and school and even the upcoming holidays. Ella loved having her mom all to herself, but she wanted to ask a question—one she had wanted to ask ever since her daddy died. She gently touched the locket she never took off anymore. Ella thought about trying to ease into the question burning in her mind, but decided to just throw it out there before she lost her nerve. It was now or never.

"Why did he do it, Mom? Didn't he love us enough?"

Startled by Ella's question, Lucy almost repeated the 'terrible accident' lie that she and Memaw cooked up to shelter the children, but now she knew that Ella knew the truth—had probably always known the truth. What a horrible burden she caused her child to bear alone. She snuggled her daughter closer.

"Oh baby, your daddy loved you and your brothers and me more than his heart could hold sometimes. But war does terrible things to soldiers, even long after they come home. All the things he saw and did in Afghanistan and Iraq just wouldn't leave him alone. I used to think the demons won out, that they were even stronger than his love for us, but I don't think that anymore. Now I believe he did what he did to protect us from what he was afraid he might do when he was trying not to drown in the darkness."

"I really miss him, Mom," Ella said.

"I miss him, too," Lucy said. "But I know he would want us to be happy. That's been so hard for me—moving on, feeling like it was okay for me to be happy without him."

"Are you okay, Mom?" Ella asked. "Really okay?"

"I am now," Lucy said. "And I finally understand that the best way we can honor your daddy's love is to live the kind of life he wanted for us—full of fun and laughter and lots of love."

"But how do you know?" Ella asked.

"Because today," Lucy said. "He told me."

Chapter 25

Sunday, October 28

Lucy woke up to a dark house, but the moon and stars cast enough light into the room that she could see Ella still sleeping soundly beside her. She eased out of bed as quietly as she could. They had talked and laughed and cried long past midnight. Lucy felt closer to Ella than ever before and on a different level—their bond strengthened by long overdue honesty and their shared love and sorrow for Charlie. She couldn't believe how fast her daughter was growing up.

Lucy dressed in black sweatpants, a blue t-shirt, and a grey thermal-lined sweatshirt. She pulled her hair up into a ponytail and brushed her teeth. She knew it sounded crazy when she said it out loud, but she also knew that she communicated with Charlie in that room where he died—like he had been waiting there for her all this time so they could both find closure.

She slipped out the front door with a cup of coffee in her hand and walked down the hill. Reaching over the top of the gate to lift the childproof latch, she swung it open, wandered down the dock, and stood at the end, her coffee cup balanced on the railing and a light morning breeze tickling her face. The sky turned from black to dark blue, and a soft pink hue began to tint the night clouds hovering above the marsh grass and small trees on the opposite side of the waterway. She could only imagine the view from the beach. She could faintly hear the roar of the ocean in the distance.

Sam stood at the kitchen sink looking out the window toward the water. The after-storm clouds that still lingered promised an amazing sunrise. As the blue hour lightened the sky, he could see a silhouette highlighted on the deck. He picked up his coffee cup, opened the back door, and walked down the hill.

Lucy heard his footsteps before she felt his presence. She hoped she could convince Sam not to fire her. She wanted to be Faith's nanny, to live in the cottage, to make a new start—at least for the rest of the year. But he might be scared to leave his daughter with her now.

"Hi," Sam said, walking up beside her and setting his coffee cup beside hers on the railing. "It's going to be a gorgeous sunrise."

"It is," Lucy said. "The clouds almost look like a washboard. I've never seen them like that."

As the sun rose closer to the horizon, the sky lightened, and the clouds transformed into yellow, orange, pink, and purple hues. Sam and Lucy stood silently side-by-side taking in the unfathomable beauty of a new day dawning.

Many minutes later, when the sun crested the treetops and sent shimmering light across the water, Lucy took a deep breath, bracing herself before she talked to him.

"I need to apologize," Sam said, still staring at the water with his elbows on the railing.

"What?" Lucy asked.

He turned and looked at her.

"For Friday night. I was out of line, and I don't want you to feel uncomfortable working here. I won't let it happen again."

"You still want me to work for you?" Lucy said. "After yesterday?"

"Of course," Sam said. "Why wouldn't I?"

"Because you probably think I'm crazy. Because you're worried that Faith won't be safe with me."

"Should I be worried?" Sam asked.

"No," Lucy said. "You shouldn't be. I'll take good care of her. I promise."

"I never doubted it for a minute," Sam said. "Do you want to talk about what happened yesterday?"

"No," Lucy said. "Not yet. Maybe one day."

"Fair enough," Sam said.

Lucy hesitated before speaking again.

"Can I ask you a question?" she said.

"Sure. You want to sit for a while? I don't think anybody will be up anytime soon except Lucille. She'll be singing and moving around the kitchen getting everything ready for Sunday breakfast."

"It makes her happy," Lucy said.

They sat down and Sam pushed off with his foot starting the swing swaying.

"The hat you wore when you rescued us said you were an Enduring Freedom veteran," Lucy began.

"Two tours in Afghanistan," Sam said.

"How did you handle it?" Lucy asked. "My brother won't talk about it. He's career Army and has been deployed so many times I lost count. I don't know where he is or even if he's ok."

"And Charlie?" Sam said, not knowing if she would answer or not.

"Four tours in Afghanistan and Iraq. He wouldn't talk about it. He was injured, but not severely, and he went right back. But then he got out a few years ago—as soon as he could when his time was up and he was forced to choose. He chose us."

"I was a medic," Sam said, "so I was on a different front line. My job wasn't to kill people, it was to save them. I saw horrible injuries, but my focus had to be on saving people. I think that's the only way I didn't let it follow me home."

"That makes sense, I guess," Lucy said. "Being a doctor must be very rewarding."

"Most of the time," Sam said. "When everything goes right."

The sun rose higher and the fall air warmed. They sat in companionable silence.

"It's going to be a beautiful day," Sam said. "How would you feel about going out in the boat this afternoon? We could ride up to Rich's

Inlet, anchor, and walk around on the island. I'll load up some chairs and the fishing poles and ask Lucille to pack some food for the cooler."

"We love the beach," Lucy said. "I think that would be wonderful."

"It's a plan," Sam said. "Ryan and I can run out and get your car right after breakfast, then we'll be ready. Would you like for me to bring the wooden box?"

"Yes," Lucy said, not asking which box. "Thank you."

"I better go check on Faith and make sure she didn't get up early and start driving Lucille crazy trying to help."

"I'm sure Memaw wouldn't mind at all," Lucy said. "I'll stop by the cottage to wake Ella and meet you there. You know the boys are going to go crazy when you tell them where we're going."

§ § §

Lucy dug her toes in the sand, watching and listening. She could hear high tide ocean waves roaring, inlet wakes lapping the shore when boats passed by, seagulls calling, and her children laughing. Less than two months had passed since their last trip to the beach, but a lifetime of changes transpired.

She glanced over at the beach chair beside her and smiled at the sight. Sam leaned back with his ball cap over his face, a soft snore escaping his lips, his long legs stretched out in front, heels in the sand. Faith's delighted squeal caught Lucy's attention, and she turned to see Benji chasing her in circles with a piece of soggy green seaweed dangling from his lips.

A huge sandcastle took shape on the shore, the teens and the kids pitching in. Even Memaw sat in the sand digging and dumping and shaping. Lucy couldn't remember the last time Memaw had been to the beach with them, much less seeing her sitting in the sand. Playing. This new life definitely agreed with her—she looked and acted decades younger.

Lucy slid the book she held but hadn't even started reading into

266

the pocket of her chair and joined her family in the sand. North Carolina weather was unpredictable—today they were barefoot in the sand at the end of October. Next week, they were expecting their first freeze. And the long-term forecast predicted temps in the mid-seventies for Thanksgiving. You just never knew.

"I may need some help getting up from here," Memaw said as Lucy sat down cross-legged beside her.

"Want me to bring a chair over?" Lucy asked.

"Nah, just help me when it's time to get up."

Faith ran away from Benji and climbed into Lucy's lap.

"Wook, Wucy!" she squealed, showing her the seaweed. "Benbi got it for me."

"That's lovely," Lucy said. "Why don't we put it on top of the castle?"

"Don't let her touch it!" Ella said good-heartedly. "She likes to stomp the towers down."

"You want to feed the birds?" Lucy asked Faith. "We have some leftovers from lunch."

"Yes!" Faith said, jumping up, sending sand flying.

"Give me a pull, baby girl," Memaw said.

Lucy and Faith both reached for Memaw's hand.

"Better let my big baby girl do it this time," Memaw said to Faith. "I might pull you right down in the sand with me." She reached out and tickled Faith's tummy.

They laughed and played for hours, Sam looking sheepish when he awoke from a long nap and joined them. Late in the afternoon, they loaded up and cruised back home.

§ § §

Everything fell into place after that, and days passed quickly. The plan that allowed Lucy to take her children to school in Pender County worked just fine. She'd often return to the house on days when Faith wasn't in school and find her sitting on a bar stool coloring while Memaw cleaned up the breakfast dishes.

"Wook, Wucy," she would say, proudly holding up that morning's artwork. And sometimes, when they were reading before naptime, Faith would whisper, "I wuv you my Wucy."

Lucy fell fast for the tiny toddler, but knew she must put her own children's needs first—which meant finding a permanent place to live in their school district and another job closer to that home.

But she still planned to make the most of every moment for the rest of the year.

They often ate meals together, and despite what Lucy told Ella about football games, they did go every Friday night for the rest of the season—home games and away. Even Memaw loved football.

With a really warm fall, Lucy and Faith spent hours outside. Sometimes Sam would come home to find them working in the flower beds—pulling up weeds, planting pansies, spreading pine straw. Lucy often took the boys and Faith to the Fort Fisher Aquarium, the Children's Museum, and to the park.

Ella spent every extra hour she could at the barn, working with the horses and spending time with her new best friend. True to his word, Tony gave Lucy a huge discount on her boarding fee. Lucy bought the boys new life jackets, and Ryan taught them how to fish and crab off the dock.

They worked out a smooth system for Faith when Sam was called to the hospital at night. If Faith had already gone to bed when the call came in, Ryan would listen out for her and call Lucy if Faith woke up and he needed help. If the call came in before Faith went to bed, she would spend the night at Lucy's house.

Lucy found a bed rail for her own bed to prevent Faith from falling off. When not in use, it folded down, perfectly hidden beneath the comforter. Lucy loved the nights when that precious sprite slept in her bed. It always stirred up memories of when her own children were small and loved snuggling. Lucy missed that.

Sometimes Sam would walk over when he returned from the hospital—just to give Faith a goodnight kiss without waking her, he said. More often than not, he ended up staying a while, having a cup of coffee, just talking. Lucy could tell when he needed to unwind, when the night might have been harder than usual or the outcomes not ideal. They rarely talked about his work, the conversations most often about their children. Lucy enjoyed the visits, and in a short three weeks' time, they were becoming true friends.

Wednesday, November 21

The day before Thanksgiving, Lucy walked into Memaw's kitchen after dropping her kids off at school, expecting to see Faith sitting at the counter.

"Is she still sleeping?" Lucy asked, surprised.

"Sure is," Memaw said.

"Maybe I should go check on her and see if everything's ok."

"She's fine," Memaw said, pointing at the monitor on the counter that showed Faith's room. "She's stirring a little bit. She'll come down when she's ready."

"Ok," Lucy said. "I wanted to talk to you anyway."

"What about?"

"I have a job interview on Friday," Lucy said. "At a farm near the kids' school. They might want to hire me as their financial manager—really a glorified bookkeeper. It's a good job that pays well and offers benefits. I didn't want to do the interview while the kids were out of school, but that's when they wanted me to come in. It's at 7:30 in the morning, so I could just tell the boys to come over here when they get up if that's okay with you. Ella will probably still be in bed when I get home."

"But you have a job," Memaw said. "And a beautiful place to live. I haven't seen you this happy in a long time. Why would you leave?"

"Because I can't expect to keep driving my kids back and forth to their old schools, and I can't make them leave everything they know—school or their friends. And there's a contractor building some new houses in the same neighborhood where Amelia lives. Ella would love living close to Amelia."

"Ella loves living here," Memaw said. "And the boys do, too. Have you asked them what they want?"

269

"No," Lucy said. "I have to make that decision—the one that I believe is best for us as a family. They shouldn't have to change schools because I can't find a job in their school district. That's not fair to them."

"What about you?" Memaw asked. "Do you really want to spend eight hours a day doing books for somebody else's farm instead of spending your days like you do now? You hated doing the books and paying the bills. You'd rather be outside any day."

"My Wucy!" Faith said, running in the kitchen and hugging Lucy's leg.

Lucy picked Faith up and sat her on the barstool next to her.

"I have wama pajamas," Faith said. "Just wike my book."

"And they're red, too!" Lucy said, smiling. "What do you want to do today?"

"Pwant fwowers," Faith said.

"That sounds like a great idea. Do you think Memaw might want to go with us and help pick them out?"

"Yes!" Faith said, leaning over to hug Lucy. "I wuv you, my Wucy."

"Mmm-huh," Memaw said smugly. "I rest my case."

The three of them spent the morning shopping for flowers, then eating an early lunch at Cracker Barrel before returning home and unloading their haul. Lucy snuggled with Faith in the child's bedroom rocker and read several books before tucking her in for a nap. She'd love to just sit there and hold the sleeping child the way she had with her own children. But those children needed to be picked up from school.

"She's out like a light," Lucy said, walking into the kitchen. "I'll be back as quickly as I can. Do you need some help this afternoon with preparations for tomorrow?"

"I think I have it under control," Memaw said. "But I could use your help in the morning. We'll eat about one, so I'll get an early start."

"Sure," Lucy said. "I'm making brownies tonight."

"I bet Faith would like to help you do that," Memaw said. "I'm so excited about having a huge table full of people for Thanksgiving. We'll eat in the dining room."

"Like it used to be," Lucy said, "when David and I were little and our whole family came to the farm."

"And before my Ma and Pa died," Memaw said. "Do you remember before your Great-granddaddy died?"

"I didn't," Lucy said. "Until the day I found the sifter. I remembered when I was three years old and all of you gave me my first pony. It was surreal, but I could see and hear and smell Grandpa just like he was right beside me."

"Memory is a funny thing," Memaw said.

Lucy glanced at the clock on the stove. "Gotta run," she said. "Don't want to be late."

She kissed Memaw on the cheek and went out through the garage. She didn't like driving the Suburban for personal errands, but Sam insisted. And until her auto insurance settled up, she couldn't afford the down payment on a car. She reminded herself to check on that—again.

Thanksgiving Day, November 22

Sam pushed away from the dining room table and sighed.

"You've outdone yourself today, Lucille," he said. "That was amazing."

"Are you ready for dessert?" Memaw said. "I have two cakes and three pies to choose from."

"Later," Sam said. "I couldn't hold another bite right now."

Memaw insisted Sam go relax in the den while the kids helped clear the table. He had been called to the hospital during the previous night and didn't come home until daybreak. Memaw was already in the kitchen putting the turkey in the oven when he returned, so he sat at the bar and drank a cup of coffee, nibbling on hot cornbread fritters she cooked for her dressing. He never went back to bed.

The boys carried dishes from the dining room to the kitchen, and the teenagers loaded the dishwasher. Lucy filled containers with

271

leftovers while Memaw washed up the pots and pans and the serving items she didn't want to put in the dishwasher. Faith stood on a stepstool drying pots and serving spoons. Memaw sighed a happy sigh, thinking what a perfect family they were creating.

Lucy took Faith upstairs for a nap while everyone else headed to the den to watch football and play games. When she came back down, Sam slept soundly in his recliner. Memaw and all the children were in the middle of a game of Clue. Waiting for them to finish so she could play, too, Lucy looked around the room. She had walked past it on her way to the stairs and Faith's room, but had never spent any time in there. It was warm and cozy, decorated in plush furniture that hugged your body. While she waited, she kept staring at the portrait over the fireplace. It made her uncomfortable. She knew it was Karina, but felt like she was looking at her own reflection—in a dress she'd never owned standing in a place she'd never been.

§ § §

When Lucy returned home after her interview on Friday, she smiled at the boys and Faith running around the yard with the dogs while Memaw sat in the porch swing watching them play. Ella still slept even though it was almost ten o'clock.

Lucy had spent some time after her surprisingly short interview riding through the new section of Amelia's neighborhood and picking up flyers from several of the spec homes there. She walked through a couple under construction that had not yet been locked. Her favorite would be finished by the end of the year and, with her new salary, she would be able to afford the payments—if the timber sold so she could make a hefty down payment.

And if she didn't have the other mortgage on the house that she and Charlie built. She planned to ask Memaw if she minded Lucy trying to sell that house with just one acre of the land where it sat. None of the rest of the land was mortgaged with the house. She knew she owned the legal right to sell it, but wanted Memaw's blessing and understanding.

Her mind reeled at everything that would need to fall into place for this plan to work, but she could do it. She must trust that she could.

"How did it go?" Memaw asked when Lucy sat down on the swing beside her.

"Good," Lucy said. "They offered me the job, and I found a house for the kids and me."

Seeing Lucy, Faith ran up on the porch and climbed in her lap.

"I just don't understand why you don't see what's right in front of you," Memaw said. "And what you'll be giving up if you leave."

She stood up abruptly and took a reluctant Faith by the hand.

"Let's go find your daddy," Memaw said and headed toward the house, leaving Lucy staring behind them.

After Memaw and Faith disappeared into the house, Lucy rounded up her children and told them they were going shopping for a Christmas tree and some new decorations. She sent Ella to ask Memaw to join them, but her stubborn—and apparently angry—grandmother made a lame excuse and stayed home. So, in addition to picking out the biggest tree they could fit in the cottage, Lucy and the children bought a smaller tree for Memaw.

They sorted through the family favorites in the plastic ornament boxes Lucy had salvaged from the loft of the shed, selected a few personally special ones for each of them, and moved the rest to a new clean container for Memaw's tree.

They lit the fireplace and turned on Christmas music, repeating a generations-old, day after Thanksgiving tradition. Several hours later, they stood looking satisfactorily at the fully decorated tree.

"Great job," Lucy said. "Let's have a turkey sandwich and some chips. I need to talk to you guys."

"What's up, Mom?" Ella asked.

"I have a big surprise," Lucy said. "But let's eat our sandwiches first."

They sat around their oval table overlooking the screened porch and waterway beyond, finishing off their food.

"I'm done," Nate said, brushing bread crumbs from his shirt.

"What's the surprise?" Benji asked.

"I have a new job," Lucy said proudly, "and found us a brand new house near your schools. My job is at a farm where we can board the horses."

"Why would you do that, Mom?" Ella said, near tears.

"So you don't have to change schools," Lucy explained. "And the house is in the same neighborhood with Amelia."

"I'm not moving," Nate said.

"Me neither," said Benji.

"I thought you would be happy," Lucy said. "You know this job and home are just temporary. We talked about that."

"But we could stay if you wanted to," Ella said. "You can keep working here for as long as you want. Dr. Sam said so."

"Even if I stayed, I can't keep driving you back and forth to school after Christmas. You would have to change schools in the middle of the year. You wouldn't see your friends anymore."

"I don't care," Nate said. "I'll go to a new school. I'll make new friends. But I love living here. I don't want to leave. Why would you make us leave?"

He ran out the front door with Benji right behind him.

"Why are you trying to ruin our lives, Mom?" Ella asked, standing up and heading toward the front door. "I'm going to the farm to see my real friends."

Lucy stood speechless at the open front door watching her daughter running away and her boys riding their bikes up and down the driveway at breakneck speed. She sat down on the front porch swing wondering how everything went so wrong.

A short time later, Ella and Susie rode up on their bikes and asked if Ella could spend the night at Susie's house. Not wanting to start another argument, Lucy acquiesced. Within minutes, the girls rode off on their bikes, Ella's clothes in a pack on her back.

Lucy's phone rang, and she was relieved to see Memaw's name pop up.

"Memaw said we could have a sleepover at her house," Nate said. "We already got clothes here."

"Ok," Lucy said. "If that's what you want to do. I'll see you at Saturday breakfast. I love you."

"Yeah," Nate said. "Benji said good night."

"Night," Lucy said.

Lucy put on her coat and walked down to the dock. Sitting in the swing under the gazebo lights, she closed her eyes and listened for the ocean in the distance. The steady cadence of pounding waves calmed her. The children just needed some time, she told herself. She had spent adequate time processing her plan, but then she just sprang it on her children without warning.

She didn't have to sign the job contract for a couple of weeks. That gave her time to think, but she shouldn't let her children's outburst keep her from doing what was right for them even if they didn't understand. That meant moving ahead with her plans and probably punishing all three of them for the way they acted when she told them. But she couldn't punish Memaw.

Sam didn't know what was going on, but he knew Lucille was not happy with Lucy and neither were her children. It wasn't any of his business, he told himself, so he needed to just stay out of it. But when he saw her sitting on the dock all alone—long into the night—he just couldn't help himself. Maybe she needed someone to talk to. He was sure she'd let him know pretty fast if she didn't. Sam grabbed his coat and a couple of beers, then walked down the dock to the gazebo.

She accepted the beer without speaking.

"You wanna talk?" he asked her.

"No," she said.

"Do you mind if I sit with you?"

"Your dock," she said.

Alright, he thought, this was going to be harder than he expected. They sat in silence until they both finished their beer. He took her bottle without saying anything and tossed them both in the recycle can on the dock. Then he sat back down.

"I love listening to the ocean," Lucy said. "Sometimes you can hear the actual waves pounding and sometimes it's just white noise."

"Me too," Sam said. "I come here to think."

"Does it always help?" Lucy asked.

"No, not always," Sam admitted, "but often."

"I want to ask you something," Lucy said after several more minutes of silence.

"Ok," Sam said.

"I saw Karina's portrait on your mantel yesterday."

Well, that was not what he expected, Sam thought, waiting for Lucy to continue.

"Why, out of all the families you rescued, did you focus on my family?" Lucy asked. "Was it because we could be twins? Did you hire me to take care of Faith because I look like her mother? Are you being so nice to me because you miss your wife? Did you kiss me at the ballgame wishing I were her?"

Sam took a deep breath and answered carefully.

"When I saw you looking out the window of that loft, you did take my breath away," Sam said. "And maybe I wanted to keep coming back to the shelter to see you because you reminded me so much of Karina."

"I need to leave," Lucy said, standing up.

Sam reached up, and she flinched, pulling her arm out of reach. He dropped his hand.

"Wait. Please," he said. "Let me finish."

She didn't sit back down, but she didn't walk away. Sam stood up, too. He walked to the railing and hoped she would follow. Eventually she did. They stood there together looking down into the water instead of at each other.

"The more I saw you and got to know you," Sam said, "the less you reminded me of Karina. You may look alike, but your personalities are totally different. You're the strongest, sassiest, most obstinate person I've ever met. You're frustrating, but fearless and faithful and forever thinking about everyone but yourself."

Out of the corner of his eye, Sam saw Lucy turn. He watched her walk to the swing, then followed and sat down beside her. He wanted to take her hand, but didn't dare.

"I hired you to take care of Faith because I saw a depth of

devotion to your children that I wanted for her and hoped you could give her just half of what you give your children. I hired you because I am impressed by your children. Even after all they've been through, they are smart, and carefree, and polite. That's amazing, Lucy."

"They aren't always," Lucy said.

"Everybody has a bad day now and then," Sam said. "But you have good children, and it's because you are such a good mother—because you love without limits. I want Faith to learn that kind of love from you. I want her to learn from Lucy Brown."

Lucy didn't answer. He felt her waiting for answers to her other questions.

"I do miss my wife," Sam said. "Just like I know you miss your husband. And maybe at first I liked being around you because you looked like her, and I could come home to her closet full of clothes and pretend she wasn't gone. But all that changed. I'm not looking for anybody to replace my wife, Lucy. I like being around you because I like you and your kids and your crazy grandmother. I absolutely love that woman. And I enjoy the time we spend together like a family even if we aren't really a family. But I hope we're friends. I feel like we are, or can be. And the kids certainly are. We work well together, Lucy—you and me and Memaw and all the kids."

She looked up at him.

"We do," she said, "and we are friends."

Sam didn't say anything else until Lucy raised her eyebrows to question him.

"Ok." Sam said. "I kissed you because I was excited about the game and you are beautiful and your smile lights up everything around you. I kissed you because of who you are."

Lucy smiled ever so slightly.

"But I know I shouldn't have done that," Sam said. "You are working for me, and I was out of line. It's not fair to you and complicates everything. I already apologized, but I apologize again. Will you forgive me?"

"I already have," Lucy said.

"Friends?" he asked.

"Friends," she said. "You want a cup of coffee?"

§ § §

Lucy walked over to share Saturday morning breakfast with everybody like they had done ever since she moved into the cottage. The only person missing was Ella, who would come home later in the day.

Lucy didn't punish her children, and by that afternoon they were pretty much acting normal again—the boys playing nonstop and Ella rolling her eyes when anybody said something she thought was lame. Lucy knew they needed time. Then they'd realize that she was right, and that her decision would be the best thing for their family.

But she still needed to convince Memaw.

Just as they were all sitting down to supper together, Sam's pager went off. He looked at it, then stood up.

"Sorry," he said. "Gotta go."

He kissed Faith on top of her head and said, "See you later munchkin."

Sam pulled out his cell phone to call the hospital on his way out the door.

"Yay!" Faith said. "I spend the night wif Wucy."

Chapter 26

Sunday, November 25

Sam pulled into the garage and listened to the door rattle down behind him. He leaned his forehead against his hands gripping the top of the steering wheel. The exhaustion settling in every bone and every muscle felt like hundred pound barbells weighing him down. When he eventually found the strength to climb out of the car, Ryan's truck parked next to the Suburban brought welcome relief. He could never rest on Saturday nights until Ryan returned from his date or an evening out with his friends.

He entered a dark house, lit only over the kitchen sink. No light shone beneath Lucille's door, and no sounds came down from upstairs. The clock showed 2 a.m., and he knew everyone was sleeping. Not even Rex and Roxie bothered greeting him at this ungodly hour.

He wanted a cup of coffee, but needed sleep more. Taking a glass from the cabinet next to the sink, he filled it with water and stood staring out the window. A new moon cast little light over the water and the yard. A light frost sparkled on the ground. He glanced over at the cottage, expecting it to be dark as well, but the Christmas tree glowed colorfully in the window.

Sam walked out the back door and down the cobblestone walk. Reaching the front door, he knew he shouldn't knock. Not now. Not at 2 a.m. He knew he needed to turn away and go back to his house. But something drew him to the sidelights.

He could see Lucy asleep in her recliner, Faith cuddled in her lap, a quilt drawn up over them both. Multi-colored lights from the tree and a flickering fire in the fireplace cast a soft glow in the room. Lucy's hair—so often in a ponytail—hung curling down past her shoulders blending perfectly where it draped over his daughter's hair. He could hardly tell where Lucy's stopped and Faith's began.

Lucy stirred and readjusted Faith on her lap. She opened her eyes and looked around the room, first at the fireplace and then the tree. Everything was fine. As her gaze took in the rest of the room, she startled seeing Sam standing at the door. But then he smiled—not the sparkling smile he usually flashed her way, but a sorrowful smile. She spoke into the remote security system to unlock the door and motioned for him to come in.

"Bad dream," Lucy said softly, stroking Faith's hair. "We drank some hot chocolate then rocked a bit. She drifted off to sleep fairly fast, but felt so good in my arms, I didn't want to put her down. We've been snuggling for a couple of hours. I hope you don't mind my spoiling her when she spends the night."

"Of course not," Sam said. He sounded exhausted.

"Rough night?" Lucy asked.

He only nodded, then sat down on the couch, leaning his head back with his fingers clasped atop. Lucy recognized the posture as something he did when he was worried or wanting to talk.

"Wanna tell me about it?" she asked.

"I don't know," he said. In the flickering light, Lucy thought she saw his eyes glistening with unshed tears. She had never seen Sam cry.

She simply waited, silent but attentive.

"I froze tonight," he said. "And that could have had devastating consequences."

"But it didn't?"

"No," he said. "Thank God."

She waited again, knowing he would continue when he was ready.

"She had a difficult pregnancy," he said. "I put her on bed rest several weeks ago. She came to see me twice a week, and everything was going well. Tonight she went into labor three weeks early, but that's not unusual with twins. She labored for hours, also not unusual with a first pregnancy. The twins were perfect—a boy and a girl—small, but perfect and healthy with strong heart beats and lungs.

"But when I started to deliver the second placenta, she hemorrhaged. Blood poured out, puddling on the floor. I couldn't locate why."

Sam stayed silent for several seconds. Lucy waited.

"Suddenly, she wasn't my patient—she was my wife. I saw Karina lying there, bleeding to death after Faith was born. The flashback only lasted a second—I'm not even sure anyone else noticed. But I knew. And I wasn't going to lose her a second time."

Lucy remained quiet, listening and watching. Sam leaned forward on the couch, elbows on his knees, head in his hands, fingers twisted in his hair, shoulders shaking as he sobbed.

"But you saved her," Lucy said, lowering the foot of the recliner and adjusting Faith in her lap so she could reach over and touch him—just lightly on the shoulder.

"You saved her, Sam."

"I didn't save Karina," he said. "I didn't."

Lucy laid Faith on the couch and covered her with the quilt. Then she knelt down in front of Sam and wrapped her arms around his muscular body. She held him until the sobbing stopped.

"I'm sorry," Sam said, sitting up and swiping his sleeve across his face to dry his tears. "I didn't mean to lose it like that."

"Don't apologize," Lucy said. "I've sobbed on your shoulders often enough. Time for me to return the favor. It's what friends do."

"But men aren't supposed to cry," he said.

"Who in the world ever taught you that?" Lucy retorted.

"We just aren't," he said. "I have to be the strong one—for Ryan and Faith."

"I hope you haven't fed that bull to Ryan," Lucy said, suddenly perturbed.

Sam looked at her, his eyes swollen and red. He was as handsome as she had ever seen him. But how could he be so clueless?

"Crying shows that you care," Lucy said. "That people are important to you. It makes you human. And it shows an incomparable strength of character. Real men cry, Sam—strong men cry. You know they do. Don't you ever think that caring enough to cry is a sign of weakness, and don't you dare burden Ryan with that lie."

"I cried when he was born," Sam said. "As much as I loved Karina—stronger than any love I had ever felt before her—seeing my son's tiny face filled me with overwhelming joy and gratitude and love. I never knew that kind of all-encompassing love even existed. I just couldn't hold back the tears. Karina said it made me sexy."

Lucy smiled at him.

"I had forgotten that," Sam said.

"I cried each time my babies were born," Lucy said, "And I doubt seriously if I looked sexy. But I know what you mean about that overwhelming love—like nothing you knew your heart could hold. Worthy of a waterfall of emotions."

"I didn't have time to cry joyful tears when Faith was born," Sam said. "Everything happened so fast. I wasn't Karina's attending OB—she wanted me to just be the daddy. When her doctor delivered Faith and handed her to me, I heard her miraculous cry, and laid her on her mother's chest. Karina kissed Faith's head, and I cut the cord. But then an audible gasp escaped from the attending nurse.

"And everybody was suddenly moving—I know they moved quickly, but when I see it in my mind, I see it all in slow motion. The nurse took Faith from her mother's arms, wrapped her in a blanket, placed her in the bassinet, and rolled her from the room. Karina's eyes filled with fear, and her doctor yelled out orders. I turned toward the end of the bed and stepped in blood. Karina reached for my hand, and I moved back to her side. I leaned in close, kissed her on the forehead, and watched the color drain from her face."

"Did you cry for Karina?" Lucy asked, fighting back tears of her own.

"I couldn't," Sam said. "I needed to be strong for Ryan and Faith."

"Not even in private? Not even when your children were asleep and you crawled in the bed that the two of you shared, reaching for the other half of you who wasn't there anymore, who would never be there again?"

"No," Sam said. "I never could."

"But tonight you did," Lucy said. "After all these years, tonight you finally did."

Sam looked up at her—the woman who came into their lives during a disaster and cracked open their future.

"I hope Faith won't be too disappointed when she wakes up," Sam said, "but I think I'll take her back home with me now. I need to hold her a while."

"Good night, Sam," Lucy said. "We'll see you for Sunday breakfast."

"Lucille would have your hide if you didn't," Sam said, thinking how much he enjoyed the little traditions they were creating.

He lifted his sleeping daughter and shifted her so that her head rested on his shoulder and her body in the crook of his arm. Lucy wrapped the quilt around her.

"I'll get it tomorrow," Lucy said.

"Good night, Lucy," Sam said. "And thank you—for everything."

Lucy closed the door behind them and walked over to unplug the tree. She stood at the window and watched Sam strolling down the cobblestone walkway, up the steps of the deck, and into his home.

She felt her world tilt on its axis—again.

§ § §

Sam carried Faith upstairs and laid her in his bed, needing to keep her close.

"Where's my Wucy?" Faith said, sitting up in the bed. "I want to sweep wif my Wucy."

"I know, sweetie," Sam said. "But Daddy needed you to come home tonight. Want to rock?"

"I want my Wucy."

She started to cry softly, so Sam picked her up and hugged her.

"You want to look at Lucy's house?" he asked, walking out the French doors onto the covered porch. He hated to hear her cry.

"I can't see it," Faith said. "It's dark."

"That's because it's nighttime and everybody is asleep," Sam said. "We need to go to sleep, too. But if you look real close, you can see the flowers you helped Lucy plant at her house. See the little lights shining on them?"

"I'm a good helper," Faith said. "Wucy told me."

Sam sat down in the wicker porch rocker and snuggled Faith close. "I know you are."

"I help Memaw, too," Faith said, yawning and rubbing her eyes.

"I know you do," Sam said. "We need to get a little sleep now, ok? Memaw might need your help in the morning, and you don't want to be too tired."

"I want to sweep with my Wucy," Faith said. "I wuv her."

"I know, baby girl," he said. "I think we all do."

Sam rocked, stroking Faith's soft curls and singing the only words he could remember from her favorite bedtime song, *You Are My Sunshine*. He didn't know the verses, so he sang the same refrain over and over until Faith felt limp in his arms. He sat and held her for a long time before he took her inside and tucked her in his bed. This time she didn't stir.

He sat on the side of the bed and took off his shoes and socks. When he stood, he picked up the small framed photo on his nightstand—Karina on the beach at sunrise wearing a flowing orange dress, cradling her swollen belly in her hands. Her long blonde hair fell in golden curls around her face and across her shoulders. That photo shoot had been just two days before Faith was born. Hugging the photo to his chest, Sam looked back at their daughter, the same blonde curls spread out across the pillow. Karina surely would have loved that little bundle of sunshine they created.

Sam opened the double doors to their huge walk-in closet—his clothes on one side and Karina's still on the other. He had not been able to even consider doing anything with her clothes or shoes or her prized collection of purses. Was it time? He looked back at the photo he still held in his hands and felt a calm acceptance flow through him.

Changing into a baggy t-shirt and flannel pajama pants, Sam

closed the closet door and climbed in bed beside his daughter. He fell asleep, assured by her soft steady breathing.

The next morning, before heading down to breakfast, Sam knocked on Ryan's door and asked if they could talk. They sat on the side of Ryan's bed, Sam trying to figure out how to begin.

"What's up, Dad?" Ryan asked. "Am I in trouble for something I don't know I did wrong?"

"Of course not," Sam said. "Unless you did something I should know about."

"Nah," Ryan said. "What did you want to talk about?"

"I made a decision last night," Sam said, "but I wanted to talk to you about it before I followed through."

"Ok," Ryan said.

"You know I'll always love your mother, don't you, son?"

"Of course, I do, Dad. I will, too."

"But I think it's time for me to donate her clothes to charity." There, he'd said it.

"I think that's a great idea," Ryan said. "Do you need some help?"

"Huh?" Sam said, bewildered. He thought Ryan would balk.

"Do you want me to help you?" Ryan repeated.

"If you want to," Sam said. "Are you really okay with it?"

"Keeping her clothes isn't going to bring her back, Dad." Ryan said. "And I don't know how you've walked into that closet every day for over three years staring at them. That's not helping anything. And it's not what she would have wanted you to do. She would have wanted you to be happy again."

"When did you get so smart?"

"Good parenting, I guess," Ryan said, giving his dad a little shove on his shoulder. "From you and Mom. I know you sometimes still think I'm just a kid, but I figured out a while ago that the best way for me to remember how much Mom cared about us is to live life the way she did—enjoy every day and be excited to see what the next day brings."

"She did that, didn't she?"

"Yeah," Ryan said. "She did."

"So you don't mind if I pack up her stuff?"

"Not at all," Ryan said. "I think you should donate it to that consignment shop where she volunteered, the one for the women's shelter. That would make her happy, be a way for her to keep giving to them."

"I like that idea," Sam said.

"Does this mean you're finally going to ask Ms. Lucy on a date?" Ryan asked.

"What?"

"It's time for you to be happy Dad, and being around her obviously makes you happy even though you fight it. You haven't fooled me or Memaw."

"But she works for me," Sam said. "I don't know how to navigate that."

"But if she gets another job, that issue will be resolved," Ryan said. "Ella told me she interviewed on Friday, and they offered her the job. That's why her kids were so mad at her."

"Because they'll move away," Sam said. "Faith would miss her so much."

"Admit it, Dad. You would miss her, too. And so would I," Ryan said. "You have a real dilemma. Talk her into staying, then tell her how you feel as a person without crossing the line as her employer, or let her leave without a fight and eliminate any possibility of sexual harassment because she works for you. But then you take the risk of making her feel like she didn't do a good job or that you don't want them around."

"I do want them around," Sam said. "All of them. I don't want them to move."

"Then offer to rent her the cottage," Ryan said.

Wednesday, December 5

Lucy knew she needed to talk to Sam. Only two days remained before she was supposed to sign the contract for her new job, and less than four weeks to work out new living arrangements and buy a car.

The timber company still couldn't cut her timber because the water just wouldn't dry up, and prospects for that happening anytime soon didn't look good. An excited weatherman said on television that their area was heading for a record breaking rainfall—over one hundred inches for the year. That made Lucy so mad she turned off the television. She wasn't furious because of the rain. She was livid watching the obvious glee that meteorologist exhibited without a thought for all the people who were homeless because of that rain and the hardships more rain would cause for them.

She hadn't heard anything from FEMA even though she tried to contact them repeatedly. And she lacked the courage to talk to Memaw about trying to sell the little house with an acre of land. Her grandmother still thought she was making a terrible mistake by taking a new job.

Ella slipped back into the mopey withdrawn teenager she had been after her daddy died—only happy with her horse. Lucy kept trying to tell her that Ace would be even closer when they moved—at the very farm where Lucy worked—and that she could ride whenever she wanted. But Ella still walked around sulking every single day.

The boys just pretended nothing was going to change.

Sam usually left his office by three on Wednesday afternoon, but at four o'clock he still wasn't home. Lucy watched for him while she pushed Faith in the swing and the boys fished off the dock—outside activity perks of an unusually warm December.

When Memaw called them in to supper, Sam was still not home.

"Where's dad?" Ryan asked, pulling out his chair.

"He just sent me a message," Memaw said. "He has two women in labor—probably delivering a couple of hours apart if his guess is right. He's just going to grab a bite to eat and stay close to the hospital instead of coming home. Try to catch a nap in the doctor's lounge in case it's a longer night than he anticipates."

"Do all doctors do that nowadays?" Lucy asked. "I remember the nurses taking care of me most of the time, and my doctor popping in when I was about to deliver."

"He does if the mother had any problems during her pregnancy,"

287

Ryan said. "He wants to be close just in case."

Lucy thought about the night Sam finally cried for Karina.

"I understand," Lucy said. "He's a very dedicated doctor."

"He's a good man," Memaw said, staring straight at Lucy.

"Well," Lucy said, looking at Faith. "I guess you get to have a sleepover."

"Daddy better not get me," Faith said.

§ § §

Lucy was sitting on the front porch when she saw Sam's headlights. It was almost midnight, but she wanted to be up in case he needed to talk. She texted him to let him know. In just a few minutes, she saw him striding toward her.

"Hi," she said. "Need a cup of coffee?"

"Probably shouldn't," Sam said, sitting down in the swing beside her. "I really need sleep."

"Long night, huh," Lucy said.

"Yeah, but it was a good one," Sam said. "Two fat healthy babies, two happy moms, and two textbook deliveries."

"I'm glad," Lucy said. "I have a message for you from your daughter."

"What did she say?"

"That her daddy better not get her. She wants to wake up in my bed, not hers or yours."

"I don't blame her."

"Huh?" Lucy said.

"Sorry, that came out wrong," Sam said, smiling. Lucy thought he actually blushed.

"I was hoping you'd get home early today," Lucy said. "I need to talk to you about something."

"We can talk now," Sam said. "I never can go to sleep for a couple of hours after I get home anyway."

Lucy sat silently for a few minutes.

"Or not," Sam said.

"Sorry," Lucy said. "I was just trying to figure out how to start."

"I'm listening,"

"I love working here," Lucy said. "And I love Faith."

"She loves you, too," Sam said. "These last few weeks have been better for her than I ever dreamed they could be."

Lucy sat silent again.

"I hear a big 'but' coming," Sam said.

"I have a job offer," Lucy said. "Financial manager for a farm near the children's school. It's really just a glorified name for being their bookkeeper, but if I take it and can buy the house I've been looking at, the kids won't have to change schools in the middle of the year."

"Is that what you want?" Sam asked.

"It's the best thing for my children," Lucy said. "It's what I need to do."

"And they're happy about it?" Sam asked.

"Now you sound like Memaw," Lucy said. "Has she been talking to you?"

"No," Sam responded. "She hasn't said a word."

"No, they're not happy right now," Lucy said. "But I know how disruptive it can be to change schools and leave all your friends. I had to do that when my parents died, and it was just awful. I don't want them to go through that."

"But if they change schools, they still have their mother, and Memaw, and they'll be living in a place they love surrounded by people who love them. That doesn't sound so terrible to me."

"Not when you put it that way."

"Do you want to be a financial manager, Lucy? Is that what will make you happy?"

"It's not my dream job if that's what you mean," Lucy said. "But I'm proud of myself for being able to find a good paying job with medical benefits so I can support my family even though I never worked anywhere but the farm and don't have an education."

"You should be proud of that," Sam said. "But you should also be happy. Are you happy working here, Lucy?"

"Yes."

"Do you think raising a child is an important job?"

"Yes, of course, I do."

"More important even, than crunching numbers for a big farm operation? Working eight hours a day in an office instead of spending time outdoors and planting flowers and nurturing the most important little person in my life?"

"That's not fair."

"I'm not trying to be fair, Lucy. I have a stake in this decision of yours, and I'm going to fight for what I want."

Lucy looked at him.

"What do you want?" she asked.

"I want you to stay, Lucy. I want you to take care of my daughter and eat dinner with us every night and breakfast with us on weekends. I want you to ride in the boat and walk on the beach. I want us to spend time together—you and me and Memaw and all of our children."

He leaned in and kissed her softly on the lips.

"And I want to spend time with you, Lucy. Just us."

"I'm not ready for that," Lucy said quickly.

"I know we both have a lot of baggage," Sam said. "But you've helped me move forward, and I want to help you, too. And I hope that forward movement brings you closer to me. But, more than anything else, I want you to be happy."

Lucy didn't respond. She didn't know how to answer him.

"I have a proposal for you, Lucy," Sam said.

Her eyes grew wide.

"Not that kind of proposal," Sam said. "Just hear me out. If the job at the farm will make you happy, then take it. But think about staying here in the cottage instead of moving."

"I was going to ask if I could rent from you until my new house is finished," Lucy said. "I finally got a check from the auto insurance company today and can buy my own car to drive back and forth."

"Then that problem is solved," Sam said.

"Thank you," Lucy said. "That takes a big burden off my shoulders."

"If you don't feel comfortable working for me—knowing how I feel about you—then by all means take that job at the farm. I don't want anything to prevent us from exploring where our relationship could go when the time is right, when we're both ready," Sam said.

He paused and Lucy didn't respond.

"But if you can stay, if you can be Faith's nanny and not feel uncomfortable if I occasionally want to take you to dinner, then please don't leave. We all need you, Lucy."

"I'm so confused," Lucy said.

"When do you have to decide?"

"I'm supposed to sign the contract in a couple of days," Lucy said.

"Go snuggle up to my daughter and sleep on it," Sam said, brushing her cheek with the tips of his fingers. "Talk to your children, talk to Lucille, talk to me again if you want to. But just think about what will make you happy, Lucy. You."

"I will," Lucy said. "Good night."

Sam took her face in his hands and kissed her lightly on the forehead.

"Good night our Wucy," he said.

Sunday, December 9

The unusually warm weather continued. As had become a tradition very quickly, Memaw planned a big Sunday brunch, and they all sat around the table talking about their week. Lucy looked from one person to another and marveled at the unlikely group of people who had bonded inexplicably—refugees and rescuers now sharing their days and their meals, their thoughts and fears and laughter and tears. She wondered how her decision would change that delicate balance that connected them.

When the lively conversation began to wind down, Lucy knew it was time.

"I have news," she said.

Lucy waited a few seconds, but nobody said anything, so she

continued.

"By now you all know that I was offered a fantastic job and found a wonderful new house close by the farm where I would be working. Ace and Brady can live at the farm, too, and none of you would have to change schools in the middle of the year or leave all your friends."

No one voiced an opinion, but Lucy could see apprehension and sadness on the silent faces staring back at her.

"I hope I made the right decision," Lucy said.

Everyone waited for her to continue.

"Well?" Sam finally said.

"Well," Lucy said. "It's a really good job. And the new house is nice."

"Mom," Ella whined.

"I decided," Lucy said. "That the best place for all of us to be is right here with this crazy new unorthodox but absolutely fantastic family we've created. I turned down the job."

After all the whooping and hollering and hugs subsided, Sam said, "Let's take the boat to the beach and celebrate."

They sped down the waterway to the island and spent the afternoon fishing, walking along the shore, shell hunting, and feeding the birds. When they returned from a long walk, Sam and Lucy and Memaw collapsed in their chairs. After a few moments, Lucy smiled as she saw Sam and Memaw both close their eyes. She then turned her attention to the wonder around her.

The warm winter sun beat down on the still tanned backs of her boys trying to help Faith create another sandcastle. Calls of the gulls swooping through the sky rivaled Faith's squeals as she stomped the castle towers and ran from the boys. They chased her around in the sand, pretending not to be able to catch her. Jovial admonishments rang out from Ella and Ryan when the younger kids ran too close and slung sand up on the blanket where the teenagers played a game of cards.

Lucy drew in a slow deep breath then let out a contented sigh as she leaned her head back to watch a formation of pelicans soaring overhead, their dark bodies and white throats contrasting sharply to the clear azure sky as they dipped and turned out over the water.

"Pelican Patrol," Lucy whispered with a smile.

Memaw stirred, sat up, and looked around. "This is just about perfect," she said.

"Yes, it is," Lucy agreed, digging her toes in the sand.

ABOUT THE AUTHOR

Cindy Horrell Ramsey lives on a barrier island in North Carolina where she loves to ride her bike, hunt for shells, and walk on the beach—especially at sunrise, sunset, or during heavy fog. Ramsey enjoyed an eclectic working career that feeds her writing as does her love of nature and life in the South. Ramsey earned a BA in English and a Master of Fine Arts in Creative Writing from the University of North Carolina Wilmington. While fueled by her literary training, Ramsey's books lean more toward commercial accessibility. Varying in content and genre, they all share one thing in common—Ramsey writes about things that matter.

www.ingramcontent.com/pod-product-compliance
Lightning Source LLC
Chambersburg PA
CBHW071449110726
47908CB00003B/565